Praise for *The Way It Should Be*

"The lives of estranged sisters collide in a summer that at first seems anything but the way it should be. Christina Suzann Nelson's beautifully written tale of the complicated nature of family, the power of faith, and the ultimate cost of self-sacrifice for those we love will have readers considering complex questions long after closing the cover."

—Lisa Wingate, #1 *New York Times* bestselling author of *Before We Were Yours* and *The Book of Lost Friends*

"In *The Way It Should Be*, Christina Suzann Nelson doesn't shy away from the horrors of addiction nor the heartache of the foster system and family brokenness. But in the midst of the hurt, Nelson offers pictures of grace, glimpses of beauty, and the hope of redemption. I loved getting to know Eve and Zara, Tiff and Bruce, and Charlotte and Sammy, and I hope for good things for all of them!"

—Lauren Denton, *USA Today* bestselling author of *The Hideaway*

"Christina Suzann Nelson's books rise like cream to the top of my to-be-read pile. Her stories are always so unique and thoughtful, with characters that are as complex as they are compelling. If you want a book that will not only entertain and keep you turning pages but that will make you think deeply about what's truly important, you can't miss with a Nelson novel."

—Deborah Raney, author of *A Nest of Sparrows* and the CHANDLER SISTERS NOVELS series

"Nelson once again delivers a story with heart, grit, and compassion. *The Way It Should Be* reminds readers of beauty in the midst of pain, hope in the thick of adversity, and the power of love to restore and redeem. A stunning read."

—Susie Finkbeiner, author of *Stories That Bind Us*

D0207738

"According to Christina Suzann Nelson, 'everyone has vulnerable places.' And with a sensitive hand, that's just what she helps readers explore—the hurts that throb with every heartbeat. Nelson's engaging page-turner is fictional, but this story about three women searching for forgiveness, reconciliation, and hope strikes awfully close to home."

—Robin W. Pearson, author *A Long Time Comin'* and *'Til I Want No More*

the way it should be

Christina Suzann Nelson

BETHANYHOUSE
a division of Baker Publishing Group
Minneapolis, Minnesota

Published by Bethany House Publishers
11400 Hampshire Avenue South
Bloomington, Minnesota 55438
www.bethanyhouse.com

Bethany House Publishers is a division of
Baker Publishing Group, Grand Rapids, Michigan

Printed in the United States of America

Library of Congress Cataloging-in-Publication Data
Names: Nelson, Christina Suzann, author.
Title: The way it should be / Christina Suzann Nelson.
Description: Minneapolis, Minnesota : Bethany House, a division of Baker Publishing Group, [2021] |
Identifiers: LCCN 2020040101 | ISBN 9780764235399 (trade paperback) | ISBN 9780764238161 (casebound) | ISBN 9781493429936 (ebook)
Subjects: GSAFD: Christian fiction. | LCGFT: Novels.
Classification: LCC PS3614.E44536 W39 2021 | DDC 813/.6—dc23
LC record available at https://lccn.loc.gov/2020040101

Cover design by Kathleen Lynch / Black Kat Design
Cover image by Nilufer Barin / Trevillion Images

Author is represented by the Books & Such Literary Agency.

21 22 23 24 25 26 27   7 6 5 4 3 2 1

This book is dedicated to
Ryan, Joshua, Aleasha, Emma, Makayla, and Violet.
The pieces of my heart.

CHAPTER ONE

THE MOST BEAUTIFUL THINGS are those that survive a storm and find their glory in the restoration. That thought came to Zara Mahoney's mind as she turned off the gravel lane and onto the farm—their farm, hers and Chad's. Most of the things she loved dearly, the items she'd brought with her through the years, were old and weathered. They showed the strain of time and the softening of experience. Even the 1968 Ford pickup she drove was what many would call a relic. But when she looked at its chipped teal paint, the smattering of rust, and the duct-taped bench seat, she saw resilience and strength.

That old house and overgrown land energized her. Underneath the layers of neglect, there was a future that she would share with her new husband. That place, though it looked fragile, wasn't an ending, but a great and powerful beginning.

Zara twirled the new set of keys around her index finger and scanned the overgrown twenty acres of land, Chad and Zara Mahoney's very own home.

She and Chad were college sweethearts. They'd met on campus outside the building where a few of her business courses and most of his accounting lectures were held. He was the first person who shared her excitement over her plans to take her degree in business and minor in botany and grow them into a company that provided natural products made by her own hands. He'd even come up with the name, Zara's Garden.

Her fingers yearned to pull back the peeling white paint and hack away at the rambling blackberry bushes, but the treetops swirled as the wind picked up, pushing loose hair over her face. If she was going to get this load of boxes inside before the rain started and turned cardboard to mush, she couldn't stand around daydreaming. Not even as she caught a glimpse of purple crocuses emerging from the soil near the house's foundation. There would be time. A lifetime.

The key slid easily into the worn lock, clicking as it turned. The moist air of a Willamette Valley winter had swollen the wood, fitting the door and its frame together in a tight embrace. As Zara tugged a few more times, the knob slipped from her grip and the entrance flew open, almost throwing her off the brittle porch.

Beep, beep.

A mail truck bumped through the last of the potholes, inching toward her until it stopped a few feet away. The man who stepped out was the image of Santa Claus on a tropical vacation. His short-sleeved Hawaiian shirt pushed the limits of the buttons above his khaki pants. A fluffy white beard nearly covered his face, and shaggy hair tumbled from his head. "Hey there. You the new owner?"

"I am." She stretched her hand out to shake his. "I'm Zara Brookes." *Nope.* "I'm sorry. Zara Mahoney."

One crazy caterpillar eyebrow cocked.

"I . . . we just got married. Last week. My husband and I." The words were still new on her tongue and had a delightfully sweet taste.

He nodded. "Well then, congratulations, Mrs. Mahoney."

"I was heading to check the mailbox as soon as I finished unloading a few things. Sorry you had to come all the way down the driveway."

He rubbed the back of his neck. "I think I made it through without whiplash, but it was close." His eyes smiled. Leaning into his truck, the man pulled out a mailbox door. "I thought you'd prefer to have your letters delivered rather than left to the wind and rain." He handed Zara the warped metal with one hinge still attached. "It's supposed to get nasty again by the end of the week." His gaze lifted to the sky. "You've got to love these Oregon springs. The weather jumps around more than a toddler with a belly full of sugar."

Zara took the salvaged material, mentally adding *mailbox* to her growing list of projects. "Yikes. The blessings of homeownership, huh?" She grinned. It would take a lot more than a broken mailbox to bring her down from the clouds today.

He bobbed his head. "Underneath it all, I think you picked a good one. This place has solid bones." He climbed into the cab and handed a stack of letters through the window. "I'm looking forward to seeing what you do with the old house."

"Thank you." She waved as he drove away, the truck lurching from one side to the next on the uneven road.

Tossing the mailbox door into the bed of her pickup, Zara dropped the tailgate and tugged the first of her boxes into her arms, the mail stacked on top. By the time she made it through the front door, her biceps screamed. She'd wake up sore tomorrow, but this was so worth the pain. Tonight, she and Chad would have their very first dinner together in their new home.

Zara scrunched her nose as she ventured farther into the house. It had been shut up since they took their final walk-through a few weeks earlier. Now absent of the synthetic floral scents of room freshener, the inside smelled damp and mustier than it had on any of the visits with the real estate agent.

She lowered the box, letting it drop the last half foot onto the cracked tile, then tossed the mail on the counter. Chad would be home from his first mandatory meeting at Emerald and Irving

Financial in three hours. That's how long she had to make sure he didn't question this investment on their first night.

Zara's next load included two smaller boxes with a watery jar of seeds balanced on top. Water waved back and forth as she took the stairs into the house. On the kitchen threshold, she tripped, catching herself before she lost her grip. Four more steps forward, and Zara's toe rammed the first box, still sitting on the floor. Agony shot up through her shin, and the jar tumbled.

Glass shattered on impact with the unforgiving surface. Flat black seeds the size and shape of beetles flew to all corners of the kitchen. She had waited weeks for these treasures to arrive. If she had to wait for another batch, it would ruin her critical planting timeline.

Zara shoved the boxes onto another counter and slammed the door shut. As she did, the stack of mail lifted and fluttered to the floor, each piece drawing up glass-laced water.

Dropping to her knees, Zara picked up each seed while cold water on chilly tile saturated her jeans. More than a few seeds had floated under the edge of the cabinets. When Zara located the twenty-fifth and final holdout, she laid them on the worn grooved cutting board. The seeds needed to be relocated to trays of soil placed on a heating pad before she could start preparing Chad's and her celebratory dinner.

Yanking open the flaps on the largest box, Zara freed a few towels from the items they were protecting, then tossed them on the spreading pond underfoot.

With her thumb and forefinger, she picked up the pieces of mail and shook them over the sink. A bill for the previous owner, junk mail, a flyer, a welcome home card, and . . . her breath stilled. All the fragile fragments of her dreams shuddered. This was the one thing she'd taken for granted, not allowing fear and dysfunction to steal what she'd built. But all it took was a glance at this envelope for the past's hatred, sorrow, and loss to invade her new life.

Standing on legs that felt like they'd run a marathon, she rinsed her hands and toweled them dry. There was nothing to be afraid of.

She reached for the envelope and tore it open. The letter, one side soaked in seed water, stuck to the inside, then finally came free. Zara read over the blurring words.

It was from her mother, an inmate in the women's correctional facility just a few hours north of Zara and Chad's new farm. How had she gotten the new address?

Zara could toss this in the trash, an action she almost always wished she'd done immediately after reading any of her mother's spiteful notes, which let old hurts rise to the surface once again.

Yet with the pain, sweet memories of her little brother came back in a rush, followed by the bottomless grief of losing him. Every tiny bit of Tyson had been a precious gift, everything except for the gene that ultimately took his young life and destroyed their family. She and her sister, Eve, had only been fourteen when he died.

Zara's phone buzzed. She snatched it from the counter and answered.

"Is this Zara Brookes?" The voice on the other end sounded professional but not in a let-me-sell-you-something kind of way.

"It is." She didn't correct the last name.

"Hello, Zara. This is Collette from Dr. Mackenzie's office. He asked me to call you with the results of your recent tests."

Zara's heart fluttered. "Okay." The shaking in her voice only sent her nerves further into panic, even though her doctor had said this was the responsible thing to do. Before they started a family, Chad and Zara should know for sure if she was a carrier for the gene that had caused her brother's death. These tests would put the niggling questions away, not letting them poke at her like splinters for the rest of her life.

"Everything looked good as far as your health goes, but I'm afraid you did test positive as a carrier for Hunter syndrome."

Positive.

The letter, still in one hand, drifted to the floor.

Tears washed over her cheeks and crumpled her fragile hope. It had only taken a second to destroy her fairy-tale future.

She ended the call, picked up the paper, and stuffed it into a bag she'd use for trash.

A DARK CLOUD seemed to have covered the sun. No matter what Zara did, the seriousness of that one word permeated every movement she made. *Positive.*

Zara opened a box of jars in a room that might have been used for dining in the farmhouse's heyday. Each glass container appeared colored by the dried herbs stored inside. She lined them up on a folding table she'd erected along a wall. One by one, Zara unscrewed the lids, inhaling the fragrance of the individual plants.

Lavender was a favorite. It softened the sharp points of her drifting thoughts. She left the top off this container, as well as that for the dried rose petals. Within a few hours, those scents would permeate the room, reviving the stale air.

They'd need to add plenty of shelving in here. But before that, she'd coat these walls with fresh paint. And prior to that, Zara would need to repair the deep divots in the worn and chipped plaster.

Her vision for this room, and nearly every other square foot of the farm, emerged from her imagination already detailed and clear, a design etched in the depths of her mind. What she didn't see, the part she kept trying to push away, was how she'd afford all this if Chad decided her brokenness was more than their wedding vows covered. And how she would survive another loss of that magnitude.

Zara bent forward, her hands clutching at her chest. Chad Mahoney was the best part of her day. He was the first person to really choose her and care about her dreams. But that same man wanted a large family, a dog, the picket fence, the loud and crazy of it all.

The reality of Hunter syndrome would steal their joy just like it took her brother's life, her twin's sobriety, and her mother's last bit of mental health. Zara couldn't watch it take Chad's dreams too.

"Hey there." His voice boomed through the unfurnished house. "Where are you?"

Zara blinked back tears she hadn't bothered with before, then yanked her cell phone from her pocket. He was an hour earlier than expected. And she wasn't ready to face him.

"There you are." The floor groaned under his feet as Chad entered the room and wrapped his arms around her. "The honeymoon ruined me. I couldn't wait to get back to you." He nuzzled closer. "It's kind of chilly in here. Did you turn on the heat?"

Zara relaxed against his chest. "I've been working. Didn't even notice it getting colder."

Chad held her at arm's length. "I've got a surprise for you." His grin creased tiny lines around his eyes. "Come see." Dropping one of her hands, he pulled her forward by the other.

Outside, the air had turned damp and icy. It wove through the knit of Zara's long-sleeved T-shirt, and goose bumps burst out along her arms. "What is it?" She wriggled her fingers free from his grip and hugged herself.

Two feet away from his nearly new SUV, Chad stopped and turned toward her. Evening was closing in, but light from the farmhouse window reflected in his eyes. "Are you ready?"

Zara blew out a breath, which turned into a puff of steam. "I'm ready to head inside." The sarcastic tone in her voice scratched at her nerves until she punctuated her words with a smile. "Okay. Let me see what you brought."

He gave a boyish grin. "It's not so much a *what* as a *who*."

Tiny bubbles tickled her stomach. She glided past Chad and

pulled open the hatch, revealing a small crate. "What is it?" Zara's fingers trailed over the rough plastic exterior.

"I guess you'd better take a look." As Chad pulled the crate toward the bumper, something inside moved.

In the shadows, she could just make out a ball of brown fluff. Pinching the latch, she released the crate's door, then reached in for the softest puppy she'd ever felt. Holding him to her face, she inhaled the sweet scent emanating from him.

The puppy yawned, then snuffled into her neck as if his nap had been cut short.

"You got me a puppy." Zara looked up at Chad, but her vision blurred. All her life, she'd wanted a puppy. The closest she'd managed was walking an elderly neighbor's even more elderly dog each morning when she was in middle school. That stopped when the woman's family moved them both away. "Thank you."

"I worry about you out here on your own while I'm at work." He shrugged. "Now that I really look at him, though, he might not have been a wise choice for a watchdog."

"I love him." The dog's hot breath warmed the side of her face.

"You go on inside. I have his supplies in the back seat." Chad planted a kiss on her cheek and rubbed his hand over the puppy's head.

A drop of rain plopped onto Zara's right shoulder, and cold shuddered across her back. She pressed the little dog closer to her chest, her hand cupped over his head like a cap, and jogged back to the house.

Inside, Zara switched on the thermostat. A moment later, the house filled with the scent of burning dust and dry heat. It brought back early childhood memories of her grandparents' cabin, a tiny, musty place in the middle of the Cascade Pass. Zara and her twin sister had dreamed of living out there one day.

So many things and people were gone now.

Chad shook off his jacket and laid it over the back of a chair. "The dog food is on the porch. Where should I put the crate?"

Her eyes locked on his. She knew loss. She'd survived it countless times, but the desire to keep her new truth hidden and put off the pain of possibly losing Chad was almost more than she could withstand.

"Zara?" The skin above his nose pinched. "The crate?"

"By the wood stove is fine for now." In only a few minutes, she'd let her heart get hijacked by a ten-pound ball of fluff. Overattachment had to be an authentic disorder. She couldn't bear the thought of putting him in that doggy dungeon.

"He's going to need a name." Chad set down the crate and scratched the back of his head. "And it shouldn't be anything on my list for our future children."

Zara's stomach twisted. "We need to talk." She sat on the floor, her gaze remaining glued to the perfect distraction. "I went ahead with the genetic testing."

Chad's presence behind her was a tower standing ready to collapse and land on her head. "The one for Hunter syndrome? I thought we'd decided it wasn't necessary since Tyson had a different father."

"I just thought it would be good to get it done, like having the test would protect us from something. Turns out, it didn't."

"You're saying it came back positive?" His words were steady but squeezed.

"Having a different dad didn't save me. I got a call from my doctor today. I'm a carrier." The puppy ran over and slid into her bent leg. "I'm so sorry, Chad. I should have found out earlier, before we got married or even serious."

"Is there a cure or a treatment? What do you know about Hunter syndrome?" He sat behind her, wrapping his arms around her chest and pulling Zara close to him. "Maybe it's not such a big thing anymore."

Always the one with the positive outlook. Zara couldn't fault him for that. He didn't know the world the way she did.

"A woman I work with is married to a genetic specialist," he offered. "We'll make an appointment. We just need more information."

She'd go with him, but only to soften the blow.

The puppy sniffed a clump of spilled sage, lifted his nose, and peed on the floor.

CHAPTER TWO

ONLY A FEW DAYS PASSED before Zara found herself waiting in a medical facility for answers. Chad must have cashed in more than a few favors at work to get the appointment with the genetic specialist inside a week. That first night, Zara and Chad had agreed to put a ban on further Google searches, realizing a bit too late that the information on the web was high on shock value and low on usable material.

After fifteen minutes in the waiting room that felt like hours, they were escorted down a hall and into Dr. Cramer's private office. Degrees and certificates lined the walls above waist-high bookshelves. Though the room had a somewhat personal feel, the pictures seemed oddly lacking in family images. Maybe smiling faces were too much for the kinds of broken, mutated patients seen here. Patients like Zara.

She dug into her purse and pulled out two fun-sized Snickers bars. Some people drank or used drugs when faced with this kind of life-leveling stress. Zara had a verified chocolate addiction. Seriously, who really cared about something so trivial? It wasn't like she couldn't give up sugar. She could. If she really wanted to.

Chad wrapped his hand over hers, sending a shiver of surprise across her skin. Somehow, she'd managed to eat both candies in the time she'd been lost in a mental list of excuses.

"There's nothing to worry about." His thumb stroked the inner ridge of her hand. "We'll deal with this together, just like whatever else comes up in our lives. We're a team now."

Zara bit at the inside of her lower lip, forcing emotion into compliance with the sting of pain. "Don't say that. It really isn't too late." Nine days was a tiny blip in the length of most lives. They could walk away. Pretend their wedding never took place. If sins really did visit the second and third generations, wouldn't that mean tragedy and dysfunction came along for the show? "You're not bound to me. My life is going to keep taking me down. It's not what you signed up for."

"No way." Chad shook his head, his jaw tense and lips tight. "We made a commitment. You and I are tied together forever." He put a stiff arm around her, pulling her close and kissing the top of her head. "You're the one for me. I signed up for the whole thing. The trials we have and will have don't change that."

The gene inside of Zara felt like something dirty, distasteful. It was a stowaway that could sink the entire ship. If only she could throw it overboard. "I'm not who you thought I was when we took those vows."

"Ha. I'm betting there are more than a few things about me that you haven't discovered yet. I know you think I'm pretty studly, but you might not be too impressed the first time I have to deal with a bat." He gave an exaggerated shiver for her benefit.

"That's not a comparable flaw." Zara's head relaxed onto his shoulder. "Unless you have some genetic time bomb of your own, we aren't even."

A deep voice echoed behind them. "I'm sure I can find one, if I look hard enough." Dr. Cramer came around his desk and sat down. "We all have some sort of genetic abnormality. You'd have to go back to Adam and Eve to find a person with perfectly formed

DNA. Usually, we don't notice many of these things until sperm and an egg with the same mutations come together."

Chad leaned forward in his seat, his arm leaving cold behind in its absence from Zara's shoulder. "Does that mean we're safe if I don't carry the Hunter gene?"

Dr. Cramer's face grew serious. "There are a few times when it doesn't take two to tango. In the case of Hunter syndrome, we're talking about an X-linked recessive syndrome. The mutation only occurs on the X chromosome. For a woman, this means she doesn't have to worry about getting the disease, because her other X chromosome will take over where the malformed one is weak. But for a guy who inherits the gene, there is no other X chromosome to make up the difference. For them, the gene equals Hunter syndrome, and I'm not going to downplay this: It's serious and fatal."

Flashes of her brother's face came with a burst of deep grief. The way his voice changed, slurred. The features that weren't quite what they'd been when he was a toddler. And the agony he faced until the day he died. Tyson had been only six years old. A child whose life didn't have time to be lived.

Chad's arm reached across her again, settling on the outside of Zara's opposite thigh. "Is there anything we can do to prevent having an affected child?"

Dr. Cramer blinked red eyelashes.

"You could do everything in your power to have only girls. Sperm sorting is widely used. It's not a guarantee, but it changes your odds significantly."

Chad cleared his throat. "So any boy we had would get the disease?"

She made the mistake of looking at Chad's face. His skin had paled to a pasty, washed-out hue, dreams of a son flowing away with his usually rosy color. She couldn't do this to him. He deserved the opportunity to pass down all the rich Mahoney traditions the way his father had.

Dr. Cramer stood and came around the desk. He half sat on the edge closest to Zara. "No. You're still looking at a fifty-fifty chance of an affected son. I did a little reading on recent studies before this appointment. There are some promising advancements in gene therapy. Hope is coming for patients with this disease, but I can't make any promises as to when." He crossed his arms. "Zara, from what you've told me, your brother had the most severe form. It's not always like that, but it is a rough life. It's not my job to make decisions for you."

There was no decision to be made. She couldn't take even a tiny risk that her child would suffer because she wanted to gamble with his life. Zara stood. "Thank you for your time. You've been a great help."

Without a look back, Zara walked out the door.

Alone.

The genetics center sat next to the hospital, both buildings on a hill overlooking the valley. As she stepped into the damp chill, she was overwhelmed by the view. How could so much beauty exist in the midst of such pain?

Reaching the SUV, she realized her mistake. No keys. And no escape.

Zara hadn't believed Chad when he'd tried to motivate her that morning with his belief that good would come from their appointment. Good didn't cling to her life like it did to his. She'd always known, somewhere in the shadow of her thoughts, that tragedy would tear them apart.

Welcome to reality. She didn't wish any bad on her husband. She only needed him to understand that life didn't always have a silver lining. For some people, it was unwaveringly difficult. Hardship and loss were attached to their actual DNA. And now she even had a name for it. Hunter syndrome.

Zara leaned up against the passenger door and let her purse fall to the wet asphalt.

By the time Chad arrived, she'd discovered a hole in her shoe that must have absorbed half the puddles between the building and the car. Her foot had gone from cold to freezing to numb and probably pruned.

He walked across the parking lot with a file under his arm and the look of a man ready to face a challenge. But she wasn't a challenge he should try to conquer. She was as dangerous as a Himalayan peak, and she could feel her lungs burning with the need for oxygen.

"I worried you left without me." He pulled the keys from his pocket and pressed the button on the fob, releasing the locks. "Are you all right?"

She flung open the door. "I'm fine. Could you take me home, please?"

He stood beside her as she buckled her seatbelt. It's not like she was a child who needed assistance. "Zara, this isn't all bad. There are many options." He dropped the folder on her lap and shut the door.

Chad climbed in his side, eyeing the information still unopened on her legs. "Just check out some of that literature. Did you know there are embryos available for adoption? Seriously, we could adopt, and you'd still have the whole pregnancy thing."

She let her hand settle on the smooth surface of the folder. Pregnancy wasn't something she'd dreamed of. She hadn't even given it much thought. When Zara pictured them together, growing their family, she saw children playing on the farm, 4-H projects, and tree forts. This broken gene forced her to ponder stages of life she wasn't ready to consider, much less commit to giving up or salvaging.

"There are so many things we can do." He started the engine and backed out of the parking space. "To be honest, I was really worried coming into this. I mean, I had no idea what we were going to do. But now, it's so clear. Why on earth would we need to have biological children? My mother was adopted. She and my grandma were so close. It's not like sharing DNA created that bond. It was love." He wrapped his hand around Zara's knee and squeezed. "We have plenty of that."

Zara was the older half of a set of identical twins. She'd never imagined a family that didn't look like a reflection of herself, but biology hadn't held her and Eve together any more than it had pushed Chad's mother and grandmother apart.

"Are you sure you can give up something as basic as having your own child?"

"No matter how our kids come into our family, they'll be our own." His lips pressed together as if they were holding back the emotion that shone in his eyes.

A seed of hope expanded in Zara's chest until it curled into a tiny sprout.

Eve
May 3, 2019

The baby's screams woke me up this morning. My brain is still pounding. I love him, but I want him to quit howling all the time. Sweat's dripping down my hairline, and I'm pretty sure I'm going to die soon if things don't change.

At least it's quiet now. Charlotte is feeding her brother what's left of the evaporated milk mixed with water. She's pretty capable for a five-year-old. I'm grateful for that. Yet she still drags around the scrap of what was her blanket and chews all the time on her thumbnail.

I'm doing the best I can.

The two of them, they're always hungry.

All we have to eat is a can of pork and beans. I promised Charlotte we'd have more by tomorrow, but I'm not sure that's true.

Why hasn't Joey come back? I know he's got business, and

I shouldn't complain when he lets us stay here. But it's been so long, and I don't dare go to the food bank. Last time, he was so mad, I thought he'd kill us all. He said it made him look bad, but what would his people say if they saw us now?

The person I saw in the mirror this morning was unrecognizable. I'm a ghost of who I was.

Food isn't the only thing we're running out of. Inside the cup that holds our toothbrushes, there are just two more balloons of heroin. Only enough to get through tonight, so I can do what has to be done to feed my kids.

CHAPTER THREE

TIFF BRADLEY STEPPED from the state-of-the-art kitchen that once gave her joy and satisfaction into her three-car garage, the place where she now found solace. Sweeping her gaze over the neatly lined shelves, she thought about her ministry, and hope hummed inside of her. There was so much here, so many ways she could serve those the world had turned its back on. Behind the solid door of her bolted-down safe was what, to some, could mean another chance to start over. Those syringes of Narcan could quickly reverse an overdose, possibly giving the recipient the needed chance to start over.

Her heartbeat quickened as she pondered the people who gave so much despite many of them having little, and all so that she could have the privilege of serving on the streets. It was the purpose of her life now, the reason she kept moving.

Yet none of these things could bring back her sweet Lindsay, her only daughter. With the help of God, they might, however, bring back someone else's little girl.

Tiff walked past her nearly new Lexus and her husband's prized Tesla, then popped the trunk of the rusted 1994 Toyota and took a quick inventory of the supplies still packed from last night. She'd barely touched the bags of hygiene products and the variety of packaged foods in here.

She took the full totes and transferred them to the back seat, removing the empty ones from there. After restocking these, she nestled them back into the trunk, thankful the new seal was working and that rain no longer seeped into this space.

There were always more items in her car than she could hand out in one night, but too much was better than too little. Before opening the garage door, Tiff ran her thumb over a stack of flyers, pulling half an inch from the pile. Two photographs of Lindsay looked back at her. In the first, she was just a little girl, holding her brother, Brandt, as a newborn. She was grinning as if Brandt were the greatest gift she could ever receive. The second was the last picture Tiff had of her daughter. In it, Lindsay's hair was no longer silky and smooth, rather her skin was blotchy and her eyes sunken. Tiff had both of these pictures on the pages in hopes that people could see addicts were once innocent children who remained someone's child. Next to the Narcan locked in her glove compartment, these were the most important things she carried. Each sheet told the story of her lost daughter and gave phone numbers for resources and support. Maybe someday she'd meet a person who knew Lindsay, someone who was willing to tell her more about what had happened to her baby.

Everyone should get another chance.

Tiff shook off the sadness, setting her mind on her mission. It was Friday. Friday meant heading to the east side of town, near the freeway. It was a place closer to hell than any kind of community, but it was where she often found the women who needed someone to care. The daughters of distraught mothers and the girls who grew up into a cold existence without the love of a mom, they were ignored by the world. Either way, these women needed to feel even the tiniest bit of compassion from someone, and Tiff needed to give it.

They didn't live in an overly large community. The town of Canyon Ridge had a population just under eighty thousand, but that didn't stop the drugs, the violence, or the human trafficking.

Tiff climbed into the car, the musty scent of a past owner's cigarettes still clinging to the interior, and pressed the garage door button. It glided up like silk over nylons, without the tiniest hesitation.

The dark of the night was broken only by the thin line of driveway lights. They stretched away from the garage and past the locked gate that kept the life she injected herself into far away from her home. That barricade hadn't been enough to save Lindsay from the dangers outside the security of their property. And it wasn't enough to protect what was left of their family—only Bruce, Brandt, and her—from sliding away in the aftermath of heroin's influence. Yet still it stood, a monument to failed safeguards.

Tiff breathed a prayer as she turned past the last block of relative safety and into what she called her personal war zone. Anyone who wasn't a soldier in these times was living life with closed eyes. She'd been one of the walking zombies, spending her days as a private school volunteer, hosting fundraiser teas, watching her husband's career grow.

Right under their noses, right there in front of their manicured lives, her Lindsay had fallen.

Tiff had to think of the loss as a fall. It was too painful to consider the many points at which she could have held out her hand and ordered her daughter into her arms and away from the cliffs where she teetered. In those days, Tiff was still naïve enough to believe Christian school tuition was the price they paid to keep their children away from the horrors all good families worked hard to avoid.

Her final turn took her onto a street where even the lights seemed dimmer than those a mere mile to the west. The sidewalks were lined with tents and cots, makeshift beds, scraggly dogs.

Here, a newspaper wasn't something to peruse while sipping a half-caf latte. It was shelter, bedding, and barrier.

Conway and Esther, a couple she'd seen weekly for as long as she'd searched these streets, huddled in a doorway, their black and gray mutt snarling at each wanderer who shuffled by.

Tiff cranked down the passenger window and let the fingers of cold air reach for her. Leaning over the console, she picked up two bags. "Esther, it's me, Tiff. You up for some food tonight?"

Esther slid from the cocoon of soiled bedding, careful not to disturb Conway. "Bless you. I haven't been able to leave him all day." She looked back at the man she'd spent her entire homeless life beside. "He's not doin' good. Can't get him to eat much, and he's sleepin' all the time."

"Has he been seen at the clinic?" Tiff pulled a sample bag of dog food from the box on the floorboard. This donation from a local veterinarian had been a blessing to so many out on the streets, where a dog was their closest companion.

When Esther turned back to Tiff, her deep-set eyes reflected the streetlight above them. "Won't go. Says he's ready to die." She twisted her lips around a toothless mouth. "I ain't ready to be without him."

Tiff covered Esther's hand with her own. A moment like this, of tenderness and truth, was rare out here. It took the dignity and horror of death to break down the walls built as protection from the world. Conway wouldn't be the first to vanish from the streets, but he would be the first homeless man Tiff would mourn. Maybe his life hadn't always been innocent, but she knew him as a man who loved the woman he stood by and harmed no one. Somewhere under his mounds of wiry eyebrows and grayed beard that had grown down over his neck was a man with a story Tiff didn't really know and likely wouldn't be told.

The dog yipped.

"I got to get back. Thank you." Esther took the bags and hob-bled toward the few square feet she and Conway called home.

Tiff had pleaded with them and with local agencies to help get these two off the streets. Yet week after week, she'd find Conway and Esther out there. In a way beyond her understanding, this was their community. Leaving would have been walking away from all they knew.

Tiff eased away from the curb and drove a couple of blocks farther, turning into a parking lot behind an abandoned store-front. She parked under the only working streetlight and waited. The girls always found her. That's what worked best. They had an established relationship, a kind of trust that had grown into a motherly protectiveness on Tiff's part and something akin to that on the women's.

From the shadows, Theresa appeared, as though walking out of another universe. She shuffled, her fifty-year-old body not suited for this harsh nightlife, but she'd told Tiff that after more than twenty years as a prostitute, there wasn't any other life she remembered and nowhere to return. But Tiff hadn't given up on her. She'd be available when Theresa was ready.

Behind Theresa, a waif-like girl followed, her arms crossed against her exposed middle, shoulders slumped, and blond hair falling over a pocked face.

Tiff unrolled her window and held her hand out to Theresa. "Hey, friend. How are you doing tonight?"

Theresa's cold, bony fingers wrapped around Tiff's. They were hands that, if they'd been born into another family, could have been the instruments of a great pianist. "Only got a second. This girl here"—she shrugged toward the blonde—"she's wanting to join our little club, if you know what I mean. Paulie's gonna be here any minute. Can you get her out before she does something stupid? She's got kids."

There was one promise Tiff had made to her husband and son.

One tiny compromise at Brandt's suggestion. She'd agreed not to let anyone into the car with her.

The younger woman tugged at the hem of her short dress, her eyes darting everywhere but toward Tiff. She was about the age Lindsay would have been, the same shade of hair tossed with gentle waves. Tiff's commitment about the car would have to become another of the many she'd broken. If this were Lindsay, Tiff would certainly hope that someone kind would take her out of the situation. "Climb in." Tiff reached across the car and pulled up the passenger side lock.

The girl whipped her focus from Theresa to the car, her feet not moving.

Theresa banged her fist on the roof of the already dented vehicle. "Listen up—you get in that car right now, or I'll be sure you never get your supply again, you hear me?"

A shiver ran through the younger woman, but she did as she'd been told, finally hunkering in the seat like a scolded child.

"Get going." Theresa lifted her chin. For a second, Tiff thought she spotted longing in Theresa's dulled eyes, but it was gone in an instant.

Tiff drove half a mile before she came up with something to say to her silent passenger. "You have children?" As soon as the words broke the stillness, she regretted them, wishing there were a way to pull the haphazard syllables back. They held the tinge of judgment, as if the young woman beside her was unworthy to be a mother.

"I do." Her head came up for a moment. "They're safe. My neighbor watches out for them." She folded back over, her finger picking at a loose thread at the hem of her dress.

"I didn't mean to imply anything. Just trying to make conversation." The bright lights of a shopping center beamed ahead. "How about a cup of coffee? I know I could really use one." Tiff bit her bottom lip. The girl's nerves and body were as jumpy as a tree frog. Caffeine on top of whatever she'd taken wouldn't be much help. "Or hot chocolate?"

Her hands rubbed up each arm, stopping only to grasp the opposite shoulders. "I don't know what else to do."

It was an opening, an opportunity handed down by God. Tiff pulled into a twenty-four-hour coffee shop. "Why don't you let me help you? I may have some ideas you haven't thought of yet. What's your name?"

"Eve."

"I'm Tiff. And all I want to do is help you out." Tiff ventured a connection, touching Eve's barely covered shoulder.

The girl trembled, but she nodded, an almost imperceptible motion.

"Come on. My treat. Then I'll take you home." Tiff took her wallet from under the seat and tucked it into her jacket pocket.

The coffee shop was more of a diner than the typical Canyon Ridge hipster hangout. No worries of running into the brew-lover crowd here. Hard-working people sat at scarred counters and drank black coffee without speaking while a replay of the latest game flickered on a muted television in the corner.

"Let's take a seat over there, near the back." Tiff pointed. "We should be able to talk without everyone else listening in." She tried a conspiratorial wink, but the gesture was pointless with Eve's eyes trained on the floor.

The moment they slid onto cracked vinyl benches, a server appeared, her hands empty. "Do you know what you want, or should I grab some menus?"

"I'd like a cup of coffee and a slice of pie." Tiff stretched to see the options in the rotating cooler. "Do you have coconut cream?"

"One piece left. You're in luck." She twisted her neck as though trying to relieve tension, then straightened the name tag that said *Sally* on her chest. "How about you?" Sally's eyes narrowed as she took a good look at Eve.

"Nothing. I'm good." Eve's gaze remained low, as if the

scratched table in front of her was something more than a flat surface to hold food.

"Are you sure? Get anything you want. It's my treat, remember?" Tiff placed both palms on the cool surface, an act she hoped would be interpreted as a sign of safety.

Eve rubbed her lips together like the way Lindsay would stick her tongue out and move it back and forth while she concentrated. "Would a hot chocolate be okay?"

"More than okay. It's such a good choice, I'd like to change my order." Tiff looked back at the server. "Could I get a cocoa instead of that coffee? And please bring two forks with the pie."

Sally glanced from Tiff to Eve and back again. "Whatever you'd like." Her tone was gilded with a layer of judgment. Eve probably dealt with that attitude every day of her life. Tiff had only a glimpse of what that felt like. She was a mother who had lost her daughter to the streets, and a woman who dared to cross the line between privilege and poverty. The church where she'd raised Lindsay and Brandt and where her husband served as an elder had become a den of lions for Tiff. The pressure to "just get over it" and move on with the life of a respectable Christian woman with a high-powered husband made worship feel more like sitting through her own trial.

Dishes clanked at the table next to them as Sally piled used plates and cups before heading to the kitchen.

"Eve, I know we just met, but I'd like to help you out if I can. If nothing else, I'm a good listener."

Eve picked at her cuticles until one began to bleed.

Pulling a paper napkin from the dispenser, Tiff handed it to her. "You were making a very dangerous decision tonight. I don't believe it's the kind of thing you'd do without feeling like it was your only option. I don't know if you use regularly, or if this is what you felt like you needed to get through the night. But help is available."

Eve wrapped the napkin tight around her finger and shook her head. "You wouldn't understand."

"Maybe not, but I'd like to try." Tiff glided her arm across the table, letting her finger land on the edge of Eve's forearm.

"Here you go." Sally positioned a cocoa in front of each of them, not apologizing for the spill over the side of Eve's cup. She set the pie and two forks on Tiff's side. "Holler if you need anything else."

Tiff forced a smile that conflicted with the irritation she was feeling. "I think that will be all. Thank you."

Eve eyed the pie. She swallowed hard, then wrapped both hands around her cup, slurping the whipped cream. "Thank you for this."

"Of course." Tiff pushed the plate closer to Eve.

Eve brushed away a white mustache with the back of her hand. "My boyfriend took off on us. I have bills. They're going to turn off the lights, and my kids, they're hungry all the time." Her head shot up. "I take good care of them. This doesn't usually happen. He always comes back before it gets like this." She rubbed at her temples.

"I have some food in the car. They're only sack lunch kinds of things, but you can take some with you." Tiff shoved the pie all the way to Eve's side. "Let me help you."

This was what it looked like when Tiff got in over her head. She felt the rise of the waters, heard the warnings from her husband, the reality that, this time, she was letting it become far too personal.

When Eve looked up again, her vacant eyes shone with tears. She nodded. "Thank you."

"Can I pick you up tomorrow? We can get you plugged in with some people who can help."

Eve's spine curved, dropping her face farther from Tiff's view.

"I'd like to get you and the kids a few groceries while we're out, if that's okay with you."

"Why?" She nudged the cocoa away and wrapped her arms against her chest.

Nothing came without strings on the streets. Tiff had spent many months developing her relationships with each of the women she met regularly. Trust grew as slowly as the cedar trees she and Bruce had planted ten years earlier, still dwarfed by the landscape around them. She'd jumped into this thing with Eve as if they'd met on the women's ministry board at church.

"I'm sorry." There was nothing left for Tiff to do but be honest. "You remind me of my daughter. It's been years since Lindsay walked out of our home. I hope and pray every day that someone out there was able to care for her. I want to help you because it helps me deal with my daughter's absence." She brushed a tear from her cheek.

"My girl is five."

"That's a precious age. I bet she's full of questions." Tiff closed her eyes for a moment and thought of Lindsay at that age, blowing bubbles while their golden retriever jumped and twisted to attack each one. Lindsay never faded. She was as alive as ever in Tiff's heart and mind. Until she opened her eyes and found a scared young woman blinking back her own tears.

Tiff reached across the table and covered Eve's hand with her own. "Let me help. Please."

TIFF PARKED THE CAR along the curb at the front of Eve's apartment building. The owner was running a real mess there. But to report him only meant fines he'd pass on to tenants, who couldn't pay. "I'll watch to make sure you get inside safely."

Eve's mouth cocked in an awkward half smile. "The walk from your car to my apartment is nothing."

"Then I'll see you tomorrow." It was more of a question than a statement.

Eve leaned forward, her gaze pointed toward the second story. Curtains spread, and a man filled the window, his silhouette black in front of the only light. She clenched her arms around herself, her body shaking. "I have to go. He's back." Flinging the door open, she jumped out and jogged up the steps, her head down as she tried to lengthen the hem of her skirt while she moved.

A moment after Eve entered, the curtains flew shut.

Tiff's heart raced for the young woman she'd only just met—and for her children. She squeezed her fingers around the steering wheel until she felt the ache in her joints. The more Tiff worked out in the world, the more she knew how little real power she possessed. Tiff and her family on the hill were feeble excuses when it came to the things that truly mattered. The best she could hope for was for God to use her to fulfill a tiny speck of His plan.

Eve

May 4, 2019, early morning

Joey was so mad, he went out for a hit, but he assured me he'd be coming back to deal with me.

I fed the kids some of the food from Tiff's paper bags, then got them back to sleep. I'm hoping their full tummies will keep them from waking when Joey returns.

I made a big mistake. I dared to get my hopes up for a minute. And I forgot that I'm not worth anything more than the needle I plunged into my arm last night. Joey will be sure I don't forget what I am.

All I had to do was be patient. One more day, and he was back. I'm so stupid.

And now I can hear his boots pounding up the cement steps. I don't even have to look to know it's him. This is big trouble.

CHAPTER FOUR

TIFF SIPPED FROM HER FAVORITE COFFEE CUP, an eclectic blend of bright colors and handcrafted pottery. Sleep hadn't arrived the night before, no matter how she'd attempted to rein in her thoughts. Her mind kept sliding back to Eve. The young woman was so small, so broken and fragile. And the man in the window had been the picture of force and anger.

She couldn't wait another minute. Tiff set the cup in the bottom of the polished kitchen sink and threw on her jacket.

Bruce entered the room with a presence that had served him well in the courtroom, all power and purpose. "You're up early. Does that mean you're finally joining me on the golf course?"

She turned her back, pretending to be immersed in the task of washing the mug. How many times had he asked her to join him in the last few months? She'd lost track, but there had been many. He didn't understand her need to work with the lost women. It was as if he'd put Lindsay away and her loss wasn't killing him every minute of the day. Tiff was unable to comprehend that ability to keep moving as if the very heart of their family hadn't disappeared. "Actually."

"Tiff. Don't even say it. You have more important things to

do. Fine." His hand slapped against the counter. "I don't know why I even bother."

Tiff blew out a breath to compose herself, then turned to him. "Just let me get changed into my golf clothes." By sheer will, she curved her lips into a smile. She did love him, or at least she had once upon a time. When they were a happy family of four and she was still blind to the rest of the world. And when her baby girl was within the walls of their home, in what they thought was safety. She could never go back to the person she was then, but for his sake and for the hope that the future would hold some level of peace, she could put on a show every now and then.

In the bedroom, Tiff pulled her once-loved golf shirt from a hanger in the back of her walk-in closet. It hung on her now, as if it belonged to another woman. Maybe it did. She finished dressing and found her clubs and shoes, then met her husband in the garage.

From behind, she could make out the clenched muscles in his jaw as he looked over the shelves of supplies.

"I'm ready. Can you help me get this into the trunk?" Tiff flung out the stand of the golf bag with her foot.

When Bruce turned, his mouth was a ridged line. He wouldn't say anything—he'd stopped trying months ago, given up his arguments against her new purpose. Even so, the temperature between them had cooled to an icy chill.

FOUR HOURS OF GOLF. How had Tiff ever enjoyed this? Time moved like cold molasses while she and Bruce took turns hitting a ball with a club. The entire game was pointless, tedious, and even a touch pretentious. All around them, men and women roamed the hillsides in carts with the sole purpose of getting a tiny ball into a slightly less tiny hole.

Tiff deposited her clubs in the closet, where she hoped they would stay for a very long time.

"Now, wasn't that a wonderful way to spend a Saturday?" Bruce stretched as if he'd finished a marathon. "The best way to cap off this beautiful day is with a nap in my chair and more golf on the television. Care to join me?" He winked.

"As enticing as that sounds, I have a few errands to run. I'll be back in a couple hours." Tiff moved toward the bedroom, hoping to avoid any questions.

"Take the Lexus." His voice had grown flat.

Those three words said everything he wanted to say about where she was going. "It really needs the oil changed. I'd better take the Toyota."

"Nonsense. You can get that taken care of while you're out."

Tiff nodded. He was pushing her to admit her errands involved the same kind of work she did at night, but Tiff wouldn't crack. If he wanted her to take the Lexus, she would. But he didn't need to know where she was taking it. "You're right. I'll do that." She left the room before he could ask any questions.

TIFF PULLED UP to Eve's apartment building, but in the light of day, it looked even shabbier than it had the night before. She parked the ridiculous Lexus next to a Pontiac with two flat tires and more rust than paint. It would serve Bruce right if she *accidentally* forgot to engage the locks and security system. Or that would just give him more ammunition in his fight against her calling.

The path to the stairs zigzagged around puddles and potholes until she was faced with the rickety railing and steps. The curtains that had snapped shut so hard the night before were now hanging crooked, as if the rod had been pulled from its brackets.

Tiff knocked on the apartment door and heard the sobs of a

small child on the other side. No one came, so she knocked again. "Eve, it's me . . . Tiff. Are you in there?"

A lock clicked, and the door creaked open a few inches. One eye, only a few feet off the ground, peered through the opening.

"Hi there. You must be Eve's little girl. Is your mom home?"

Tears flooded over the child's lashes.

Tiff's heart pounded until her pulse crashed in her ears. Something wasn't right. "Honey, would it be okay if I came in?"

The door opened farther. Behind the little girl, another child sat on the floor, wearing only a diaper. With each sob, the toddler's bottom lip quivered.

"Sweetheart, where's your mama?" Tiff took one of the girl's hands in her own.

She pointed to the corner.

Tiff's stomach lurched.

Up against the wall, Eve lay propped, an eye nearly swollen shut. Her lip had a severe cut, and blood had soaked into the front of the dress she'd been wearing the night before. One sleeve was torn from the shoulder and hung over her wrist and hand, and her shoes were gone.

Tiff rushed over, watching Eve for signs of life. Her chest rose and fell in shallow breaths as blood continued to ooze from a gash beside her injured eye. Tiff reached into her pocket and took out her cell phone, dialing 9-1-1.

"What's your emergency?"

"There's a woman here who's been beaten. She needs help immediately. Please send an ambulance." Tiff touched her palm to Eve's ankle, one of the only spots she could see that wasn't ravaged.

"What's your address?"

"I don't know. We're near the McDonald's on the east side of town. A couple blocks back in an apartment building."

The little girl who'd opened the door curled up on the floor near her mother's hardly moving body.

"I'm sure you can see my location from this call. It's apartment 84A. Just get help here fast, please." Tiff set the phone on the arm of a stained sofa and motioned for the children. "Your mama needs to rest. People are coming to help her."

Tears streamed down their faces. The scent of a very dirty diaper and blood mixed in the small room.

Eve's eyes fluttered. "Help."

"I'm here, Eve. It's Tiff. You're going to be okay."

"He'll be back." Her voice was a raspy whisper.

"But you won't be here. We're going to move you somewhere safe." Tiff's nose tingled with emotion. She glanced over her shoulder at the door. There was no escape if he returned. How could she get the two small children out of there safely?

"My bag . . . I need my orange bag." Eve's eyes closed again as she seemed to lose consciousness.

Sounds echoed outside, and the floor vibrated. Tiff's heart hammered in her throat. A moment later, EMTs entered the small living room, bringing a thin layer of safety with them.

Tiff pulled the children away from the scene. "Can you help me find your mama's bag?"

"It's her books." The little girl walked into the bedroom and pulled a tote from a crate in the corner of the closet. Three spiral notebooks with worn or missing covers slid onto the stained rust-colored carpet. "She writes in them all the time."

Tiff replaced the few that had fallen and lifted the bag; its weight felt right for a lifetime of thoughts and memories. "Do you have a grandma or grandpa close by?"

The girl's gaze dropped to the floor. "We might have an aunt Zara."

Tiff latched on to this. "Do you know your aunt's phone number? We could call her and tell her about your mom's accident."

The girl shook her head. "We don't have any family but us." She wrapped her skinny arms around her brother. "I need to change Sammy."

The noise from the living room pounded through the tissue-thin walls.

Tiff dug her fingers into the sleeves of her sweater. She was sure Eve had mentioned the children by name the night before, but she couldn't remember. Maybe she hadn't. There'd been a time when Tiff would know this information, but women on the streets didn't like questions, and she'd adjusted to that. "Sammy is such a wonderful name. What's yours?"

The girl laid her brother down on a soiled blanket and tugged a couple of wipes out of a sandwich bag. "Charlotte. My mom calls me Charlie sometimes."

Tiff retrieved a diaper from the pile in the corner of the room, feeling like a fool because this five-year-old was doing a job she should have handled.

Charlotte took the diaper and unfolded it, ready to slide it under Sammy at the right time.

"Charlotte is another pretty name. Your mom did a fine job picking those two."

The little girl shrugged her shoulders and yanked the dirty diaper out from under her brother as if she'd done it a hundred times.

Tiff placed the new one beneath Sammy, who dug at his belly button, unbothered by all the attention he was getting.

A knock at the open door drew their attention. Charlotte pulled Sammy into her arms and scooted into the corner.

A police officer filled the doorway, his hands empty and held in front of his body as if to present himself as safe. "Hey there. I'm Officer Wilson. Do you mind if I come in?" He kept his light blue eyes trained on the kids.

Charlotte ducked her face, nuzzling it into Sammy's neck.

A sense of protectiveness fell over Tiff, as if she owed Eve and the kids her loyalty. She got to her feet and stepped between the children and the officer. "I'm Tiff Bradley. Is there something I can help with?"

"Oh, Mrs. Bradley. I thought you looked familiar. I've seen you down at the soup kitchen." He pointed at his uniform. "You might recognize me without all of this."

Tiff squinted to take in his features. "Aaron?"

He nodded.

"I had no idea you were a police officer."

"It's not something I make known when I'm volunteering. A lot of people who go through the mission don't care for us." His eyes darkened, as if a cloud had passed over the sun.

"That's a shame." Tiff looked from Aaron to the children. "Can we talk outside for a minute?"

He motioned for her to step ahead of him. "Kiddos, can you both stay in this room for a few minutes? Mrs. Bradley will be right back."

The EMTs had Eve buckled onto a stretcher that they pushed out the door. Tiff cringed as she thought of the ride down the wobbly stairs on a gurney.

Aaron took a notebook from his breast pocket. "How long have you known"—he glanced down at the paper—"Eve Brookes?"

She rubbed her palms together, creating heat with the friction. "I met her last night. She was desperate and took to the streets. I brought her home."

"About what time was that?"

She ran her tongue over the edge of her teeth as she sorted through the night before. "About one in the morning. Maybe a little later."

"Did you see or hear anything you were concerned about?"

Sickness swelled in her stomach again. Tiff tipped her chin and looked up at Aaron. "Well, everything. Eve said she had two children and her boyfriend was gone. It sounded like he'd left her without any money. She had to pay rent and get food for the kids. But when we got here, there was a man in the window."

"Was it the boyfriend?"

"I assume so. She seemed frightened. I should have stayed."

She covered her mouth with cupped hands. All it would have taken was some courage. When Tiff closed her eyes, her mind replayed the image of Eve, beaten and bleeding, her little ones witnessing it all. Had they been assaulted too? "What's going to happen to the children?"

"I've contacted the Oregon Department of Human Services. I'll be taking them to the office. A caseworker will find them a safe placement. Would you be willing to ride along with me? The children seemed scared when I introduced myself."

"Of course. Let me help them get a few things together." Tiff wrapped her arms around her middle. The smell of blood and sweat and poverty floated in the air, but the kids would be safe tonight. She kept repeating that to herself, because it was the only thing keeping the grip of guilt in check.

CHAPTER FIVE

SPROUTS APPEARED as semicircles pushing through the dark soil in the starter trays. Seven so far. Zara rubbed her fingertip and thumb together, itching to push back the top layer and find the hidden seeds.

She spritzed the tiny sprouts with water from an old pump sprayer with *Zara* written across the side. A glance at her fitness tracker showed the date. May 5 meant it would be considered safe to set the little seedlings out in the soil, where they would flourish. Each baby plant needed its first set of true leaves before that could happen, though, along with some time to toughen up with daily trips into the outside world.

Looking at their tenderness, it was hard to imagine they'd grow to form the large pods with the rough texture that made up a loofah sponge.

Next year, she'd have the greenhouse cleaned and repaired, allowing her to start maybe fifty to a hundred loofahs and so many other plants. Chad was planning to help her erect a sturdy trellis for the tendrils to grab hold of as these plants grew. While the talk of the future and children had thrown her husband into a state of family planning, Zara was even more content to spend her days nurturing the farm. No matter how they decided to move forward with kids, the decision didn't need to be made right now.

Chad sidled up beside her and dropped a stack of thank-you cards on the counter. "My half is done." He kissed the skin behind her right ear. "It's not that I'm ungrateful, but did we even register for a clock?"

Zara laughed, and the accompanying snort caught her off guard. This was going to be a joke in their home for many years. Though their wedding had been small, only about fifty of their closest friends and Chad's family, somehow they had received twelve clocks from that meager crowd. Maybe it was a statement the group was trying to make. "You're showing me up. I'm only about halfway through with mine."

"I wonder if that has anything to do with you staring at these plants for hours a day?"

"Ha-ha." She shook her head. "I'm just excited. This is a dream come true. Think of all the products we'll have this fall." She wrapped her arm around his waist. "I can't believe this is really happening. That we're really here, in this life. It's so perfect." *Except for that gene.* But she wasn't going to bring up the topic again and ruin this moment. If Zara hadn't gotten tested, everything *would* be perfect. Even if they never had children, her life was far better than she had ever imagined it could be.

Before she'd met Chad, Zara had been without a family for years. Her sister, if she was even alive, was out there somewhere doing whatever she pleased with no regard for anyone but herself. Their mother was locked away and might as well be dead—it wasn't like Wanda had ever been very lively. And Tyson—he'd been gone so long, Zara could barely remember his face without pulling out the three old photographs she kept in the bottom of an ancient jewelry box featuring a ballerina who hadn't twirled in a decade.

"Something smells really good." Chad leaned over the Crock-Pot, inhaling.

"I thought I'd give one of your mom's gifts a try since she's coming over tonight." Her dinners might come from this contraption every time she made them. Why hadn't she known cooking could be so easy? Of course, they hadn't *eaten* the yummy-smelling chicken yet. She should hold her newfound culinary confidence in check. But Zara's usual fare had a smoky quality that wasn't at all appetizing, and Sharon had assured her it was nearly impossible to burn food in a slow cooker.

"Since you made the grub, I've got the table and dishes." He pulled three plates from the open cupboard.

"Wait. We should use the new ones. And all of our gifts are stacked on the table, so I think you've volunteered for more than you bargained for."

He tipped his head to the side. "So just find the new plates in the pile?"

"And wash them. Of course."

He smacked his forehead with the palm of his hand. "Of course."

Chad headed off to find their table with Pickles, the name they'd finally settled on for the puppy, attached to his ankle.

What more could she do to make this old house seem like a home before her mother-in-law arrived? Sharon had never been one to judge, but Zara ached for her to be impressed. She wanted Sharon to think her son had made a wonderful decision in marrying Zara, even if Zara herself doubted his choice.

Unable to resist a peek, she unlatched the lid of the Crock-Pot. Her better sense told her this was not the thing to do, but she needed confirmation that the chicken was cooking in there. Sharon would be pulling in soon. As Zara opened the top, steam rolled out with the warm, homey feel of someone else's kitchen. She stabbed a fork into the flesh and pulled back a chunk of dark meat. It came away from the bone with ease. Plunking the bite into her mouth, she jumped back, turned to the sink, and spit. *Slow cooker* did not mean less heat. The burned patch on her tongue should help her remember that for a long time. Zara turned on the faucet and swigged cold well water that tasted like licking the bottom of a rusty pan. Yet her mouth still burned.

A crash from somewhere out of sight stole her attention. *Oh please, don't let it be the dishes.* She jogged into the dining room.

Chad stood at the window, pressing his cheek against the glass to get a better view.

"What is it?" Zara tried to see what he saw.

"Looks like the gutter along the back porch is done." He straightened. "It might have taken a chunk of roof with it."

Zara twisted her hair around and held it in a mound on top of her head. "That was not on the list."

"I have a feeling this place is going to determine its own order of repairs for a while. Right now, the roof is crying the loudest." He shook his head as he walked out of the room.

Snatching Pickles off the floor, Zara followed. From the mudroom, the view was disheartening. The gutter swayed in the breeze, rain spraying off the end. Chunks of rotten wood littered the porch, and a flap of roofing waved from the eaves.

"I'm going to get a tarp up there and check out the damage." Chad twisted and looked at her with pleading eyes. "Do we have a tarp?"

She shrugged. "I don't think so. Wasn't there one in the wedding gifts?"

He shook his head at her pathetic attempt to lighten the mood. "I'll be back in twenty minutes. Can dinner hold?"

"I guess." Zara forced a smile. Crumbling or not, this house was still her dream. "I love you."

His lip quirked. "Nice try." He kissed the top of her head before pulling on his jacket. As Chad opened the door to leave, his mom stepped in. "Hey, Mom. I'll be back in a few. The reality of homeownership just struck." He gave her a quick hug, grabbed his keys from the hook, and left.

"What's that about?" Sharon removed her teal raincoat and folded it over one arm.

"We had a little issue with the gutter." So much for making the place feel homey. Zara pointed out the back window.

"Wow. That's a fine start." Her smile was kind and genuine. It was something Zara loved about Sharon. Though she couldn't help bracing for her judgment, it never came. "If we have a few minutes, maybe I can get your gown and veil. I wanted to have them cleaned and sealed for you, if you don't mind."

Zara was torn between wanting to dive into this woman's open invitation to mother her and the fear that it was a trap. Her own mother's words could never be trusted. "That's so generous of you, but I don't want you to put yourself out. I can do it." Though more than two weeks post wedding, she still hadn't.

"And so can I, if it's okay. Ted's mother did this for me. Let me return the favor." Her hand brushed Zara's arm.

Zara found herself nodding before her brain had a chance to fully untangle the twists and turns of the offer.

"Are they handy?"

It was a little embarrassing just how handy the dress and veil actually were. Zara's gown was still lying over a chair in the living room. "They are."

"Wonderful. I can get them into my car before the next dump of rain." Sharon rubbed her palms together as though Zara had set a grand meal in front of her and not just taken her up on an offer of help.

Sharon followed her into the other room, where she picked up the dress by the hanger and draped it over her arm. The veil shifted from the top and slid to the floor. Zara's breath faltered.

For a moment, all she could do was stare at the handmade lace, remembering the woman who had worn it before her.

"It's so beautiful. And you looked perfect wearing it." Sharon bent down and picked up the veil by the crown. She handled it with care, as though it were a treasured item passed down in her own family.

"My grandmother was a good woman. I wish she could have been there for my wedding." Zara blinked away a tear.

"I'm sure she would have been so proud, like I am." Sharon placed the piece on Zara's head, tucking loose strands of hair behind her ears. "You are so beautiful, inside and out."

"I bet you say that to all your daughters-in-law."

"Maybe so, but, Zara, you are special. You're the perfect match for my Chad." She ran a thumb over Zara's cheek. "God created you and my son for each other. I have no doubts."

Zara felt the shift in her expression and tried to turn away, acting as though she needed to catch another sight of the view out the window. Anything to keep Sharon from seeing the fears rising to the surface.

"You didn't ask for my thoughts, but I feel led to give them anyway." Sharon stood beside her, looking out into the darkening day, their reflections in the window. "I had a rough time as a child. I was moved from one home to another before I was finally adopted. When Ted came around, I didn't know how to trust him. It wasn't in me. I'd been robbed of the chance to understand that kind of love." She took Zara's hand in hers without shifting her gaze away from the shadowed field outside. "It took time, but healing happened."

Zara's face tingled, and tears pulsed behind her eyes. She bit her lip to hold back the tsunami of emotions.

"Sweet girl, let me help you." Sharon's voice shook.

Zara turned toward the much shorter woman. Gray tendrils curled around Sharon's lightly lined face. "How do you keep going? How do you do it without Ted?"

Tears shone in Sharon's eyes. "It's not easy, but the pain and sadness of losing him is a price I'm glad to pay for the time we had together."

The muscles in Zara's shoulders softened. If she could some-day be a little like her mother-in-law, then the past would be redeemed. Her life would have proved worthy.

CHAPTER SIX

TIFF RUBBED THE TENDER SKIN beneath her right eye, trying to push away the heavy weight of exhaustion.

Eve's hospital room was filled with steady beeps and swishes as equipment monitored her improvement. Though there wasn't much to do in there, it beat the days Tiff had spent waiting for Eve to be released from ICU and placed in a regular room. HIPAA prevented the healthcare providers from sharing details about Eve's condition, but after so many hours blending into the background, Tiff had overheard enough to know the young mom's condition was serious.

Officer Aaron Wilson stepped around the curtain dividing Eve's half of the room from the bed occupied by a nearly unconscious elderly woman. "How's she doing today?"

Tiff shook her head. "She hasn't been awake since they brought her here. She's still coming out of the sedation. Any word on the children?"

"I know they found a temporary placement. That's about it." He crossed his arms and looked down at Eve's thin frame.

Six calls to DHS had only served to get Tiff's anger surging. She'd pushed the scant information she had—that the kids had an aunt named Zara. How hard could it be to find someone with that name? The case manager assured Tiff the children would be safe until a suitable family member could be reached. Maybe this would be Eve's chance to reconnect and start over.

"We've lost a lot of time on this case." Aaron sighed. "I need information only Eve can give."

"What about Charlotte? She must know what happened." Though the thought of the child being questioned tore at Tiff's middle.

"I'm sure she does, but she's not talking, and the little guy doesn't have the vocabulary to help." Sadness washed over his features. The man must have seen the worst in their community, but he still had a tender heart. "Those kids have had more than anyone's share of trauma in their short lives. I can't imagine."

"Me neither." When Tiff closed her eyes, she could see the children's faces. The eyes of a five-year-old should never have contained so much of a chill, but Charlotte had survived. How many kids were out there just making it from one day to the next?

Looking back at Eve's face, still battered and swollen, Tiff's heart split between compassion and fury. It was one thing to throw your life away, but to do that to your children? How could any mother allow her kids to suffer the way Charlotte and Sammy had? Yet who was there to protect Eve? She was not much more than a child herself.

The kids, hidden wherever they were, had not been part of Tiff's mission. They were an area she couldn't touch or consider. How many of the women on the streets had children? How many of those kids were living in war zones?

Tiff might have been able to overlook this need before, but now it had crashed into her world.

Eve moaned.

"Looks like Sleeping Beauty is finally coming to." Aaron scratched the back of his neck.

Tiff dissected his words, looking for sarcasm, but there was none.

He pulled his notebook free of his pocket. "Eve, can you hear me? This is Officer Wilson. I was at your home the morning Mrs. Bradley discovered you."

Eve's eyes blinked. The right one slowly opened, but swelling forced the left shut.

"What's this?" Her voice was a barely audible scratch. She pulled away, attempting to roll toward Tiff. "What's going on? Where are my kids?" She raised an IV-tethered hand to her weeping eye.

"Eve, do you remember me?" Tiff leaned over, putting her face in view of the woman's better eye. "We had cocoa the other night."

"Yeah." She moved back an inch. "Where's Charlie and Sammy?"

Tiff looked to Aaron. She couldn't bring herself to say *foster care* to the woman who'd just survived being beaten to the point of nearly losing her life.

"Ms. Brookes, you were very badly injured. We were unable to locate your family, so the children have been staying with a certified couple. They're being well cared for."

"I've lost them." A tear rolled down her face. "You put them in foster care?"

"There wasn't another choice." His voice was soothing yet firm and factual. No room for discussion or compromise.

"I want them back." She tried to lift herself up on the mattress but cringed and backed down. "They're my children."

"That's between you, their caseworker, and the judge."

Tiff's chest tightened. "I'll help you however I can."

Eve took her in. "You don't even know me. Why do you want to get all into my mess?"

"Because." Tiff scrambled for the truth. "Because I care about you and the kids. Because we all deserve another chance. I want to help you get yours." If only Tiff could have another chance to mend the broken place between her heart and Lindsay's. "Look." She bent and, from her purse, pulled out a fresh spiral notebook and a package of four colored gel pens. "I have the tote you asked me to get. It's at my house for safekeeping, but I thought you might want to have a notebook to write in while you recover."

"You read my journals?"

"No. Charlotte told me what they were. I haven't opened a single one."

Eve's head bobbed in a fractional nod, and she took the offering, placing the items on her blanket-covered lap, her hand on top as if protecting something vital.

"Ms. Brookes, we need to talk about what happened the night you were injured." Aaron removed his notebook again and flipped to a clean page. "Let's start with your name, birthdate, and age."

Eve gave the information without argument, but when it came to naming her abuser, her lips tightened, forming a pale line.

"Listen, we have his name from two other sources. I just need you to confirm that he was the man who hurt you."

Eve gathered the notebook and blanket tightly to her chest and turned her gaze toward the wall. Her tongue ran over the stitches holding her lip together.

Aaron blew out a hard breath. "You're not helping yourself or your children by staying quiet." He took a business card from his pocket and placed it on the bedside table. "Joey is dangerous. We can help you. Call me if you decide it's time to put this guy away." He nodded toward Tiff and left the room.

In the last few years, Tiff had grown tough. Her emotions rarely took hold when she saw the sadness that drugs and poverty created. But there was something different in this room, a feeling of motherliness taking over, as if the broken woman in the hospital bed were Tiff's own daughter. The walls she'd built to hold back the scenarios Lindsay could have faced out in the world crumbled a bit, and a tear slid over her cheek. Tiff brushed it away with the back of her hand and looked away.

From the window, Oregon shone with lush greens and towering trees. Up there, on top of a hill, poverty was hidden. Life on the streets was shadowed. For the first time in longer than she could remember, Tiff wished she could go back to being ignorant.

Eve
May 7, 2019

One day is just like the other—miserable. I'm in a hospital, more alone than ever. It's hard to write. The room swirls and tosses, but I feel like I have to get my words on the page.

Bright lights cut into my brain. I can't stand this pain. It's everywhere, in my body and in my heart. It's crawling along my skin, digging into my flesh. My stomach is angry. I need a hit. I'll die without it.

The beeps of the machines pierce my ears like strong gusts of wind, coming closer and closer.

I'm going to die in the hospital because they won't give me what I need to survive.

TIFF MUST HAVE DOZED OFF in the chair in Eve's hospital room. The sound of rustling and sobs was disorienting for a moment. Blinking, she shifted the room into focus. "Eve, do you need something?"

"I'm going to be sick." Her arms flailed and reached out.

Tiff shot up, grabbing the blue bin and holding it under Eve's chin.

She heaved and gagged, not giving up much more than needed fluids. Finally, the convulsions stopped, and tears ran down her face. "I'm sick. I need help."

"What do you need?" Tiff punched the call button and set the tray aside.

"I need something strong for the pain. My head." She curled onto her side, forming a ball with her body. "Please make them give me something."

The curtain squawked along its runner as a nurse drew it to the side. "What's going on in here?" Her words were clipped but bright. "Do you need help?"

Tiff touched her fingers to Eve's clammy arm. "She says she's in a lot of pain, and she just vomited. Can she get some medication?" She set the container near the sink.

The nurse tilted her head. "It's going to be like that, I'm afraid. The doctor ordered no narcotics, but he prescribed a high-level ibuprofen. Unfortunately, the next dose isn't for a couple of hours."

"I need something stronger." Eve moaned.

The nurse checked the IV, then ran a washcloth under the water in the sink. She wrung it out and placed it on Eve's forehead. "I know you feel like you need the drugs, but give it a couple days, and you'll start to feel better. Detoxing is tough on the body, but it's worth it."

Detox. On top of all the injuries and heartbreak.

Detox held a lock on so many women's futures. They wanted to do something else, but detoxing was so frightening and painful, it kept them chained to heroin out of fear they'd die without it—or fear that they wouldn't. It was too much to escape. Even if more clinics offered medically supervised detox, there'd still be a cost, both in money and in pride.

The nurse patted Tiff's arm. Her eyes were sad and sympathetic, a combination that would break Tiff's heart if she were in Eve's position. "You're a good friend. She'll need one of those." She turned away, taking the tub and leaving the room.

Tiff pulled a chair next to the bed, then turned the cloth on Eve's forehead to the cooler side. "I noticed you were on something the other night, but I wasn't sure what. Do you want to tell me about it?"

"I don't know what you're talking about." Eve covered her face with an arm.

"Listen, I'll help you. I'll do whatever I can, but there's one thing we need to agree on. You must be honest with me."

Another tap at the door.

Tiff turned her body. "Yes?"

A woman in slacks and a button-up shirt walked in, a canvas bag hanging from her left hand. "Hello. Is this Eve?"

Tiff nodded.

"Hi. I'm Cheri Jerome. I work with the Department of Human Services on the Child Protective Services side."

Eve's face shifted just enough to get a look over her arm.

"Eve, I know you've been through a lot, but we need to talk about Charlotte and Sammy. Are you up for that?"

She rolled to her back and pressed the bed controls until she sat up, then hugged her knees to her chest. Sweat still beaded across her collarbone and her body trembled, but she made an effort to smooth her hair.

"Is this a relative of yours?" Cheri looked to Tiff as if the question was hers to answer.

Tiff shook her head.

"Well, I'm going to need your permission to talk in front of her. What do you think, Eve?"

Tiff stood to leave. This wasn't her business, and she was in far too deep already.

"Stay." Eve's voice was scratchy but stronger than earlier. "Please."

Tiff sat back down, wrapping her fingers around Eve's nearly translucent hand.

"Okay then." Cheri set her bag on the small bedside table. "The kids have been put into the care and custody of the state. From what I've seen, this is the first time this has happened. Is that correct?"

Eve nodded. "I want my babies back." A tear slid down her cheek.

"I'm sure you do. That's our goal too, and I'm here to help you reach it. There are steps you're going to have to accomplish before we can deem you safe to parent. Do you understand?"

"I've never hurt my babies. I haven't laid a hand on them." Her face reddened under the array of blues, greens, and yellows.

"And we have no reason to believe you've physically abused them. Eve, there are other ways that children get hurt, and they can be just as devastating to a child as a beating. Charlotte and Sammy have witnessed domestic violence. Is that correct?"

Eve's mouth dropped open, and her gaze descended to the floor.

"It's my job to help you and your kids. We'll set out a plan, and once you've completed the necessary steps, your children will be returned to you." Cheri dug into the pocket of her bag and pulled out an official-looking sheet. "You're going to need to attend drug treatment classes, have clean urine tests, find a job so you can support your kids in a legal way, and also obtain safe and secure housing." She took a breath. "I know this sounds hard, but you and your children are worth it. Am I right?"

Eve rested her hand on her stomach, her eyes flooded with tears. She nodded, but the motion was almost invisible.

"Do you have a place to go when you're released?"

Eve brushed her teeth over the stiches in her bottom lip.

"I've been in touch with an emergency shelter." Tiff swallowed. "They're holding a bed for her. Eve can stay there till something opens up in temporary women's housing. "

"That's wonderful." Cheri winked. "It's not easy getting in these days. Eve, you're being given a chance at a better life. It's up to you to take it."

Eve rolled back onto her side, her body quaking.

The show of sincere agony tore at Tiff's heart. "I'll walk you out. I want to ask about getting Eve a blanket from the warmer."

Outside the room, the hospital felt alive and hopeful. Tiff had the ability and right to walk in and out of this daily desperation. She could return to her warm, beautiful home after driving the streets at night. Back to a place where there was safety and security, hot water and electricity. If she ever had a need, it could be met with a few keystrokes and two-day delivery. After all the time she'd spent trying to make a difference, what had she really changed in her own life?

"It's so kind of you to help Eve." Cheri lifted the strap of her bag over her neck and crossed her arms. "You need to know, this isn't going to be easy, and that girl in there isn't a stray puppy. She's an addict. Addicts lie, cheat, and steal. They say they're going to do whatever is needed to get their kids back and keep them safe; then they turn around and skip a visit in exchange for a hit."

"I found her. I was the one who called the ambulance. It was one of the most frightening things I've ever seen." Tiff tucked loose hair behind her ear. "I have to believe it was a wake-up call for Eve." It certainly was for Tiff. She needed to give more and go deeper. She had to do this, because she needed to believe someone, somewhere had done the same for Lindsay.

CHAPTER SEVEN

Eve

May 9, 2019

The lady who gave me this journal keeps hanging around here. She's so kind. I can't think of anything I can give her back. The truth is, her caring only makes this whole thing harder. I have a long history of being a fool. I fall for people who act like they care. It's like I'm a desperate old dog, willing to put up with anyone who will show me some attention. Even if they beat me.

Every bit of my body aches. The muscles, the bruises, the healing cuts. None of it feels worse than my heart, though. The state has my kids. My man is on the run. And the doctor tells me I've lost the baby I didn't even realize I was carrying.

How did I not know?

I'll never get to hold this little one. I can never make up for what I've done to him.

I don't know how I can ever make it up to Charlotte and Sammy, either. Bad things can happen to kids in the system. Horrible things.

I can't keep writing. There's a twisting in my stomach, and

*my head pounds. I just need a little something to stop the pain
and get me through. But not too much. It's better to come off
heroin slowly. I'll die if I'm forced to white-knuckle this. And if I
die, what will happen to my kids?*

TIFF NUDGED THE DOOR OPEN with her shoulder and entered
Eve's room. "Knock, knock. I brought you some clothes to wear
when they release you."

Eve slapped her journal shut, her eyes wide. "When? Do you
know when I can leave?"

"I thought you might. It sounds like it will be soon, but I
don't have any details. I spoke to the director of the emergency
shelter. They still have a bed for you. It's not perfect, but try
to remember this is just for now. We'll get you into temporary
women's housing as soon as we can." She laid a stack of jeans,
T-shirts, and other essentials on the chair—three outfits. As a
precaution, Tiff had slid a card with her contact information
into every pocket. Tiff had assumed Eve would not have easy
access to the things she'd left in the apartment. Apparently, rent
hadn't been paid for some time, and the eviction was already in
process. After the assault, the landlord would be able to expedite
the process. She'd be checking with an attorney, but Tiff knew
how these things usually worked out, and it wouldn't be in Eve's
favor. "Have you thought about reaching out to your family?
They might be able to help."

Eve rubbed her fingers in circles along the sides of her head.
"No. I mean, thanks for the clothes. I can't pay you back." Her
eyes searched the room as though needing somewhere to anchor
other than on Tiff.

"The clothes are a gift. Don't worry about the cost. When the
doctor gives the okay, I'll drive you to the shelter. You'll need
some extra help for a bit. I'm planning to check in each day."

Tiff slid her index finger over her bottom lip. "It's not going to be easy, but you can do this. I know you love your kids. They're counting on you."

Eve's eyes grew darker. "I'll make it right for them. Can you tell them I will?"

"You can tell them yourself. Cheri said she'll set up a visit for you as soon as you're ready. It would be good, especially for Charlotte, to see you're recovering. The last time she saw you was the day of the . . . accident. She needs to see you're okay."

A shiver spread over Tiff's skin. What she'd seen that morning had kept her up late into that night and many of the next, waking her with nightmares whenever she drifted off to sleep. The smell of blood and the look of horror cloned on the faces of the children—the trauma they had witnessed could haunt their lives forever, a moment that could send them on a life journey that would either include a long and painful healing process or a repeat performance for their own children. A cycle of dysfunction and misery like that only stopped when it was forced to halt.

If Tiff had a wish, it would be to end this spiral before it consumed another generation.

THEY WERE GROWING. The first leaves of the loofah plants uncurled as the sprouts straightened and stood like proud soldiers in pristine emerald green uniforms. It took all of Zara's self-control not to assign names to each individual plant. With all the watching, waiting, and caring she'd done for them over the last few weeks, they were like members of her little family.

Her life, the way it was at that very moment, was the dream she feared too fragile to bloom. Yet here she was, Zara Brookes Mahoney, living in this old farmhouse, its walls full of untold stories, its rooms as ready for change as a freshly plowed plot of ground. And she shared this true-life fantasy with her handsome husband, a man who would work alongside her and then fold her into his arms at night. They had years to cultivate this property and grow their house into a home. Chad had turned her life into an endless honeymoon.

Zara washed her hands and dried them on a hand-embroidered tea towel Sharon had made for their home. The towel was simple and quaint. The perfect match to the vision Zara had for this place.

Pickles bounded into the kitchen, his back legs working faster than his front until he rolled into a pile at her feet. Gathering him up, Zara inhaled the sweet scent that only came from newness. His tongue flapped like a toddler on caffeine, slapping her face from her eyes to her nose.

Chad kissed her forehead, his mouth rough with morning stubble. "Okay, buddy. Let's get the day off right." He took Pickles and stepped out the back door.

Zara sipped her coffee and stared out the kitchen window, watching Chad try to coax the puppy into doing his business before they headed to Sharon's. She had agreed to dog-sit while Zara and Chad sanded and refinished the hardwood on the first floor. There was a good chance she and Chad would be sleeping in the back of the SUV for a few nights until the fumes dissipated.

Zara's hands warmed against the mug, adding to the odd sense she'd had all morning. She felt . . . settled. As if her life was, for the first time ever, falling into place. Chad had blessed her more than he would ever know by marrying her. The anxiety she'd been fighting since discovering she carried the Hunter syndrome gene had leveled off, and she was beginning to accept the truth—for now. It wasn't like she was ready for kids, anyway. The agony would revisit, she was sure. For the time being, Zara was going to live like a teen, assuming nothing bad could happen. Except that had never been her way. Her twin sister's way, yes—and look what had happened to her.

Zara had always been a worrier. It was amazing she'd ever agreed to get married. It would have been just like her to sabotage her future by running away. Now she was committed. No turning back.

The door opened and Chad came in, the puppy held out and away from his chest. "Well, I convinced him to do half of what he was supposed to do. I'm sure Mom will let me know when the other half lands on her carpet." His nose wrinkled.

She grabbed the rag they kept by the door and wiped all four paws. "Maybe we'll get lucky this time." She grinned. Housebreaking wasn't going well. Another wonderful reason to hold off on children. With the skills they currently had, their kids would be heading to college in diapers.

"You look gorgeous." He kissed her forehead, then took a sip from her coffee mug. "This is my favorite morning." He winked. "I'm going to take the dog stuff out to the car. Are you about ready?"

"Just let me do a final check on the plants. I'm going to cover them before we start the refinishing."

Chad chuckled. "They are plants. You know that, right?"

"Very funny. I'll be out in a minute."

The door clicked behind him, and Zara immediately smelled another task. "Well, dog, at least you didn't do that at Grandma's." She probably should scold him or something. Did people really rub dog's noses in it? *Yuck.* As she bagged up the mess, someone honked outside. Chad must have been in a huge hurry to get moving.

A moment later, he opened the door. "Whoa. What happened in here?" He waved his hand in front of his nose. "That's nasty."

She nodded. "At least he didn't save it for your mom."

"I'll help." He tossed a stack of papers on the counter. "The mailman was here. He said the box door was hanging on one hinge again."

Zara blew out a breath that lifted her bangs from her eyes. "I thought I'd fixed it last time."

"We'll take care of it when we get back."

She took another look at the sprouting loofahs.

"Don't worry. All this will be here when we get back home."

Home. Their home.

ZARA'S BACK WAS ON FIRE. Too many days of sanding, sweeping, running a shop vac, and finally, painting on new layers of finish had left their hardwood floors shining like they must have when they were brand-new. But the effort had also tweaked every rarely used muscle in her body. And now that Chad was home from work, they still had another coat to apply.

In the kitchen, she folded herself over, letting her arms dangle like a rag doll's. The release was painful and blissful all at once.

Something, a paper or envelope, stuck out from between the shelf and the wall. It had slipped back there, wedging itself in so tight that it took a good yank to release.

Zara straightened, her mind going off on a million little imaginary paths. What if the letter was placed there by the original builder of the house and had finally just worked its way free from a hundred years of hiding? Or maybe the contents held the solution to a long-forgotten mystery.

She snagged it before Chad came in and ruined the fun with his accountant-like factual thinking. His wildest suggestion would be the electric bill or maybe junk mail.

The envelope had barely a ding on the edges, telling her Chad would have come out on top in a competition. But just because the practical guess was usually the right one didn't make this any less entertaining.

Turning it over in her hand, Zara could see her maiden name. It was not a bill, and it seemed to be from the government. What could the Department of Human Services want with her?

For a moment, she considered waiting for Chad, but she was sure, or at least semi sure, that it was nothing. Weaving her finger under the seal, she ripped it open and tugged out a short letter.

The words lost focus as Zara stumbled and grasped the side of the sink, the paper floating to the floor. Tingles rolled over her face like she was going to cry, but her eyes remained dry.

"I think this project is increasing my love of office work." Chad brushed past her, cupped his hands under the faucet, and took a drink.

Zara's body had gone into some kind of an upright coma. Even her mouth was disconnected from her brain. She strained to get words off her tongue, but what could she say?

"Are you okay?" Chad stopped wiping his hands on the kitchen towel and stared into her eyes.

And here came the tears. Washing over her cheeks and along her jawline. Zara pointed to the paper that had landed near the door.

He snatched it up, reading the words that were no longer harmless groupings of letters on a page.

"Who are these children? Do you know them?" He lowered the letter, his gaze returning to her.

It felt like an accusation, like she'd done something, and they were both to be held accountable. But she hadn't. She wasn't even sure this could really be happening. *Charlotte and Samuel.* Zara had never heard those names before. No. That wasn't true. Her sister's favorite baby doll had been named Charlotte. Eve had carried her everywhere until the day she set her down at the grocery store and their mother refused to go back for her.

"Charlotte and Samuel have to be Eve's children." And Zara was the aunt who hadn't even known they existed. How could the state ask if she was willing to be a caretaker for these two? They might as well scoop someone off the street. She and Chad were as good as perfect strangers.

"Wow." He stood in front of Zara, stunned into his own silence. It took what felt like hours before he stepped forward and brought her to his chest. "What do you want to do?"

Was that a question she was supposed to have an answer for? These two children had come out of nowhere, like God had snapped His fingers and they appeared. She pushed back, Chad's warmth evaporating from her skin, and took the paper from his hand. "I don't know anything about them—not even how old they are. What's happened to these kids? And where is Eve? Why didn't she call before things got this bad?"

The answer to that question punched her hard in the heart. The last time she saw Eve, not long after starting college, Zara had told her she was done. She wouldn't see her or hear from her until Eve decided to get her life together. Zara had thought that was tough love, that maybe if she didn't help her sister, Eve would find the strength to kick her addictions and start fresh. Honestly, Zara believed that Eve wouldn't be able to live without her, and she'd have to get clean.

But Zara had put herself in a seat of honor, and it turned out she was just another person. If Eve could have gotten clean because she didn't want to lose Zara, she could have gotten clean so she wouldn't lose herself.

Zara didn't have the strength to watch the other half of her die.

Chad laced his fingers into hers and guided Zara out the door and into the front seat of his SUV. They sat staring out the window at raindrops merging on the windshield until they grew too heavy and slid down the glass.

"We're going to remember this day forever." He pulled the lever on the side of his seat and reclined. "It will always be that day when all the furniture was stacked, the house stunk like chemicals, and we found out about two kids who needed a place to stay for a while."

Zara's stomach balled tight, forming pressure below her diaphragm. "You're actually considering this?"

"I'm not sure how we can't. Whatever happened, it's not their fault. The caseworker's name and number are on the letter. I think you should take the first step and call." His thumb rubbed back and forth over the side of her hand, but his eyes remained fixed on the windshield.

"These aren't our children. It's not a way to start our family."

He gripped her hand tighter and ran it along his rough chin. "This isn't about us."

His words left a guilty hole in her heart. These kids needed someone. They'd been put into the foster care system, staying with who knows who. But it was a little about her, wasn't it? Why did she have to give up her perfect life because her sister had screwed up?

Zara flipped off her shoes, reclined her seat, and pressed her bare toes to the windshield.

"We don't have to make any decisions today. Just collect information. When we have all the facts, we'll be better able to choose what makes the most sense." He nodded his head as if making a plan would take away the sting that followed a yes or a no.

"I know it's selfish, but what about us?"

"Us?"

"This was supposed to be our time, just the two of us living the dream."

A deep chuckle rumbled in his chest. "Babe, we're always going to be living the dream together. It might look a little different than we thought, but we're a team."

She rolled her head to the side and stared into his eyes. "I feel like you're mixing your metaphors."

He shrugged and raised their hands together. "Victory is ours?"

"Not even close." Zara blew out so hard she fogged the windshield. "I'll call the caseworker and ask about the kids." It was tiny, but it also felt like a grand relinquishment. If they moved forward, the first children they would bring into their home wouldn't even be theirs. She knew it was irrational, just like the way she had to celebrate birthdays on the actual day and refused to eat out on holidays. Maybe her hesitation, her clamping on to the plan she'd had for their lives, was just another way to keep her life from becoming anything like the one her mother lived. Wasn't that a worthy pursuit?

"We need a list. All the questions we can think of." Chad nodded his head as though making this major life decision into a structured goal would make it easier. "We need to know the process to become foster parents. How old are they? Do they know you exist? Have they been hurt?"

Zara swallowed past the knot that seemed to be tied in her throat. Each question made her feel more and more like the heartless woman she must be to even think about saying no. Knowing what she knew, how could she leave any child in the system? If the kids weren't with them, they would be with strangers. *Trained strangers who purposely set out to care for children in need.*

"I don't know what's wrong with me. My mind is flying from all the reasons we should take them to all the reasons we are absolutely not the people for this task." She tapped her knuckles against her forehead. "What kind of a person would say no? But what if it's too much for us and someone else could do a better job? I'm not a person who believes love is genetic, yet . . . I don't even know."

Chad took her left hand away from her face and threaded his fingers between hers. "I believe God will give us the answer. Why don't you call the caseworker, ask all your questions, and set up a time for us to meet the kids?"

Cold spread over her. This wasn't one of the scenarios Zara had worked through in her imagination. She wouldn't wake up and think she'd just had the craziest dream yet. This was real and present, and they couldn't ever go back to the way things were before she'd opened that envelope.

CHAPTER EIGHT

TIFF DROPPED HER KEYS into the dish by the garage door.

"Where have you been?" Bruce smacked the handle on their kitchen sink faucet. Water continued to drip into a large bowl set in the bottom of the basin. The heavy scent of Indian takeout permeated the air. "I've been trying to get ahold of you for hours."

She turned her cell phone over in her hand. Seven missed calls, each one from her husband. *Oops.* "I'm sorry. I was at the hospital and had the volume off. I guess I didn't notice it vibrating."

"And you didn't notice dinnertime again?"

Her spine straightened. "Excuse me. I didn't realize feeding you was my responsibility."

"I work hard. I make the money to get all the nice things you have. And I'd like to have dinner with my wife." His shoulders fell, and his voice softened. "I'm not asking you to make me a meal every night. I just want some company. We can go out. I can get food on the way home. But you could at least be here."

"I'm sorry. Time got away from me." This feeling of being tugged in two directions at once was oh so familiar. She'd felt the same way when Lindsay and Brandt were children. One would have a baseball game, and the other a dance competition. It was bad enough choosing between her children, but it was nearly impossible to find time for Bruce alone. Throughout those years, they'd promised each other that their time was coming. Bruce's job would get easier, and he'd be home earlier. The kids would grow up, freeing them to be together. Maybe things would be different now if they'd made the room in their schedules back then. "It will get easier." Tiff repeated the worn-out saying. But would it really?

He shook his head. "You don't believe that. I can see it written all over your face."

"I do. I'll make time for you. Didn't I go golfing last week?"

"Against your will."

"It was fun."

"Don't. I can't stand your pity."

She glanced toward the garage door before she was able to think better of it.

"Seriously?" The vein in his neck grew pronounced.

"What?"

"You're heading out tonight, aren't you?" Color painted his face a frightening shade of red.

"It's Monday."

Silence thickened the air.

"I have a responsibility to go."

Bruce crossed his arms in front of his chest. The bulge of his belly was starting to grow, and the hair at his temples had turned gray. They weren't the young parents they had been or the newlyweds before that.

"Please, don't be mad." She touched his arm. Beneath her fingers, his muscle tightened.

"Go. I'll watch television until I fall asleep, like almost every other night. It's the dream of all men, you know." He pulled away and headed to his recliner, which sat next to its twin—the one he'd bought for Tiff. A gift she rarely used. But she wasn't ready to sit until she died when she had an opportunity to make things a little better in the world. She was fifty . . . something. Not ninety.

The surround sound blasted to life, and the house became an extension of a professional basketball arena. She should go in and spend a few minutes watching the pointless game with her husband, but she didn't. Instead, she walked toward the garage, leaving his dishes in the sink and his takeout containers open on the granite countertop, not even bothering to change her clothes.

What was wrong with her? She'd rather spend her evening with Esther and Conway. Maybe she could convince him to go to the clinic. And she wanted to see Theresa with her own eyes and make sure she was okay. These people counted on Tiff, and in many ways, Tiff counted on them. They felt more like family than Bruce and Brandt had over the last Lindsay-less seven years.

Eve

May 13, 2019

Everything in this room beeps, and it's breaking the thin glass in my head. My muscles ache as if they're being torn apart. I try to take a deep breath, but even that hurts. My kids need me alive. But if I stay here, I'm going to die. Why doesn't anyone care?

If I throw up one more time, there'll be nothing left of me. The nurse said she was getting an order for antinausea medicine, but that's not what I need.

This is the first time today that I've been alone in my room. It's what I wanted all along, but now I feel the demons coming after me. As the sun sets, I sense them set free to devour me.

I'm trying to get my nerve up to rip the IV out of my hand. I have rights. They can't keep me here. I'm not a child, and I'm not waiting on some judgmental doctor to tell me what I can and can't do.

Tiff left me clothes. I wonder what life must be like for a

woman with a name like Tiff. It seems like you'd be guaranteed
a certain amount of privilege just by the sound of it. I tried
to give my kids those kinds of names, ones that wouldn't fit
in where we live. Whatever it takes to push them into a better
world.

I can't stop crying and throwing up, and I can't get free of
the invisible strap that's growing tighter around my chest. I
need Charlotte and Sammy back. And I'll get them. I only need
enough to stop being sick. Then I can figure out what to do
next.

I'm not going to make it much longer. Getting out of here is
my only hope.

An alarm has just gone off somewhere down the hall. People
are rushing that direction. This is my chance. I'm going.

TIFF DECIDED TO SWING BY the hospital before heading out to
the streets. She had called in a few favors to get Eve a place to stay
at a decent women's shelter, but that wasn't a long-term solution,
and it wouldn't be available until next week. Their practice was
to allow the women to stay for one month before requiring them
to move into something more permanent. With God's help, that
would permit Eve time to acquire employment and safe housing.

Tiff parked the car in the lot below the towering building, slung
her purse over her shoulder, and locked the doors.

Typically there was a sweet-smelling breeze up here that she
might have enjoyed. Today's pounding late-spring rain made her
wonder how those who lived in the elements survived.

The parking area was blanketed in the soft lighting of
streetlamps placed close together and filtered through the storm.
Up ahead, someone huddled in the corner of the bus stop shelter. Tiff glanced back at her car. She had sacks of food and other

items in there, yet water was already soaking through her jacket and chilling her skin.

As she approached, Tiff was struck by how very small the person was. For a moment, she was stunned that someone would allow a child to be there alone; then the outline of the face came into focus. It was Eve.

The bottom dropped out of Tiff's carefully planned future for the young woman. And less than a day from Eve's scheduled release. One more day, and she was running anyway.

Tiff eased down onto the bench next to her, letting her bag settle at her feet. "Hey."

Eve's face turned to Tiff, shock registering in her eyes.

"What are you doing out here, Eve?"

Her shoulders rose and fell in a shrug that was probably meant to look tough but failed.

"I understand wanting to get out of there. I really do. But you need to look at this from the perspective of your kids. If you show the state that you're not even willing to get a clean bill of health, they aren't likely to want to give your children back to you."

Tiff's words must have hit her where it hurt. Eve dropped her face into her hands, her shoulders bouncing with sobs.

"I've been talking to a lot of people. There's an emergency shelter where you can stay for a few days. After that, there will be a bed available in very nice temporary housing. They'll help you get your feet under you and start over. I'll help too, but you need to go back inside for tonight." Under her rib cage, Tiff's heart beat like a marching band. She wasn't a counselor. That point had been proven with her own daughter.

Eve's arms wrapped tight around her chest, as if she was trying to control the shivers that coursed through her like seizures. Maybe she had come through the beating with her life, but heroin was still in the fight.

Standing, Tiff held out her hand. "Do this for your kids. And for you. There's a better life for your family. I promise."

"I can't do it. I'm just going to let them down." Eve still hadn't looked Tiff in the eye.

Kneeling, Tiff felt the wet concrete press into her right knee as she crouched down to eye level. "You can't do it alone. No one can. But there's help." She wanted to tell her that God would walk her through this, but there was a check in her spirit that told her this wasn't the right time. Tonight, Eve wouldn't be able to hear truth over the roar of the devil that was this addiction. "Come with me. One step at a time, we'll get you and the kids to the other side of this."

Eve didn't take her hand, but she did rise. It was a beginning, and that was all Tiff could ask for right now.

TIFF WOKE UP with a deluxe-sized kink in her neck from sleeping on the hospital chair, but when she looked over at the bed, Eve was still there. Her mission had been a success, though Tiff's relationship with Bruce had taken a blow.

She'd exchanged a series of terse texts with her husband last night. He wasn't willing to understand her need to stay with Eve. What had happened to their marriage? It had once been so good, but now, everything was a struggle. And she was such a different person than the one he married. A lot of the blame should land on her, but people changed. Wasn't that part of what made love beautiful, the choice to keep caring as you grew?

A nurse Eve hadn't had before walked in with a folder and a clipboard. "Looks like you're out of here for real this morning." Her grin lit up the room that had been filled with trepidation through the night. She stood by Eve's bedside. "I know you're ready to be away from this place. I hope you're able to get some good sleep once you're home."

Eve's eyes rounded, as if the mention of home brought on a battalion of fears.

"Will there be someone who can look in on you, make sure you have what you need?"

Tiff stood and came to the other side of the bed. "I'll be looking in on her." Her smile did not earn one in return from Eve.

"Wonderful. I'm glad your mom is around for you." The nurse shuffled through the papers in her arms while Tiff tried to find the words to correct her, but Eve said nothing, so Tiff took her lead. The nurse continued through the discharge instructions, had Eve sign a few papers, then told them to press the call button when Eve was dressed and ready to go.

Time seemed to fly forward, and before Tiff was ready to think through the next steps, she was in her car with Eve buckled into the passenger side. They didn't talk much as they made their way through traffic to a crummy emergency accommodation. If Eve could make it here for a couple of nights, Lyla had assured Tiff there would be a room at the women's shelter she ran. There, Eve would be as far away from the people who wanted her to stay a slave to her harmful lifestyle as she could be in Canyon Ridge.

ZARA DIPPED HER HAND into the dirt. The soil was rich and dark beneath the sod. As soon as possible, Chad would rent a tiller and tear up the space she'd roped off, but Zara was preparing the land for the loofah plants on her own strength. She shoveled another scoop of grass, divided it from the earth, and dumped it into her wagon to be unloaded at her new compost site.

Today the sun shone warm, a prelude to summer's coming arrival. It felt like the months would stretch on forever, but fall always came too quickly. Zara wiped her forearm across her face, feeling the dirt mix with sweat above her brow. This was hard work, and she loved it. She loved the smell of the earth, the ache in her muscles, and the ever-changing view out here on her own little farm. Soon, lavender, sage, mint, and chamomile would grow in uniform rows. She could almost smell the perfection as she pictured the place in its glory.

Her phone buzzed against her hip, shattering the dream. It must be the caseworker. Zara had left three messages already.

Zara glanced at the screen before holding it to her face. The number was one she didn't recognize. "Hello?"

"Hello. This is Rebecca Stevens from The Bees are the Buzz. Is this Zara Mahoney?"

"Yes." A grin tugged at her cheeks. She'd been waiting for this call, hopeful but not optimistic.

"Good news, Zara. We had a cancellation, and we'll be able to set you up with bees after all."

"Thank you. This is so great." Now she could add honey to her product list. Zara imagined what she could do with homegrown honey. Not only could she offer food-grade honey for sale, but she could make lotions and soaps. She'd even been working on a recipe for a foaming honey bath bomb.

"The driver will be in your area tomorrow morning. I know it's short notice, but do you think that would work?"

"Absolutely." Her gaze swung around the farm, searching out the best location for the hives. They would be perfect at the distant end of the property, far away from their normal life activities.

"All right, then. He'll call when he's about thirty minutes away. Have a wonderful afternoon." The line disconnected.

Zara did a happy dance around the plot of land she'd been turning over. The phone buzzed again. "Hello." She was out of breath but hoped the lady from the bee place wouldn't notice. "Did you forget something?"

"I'm calling for Zara Mahoney?" This voice was different, understated and serious.

She took the phone away from her face. The number was also different. She'd just assumed it was the bee place again. "It is. How can I help you?"

"This is Cheri Jerome from DHS. I received your calls but just finally had a moment to get back to you."

All the excitement drained from Zara's body, leeching from her feet into the soil. "Yes, I got a letter about my niece and nephew. It said they're in foster care."

"I'm glad you contacted us. Charlotte and Samuel are in a temporary placement. We can only keep them there for a short while. I'm afraid we just don't have enough foster parents in our county. If we could move them to you, that would be best for the children and your sister."

"What's my sister done?" Tension climbed up her spine and clenched the muscles in her neck.

"I'm afraid I can't go into details about Eve. She has the right to some confidentiality."

Zara's body flamed with too much sun and not enough choices. She walked closer to the house and sat in a camp chair under the shade of a giant oak. "I don't know."

"I'm sorry. What don't you know?"

"Well, for starters, I don't know the children. I've never met them. And I don't know what to do." She struggled to remember all the questions on the list that remained on her bedside table. "Are they okay?"

"They've just been brought into foster care. I'm sure they're scared and worried."

"Have you asked them about me? Do they want to come here?"

"Zara, I'm not in the custom of asking children if they'd like to do things I'm not sure I can even make happen. We need to know if you can be a resource for them first. Are you employed? Is there anyone else in your home? Do you have a safe home?"

"I—my husband and I—moved onto a farm recently."

"That sounds wonderful. I'll get you in touch with a certifier in your county. They can come out and do the paper work to get you okayed as soon as possible, if you fit the qualifications."

This was no longer about Chad and Zara deciding if they were willing to do something good. It was about if they were even good enough to be involved. "We're not bad people."

"You'll have to excuse me, but I hear that all day long from parents who've hurt their children. There are procedures, and we will follow them, because in my job, the consequences can be fatal. Once I send the email, your certifier should get in touch with you right away. Is there anything else?"

"Can we meet them before we decide? This is a lot to process."

"I'm sure it is. It's a lot for these children too."

The weight of her statement sat heavy on Zara's shoulders.

"I'll see what I can arrange."

"Thank you." Her skin had gone from burning to numb. And she was thanking a woman who might have pushed her into a black hole of mistakes. But then again, Charlotte and Samuel didn't get a choice, either. Why should Zara?

CHAPTER NINE

ZARA WIPED THE PERSPIRATION from the back of her neck.

A few days had ticked by with no word from the caseworker or the certifier who she was told would call. At least it was a Saturday, relieving the panic each time her phone hummed. They'd worked nonstop since the sun rose that morning. Chad completed the tilling, and Zara had cut some of the brush along the foundation of what was once a very large barn.

Zara sat on the edge of the exposed cement and surveyed the progress. Closer to the house, Chad rinsed the dirt off the tiller's tines. When he finished, he sprayed a heavy mist into the air, then tilted his head back while water floated down in a shimmering mirage, landing on his skin. It looked too tempting to resist. She was like an egg baking on the sidewalk.

In a burst of spontaneity, Zara dropped her clippers and gloves and jogged toward the house and her husband.

He must have heard her coming. Chad turned her way, pointing the hose as if this had been his plan all along. In a flash, she was covered in a stream of ice-cold well water. It saturated her denim shorts and dripped along her hot scalp. Charging forward, she got to him, lunging into his arms and sharing the wet chill.

The hose dropped, water filling her tennis shoes, as he pulled her close and kissed her with warm lips. "This is the dream," he murmured.

She couldn't agree more. She was tired. Her muscles ached. And she thought she'd gotten a sunburn on the top of her head. Everything was exactly how Zara had pictured it would be.

He leaned back. "I have a surprise for you." There was a twinkle in his eye that made her feel like a child at Disneyland.

"What is it? And don't you dare say I have to wait." Zara tugged her soaked T-shirt away from her skin, then let it slap back into place.

"Well." He rubbed his hand across his jawline. "I know a guy who knows a guy."

"Cute. What does this guy have to do with anything?"

"Equipment. I've been looking at that field of blackberries. We're going to need the right kind of equipment to clear it and keep it under control."

They'd already gone over this more than once. A tractor would save a ton of man hours, but it was not in the budget. It could be five or more years before they could justify a purchase like that, even if they found a used one that still had some life in it. "Did you happen to dig up a pile of money while you were tilling the garden?"

His cheek twitched. "Nope."

"Then what?"

"Goats." A full grin brightened his face.

Zara's heart beat strong and fast. "Seriously? That's brilliant. And I've always wanted a goat."

"I know. That's why I agreed to this. It's a small herd. The guy who owned them passed away suddenly. His son doesn't know what to do with them, but he thought his dad would want them to stay together."

"When you say herd, you mean like three?"

"Or . . . I could mean seven." He wrinkled his nose. "But they were free."

Zara's mouth fell open. She looked down at the small structure that remained near where the original barn had been. They'd need to add on. And there would be fencing to deal with. "How much time do we have to prepare?"

"Not much. The guy just called. He wants them moved as soon as possible." Chad pressed his finger against the side of his nose. "I said we could be there this afternoon."

Spontaneous, jumping without thinking first—that was usually Zara, not her responsible husband. She was stunned by the generosity and absurdity of this plan all at the same time. A glance at her watch told her they would have more work than time. "I guess we'd better get moving, then."

Chad grabbed her hand, taking in the wedding ring. "I want to give you everything you've ever dreamed of."

"You already have." She tipped her chin up and kissed his cheek.

After showering and putting on fresh clothes, something she was sure would be pointless in a couple of hours, Zara was ready to head out on the next adventure. She found Chad outside fastening a bungee cord to the no-longer-functioning latch on the pickup canopy.

"There you are." He was wearing a lightweight flannel shirt over a T-shirt and jeans, and he looked about as rugged as any man who worked in finance could. "Are you ready to be a goat herder?"

"Is anyone ever ready for such a thing?" She tossed him the keys. "You drive."

They bumped along the driveway, the air whipping hair around her face and a country station playing on the AM-only radio. Chad's right hand reached across the bench seat and took hers, and Zara wondered if his thoughts had strayed to Charlotte and Samuel as hers had.

They were only about fifteen minutes from their house when Chad pulled off the main road and into a driveway that probably required four-wheel drive in the winter. A gate crossed the lane, but it had been left open, presumably for them. At the end of the road, they found a man standing by a minivan. He had the washed-out look of someone who'd recently been through a rough time. As they approached, he raised a hand in greeting.

Chad parked alongside the van and cut the engine. Getting out, he walked up to the guy and stuck out his hand. "You must be Logan."

"I sure am. You're here for the goats?"

Zara hustled to join them. "We are. Thank you for this. I promise we'll take good care of them."

Logan looked away for a moment. "I appreciate that. These animals meant a whole lot to my dad." He walked down a path leading to a steel-sided barn.

Before they opened the main door, the bleating began.

"They seem to miss Dad as much as I do." Logan turned the knob and flipped the inside light switch.

The inside of the barn smelled of hay and dust. It was divided into two sections. They walked into the half where bales were stacked along one wall and two silver garbage cans were lined up. Pegs held a variety of leashes and collars.

Through the middle, a plank fence cut the goats off from the supplies. Zara stepped forward and was greeted by a tall white goat with no ears. The goat hopped her front feet onto the railing and stretched forward. In an instant, Zara was in love. She rubbed her hand down the sleek neck while straight white teeth nibbled at the neck of her T-shirt.

"That's Tiny. She's a LaMancha and the mother of that little squirt over there." He pointed to a small speckled kid standing on the back of a full-bellied gray goat. "As you can see, my dad didn't hold to one breed over another. He mainly took in any who needed a home. The one underneath the kid is a pygmy. So is the caramel one coming closer." He reached his hand over the fence and scratched the little goat behind the ear.

"What about this one?" Chad had made a good friend of a black goat with white ears, its teeth jutting over her upper lip, her eyes closed in pleasure as he gave her a soft rubdown.

"Lucille. She's a Nubian. And the only goat I actually thought about keeping." He ran a finger over her velvety ear. "I just couldn't break up the family, though." He stepped back and pulled a paper from his shirt pocket. "I've copied their health information for you." He handed Zara the papers, then went to the wall, collecting collars and leashes.

Twenty minutes later, they had a truck bed full of goats and a pile of starter supplies taking up the space between their seats. Chad gave Logan a last handshake before climbing into the cab.

"Take it slow. I don't want any of them to fall over back there." Zara tried to see through the tiny window in the canopy, but dirt and grime blocked most of the view. "I can't believe you're okay with seven goats."

"You heard the man. It's not right to break them up."

Her mind swung back to the children. "Do you think Charlotte and Samuel would stay together if we didn't take them?"

He shook his head. "I have no idea."

They rumbled down the road, both of them silent amongst the squawk of the pickup and the muffled bleating of their new herd. Finally, Zara turned to look at Chad over a stack of feed bags. "I really don't want to do this." It was out, but the depth and weight of the words still burdened her.

"The goats?"

"No. The children. Does that make me horrible?" She'd asked the question knowing it would lead to his reassurance.

"I hope it doesn't, because I find myself feeling that way sometimes too. I'm loving this time with just you and me." He reached over the mountain between them and squeezed her shoulder. "I don't know. I prayed about it last night. But I'm no closer to an answer."

His hand left her as they turned onto the driveway, Chad

needing both hands to maneuver the corners in her old truck. There was no right answer. She felt like they were trapped. Whatever they chose would lead to some kind of loss. This wasn't what the honeymoon year was supposed to be like.

Chad backed up as close as they could get to the animal shed. "It won't take long for these guys to open up the land." He cut the engine, and the door squeaked open.

Zara's phone buzzed. Another unfamiliar number, but surely not DHS on a weekend. "Hello."

"Is this Zara?" The voice on the other end was kindergarten-teacher perky.

"Yes."

"Great. This Rita Goodman. I'm the foster mama to your niece and nephew."

"Oh. Are they okay?" Her heart thundered.

"They're doing very well, but I'm sure they'd love to see you."

"Did they say that? I've never met the kids." It all felt wrong inside. Something seemed to tighten around her ribs, squeezing her lungs. "Thank you for taking care of them." What a lame thing to say, but she was dry of words.

"My parents live in Salem. I was coming down tomorrow for a visit with them. Cheri says you live about an hour or so from there?"

"Yes."

"Would you be available to meet at the park near the carousel?"

Zara stepped out of the truck and breathed in the fresh air that still felt devoid of sufficient oxygen. "Tomorrow?"

"I was thinking sometime around two. What do you think?"

They couldn't, wouldn't. This was truly asking too much. It wasn't fair. Then she remembered that it wasn't fair to any of them. At least they all had that in common. "We can be there." Her gaze locked with Chad's, and she felt as if he were the other half of her team. No matter what they did, they were in this together.

Chad set a bag of feed near the collapsing livestock fence and came in close to her side. His breath warmed her neck as he tried to hear the other end of the conversation.

"That's so great. These guys are going to be very excited." Rita paused, leaving Zara in a search for the next thing she was supposed to say, but sooner than she could find it, Rita spoke again. "Before I tell them, can you promise me you'll be there?"

Zara's vision blurred. "Of course. We will definitely be there. I promise."

"Thank you."

After their good-byes, the call disconnected, leaving Chad and Zara staring at each other while seven goats bellowed to be unloaded.

"Tell me it's going to be okay." All the strength she thought she'd gained in her adulthood was shattering under the pressure of this situation. Where was her sister? What had happened to her and to her children? And *why* hadn't she asked Zara for help?

Chad put his arm around her shoulders. "It's going to be okay."

But this time, his words didn't bring her any comfort.

CHAPTER TEN

Eve
May 18, 2019

>   *Warmth spreads like a current of pleasure from my heart to*
> *the tips of my fingers and toes. All my pain washes away on soft*
> *waves. Nothing can touch me here. I'm floating and drifting,*
> *finally free.*

FOR TIFF, SATURDAY NIGHTS were always hectic, especially with summer approaching and the evenings growing warm. It brought the users out of the hovels where they congregated to stay warm during the cold months. Those who wanted to take advantage of them became more visible too.

The numbers were always the same; it was the faces that changed. As overdoses took the lives of soul after soul, their places were filled with new people. It was a cycle that destroyed parents and children, families and entire communities. It was an ugliness she couldn't do anything about, except maybe remind whoever she could that they were loved by God, possibly by family, and absolutely by her.

It wasn't enough.

Eve had left the emergency shelter.

Tiff's eyes had been trained on the faces of the women she passed, hoping to spot Eve but dreading it all the same. Maybe she'd contacted someone to help her get out of the grip addiction held on her. More likely, she was out there somewhere.

Pulling into the same parking lot she had the night she met Eve, it was hard to believe two weeks had passed. Before she lost her daughter, Tiff never would have believed her heart capable of loving a stranger with so much stacked against her, and to love her so quickly. But she had. There was something about Eve that reminded Tiff of Lindsay. If Tiff couldn't make a way for Eve to have a future, she would have a very hard time walking away.

At the back of the building, Tiff motioned to Theresa.

The woman took a quick look around, then came to her car window. "You got any of those protein bars? I'm about starved."

Tiff took a bagged meal, tossed in an extra bar, and handed it to Theresa. "You haven't seen Eve around here, have you?"

The bag crunched as she dug through the contents. "Who's that?"

"The girl from a couple weeks ago. The one I took out of here?"

Theresa scratched at a bite along the side of her arm, then tore open a protein bar. "I've seen her. I'd hoped for better but expected exactly what happened. Looks like she's been beaten to the edge of life."

Maybe it had been too early to leave the hospital. Tiff's stomach, sour with the pent-up fear, grew worse. "Can you give me any help finding her?"

"I don't understand you. She's a lost cause. Once they get that bad . . ." The lines on her face spoke the words she didn't. "You got a nice home somewhere. You come down here in that old beater of a car, but I recognize a good life when I see it. Why mess with this? Your girl isn't out here."

Tiff reached her hand out the window and did something she rarely did. She made physical contact. At the touch on her arm, Theresa flinched, but within seconds, her muscles softened. "I'm not here looking for Lindsay. I love all of you. It's hard to explain, but somewhere along the line, God gave me a heart for you—you have a kind of strength I can't imagine possessing."

Theresa tugged away. "You don't know what you're talking about. I'm nothing. Nobody out here is. Take a look at Eve if you want to see the truth. She's huddled next to the dumpster in the alley." Her voice grew gritty. "Get back to your own people." She turned and walked toward the wall where four other women stood waiting to sell their bodies for another night of survival.

Tiff's gaze swept the shadows, landing on the darkened entrance to the alley. Her heart screamed to retrieve this young woman who needed another chance as much as Tiff longed to give her one. At the same time, she heard her husband's voice of warning. *"It's too dangerous in the dark."* Tiff would not be heard if she called for help.

A squad car circled through the parking area, scattering any potential customers for the moment. Tiff could wave the car over and ask the officer to escort her into the alley, but that would only draw a thicker line between her and Theresa, as well as anyone else out there.

Relationships took a long time to form. In that neighborhood, they took an eternity.

She watched the taillights fade, her decision made by her indecision. She was going in. Tiff got out of her car and took three strides forward, her shoulders back. "Lord, please be the strength I need in this moment." Five more steps, and she would be able to see around the corner, though not into the depths.

A shadow moved, coming closer.

Tiff's feet grew heavy, sealed to the surface of the earth as if gravity had multiplied itself by eleven. Waves of sound crashed against her eardrums, the pounding of her own blood.

Before she could scream or force her legs to advance or retreat, the figure stumbled into the dim light. Even in the shadows, Tiff could see the bruising still spread across the right side of her face. She moved forward, taking Eve by the arm and guiding her to the passenger side of her car. "What have you done, Eve?"

"I'm fine." Her words were slurred, her eyes barely open. "Just sleepy." With a jolt, her head tipped back, a delirious smile on her lax face.

Opening the door, Tiff slid Eve onto the seat and pulled the safety belt across her waist, buckling it tight. The young woman's head fell forward. She'd taken too much heroin, but she was still responsive. Tiff lifted the latch and reclined the chair back as far as it would go. "Just stay put. I'm going to get you some help."

"I'm fine, really." Eve's eyes fluttered shut again, and she hummed a child's lullaby.

"What do you think you're doing with her?" A woman Tiff only knew as Star approached the car.

Tiff shut the passenger side door, hoping Eve would stay zoned out enough not to try and get out. "I'm going to get her some help."

Star's hands were fisted into her sides. "What's so special about that one? You think she's your girl or something?"

The question knocked Tiff back a step. "No. I'm only trying to help."

Star tossed her head back. "That's a good one. I don't see you throwing any of these other junkies in your carriage for a ride." She looked over her shoulder. "What do you think, girls? Would this rich lady ever take you for a ride?"

The poison in Star's glare shook Tiff's sense of morality. She didn't know why Eve was different. There were no words to put to the feelings. It was like God was calling Tiff to her. If she didn't do all she could, she'd never be able to manage the rest of her life.

But why not? And why not Theresa? Why not Star? Why not any of the other women and men out here trying to survive under the sentence of poverty and addiction?

She ached to go to them, to explain a situation she had no explanation for, but instead circled her rusty car and slipped in behind the steering wheel.

Before she could make a plan or reconsider what she was doing, Tiff drove away from the parking area and headed toward that same diner she'd taken Eve to the first night. The girl was in no shape to go in, but it felt like safety and was far enough away from where she'd picked her up to give them both a new perspective.

The lights from the restaurant cast a glow that joined the intermittent illumination of the beams in the parking lot. The same waitress poured coffee into the mug of an old man.

Tiff let a held breath retreat in a heavy sigh. "Eve, how are you doing?"

Her eyes were still heavy, but she was able to make eye contact with Tiff for a moment. "I don't know." She folded over, her face buried in her too-thin hands. "I need help. I miss my kids."

Tiff let her own head rest against the cool window. She missed her kids? Then why was she doing this to herself and to them? The rage Tiff had felt at Lindsay when she stole from Tiff's purse to pay for her habit came to a simmer again. But this time, there was more at stake than money Tiff could spare anyway. Charlotte and Sammy were somewhere in foster care. They hadn't seen their mother since she left in an ambulance. How could anyone grow up feeling worthy of God's love when they were left behind so the parent who was supposed to love them could chase a high?

"I need to get my kids back." Eve's words were muffled by racking sobs. "They're mine. No one has the right to take them away from me."

Turning back to this girl, Tiff was struck by the ridiculousness of her thought process. Maybe it was the heroin speaking, but she couldn't really think the kids should stay with her under these circumstances. "If you want to get your kids back, I'll help you, but you'll have to get clean. They aren't safe if you're using. Do you understand?" Her words came out with a firmness she didn't really feel. It was possible the woman before her couldn't ever be someone who should have her children back.

"I know. I want to get help. I don't want to be like this." She turned toward Tiff, and the light from the diner reflected in her steely blue eyes. There was desperation there. And heartbreak. And love. How could Tiff not do everything in her power to give this woman, this girl, every chance at a happy future?

"If you mean it, then we need to get you into a detox center. Will you go?" Tiff kept her voice firm, but underneath, her mom heart was tearing open again at the weakened healing points. There'd been a time when she'd posed a similar question to Lindsay.

Suddenly, Tiff was there again, in her own kitchen, her daughter in a pile on the floor. Lindsay had looked up, tears streaming down her face, begging Tiff to understand why she needed to go, that she was sick. Back then, Tiff hadn't really understood that withdrawals also held the potential for death. She'd held Lindsay hostage for three days, never letting her out of her sight. Tiff had thought she could fix her, cure her of the evil she'd let into their lives. All her daughter had to do was agree to rehab.

There was so much Tiff hadn't known. Probably so much she still didn't comprehend.

Lindsay had finally given in. She'd agreed to go to the treatment center. But she'd agreed for her mother, or to get away from her. Two days later, she was gone, disappeared after signing herself out. Tiff had raged at the person behind the desk until they'd threatened to call the police . . . on her.

"Eve. This needs to be your decision alone. Do you understand what I'm saying?"

Her head bobbed.

"You want to detox." It sounded more like a statement than a question.

"I'm scared." She wrapped her arms around her middle, rolling up into a tight ball. "But I need help. I need my kids."

Tiff turned the key, and the engine started with a sputter. "Then let's do this. I'll help you any way I can. I promise you that."

The transmission ground as she put the car in gear. Wilma Steadman Detox Center was the only facility nearby. Though Tiff had never entered the building, she'd heard it was as good as any that would take those who didn't have a vault of gold to draw from.

Only a few minutes passed before she parallel parked outside the clinic. She held her tongue, fearing anything she could say would give Eve an excuse to change her mind. But this had to be her choice. That much Tiff had learned.

CHAPTER ELEVEN

Eve
May 19, 2019

I wrote May 19, but now I'm not so sure—I'm losing track of days. Or it could be the same one as my last writing. Either way, it's early.

I think I went too far this time. Or maybe I needed a little more. It doesn't matter. I have to make a commitment. Die or live. It shouldn't be so hard to decide. If I listed all the reasons to end my life, they would fill pages, but there are only two words I can write under Stay Alive—Charlotte and Sammy. If I'm honest, though, I'm not sure that's the right column for my kids. They deserve better than me.

I'm in a clinic now, waiting for something. I had my journal stuffed into the back of my pants. At least if I died, it would have given my body an identity.

I didn't even know I was with Tiff until I realized we were in that restaurant parking lot. Tiff seems to show up for all my worst moments. If I wasn't so sure God turned His gaze away from me years ago, I'd think she was some kind of angel.

This place is locked down tight. We had to push a button and talk through a speaker just to get in.

I'm just so tired. But I can't sleep. It's so hot, I can't breathe. And my shirt feels like it has razor blades sewn into the seams.

TIFF LOOKED BACK AT EVE. She'd been busily scratching in her journal as if the act were as important to life as breathing.

After being beeped in like they were requesting access to the White House, she'd assumed they would get service. Instead, a woman with tight curls and an even tighter smile tapped away at a keyboard on the other side of a glass barricade.

Tiff waved, knocked on the glass, and scowled, but the lady kept on with her work. The old movie *Truman* came to mind, where the main character was really inhabiting a made-up world while people on the outside watched his every move. The woman swiveled in her chair, catching papers as they shot out of the printer, seemingly unbothered by or unaware of Tiff's presence.

Eve leaned back in her chair, clawing at the neck of her T-shirt. Her face was flushed, and perspiration was gathering at her hairline.

Along one wall was a water cooler. Every thirty seconds or so, bubbles rose to the tank's surface, the gurgle joining the hum of the fan in the corner. Tiff poured a cup and held it out to Eve. "Maybe this will help."

Eve's hands shook as they took the drink.

The glass curtain slid open. "Do you have her insurance information?" The woman behind the counter had a voice that could scratch diamonds. She shoved a clipboard across the counter to Tiff.

"Eve? Do you have insurance?"

When Tiff touched Eve's leg, she jumped, then shook her head. "I should have insurance. I should have gotten it when I took the kids in for shots, but I didn't go." Tears rose in her eyes. "They were right to take them, huh? I screwed up. I've been a horrible mom." She seemed to sink farther into the chair, as though the weight of her guilt was crushing her.

"Eve? Are you okay?"

She grabbed the arms of the plastic and metal chair, gripping so hard, her muscles trembled.

Tiff looked over her shoulder at the steely-faced woman. "Can't we fill out the paper work after she's settled?"

"Nope. Paper work and payment are required prior to admittance. No exception."

Tiff knelt on the ground in front of Eve. "No Oregon Health Plan?"

"I don't think so."

The other woman broke in again. "We can get her signed up, but approval can take time. It'll be $870 to get her in here tonight."

Tiff wiped her hand across her forehead and found her own hair wet with sweat.

Eve started to rise.

"I'll pay it." The words were out of Tiff's mouth before she'd thought through the consequences to her marriage.

The woman motioned Tiff to her throne and whispered her thoughts loud enough for anyone to hear. "Save your money. This one will run. We can't give you a refund when your charity project doesn't do what you want her to."

The heat rose with the realization of what the woman had just had the nerve to say. Tiff crossed her arms tight across her chest, partially to keep from reaching through the reception window and grabbing her by the collar. Maybe it was foolhardy to assume anyone working in a detox center would be compassionate, caring, even hopeful. Yet in her wildest thoughts,

Tiff had never contemplated the possibility of cold, jaded, and sharp.

What if Lindsay had come into a place like this? What if they'd judged her to be no better than trash left on the sidewalk? People in these kinds of positions had a responsibility to the clients who had the strength to walk through the doors in search of a chance. They deserved hope.

"I'll gladly pay the bill. My friend is worth every single cent." If there were another detox center anywhere nearby, they'd be gone. But despite the drugs and trafficking that hid in the shadows, theirs wasn't a huge town. They didn't have endless resources. Their one and only option, this place, had come into the community late last year. Yet an air of hopelessness already drifted in on the distant melodies from a radio somewhere out of sight.

As though Eve's failing would be a bet she would win, the woman slid another clipboard to Tiff with a shake of her head, a Cheshire-cat grin casting amusement. "We don't take checks."

Tiff pulled her Visa from her wallet and snapped it onto the counter. She'd hear about this one when the bill came.

Sitting next to Eve, Tiff started to ask her questions as she filled out forms. It was the kind of thing a mother did for her child, but the woman beside her didn't have a mom around to help her make a change. Lindsay hadn't, either. Tiff had refused to see the seriousness of her daughter's addiction, or maybe her pride had kept Tiff from seeing Lindsay's pain. She'd never be that woman again. No matter what Bruce said, she was doing this.

Eve's hand, cold as ice, grabbed her arm. "Get your money back. I can't let you pay for this. I need to go." Shivers ran over her body, passing into Tiff's.

"It's too late. Even if you run now, the money is paid. Don't let it go to waste." Reaching her arm over Eve's shoulders, Tiff let her fingers graze the thin sleeve of the T-shirt before committing and pulling her into a gentle hug. Tension stiffened her body, but Tiff kept holding on until she felt the muscles soften and relax into her chest. "You're worth this, and so are your children."

Eve's tears soaked through Tiff's shirt and warmed her skin.

CHAPTER TWELVE

A COOL WIND GLIDED OVER the newly sprouted leaves and blew a chill through Zara's long-sleeved T-shirt. Yesterday's warmth had evaporated with her enthusiasm. She went inside through the kitchen door, then poured way too much caramel creamer into her mug and topped it off with a splash of coffee.

Zara checked the time on her phone for the one zillion and twelfth time. No matter the result, it disappointed her. She was torn between wishing the minutes wouldn't tick by and wanting to move forward and be done with the next step. They should have gone to church that morning. When she'd woken up, it felt like too big of a challenge, like she needed to reserve her strength for that afternoon's meeting with the children. Instead, the free hours had let Zara's imagination loose to cultivate acres of potentially disastrous scenarios.

The goats let out a bleating chorus as Chad's car pulled into the drive. He'd been gone longer than expected for someone picking up a new carton of half-and-half, but Chad had a way of finding someone to talk with no matter where or when he ventured into the world. It was a good thing he had that outgoing nature, or they never would have met. While Chad enjoyed new acquaintances and proceeded toward anyone he'd ever met before, Zara ducked for cover at the first sight of anyone who might want to chat. They were truly a case of opposites attracting.

The kitchen door scraped shut. Zara kept meaning to add that task to the ever-growing list of home repairs.

Chad dropped two reusable grocery bags on the counter.

"How much half-and-half do you think we need?" There was a joking tone in her voice that he hopefully wouldn't realize was forced.

Reaching into the first bag, Chad pulled out a plastic circle, like a ball but not. He passed it into Zara's hands.

"What's this?"

"According to a little girl I met in the store, it's the greatest thing in the world. You don't know what toy you get until you put some stuff in water and it bubbles off."

"That sounds horrible. What if you get something you already have?"

He shrugged. "Maybe kids trade them." His eyes sparkled like it was Christmas morning rather than the day guilt rained down. A day she'd spend with the children her sister couldn't take care of. A day that reminded Zara that she couldn't—shouldn't—have kids of her own.

Chad kept removing toys from the bags, showing off each one. "Do you think they'll like them? I want to make a good impression."

"This is just an introduction. We're not bringing them home." Stress felt like a tightening band around her chest, making breathing difficult.

He squeezed her shoulder. "I know. But we're their aunt and uncle. Just in case there are more out there, I want to be sure to tie up the favorite uncle position from the start." His face said he was being silly, but she wondered if Chad was already becoming too attached to children who were technically relatives, but in reality, strangers.

CAROUSEL MUSIC CLANGED through the park, growing louder as Chad and Zara approached the circle of bobbing horses and other animals carved from chunks of wood. So many children and no reference aside from gender and age to guide them to her niece and nephew.

A little boy flew off the end of a slide, his bottom landing in the sand. At first his eyes were large and round, then with the clapping of his father's hands, the boy burst into laughter.

Genetically, Charlotte and Samuel were half like her, another oddity of twin life. Shouldn't that come with a pull toward them, some kind of innate understanding and recognition? Yet all these little faces looked the same, and the thought of bringing two strangers into her home, especially strangers with a genetic connection, gave Zara waves of fear, the kind that pushed her to run far and fast.

Chad nodded to a woman holding a toddler. "That must be her."

"How can you possibly know that?" Zara glanced back at the car.

"Because the child in her arms has your beautiful eyes, and the woman has been scanning people like she's waiting for someone."

Slipping her hand around his upper arm, Zara resisted the urge to pull him toward the parking lot.

The woman made her way in their direction, a smile on her face even as she wiped drool from the little boy's chin with the arm of her sweatshirt. She looked like a Rita, though Zara couldn't explain why. Tight curls cut just below her ears framed her face beautifully.

Zara's gaze remained stationed on her—a glance at the child would undo her and break her resolve, potentially plunging her back into a life she didn't want.

Rita reached out her hand, introducing herself first, then Samuel. "Would you like to hold him?"

Chad's hand pressed Zara's upper back, urging her to open up.

She slipped her hands under the arms of the child, felt the weight of him as she lifted his slight body from Rita's arms. His eyes searched her as if they knew her. Held against Zara's chest, he reached his little hand to her face and rubbed tiny fingers over her cheek; then his chin wrinkled and his lower lip quivered. She wasn't the one he wanted.

Uttering calming words, Chad rubbed Samuel's back.

Heat covered Zara's skin. She forced the boy into her husband's arms.

In only a minute, the tears stopped flowing and Samuel's face transformed with grins and giggles.

Rita gave Zara a sympathetic smile. "Don't take it personally. He's been through a lot. Do you look like your sister?"

"We're identical twins."

"There you go. I'm sure it's confusing to him. My husband has Charlotte and the other kids in the sand area. Let me go talk with her for a moment and prepare her for your appearance. I'd hate for her to think her mama's come to get her."

As Rita walked away, Zara looked at the car again, then at Chad. Her husband was consumed in a nonsensical conversation that seemed to amuse not only Samuel but also Chad. How could he betray her like this, leaving her all alone to wonder why they had even come?

When Rita returned, she was holding hands with a little girl with wavy brown hair and eyes a shade darker. She looked nothing like Zara or her mother. "Charlotte, this is your aunt Zara." Rita knelt next to the girl.

Charlotte crossed her arms, her gaze running over Zara. "She doesn't look anything like my mom. She's not even slim."

Zara's mouth fell open. Slim? First of all, that was an odd thing for a little girl to say, and maybe Zara could stand to lose a pound or two—*okay, ten*—but she was a healthy-ish weight.

"And what's with the hair?"

103

Zara ran her hand over her smooth, straightened hair. "I like it this way."

"It's not how my mom does it."

Eve and Zara had never been the kind of twins who dressed alike. Apparently, DNA did not determine fashion sense. "Being twins doesn't mean we always like the same things. We're different in a lot of ways."

Charlotte's attention shifted to Chad. "Hi."

"Hello there." He squatted down, eye to eye with Charlotte. Why didn't Zara think to do that? "I'm Chad." He reached out his hand in greeting.

For a moment, Charlotte stared at it; then she reached out her left hand, and they shared an awkward shake. "Can you play with us?"

"Of course. It's the whole reason we're here." Chad winked at Zara like he hadn't even noticed the three-point snubbing she was on the wrong side of. He took Charlotte's hand, and the three of them moseyed off toward the play structure.

Rita touched the back of Zara's arm.

Zara hoped the woman didn't feel the shudder that ran over her skin at the contact. Her nerves were pulsing.

"This will give us a few minutes to talk." Rita took a seat on a short cement wall.

Joining her, Zara let her focus stray to the coolness coming through her jeans and away from the connection her husband was making with the children.

"Don't take Charlotte's words personally. She's been through a lot, and that's how she controls who gets close and how close they get."

Samuel picked up a handful of sand and shoved it in his mouth. On instinct, Zara jumped up. "Chad."

He turned.

She pointed to the toddler.

Her husband grinned as he swiped a finger through Samuel's

mouth, pulling out a clump of sand that probably contained a high level of things Zara didn't want to name.

"He's a natural."

She shifted her gaze to Rita. "But—the thing is . . . I'm not."

"You're wrong. You didn't hesitate to make sure Samuel was safe. I'm guessing you and Chad have very different personalities." She looked at her, waiting for confirmation.

"True."

"Kids can benefit from that."

"I'm just not sure we can do this, though. The kids seem happy with you. You know what you're doing. They've never even met us." The direct sunlight was not equipped to combat the chill snaking through her body. What she wanted to say—the words that were screaming through her brain—was that she didn't plan this. It wasn't what she wanted. Why couldn't she have a normal family . . . just this once?

"Listen, I get that you have the right to walk away from here and never give those two another thought. But what about them? Who puts them first?"

"You do."

A sound like air escaping a balloon came from Rita's mouth. "No. I have two other kiddos in my home right now. In three weeks, the state will be moving in their three older brothers. It's important to keep siblings together as much as possible, so I have no choice. *Your* niece and nephew will be moved to another foster home as soon as one is available. And who knows, they could be moved from that house, and maybe another." She tugged at a curl. "Kids who are moved around often develop more issues. They don't have the opportunity to heal from the trauma they've already endured."

Her words crushed Zara as surely as if she'd been put in a vise, and Rita was turning the handle, waiting for Zara's resolve to finally conform to the shape she desired. "You can't really expect us to make a decision like this with no time to think about it?"

"How much time did Charlotte get to decide if she wanted to enter the system?" Rita stood and walked in front of Zara. "I'm not trying to give you a guilt trip or to force you to take the kids. I just want you to see this from their perspective. No child chooses trauma. And no child deserves it. You have an opportunity to make a difference for them." Without waiting for Zara's response, she stepped into the sand and sat next to a couple of boys with matching curls. In a moment, Rita had become a member of their group, building alongside them.

The pit of Zara's stomach was hollow, void of any comfort, and unwilling to let her skip away from this without doing something.

Chad motioned her over.

Charlotte was clinging to his hand as if she was afraid to let him go.

"Hey, babe, can you take Samuel so I can go down the slide with Charlotte? She's concerned about doing it on her own."

Zara looked from her husband to the playground equipment. There were three slides, none bigger than any you'd find in a typical family backyard. "Sure."

Chad lifted Samuel, brushing sand from his tiny sweatpants, then handed him to Zara.

He was filthy, covered in drool and smudges of dirt, and he smelled a little sour, but he was warm. Samuel rested his head on her chest, his fingers working the fabric of her shirt, and the coldness that tried to consume her lost its bitter edge.

CHAPTER THIRTEEN

ZARA FELT EMPTY as she and Chad got into the car and headed home. Though Samuel and Charlotte were little more than strangers, they were also children, and leaving felt like walking away from their needs.

Chad blasted the air conditioning to blow away the stuffy heat that had filled the parked car, but the air sent an uncomfortable chill over her skin.

"What are you thinking?" Chad asked.

The blinker clicked a rhythm like impatient fingers drumming on a desk. "You go first."

He pulled into traffic. "Nah. There's more to this for you. It's your family. There's baggage there, and I don't want to make light of that."

"*You're* my family."

He patted her leg.

His touch made her brave. "They're just little kids. This isn't fair to them."

"You're right on that."

"But we just got married. This is supposed to be our time, the two of us. It's not really fair to us, either."

"You're right about that too."

"Oh, come on. You need to have an opinion here." She leaned back and put her feet on the dash. "I don't know what I'm thinking, or what's right. The only thing I've learned from this experience is that I'm a truly horrible and selfish person."

"You are not." There was amusement in his voice. "Anyone would have the feelings you're having."

"What about you? Are you feeling that way? Are you tempted to run until you've passed at least a hundred zip codes, changed your name, and become a hermit in a cave somewhere in the Rocky Mountains?"

He coughed as a poor attempt at covering a laugh. "Were you saving this insane side for after the wedding on purpose?"

"Ha-ha. See, we don't have the same feelings." Zara crossed her arms and let herself indulge in a good old pout.

They came up to a stoplight behind a minivan adorned with one of those stick-figure families Zara wasn't a fan of.

Chad touched her face, turning her to look at him. "Unless you feel differently, I think we should take the kids."

Zara curled her fingers around his. "I agree."

From behind them, someone honked. Chad and Zara both looked up to see the spot in front of them vacant and the light green.

Her chest tightened with a mixture of fear and excitement. The plan had been to live a life of adventure together. Those words were actually in their vows. It looked like the adventure was about to begin. "I'll call the caseworker first thing tomorrow morning, unless you think I should do it now."

"I think now would be better. A lot can happen in sixteen hours."

It certainly could. She surfed through her contacts and made the call.

"You've reached the phone of Cheri Jerome, caseworker with the Oregon Department of Human Services. I'm unable to take your call, but you can leave me a message, and I'll get back to you as soon as I can." The recording went on to give a long list of emergency options, then finally signaled for the message.

"This is Zara Mahoney and Chad . . . Mahoney. We want—" She took a moment to swallow. "We would like to start the process to become foster parents for Charlotte and Samuel. Please call me and let me know what we need to do next. Thank you."

Zara pushed the button to terminate the call. Chad was right. She'd never have the courage to back out now that she'd committed. They were in this, good or bad. Either way, it wasn't a permanent situation. And wasn't it normal to take your sister's kids in when she was in crisis? That's all this was. Eve was in crisis. It was a season, a time that would pass.

"Which room should we put them in . . . and is that okay? Do they sleep in the same room?"

Zara shrugged. "I wasn't one of those girls who babysat. I don't even know what to feed them."

"I'm sure the caseworker will give us information. That's one of her jobs, right? The two of them together couldn't weigh as much as one of the goats. We'll be fine."

"Will we?"

"I'll call my mom when we get home."

Zara's newlywed pride wanted to take offense at that statement, but Sharon was the only one she knew who was a bona fide successful parent, all the way through. "Yes. Call your mom."

Eve

May 20, 2019

I know the worst is yet to come, but my children need me.
I'm trying to focus on my kids. Already my body is screaming
as if my muscles are wrenching my bones. I want relief, but
I've tried that before and nearly died from the cure. An addict

with a methadone allergy is pathetic. I can die from the help or die from the withdrawal. Either way, I'm not sure I'm going to make it.

The door is a hazy blur of white, a passageway in a room of soft blues. I can leave whenever I want. That's the rule. It's my right. But Tiff paid so much money for me to be here. And my kids. I have to make it . . . for them.

It's getting hard to write. The shaking has started. My body is covered in sweat, but I'm freezing cold. And my stomach is starting to cramp.

TIFF WATCHED THE GARAGE DOOR LOWER, settling softly onto the cement floor. The overhead light beamed down. It would do that for one minute, then click off automatically. She stayed, waiting for the darkness.

When it came, she took a deep breath and stepped into the kitchen, inhaling the vanilla and lime scents that comforted her. The house was hers with Bruce at work. She wouldn't have to explain anything about the last couple of days, why she'd left only vague text messages, or why she'd added another bill to the credit card that wouldn't benefit her husband in any way.

Tiff's body and brain made the desire for coffee or sleep known. A look at the pot told her it had already cooled from Bruce's morning java. If she could just stay awake long enough to shower the putrid stench off her skin, she could crawl under the sheets and doze for a few hours. She stumbled through the house, setting her phone to wake her an hour before Bruce's earliest possible arrival home.

Their master bath was larger than the kitchen at Eve's old apartment. It sparkled and everything was in its proper place, thanks to the woman who came in each week and made Tiff look like the ideal homemaker. She'd thought about letting the cleaning lady go, but honestly, she had no skills for taking care of a house, and Bruce deserved better than what she gave him.

Stepping into the shower, she didn't let the luxury go unappreciated like she had for more than twenty years prior to her eyes fully opening. The water came straight down from the wide head, covering her with a warm rain. The shelves held products to make her look younger, softer, and better than who she was. Yet Tiff used only the soap, shampoo, and conditioner.

When every muscle in her body was relaxed and heated, she stepped out and wrapped herself in an ultra-big, luxurious towel. It took all her remaining energy to slip into pajamas and slide under the blankets. From the top drawer of her nightstand, she retrieved a sleep mask to block out the filtered light, then let her head drift into the comfort of the pillows.

In that space of time where reality started to ease away and the thoughts she'd been having softened and changed shape, the phone rang. Her arms were already heavy with sleep, but the ringtone sent her mind racing back to consciousness. "Hello?"

"Ms. Bradley?" There was a familiar cadence in the words, but she didn't recognize the voice.

"Yes."

"This is Cheri, the caseworker for child protective services at the DHS. We met at the hospital."

It took no imagination to hear her husband's voice reprimanding her for getting too close to one of *those* people. "Yes, Cheri, how can I help you?" Tiff pushed herself up against the headboard, keeping her legs covered by the weight of the blankets.

"I've been trying to reach Eve Brookes. The hospital tells me she was released, but I don't have an address or phone number for her. I'd like to set up her first visitation with the children. This is important for them. They need to see that their mother is okay. If Eve is planning to do the work and get her kids back, she'll need to make these visits."

"I understand." When Tiff had finally left Eve at the detox

center, she'd been in no shape to visit with anyone outside of medical professionals and clergy. "Do you have a day and time set?"

"No. I was looking for input from Eve, but the kids will be moving to a different home soon, so I'd like to get one done before that happens."

A move already. This was not okay. "I see. Well, I'll talk to her about it as soon as I can."

Tiff could hear the exaggerated sigh through the line. It wrapped around her nerves and made her want to scream. This wasn't ideal for Cheri; Tiff knew that. But it wasn't ideal for Eve or for her, either. And it definitely was not ideal for Charlotte and Sammy.

"Do you at least have an address?"

"I don't. But she'll have one shortly. Give her a chance, okay?"

"Ma'am, that's exactly what I am doing. Leave a message on my phone if I don't answer. I'd like to have this all scheduled ASAP."

"I understand."

They hung up. The quiet of the house was replaced by a ringing in her ears. If Bruce were there right now, he'd be saying exactly what Tiff knew to be true: She was in over her head. Maybe she should have been open with the caseworker and told her about the detox center, but that was Eve's story. Tiff was only a secondary character who hopefully would help the hero survive.

There was no use trying to sleep now. Her veins were humming, and her heart ached for Charlotte and Sammy—and for Eve.

She padded down the hall, past Brandt's old room, touching her fingertips to the closed door that hid where Lindsay used to sleep. She didn't go inside often. The emptiness hurt too much, but today she turned the knob and forced herself to enter.

Lindsay's bed was made, the blankets straight and even, not because this was how her daughter left them, but because Tiff couldn't bear to have the room left as it was. The mess had only served to remind her of what had happened to her daughter, the way she'd slipped away and become someone they didn't recognize. Tiff needed to remember the sweet little girl she'd been. The soccer player and ballet dancer, the one who dragged her stuffed teddy bear around until she was in second grade. She still needed to remember Lindsay by the drawing she'd created of their family, her daddy bigger than life, a heart above each of their heads, even her brother's. And by the hugs Tiff could still feel when she was in here and closed her eyes, inhaling the scent that was probably only still alive in her imagination. She couldn't help Lindsay. But she could do what she hoped someone had done for Lindsay. Tiff could step up and advocate for Eve, give her every chance of beating this addiction into the ground and restoring her family to a state that would be better than anything they'd had in the past.

From the shelf above Lindsay's desk, Tiff took the old teddy bear and squeezed it to her chest while a sob tried to choke her. She bit back her tears, knowing her grief wouldn't bring back her baby but would waste time that Eve didn't have.

Gently, she kissed the top of the bear's head, then laid him on the pillow. He seemed to stare at her as if there were words to say, but now wasn't the time for any of that. Tiff would honor her daughter by helping someone else. She understood now. It was what she should have done for Lindsay when she'd had the chance.

Returning to her own bedroom, Tiff retrieved her cell phone. Having a few favors available to her was a benefit she needed right now, and she wasn't about to hesitate when it came to cashing in.

CHAPTER FOURTEEN

THE TICK OF THE CLOCK echoed through the empty bedroom closest to the one Zara shared with Chad. She understood the caseworker being busy first thing in the morning, but two days had passed since Zara left a message, and still no word. They were making a huge sacrifice here. Was a call back really too much to expect?

Zara released the lock on the original double-hung window and watched the pane slam down, the glass crack, and huge shards hurl toward the overgrown flower beds below. For a moment, she just stood and stared at the open space. There was no way this room would pass inspection with half the glass poking out of the ground like daggers. *Great.* Even before adding this project to the list, she had more tasks than humanly possible lined up for the day.

Her phone chimed, alerting her to an email, a distraction Zara was more than happy to have.

It was from the caseworker, though Zara had no memory of giving out her email address.

Good morning,

My name is Abby Gentry. I'm one of the certifiers for your county, and I've been assigned to your case.

Your message to Cheri Jerome was passed on to me. I'm glad you've decided to move forward as a resource for Charlotte and Samuel. Unfortunately, I'm out of town until Monday. I can meet with you and your husband that afternoon at three if that works for you.

Attached you'll find a list of things we need to have in place before I can grant you temporary certification. We will continue working with you to make this permanent after the children are transitioned into your care. Please use this time to get your fingerprints done and send me the names and phone numbers of at least three references.

Thank you,
Abby Gentry

Zara opened the first attachment and scanned the list of home requirements. And here she thought she'd simply needed to clear out a room . . . and replace a broken window. Not even close. To think there were people who volunteered for this, ones who weren't thrust into the system because of a family connection. Out there in the world, some people chose to make this their lifestyle. Those kinds of people were better than she was. She hadn't thought of herself as suffering from low self-esteem, but she also knew when she'd been beaten. Zara had major doubts she'd make it through this process.

She looked up at the stained ceiling with no smoke detector. They were going to need a lot of those, and she was guessing they'd also need to paint, and get beds, and—did Samuel sleep in a bed or a crib? Diapers. They'd need diapers and a place to change him. And bottles.

The floor felt unstable. She was still staring at the ceiling, but when she looked down, there was definitely movement. Zara sank onto the carpet. Was the earth going to open up and swallow her along with this house she loved so much?

"Hellooo?" Her mother-in-law's voice wove up the stairs. "Are you up there, Zara?"

"Yes." She pushed against the wall, but the effort was too much, and she sank back into the faded shag. "Come on up."

"Well now, it looks like you're making great progress."

Zara looked around. Only Sharon would say something like that. This place was straight out of *The Money Pit*, an old movie she'd seen once. "It's a lost cause."

At nearly seventy, Sharon hadn't slowed down a bit. She sat next to Zara. "I can see why you'd feel that way. This is a big project."

"It's too big."

She patted Zara's leg. "Nothing's too big for God."

Zara buried her face in her hands. Now she had the guilt of being faithless on top of everything else. "I don't know, Sharon. There's no time, yet there's so much work, and we have nothing for kids. I don't even own a doll."

"What children need more than anything else is love. You and Chad have that."

The puppy woke from his nap in the corner of the room and pounced on a pile of old wallpaper Zara had stripped away.

Sharon stood and offered her a hand. "Let's get a list going, and I think I know where we can get some help."

As Zara rose, she was overwhelmed by what Sharon was suggesting. Help from strangers? She wasn't that kind of girl.

"Don't look like a cobra just slithered in. We have a group of people at church who are dedicated to helping foster families. I think this would be a good time for you to learn to let others lend you a hand."

She stared at her fingers, still wrapped in Sharon's. "Maybe just a few things."

"We'll make a list." She bent, rustled through her oversized purse, and came out with a tablet with a pen tucked inside the wire binding. "I have an extra twin-sized bed with a pretty good mattress." She wrote *twin* on the right side of the page. "You'll need a crib for the little guy." On the left she scribbled *crib*. "Of course there's crib sheets and all that too."

"Yep. Of course." The room had a different feel. The emptiness was overwhelming. "They need clothes, and I guess Samuel needs diapers." She remembered changing a few of her brother's when he was tiny, but that was a lifetime ago. His lifetime.

"You might want to put screens on the windows." Sharon stepped closer, her eyes growing wide. "And maybe glass."

"I didn't realize the weights weren't attached, and it dropped."

"I know a guy. He's good at this kind of thing."

Zara took a step back from her mother-in-law. She was sure she'd just seen a twinkle or sparkle. "A guy?"

"A friend." She turned away, acting like Zara's half-stripped wallpaper held great fascination. "I'll text him."

Before Zara could ask anything else, Sharon had taken out her phone and her thumbs were tapping like a teenager's. Then, as if he were waiting for her contact, the phone buzzed. "Aw. He said he'd be glad to fix the window." Another buzz. "He can be over this morning for the measurements." She smiled and walked out of the room, leaving Zara with the odd feeling that she was supposed to follow.

In the kitchen, Zara picked a box up off the counter and set it on the floor, then turned on the stove to warm some water. Sharon loved tea. She'd learned this over the last couple of years and found herself thrilled to have a basket of options and an actual teakettle to serve her mother-in-law, like a real wife. The thought made her grin. Hopefully, she'd find a way to feel like a real mom, or at least like an aunt, for the sake of Charlotte and Samuel.

But for now, she was a fraud.

Fake it till you make it. This was the phrase she'd told herself all through college. There weren't many places she'd felt like she truly belonged—aside from with Chad—and Zara wondered if her place in his life was selfish. He wouldn't have to worry about genetic diseases and dying children or becoming a foster parent overnight if he'd stayed with that woman he was dating when they'd first met. If only Zara hadn't sat next to him in their writing class.

"I have all sorts of teas to choose from." She handed the basket to Sharon, who was staring out the back window.

"Thank you. I can't believe how much progress you and Chad have made on this farm already. It's beautiful. The perfect place for my grandchildren to grow up."

Alarms sounded in Zara's brain. "We're not adopting Eve's kids."

She turned toward Zara, taking in a long inhale of a tea bag, then handing it over, the chosen one. "I know. But that doesn't mean I don't intend to grandma them. I assume this is an open position in their lives?"

Zara shrugged. "I suppose you're right." Any number of things could have happened to Zara if she hadn't had grandparents. Somehow, the thought of not having them was more shocking to her than being taken from a mother. Technically, the kids had a grandmother, but the woman who raised Zara and Eve had been incarcerated for the last few years. She was sure Sharon knew this, though the information had not come from Zara's mouth. "That means a lot to me. Grandmothers—good ones like you—they're important."

The kettle whistled like it must in all good homes, sending steam jetting into the air. Zara showered the blackberry sage tea bag in the cup with scalding water. The scent that rose to her nose was like medication for a worried soul. After handing the cup to Sharon, she made one for herself, then sat at the breakfast bar, her hands wrapped around the hot mug.

"I'll help in any way I can." Sharon took the seat next to her. "What you're doing is going to be a blessing for all four of you."

Outside the window, the breeze picked up some of the newly turned soil, sending it into a miniature tornado that danced over the uneven surface of the garden. "I don't have anything to offer them."

"You have love. I've seen the way you and Chad are together. You have plenty of love. Just give it a chance."

Her words floated in the air and settled, not like the weight Zara had let the situation become, but like hope.

"I'm scared."

Sharon's arms reached around Zara. "Of course you are. That's natural. But so is faith."

Zara let Sharon comfort her the way only her grandmother had done. Faith—*the substance of things hoped for, the evidence of things not seen*—one of the first verses she'd learned when she became a Christian. She'd thought she'd chosen faith when she married Chad and they bought this farm, but it turned out faith was something that must be committed to over and over again.

CHAPTER FIFTEEN

THE RECEPTIONIST BUZZED TIFF THROUGH before she could even press the button. On entering, she saw the cringe in the woman's expression but didn't hesitate. "What happened?"

She rose behind the counter, not bothering to come around to Tiff's side. "Ms. Bradley, there's no emergency. The doctor was able to treat the reaction right away. He's still here and would like to talk with you and Eve together."

"Where?"

"Just a moment. I'll let him know you're here." She pressed a button and talked into her headset. "Ms. Bradley has arrived." The smile she gave increased Tiff's irritation. "He said he'd be right out." She slid the glass between them shut and turned back to her computer as if she could no longer see Tiff through the window.

The door to the back of the facility opened with an ear-piercing beep. "Ms. Bradley. I'm Dr. Warren. I've been treating our friend Eve."

Our friend? Oh goodness. It was going to take dedication to like this man. "What can you tell me about the reaction she had? The message made it sound serious."

He patted her upper arm as though Tiff were an exaggerating

child. "It could have been very serious, but I was here, and Eve is fine now. Before we step into her room, I would like to let you know that she still has hives, but they will be gone within the next few hours." He stopped with one hand on the doorknob and the other on his security badge. Another buzzer and the door popped open.

Upon admission, Eve had been assured she would only be kept there of her own free will, and though Tiff believed that was true, this place certainly had a prison-like atmosphere.

Eve was wrapped in a blanket and sitting up along the side of a hospital bed. Her face and neck appeared angry with bright red swelling. As the door clicked shut, Tiff felt the urge to escape. What was she even doing there? She didn't know this woman, and as Bruce had reminded Tiff several times now, her life really wasn't any of her business.

Dr. Warren took a seat. "Eve, I've invited Ms. Bradley in for our discussion because you've indicated she's part of your recovery team. I'm so glad you have someone to walk through this with you. So many of our patients have burned all their bridges and have to step into a new life on their own. I guarantee you that your odds of success are much better with a support system."

It seemed as though he'd gotten the wrong impression and assumed Eve and Tiff were related. She could correct him, but the shadow of a girl sitting across from her needed someone, anyone, to give her a chance. Bruce might be right, but Tiff couldn't walk away from Eve. Not when she was so alone.

The doctor threaded his fingers together and leaned forward. "This isn't going to be easy. We'd hoped Suboxone would give Eve an extra boost as she came off the heroin and worked to remain clean. However, the allergic reaction she had was unfortunately a deal breaker. I believe she's through the worst of it—both the detox and the reaction—but she'll need to keep up her liquid intake, and I'd like her to stay on Benadryl for a few more days."

Tiff's pulse beat a heavy rhythm. "It sounds like you're letting her go . . . already."

"Tomorrow. You've paid for our supervision through detox. I can refer you to a residential rehab facility, but I'll let you know right now, those aren't cheap, and the ones that take Oregon Health Plan have a waiting list."

Eve shook her head. Her eyes seemed to be staring off in the distance, but she was there, taking in the conversation. "I can't go away. I'm doing this for my kids. I need to be here."

"I'll tell you my main concern." He swiveled his seat toward Eve. "You've said you don't have housing lined up. Where will you go when you leave here?"

Tiff held up her hand. "I've made some arrangements. Eve, if you're still willing, there's a room being held for you at the women's shelter. It's not a lot, but it will work while you get back on your feet."

Tears pooled in Eve's eyes and flooded over her bottom lashes.

"What do you think, Eve? It's a start, and I'll help you however I can." The temperature in the room seemed to rise as she faced what she was saying. She chose Eve, choosing what her faith called her to do. But that meant choosing to do something her husband would never agree to.

"Thank you." Eve's words were a choked cry. "I want to do this. Thank you."

"And you will."

The doctor stood, his chair squeaking as it inhaled air into the cushion. "I have to be going. I'll let you two talk out the details." He held out his hand to her. "It was nice to meet you, Ms. Bradley."

"And you too." They shook and he left without another look at Eve.

When he was gone, Tiff mustered the will to bring up the subject she couldn't with the doctor in the room. "I got a call the other day from the caseworker. She'd like to schedule a visit with the kids. Apparently, they're moving to another foster home soon.

I didn't tell her you were here. I . . . maybe I should have, but I thought that was your decision to make."

Eve nodded, but her gaze had dropped to her sock-covered feet.

"Charlotte and Sammy will be so glad to see you."

Eve covered her face with both hands, and her shoulders shuddered as she shook with wrenching sobs.

"What?" Tiff moved to sit beside her, putting an arm around her shoulder. "The kids are going to be just fine, and they'll be so proud of you for getting clean."

"They'd be better off without me."

"No. Don't say that. You are their mother. They need you." *And you need them.* Tiff's heart split open again with the loss of her own child. It was a wound that never healed, only scabbed over until the grief burst through again.

"I don't know how to be a good mom."

"It's as simple as love." But that was not entirely true. Love without wisdom could be dangerous. She was sure Eve loved her children, but that hadn't prevented the trauma that would stick with them like a stubborn stain. And Tiff had loved Lindsay with her whole heart, but she hadn't known what she'd needed and how to protect her. "I'll help any way I can." Repeating this didn't help Eve, but Tiff needed to say it again. She needed the commitment to be out loud, because without the firm verbal contract, she wouldn't be able to stand up to Bruce.

"We can do this together. I promise."

Eve

May 24, 2019

I feel like there's a chance. It's not real big, but maybe I can do this. I don't want Charlotte to end up like me or like my mom.

I hope she can be like Zara. My sister escaped somehow. I've seen her picture on Facebook. She looks like what I might have looked like if I hadn't become a junkie. She's really very pretty.

In the bathroom, I run water over my hands and slop it onto my face, washing away the tightness from my tears. The mirror reflects my sharp, bony features, the teeth that seem to stretch out from my gums, and the yellow hue of my skin. Even my hair is brittle and frizzy. Who have I become?

CHAPTER SIXTEEN

ZARA PEERED THROUGH THE WINDOW of the old oven. The glass was splattered and stained with years of culinary misfortunes, leaving it nearly impossible to see past the grime.

Chad had brought take-and-bake pizza home so they could get the rest of the house ready for the inspection. As the timer on her phone went off, Zara noticed the lack of the yummy scent she'd expected to be coming from the oven. And when she opened it, she found raw dough that may have slightly warmed.

"Hey, babe." Zara called Chad in from the living room. "I think there's an issue."

He came into the kitchen and leaned over her shoulder. "Hmm. I really prefer my pizza cooked."

"Ha-ha. Was it hot when you put them in there?"

She felt his shoulders shrug. "I think so. I guess I didn't really pay much attention. Maybe it's the circuit. I'll check it out."

Her only response was the loud grumble of her stomach. She closed the door and checked all the knobs, but the oven should have been on. The second hand on the clock ticked along in its circle, showing there was power to the appliance, but still she hoped this could be fixed with the flip of a switch in the circuit box.

"Sorry." Chad came back in and leaned against the counter. "It's not that." His nose wrinkled. "Do you smell something?"

And she did. The scent of a fire burning. Not pizza.

Chad jumped forward and pulled the oven away from the wall. Smoke snaked up from the back, just above the place where the cord went in. He tugged the plug out of the outlet and motioned for Zara to open the back door.

Smoke was really taking over then.

Chad ran out through the porch and showed up a minute later at the back door with a hand truck and gloves. As if this were a normal event, he slid the nose plate under the oven. "Push on the top while I tip this back."

She did, and he wheeled the smoking oven onto the deck before ejecting it over the edge and onto the ground. In no time, he was spraying it with the hose. That was the end of the story for the ancient stove that came with the house. Another thing to put on the list. Zara sat down on the top step and watched steam billow from the pile of useless metal.

Chad came over and sat beside her. "So, what should we have for dinner?"

She snorted as laughter took her by surprise. "The pizza's still in there."

"I've suddenly lost my appetite for Italian. Now, a can of pork and beans and a chunk of cheese, that sounds like the perfect dinner."

"That's handy, since that's about all we have." Zara melted into his side. Even though their only cooking appliance was lying in the yard, she was still happy to be by his side.

"Was a working stove on the list of items we needed?" His mouth was so close to her ear that his words sent a shiver over her skin.

"It's hard to remember. I only paid attention to the things that seemed pertinent." His cheek was rough on her hand as she rubbed it gently. "We're going to be okay, huh?"

"No problem. It's just an appliance. And kids love hot dogs."
Again, her stomach growled.

Eve

May 25, 2019

Stepping out of the detox center was both scary and exciting. I feel okay. I'm not so sick, but my legs are shaky, and I keep trembling. The clothes Tiff brought me hang like I'm nothing more than a skeleton without muscle to count on, but she keeps reminding me there's hope. I need to believe that. I need to do this for my babies.

I'm sitting in Tiff's car while she runs into a convenience store. From here, she'll drive me to the shelter where I'm supposed to stay until I can get a job and a safe place to live. I wonder if Joey knows where I am. I wonder if he's been looking for me. He's not all bad. And I'm not that easy to live with. He took me and Charlie in when we had nowhere else to go.

The cops are looking for him. They say the charges aren't up to me. That doesn't seem fair. I'm the one who got hurt. How do they know I didn't deserve it?

TIFF'S INSIDES BUZZED as she and Eve moved through the women's shelter.

The room they gave Eve was simple and sparse but clean. She would share it with two other women, and there was a restroom down the hall. The rules were strict, enforced, and posted all over the house. Eve would be expected to do chores and make progress toward independence. There were no second chances when it came to possession of illegal drugs.

Forty-two women and twelve children lived in this building run by Tiff's friend Lyla. As far as she could tell, Lyla was a saint. The woman actually lived in the building herself. That was what giving it all for Christ looked like. If Bruce and Brandt would just take a look at the real work being done in the shadows, they'd understand why Tiff had to be directly involved. Her deepest dream was to share this calling with her husband and son, to work with them and not fight against them. Christianity wasn't going to church and paying your tithe; it was living for Jesus. It was serving His people. How much better that would be as a family.

Lyla returned to the room where Tiff was putting away Eve's minimal clothing in her designated drawers. She only got two, but she could easily be fine with half of one. "I've sent our girl to tour the house with Wanda. She'll take good care of her and will be a real fine friend to have around here."

"Is the house dangerous?"

"Not in a physical way. But when you get this many women living together, especially under trying and sometimes downright frightening circumstances, they can get mean with their words. We have the occasional fight, but the women know that's grounds for immediate eviction, so I don't get a lot of that behavior. It's better than the streets by far. And we've got solid protection. That's what they need—to be safe while they change their lives. No one gets in the way of that around here. I won't allow it."

Tiff believed her. Lyla was tough. She was tall and strong and had lived out on the streets herself. She knew what was out there, and she had let Tiff know more than once that she could stand for more *education* on the subject. The guidance and mentoring Tiff had already received from Lyla were worth more than the beautiful house on the hill where she and Bruce lived.

"Eve's supposed to call her caseworker today. Here's the number." Tiff took the card from the pocket on the side of her purse and tried to hand it to Lyla.

"Nope." She shook her head. "That's not my thing. The women here have to learn how to take care of themselves. Eve will need to learn to do what's required, or she doesn't stand a chance of getting those kids back or changing her life. I'm not their mama. If anything, I'm more of a warden."

Tiff slipped the paper back into her pocket. "You do have a phone she can use, though?"

"We do. It's right out here in the open." She pointed to an old-style push-button phone on a desk in the corner. "As long as no one is waiting, she can use it as much as she needs."

This was a bit like prison. No privacy, but Tiff reminded herself that Eve would be safe here, and safety was far more than she'd had for a long time.

MONDAY MORNING WAS A BATTLE of chaos and nerves. Sharon's "friend" Walter—a man who couldn't keep his eyes off Zara's mother-in-law—replaced the window, leaving it better than it had been before Zara broke it. The foster care support group from church brought in a bed, a crib, and a dresser. Zara washed the bedding, and Chad would be home any minute with a stove they'd found on Craigslist.

Zara couldn't find a fire extinguisher with a 2A rating or above anywhere in town. It wasn't like they had a lot of shopping options. The one that met the state's standards had been ordered, and the treasury of gold it cost had been paid, but it wouldn't arrive until Friday at the earliest.

"Knock, knock."

She spun to find Trinity in her doorway. Trinity was the kind of woman Zara assumed had been very popular in high school. Zara wouldn't have garnered a look from that crowd. But Trinity was also generous and humble. She seemed to be the lead from the church group. "Come on in."

She set a cardboard box on the counter. "Look what I got."

The enthusiasm in her voice upped Zara's own excitement. She edged closer as Trinity lifted a flap. The box was stuffed with children's clothes. Zara lifted out a sundress, bright with a sunflower print. There were tiny socks and little sandals. As she took out one item at a time, the scent of fabric softener filled her heart. She could see Samuel and Charlotte in these, running through the yard, all giggles and smiles. As much as she'd like to keep a wall between them, she couldn't. Like Chad had said, they deserved all they could give them, not just the easy parts.

"And I've got a huge box of diapers in the van."

Zara patted her heart. "You didn't have to do all this."

"Neither did you. I'm doing the fun stuff, but you've agreed to be there for the hard times. This is the very least we can do to help." Trinity squeezed Zara from the side, and she realized she'd like to be friends with the woman. "I'll be right back." With all the energy of a teen cheerleader, she was out the door and hopping toward her car.

Two hours until the certifier arrived. It didn't seem to matter to Abby Gentry that today was Memorial Day, but it also meant that Chad didn't have to take more time off work. Zara tapped her phone and pulled up the tracking app. Chad was only minutes away from home. She swept the pockmarked floor again, knowing the plan to put down new flooring might be on hold for now.

Trinity returned with the diapers. "I'll take these upstairs."

"Thank you." It was hard to see her house the same way she had when she and Chad first discovered it. Back then, the broken rails, sagging gutters, and peeling paint were nothing next to the vision she'd seen for the house's future. In her mind, the siding gleamed with fresh white paint, the gutters were true, and everything was crisp with newness. Hopefully their certifier was a woman of imagination.

Gravel crunched outside as Chad pulled up in the pickup, the bed of which was starkly absent of a stove.

Zara jogged out to meet him. "What happened? Is the guy bringing it to the house?"

Chad stepped out and took off his worn baseball cap. "I got all the way over there, and he'd already sold it."

"But he knew you were coming." Her blood pressure climbed.

Chad took her hand. "Yep. But someone else came by and offered him a few extra dollars if he could take it. Nothing we can do. I looked through Craigslist again, but the closest in our price range is two hours out of town."

"No luck?" Trinity asked from the porch.

Chad shook his head.

"Oh well. I'm sure the certifier will understand." She came down the steps and joined them. "I'm so excited for your family. I'll be off now, but please let me know if there's anything else . . . besides a stove . . . that you need." Another quick hug, and Trinity was off to her van.

"Thank you." Zara hollered after her, but the words were not nearly enough to encompass the enormous amount of gratitude she felt. "Now we have to get that paper work done. Time is going by way too quickly."

ZARA STOWED THE VACUUM CLEANER just as the puppy barked at a new arrival, a trick Pickles had mastered only in the last few days and seemed very proud to show off.

Chad scooped him into his arms, gave Zara one last smile of reassurance, and opened the front door.

Abby Gentry wasn't what Zara had expected. She was all twinkle and glamour from her updo to her stilt-like heels, without which she couldn't have been much taller than a child herself. As she came toward them, she rubbed her lips together, as if smoothing out newly applied lipstick. "I'm Abby." She held out a hand with a business card.

"Nice to meet you. I'm Zara." She wove her arm through Chad's. "And this is my husband, Chad. Please come in."

They let Abby go ahead of them, giving Chad and Zara a moment to exchanged puzzled looks.

In the living room, Zara was surprised when she sat on their old stained sofa without hesitation. The skirt she wore was finely tailored and appeared costly.

Chad and Zara took the two kitchen chairs they'd moved for this purpose.

"Everything looked good with your fingerprints." Abby took a file folder out of her oversized purse. "Thank you for getting those done so quickly. Were you able to finish the questionnaire?"

Zara's stomach did a flip-flop. With shaking hands, she passed the paper work to Abby. She'd tried to be honest yet hopeful, a combination that wasn't easy when many of the questions revolved around her upbringing and extended family.

Abby glanced through. "This looks complete. I'll need to take time to interview you each separately and together. How would you like to begin?"

Their premarital counseling had nearly done Zara in, but this was going to go deeper. A storm was coming with dark skies, cold winds, and bottom-plunging questions that she would have to answer. Her entire adult life was based on the theory that she could walk away from her past and form a new life. No one else seemed to have this understanding.

"What do you think, Zara?" Chad touched her leg, and she jumped.

"I'm sorry. What was that?"

He ran a hand over her arm. "I thought we could start with the questions we can answer together."

"Perfect."

Abby laid the file out on the couch, then picked up a notebook and pencil. "This isn't going to be as bad as what I'm sure you're imagining."

She had no idea how warped and dark Zara's worries could go.

Abby started out with a series of questions that must have been designed to relieve their stress and relax them for the attack, because after about five of the easy pitches, she started in with the hardballs. There was nothing like having a woman she'd met just fifteen minutes earlier ask questions about their sex life when they'd been married only a little more than a month. This was like going-to-the-gynecologist awkward.

Zara's cheeks burned so hot, she was sure Abby was scribbling down notes about how repressed she was. But as it turned out, those questions were just teasers too.

"Neither of you have any children. Do you plan to start a family together, and if so, when would that be?"

Zara's ears began to buzz. If these were the things they had to discuss together, she feared the questions Abby would sling when she had her alone.

"We want children," Chad said. "We haven't discussed when. I mean, we have, but there are complications."

Prickles ran along Zara's skin. "It's a genetic thing. We're going to need more information before we have kids. If. I mean, we just aren't sure."

Abby set the notebook on her lap. "I know you didn't seek out being foster parents, but do you have the idea that you will be able to adopt these children?"

"No." Zara started picking at her cuticles, a habit she hadn't been able to break since childhood. "No. That's not it at all."

"Because the plan is reunification. We're mandated to do everything we can to get the kids back to their mother."

"We understand." Chad's chair squeaked as he wriggled.

"Now would be a good time to do the individual interviews." Abby's gaze seemed to bore into Zara. "Zara, how about you go first?"

"Sure." She tried to infuse a sweetness into her voice that might pass as confidence, but it came out more like a squawk.

When Chad had left and the two women were alone, Abby leaned back and crossed her thin legs. "I'd like to talk about your relationship with your sister. How much contact have you had over your adult years?"

Finally, a simple question. "None."

CHAPTER SEVENTEEN

ZARA STARED AT THE EMPTY PLACE where the stove should be. It was like a blaring siren screaming they couldn't do this. They weren't the kind of people who knew what they were doing and could manage the basic tasks required to keep young children safe.

Chad called from the living room. "We're done." There was relief in his voice, and she wondered what Abby could have asked her spotless husband with the ideal childhood.

When Zara joined them, they were already standing.

"Let's take a look around, shall we?" Abby's eyes scanned the room.

A lump hindered Zara's ability to swallow. "Upstairs first?" She'd never noticed the way the boards creaked and whined with each step on the staircase. It was all she could do not to look back and see if Abby was making notes. At the top, they crossed an open area, then entered the room that would be the kids'. "We were thinking they'd be more comfortable in the same room . . . for now."

"That seems fine. They're still quite young, but because they are different genders, this can't be a permanent thing." She stepped in and patted the bed, all made up in girly pinks with purple frills. Sharon went wild with this, surely coveting the opportunity to buy the pretty items she'd missed by having boys. "Isn't this beautiful."

Zara eased herself over to the new window, standing in front of it.

Abby looked at the outlets, and Zara gave herself a mental high-five for thinking of the childproof covers. Score one for her. Then Abby started toward the other window, reaching for the latch.

Without a thought, Zara dashed over and clamped her hand down on the mechanism.

Abby's eyes went wide.

"Sorry. This is a tricky one." Zara braced one hand on the upper window and released the lock. When she stepped slowly away, the window remained in the same location.

"I'd like to see that it opens." Abby tapped a pencil on her tablet.

"Of course." With a gentle push, the window slid down as if greased and prepared by a master carpenter. "No problem."

Behind Abby, Chad wiped his hand across his forehead in a dramatic gesture.

They went from room to room with the certifier inspecting every nook and closet, even the rooms they hadn't touched since moving in.

With each step they passed, Zara breathed a little deeper.

At last they made it downstairs and through those rooms. They stopped in the kitchen, where she pointed to the hole that should have contained an oven. "What's going on here?"

Chad shrugged. "We're getting a new stove. It should be here in the next day or two."

The confident way he said it seemed to work a miracle on Abby.

She nodded. "No problem. Let's take a quick look outside; then we'll be done."

As Zara opened the door, Pickles jetted through her legs and toward the barn. The sounds of the goats had intrigued him since they'd brought them home, but the wire fence Chad put up kept Pickles from getting to visit too closely.

"This is the garage." Zara pulled open a door. "We have tools and equipment in here, but no actual cars." She hoped to get at least a smile at that, but no. The overhead light did little to illuminate the area, but the clutter was visible enough to make any potential foster parent cringe. Most of what resided in this place came with the house. Whatever was on the far back of those shelves was a mystery, and Zara hadn't planned on investigating there until she absolutely had to.

Abby pulled a mini flashlight out of her bag and proceeded to look around like she was a crime scene investigator. "There are a lot of chemicals and dangerous tools stored in here. Do you have a plan to keep the children away from these things?"

Chad scratched at the back of his neck. "I could put locks on the doors."

"Very good. That would meet the requirements." The light was snuffed out, and Abby walked back into the sunshine. "I have just a few concerns you'll need to address. They're not huge, but I will need to come back and witness that you've brought the house into compliance. The first is the fire extinguisher. You'll need one with the proper rating."

"I've ordered one. It will be here Friday."

"That's great, but I'll need to see it. Number two: You do not have a carbon monoxide detector in the house. One will need to be installed before I can grant approval."

Chad raised his hand. He was in full school mode. "We don't have natural gas out here. It's all electric."

Abby shrugged. "It's in the rules. You must have a carbon monoxide detector."

"We'll get one." His eyebrow cocked.

"The cord to the blinds in the children's room needs to be secured, or better yet, remove the blinds."

Zara's stomach sank. She should have thought of that. When she was in high school, a friend's younger sister strangled in her crib because she was playing with the cord from her blinds. Zara wrapped her hands around the sides of her neck and looked up to the sky.

Abby cleared her throat. "Did you have a question about that, Zara?"

"No. I just feel foolish that I didn't think of it."

"No worries. This has all been sudden. We understand that. I'm here to be another set of eyes. The safer your home is, the easier it will be on you."

A puppy scream—that's the only way it could be described—came from near the barn. Chad and Zara jogged around the corner of the house. Pickles was running circles in the field, through Zara's freshly planted herbs. Behind him, a goat tore up the ground in hot pursuit.

"My plants!"

Chad hurdled over a short fence and joined in the chase.

He bent down to scoop up the puppy, looked at Zara and gave her a thumbs-up, then got knocked off his feet by a full-force ram from the loose goat.

Zara whipped her head around. Sure enough, Abby had seen it all.

Chad was back on his feet, the puppy still in his hand, his other held up between him and the goat as he inched toward the house.

"The goat isn't usually like that. Really." Zara failed to mention that this was the goat they called Bomber. "There must be a break in the fence."

Abby nodded, then scribbled down another note in that ridiculous tablet. "You'll need to show that farm animals are properly secured."

"I understand."

She made a bunch more notes, then tore off a paper and handed it to Zara. There were marks all over the thing, indicating areas where they had failed. "Can I come back Friday afternoon?"

"Of course. No problem. We'll have this all fixed." All eleven items. *Eleven.* They didn't buy the farm with children in mind, at least not an instant family. There was supposed to be time to prepare, to renovate and make this the perfect little farm. Once again, life was not going in the direction Zara had put down in her planner.

Eve
May 28, 2019

If I could do my life over again, I'd be a different woman. I'd be like Zara, even if it meant I had to be perfect at everything, judgmental, and stuck-up. That's not fair. I don't even know my sister now. Those traits might be what's needed to get out of this dump of a life. She did it. I sunk in deeper. Mom always said Zara was a snot. I did whatever I could to keep Mom happy. Zara walked away to have a life. When Mom went to jail, I was abandoned.

I just want to know how I can keep my kids from being like me.

It's crazy how my desire to do better for them is exactly what triggers my cravings. Just thinking about trying makes me desperate for the warm rush through my veins.

Not today. If I have to stay in this room until I'm strong enough to handle life without drugs, that's what I'll do. I wish someone would lock me up and keep me prisoner until I figure out how to live without heroin.

WHEN BRANDT AND LINDSAY were in middle school, the Bradleys had a weekly family tradition, Wednesday night pot roast, which they'd sit to eat as a family. Often it was the only night of the week that remained free of sports and work obligations.

This week, Tiff finally managed her first pot roast since Lindsay's disappearance. She'd tried this once not long after hearing the report of her daughter's death, but by the time she set out to actually cook the meal, a week had passed, and the meat had gone bad in the refrigerator.

The herby scents that filled the kitchen reopened the hole in her heart, but Tiff and her family had to heal and find a way to still be connected with the missing piece, gone forever.

Somehow, even with the knowledge that Lindsay wasn't coming home, Tiff couldn't help but feel her presence as she laid out the two plates, two glasses, and two sets of utensils.

A beep sounded from the security system as Bruce drove through the gate, and with his nearness came a nervous tingle in her stomach. Attempting to be vulnerable enough to fix even the tiniest bit of the gaping wound between them brought a fear so deep it ached.

She looked up as if begging the ceiling for another minute before he arrived, but God didn't hear her internal cries, or He felt His timing was better than hers.

Bruce swung the door open as though his entrance was meant to be a surprise. The look of irritation on his features quickly shifted to shock as he took in the set table. Clutched in his right hand was an envelope.

It only took seconds for Tiff to unravel that mystery. The credit card statement must have arrived.

"What's this?" He flung his bag onto the floor near the entrance.

Tiff gathered the serving utensils and set them on the table. "Pot roast night." She forced a smile.

He dropped the bill beside his plate and went to the sink, washing his hands.

"You've been right about me not making enough effort. I

wanted to show you that I really do care about you." She brought the food to the table and took a seat, unfolding her napkin and placing it on her lap.

Bruce remained silent as he came to join her. They didn't pray, at least not out loud, but they ate the meal together, even exchanging a few pleasant words.

All through the meal, Tiff trained her gaze to avoid the envelope, fearing the weight of her stare would cause the contents to explode.

Bruce used his fork to move the last of his meat through the thick gravy. "I see you paid for a detox program."

Her response stuck in her throat.

"I assume this was for the girl who was beaten. Please talk to me next time." He wiped his mouth with a napkin, then set it on his plate as he stood. "If you don't mind, I have some work to get to. Thanks for dinner."

As the door to his office clicked shut, Tiff folded forward and rested her forehead in her palms. There wasn't a lot to rejoice in, but this was something. A moment of semi peace. Maybe someday they'd find their way back to each other—except neither of them was the person they'd been when they fell madly in love.

CHAPTER EIGHTEEN

Eve
May 29, 2019

I'm scared. Terrified. I know the girl who just moved into the
bunk above me. When she came in, I acted like I was sleeping
and buried my face in the blankets. An hour must have gone
by as I waited for her breathing to grow heavy enough for me
to grab my journal and write by the light from the streetlamp
outside the window. It's got to be one in the morning by now.

I met her years ago, under the bridge that goes to the freeway.
She was Joey's girl then. I heard rumors after we got together
that she'd like to kill me. Joey is her baby daddy. She thought
that would mean something. But he loved me. He told me so.
And most of the time, he took care of me and the kids.

Joey's out there somewhere, hiding. The cops will be after
him. I feel like this is all my fault. I never should have gone out
that night. I made him feel like I didn't trust him.

How am I supposed to sleep when the mattress keeps
squeaking above me?

RITA HAD SUGGESTED THEY FACETIME with the kids. This
allowed everyone another opportunity to get used to one another

before the move. It was the best they could do with all the repairs and preparations, Chad's demanding job, and Rita's getting ready for the new kids coming into her home. Plus, Charlotte and Samuel had a visit with Eve scheduled for the next day.

Zara scooped up the wrappers from their fast-food dinner, something she felt an unbalanced amount of guilt for, and stuffed them into the trash, being sure no remnants remained to be seen from the laptop camera.

"Let's give it a trial run." Chad clicked on the app, and there they were, the two of them looking back at their own images.

This wasn't like seeing herself in the bathroom mirror. Somehow, she had to prepare herself for that reflection, giving effort to see what she needed in the glass. The camera on the computer didn't ask if she was ready, if she'd put on her confident expression and unbreakable façade. It didn't even give her the chance to brush the hair out of her face.

The image that greeted her was her sister's. She saw Eve on the screen sitting next to Chad. She saw her sadness, her worry, her need to fit in. She saw all the things in her sister that Zara had been too young to understand. Then she saw the tears fill her eyes and spill over, and she had to face reality. The person on the screen was her, but it was also Eve. Even after years apart, Eve was her missing half.

Chad brought her into his arms and stroked her hair. "Hey now. What's this about?" His words were gentle, but the question was so large and heavy.

Zara shook her head against his chest. "I don't know." But really, she just didn't have the words to help him understand. She'd abandoned her identical twin. She'd left her with their mother, with the pain of losing their brother, with the fears of what each day would bring, and she'd started her own life without inviting Eve. Zara had lived the dream, but as half a person.

A computerized ring shocked her straight, an incoming call that must be Rita.

Chad didn't touch the keyboard. His gaze remained pinned on her.

"I'm fine. Answer it." Zara leaned out of the camera's range and wiped her eyes, pushed back her hair, and took a calming breath, then popped up next to her husband with a smile covering what was missing in her heart. "Hi, Rita. How are the little ones doing?"

There was a relief in Rita's features she didn't even try to hide, like she never quite trusted that they'd hold up their end. But they would. Zara was committed to doing this for the kids, but also for Eve. She owed her sister that much. "They're wonderful. In fact, you can see for yourselves." Rita turned her head and called for Charlotte.

When the girl appeared, Zara saw something in her she'd missed before, maybe fear. She wanted to ask what was worrying her, but there were so many possible answers, almost all of which Zara could do nothing about. "Hi there."

"Hi."

"Do you remember us?"

She looked down, then made eye contact again. "I know. You're my aunt and uncle. Rita tells me about you. She says Sammy and I are coming to stay with you."

"That's right." Chad's hand curled around Zara's. "Does Samuel like to be called Sammy?"

"Yes. That's his name."

"What about you? Do you have a special name you like to be called?"

She leaned back on Rita's chest. "My mom calls me Charlie, but that's just for her, okay?"

"I understand."

Chad tilted his head. "Charlotte, do you have any questions for us? Anything you really like that you want us to know about?"

"I want to know where you were before. My mom wrote to you. Why didn't you come?"

Her gaze stared into Zara's heart and tore it apart. "I'm so sorry.

144

I didn't get any letters from your mom. I would have come if I'd known you needed help." But that was a lie. It was one of those untruths you told to avoid hurting someone else, or perhaps to keep from hurting yourself with the truth. "Charlotte, I'm really sorry. But Chad and I are here now. We're not going anywhere."

A tiny smile lifted the sides of her mouth, not enough to look joyful, but a hint that she could be okay someday. Then she was gone, out of view from the camera.

"She's going to be all right," Rita said. "It takes time for kids like Charlotte to learn trust. She's been in the midst of trauma her entire life." She turned to the side and grinned. "What do we have here?"

A moment later, Sammy's drooling face filled the entire screen. He saw them and broke into a round of perfect baby giggles. Thank God he hadn't outgrown that yet. Zara was suddenly overwhelmed with the honor that she had the fortune to be there for a bit of his life, to enjoy the times like this one when she could see her nephew giving over to the all-out wonder of living. He was perfection, the spitting image of her brother in happy, healthy days. She'd take this as evidence that Hunter syndrome didn't take every male child in her family.

By the time they ended the call—not long, as the kids' attention span could be counted in single-digit minutes—Zara was in love with both kids and ready to fight for their lives. Whether it was only for months or a year, she'd give them every bit of hope she could in that time, because life was sometimes great. And she'd been blessed enough to find that out.

CHAPTER NINETEEN

Eve

May 30, 2019

I got up early, not because I felt like it, but because I couldn't stop thinking about what would happen at the visit. I really let my kids down. I thought I was better than my mom—in some ways. But knowing they're in foster care and I can only see them with supervision in a secure location . . . it's hard for me to argue what's happening.

I tried to keep my face turned away as my roommates woke up, but when I heard the evil laugh behind me, I knew I hadn't succeeded in remaining unnoticed. This is exactly what Bonnie said: "Oh, look who's lost her sugar daddy. It's about time Joey threw out the trash."

If I hadn't been so weak, and she hadn't been so right, I would have turned around and punched her. It was then that I got the call over the speaker to come to the front desk. Tiff was there. She keeps on saving me.

When I got in the car, she had a warm cinnamon roll and coffee waiting for me. I wish I had a mom like her. But if my mom had been anything like Tiff, I wouldn't be where I am.

Before I got to see the kids, I had to sit down with the caseworker. I can't stand talking to her. She took my children away from me! And now, she gets to make all the decisions, including when and how I can see my own babies.

One of the first things she told me is that I have to start taking a drug test before each visit. What if I fail? Does that mean she won't let me see them? Don't I have a right to my own kids?

She explained the plan for Charlotte and Sammy. And I was shocked and overwhelmed and ashamed. Tomorrow they're moving from their foster home to live with Zara, my own twin who I haven't seen in years. Charlotte and Sammy haven't even met her.

I expected the visitation room to be smelly, with old toys and a ragged couch. This is what I remember from my own short trip into foster care. But the place was clean and new and looked like a fancy preschool. There were toys, things I could never get my kids, neatly tucked onto white shelves, and costumes hanging on the wall. Why would my kids want to come back to me now that they've seen how life can be? Or after they live with who I'm sure will turn out to be the good twin.

I didn't meet the foster mom, but they said she was waiting in a room down the hall. Some woman who has the job to make sure we're watched every second I'm with my kids left me in the room while she got Charlotte and Sammy. I found myself shaking, not because I needed a hit, but because I was scared. What if they didn't want to see me? What if they'd learned how horrible I am because they've spent time with one of these perfect parents?

When the door opened, Charlotte stared at me, then ran into my arms. I held her tight against my chest and felt the tears streaming over my cheeks. I told her I'm sorry. I messed up. And *that I'm doing everything I can to get our family back together again.*

When the lady handed me Sammy, I almost melted at the powdery smell of him.

There is nothing in this world I love more than my children. Nothing. Heroin, I still want every single minute, but what I feel for my children is love.

The visit ended so soon. I'd just gotten my balance when the woman, who never left us alone, said our time was up. Sammy cried so hard when she took him out of my arms, but Charlotte didn't shed a tear. That was worse.

TIFF PICKED AT THE PLASTIC on her steering wheel. Was this really the way to restore families? She drove about three blocks after dropping Eve back off at the shelter before finding a place to park and let the tears fall. The entire drive to the DHS office, Tiff had fed Eve words of encouragement. She'd told her this was the beginning of the healing. But when Eve came out of the visit, she was more broken than before. The devastation and hopelessness were clear in her eyes, the grief etched into her face.

If reunification was truly what the state wanted for families like Eve's, why did they put them through a process that stripped away a parent's last vestiges of pride?

They didn't live in a perfect world, and asking a government agency to change its ways and allow parents to be mentored rather than punished, taught rather than shamed, was probably idealistic and unattainable. That didn't stop Tiff from wanting it for Eve.

Drying her tears, she drove the rest of the way home, Eve's rounded shoulders present in her thoughts and prayers. As she approached the house, she saw her son's car parked in the driveway. Tiff's heart was swallowed by a black hole of familial failure. Pot roast night could never make up for what she'd done today. She was supposed to have a family dinner tonight to celebrate Bruce's birthday early because Brandt had to be out of town on the actual day.

Before she closed the garage door, Tiff called Bruce's favorite Italian place and put in an order, then offered an exorbitant additional fee if they'd send someone over with the food. The manager agreed without hesitation. Then she did the same with the bakery down the street. She knew the owner well, and the woman promised to send her son with the best cake left in the display.

Tiff powdered her nose and beneath both eyes, then blew out a breath she hoped would take a measure of her nerves away, but it did not.

Inside, Bruce and Brandt were watching a baseball game while Sophie, Brandt's longtime girlfriend, stared at her phone.

"I hope you guys are hungry." She threw an extra dose of enthusiasm into her voice. It was the best way to frost over her shortcomings.

Bruce looked over his shoulder and, finding Tiff without a morsel of dinner, shook his head and turned back to the television.

"Hey, Mom." Brandt leaned back in the recliner that was supposed to be hers. "Dad just suggested we order pizza. He said you've been busy with something."

"No. Not pizza tonight. We're celebrating your dad. I've made arrangements to have his favorite meal brought to the house. I thought he'd like Giovanni's better than anything I could cook."

"Ha." Bruce didn't even look back.

Tiff walked over and stood behind his chair. She set her hands on his shoulders, which tightened beneath her touch. But she wasn't giving up. "I have cake for dessert."

"What kind?" Though his voice grumbled, she could tell he was truly curious.

Unfortunately, Tiff had no idea what flavor would be arriving. "It's a surprise. You'll just have to wait until it's time to blow out the candles." At least she had a few of those around—somewhere.

The gate buzzer rang, and Tiff let the delivery person through. Only a few minutes later, the house warmed with the scents of sausage, cheeses, and Italian herbs. The restaurant had sent a generous amount of Caesar salad and toasted sourdough rolls to go with the meal. For something she'd only just put together, this dinner looked more than adequate.

Tiff set out the nice dishes, filled the glasses with ice water, and folded napkins at each setting. No one bothered to help, but that was partially her fault. This was how she'd trained her family to behave. Separate. Distant. Everyone doing their own thing.

She'd even given Sophie the idea that she was better off doing things alone. Early on, Sophie would ask to help. Every time it made Tiff think of Lindsay—not that they'd worked together on dinners, but that those were the kinds of things mothers and daughters *should* do together. Sharing that space with Sophie would be giving her something Tiff should have given her own child but didn't.

"Hey, guys, dinner is ready." Tiff stood behind the table, her apron tied around her waist as if she'd actually cooked something, their food transferred into real dishes.

Bruce came over without bothering to turn off the game. He adjusted his chair to ensure his view, then placed a napkin on his lap.

When they were all seated, Tiff looked to her husband to say the blessing, and he did, but it lacked the phrase she missed so much—"and thank you for my wife and all she does for our family." How long ago had he stopped saying that?

"This is delicious. Thank you, Mrs. B." Sophie took small helpings of everything, leaving her plate looking like it could hardly maintain the weight of a squirrel, let alone an active young woman.

Sophie had been part of Brandt's life for over two years. They would likely get married, yet Tiff hardly knew her. And she was sorry for that and so many other ways in which she'd failed, but that didn't mean she'd walk away from the women who needed someone to care. Eve was alone. Completely alone.

"How have you been, Sophie?" She set her fork on the edge of her plate and paid full attention.

Sophie swallowed and dabbed her lips with a napkin. "I'm good. I'll graduate this June, and I'm really excited about that."

Tiff tried to remember what she was majoring in but couldn't come up with the degree. "That's wonderful."

"Brandt said you've been working with a woman who was badly beaten. That's so good of you."

There was an audible grumble from Bruce.

"It's a privilege, really. Eve has no one. She's trying to get her life back on track, but without a support system, it's tough."

"Is she safe now?" Sophie leaned forward, appearing truly interested. How had Tiff missed how caring her heart was?

"Somewhat. She's staying at a shelter for now."

"Is there any way I can help?"

Brandt put up his hand. "Mom, please don't be offended, but I don't want Sophie around the people you see out there. It's not safe."

The air in the room had taken a sour turn. Brandt was missing what was true and important, but it was her own fault. "Listen, life isn't safe. I used to do all the *safe* things, and I missed what was really happening in the world."

"Lindsay is gone. I thought you just needed to do this so you could accept that, but it keeps going, and I don't understand.

Do we need to lose you too?" His voice grew louder with each word.

Sophie stood. "I get to decide what I do with my life. If I'd like to help your mom or this woman she's working with, I can do that."

"Now look what you've done." Bruce threw his napkin on the floor. "This *ministry* is tearing our family apart."

"No, Bruce. It's not what I'm doing that's tearing us apart." She shook her fisted hands. "It's guilt. We all feel it. You wonder what you could have done differently for Lindsay. Brandt probably thinks he missed something, or should have told us what was going on. I feel like I didn't get into her business enough and wish I'd been a different mother. We can go on and on, but none of it will turn back the clock. If I had it to do over again, you bet I'd do better. But all I can do now is move forward. Believe it or not, that's what I'm doing." Tiff stood so quickly, her chair started to tip. "Take a minute and really think about this. Bruce, if anyone is stuck in the past, it's you."

She picked up her keys and purse. "Don't forget to tip the cake delivery boy." Then she slammed the door on her way out.

Tiff pulled in the driveway a couple of hours later with her passion all cried out, leaving only guilt and regret in its place. They were all still hurting, still wanting to have hope, but hope had been stripped away. It had faded away a year after Lindsay walked out of their house, when Tiff got the call that she was gone forever.

Some dealer, a man who didn't care about Lindsay or anyone else, had gotten locked up. He confessed to seeing her die, not of an overdose, but from a knife to the belly. Did he really think giving that information would help him? Maybe it had—she didn't know. What was clear to Tiff was that her daughter—whose body was not recovered, whose murderer was not found—was gone and wouldn't be coming back.

Yes, she knew the streets could be dangerous at night. She understood the risks. But if Tiff could stop one mother from the deep, gushing pain she felt with every mention of her child's name, it was worth the chances she took.

Tiff pressed the button and sat listening to the garage door close behind her, the engine still running. For a moment, she wondered what it would be like to let herself slip into sleep and wake up in heaven, maybe find her baby there waiting. She missed Lindsay so much the pain was physical, like someone pressing a strong hand against her windpipe.

CHAPTER TWENTY

TIFF TURNED OFF THE ENGINE. It would be God's choice when and how to take her home.

The house was dark. She hung her keys on the hook and reached for the switch. As the room illuminated, she saw her husband, his recliner turned toward her, his expression unreadable. "What are you doing sitting in the dark?" She'd completely destroyed his birthday dinner and now braced for the fury he must be feeling. Though Bruce had never laid a hand on her in anger, he had a voice that could thunder through her bones.

"Waiting. We need to talk." Instead of anger, his words held only regret.

Tiff's legs grew weak. Had they really come to this point in their marriage? She'd thought they would be one of the couples who survived the death of a child, but they'd drifted in their own individual directions, and most of that sat firmly on her slumped shoulders. Tiff walked to his side and took a sideways seat in her own chair.

"I spoke with the new pastor the other day. I just couldn't get myself to bring up our problems to Pastor Lewis, and the new guy seemed like he knew a thing or two."

"I'm shocked." Blood buzzed through her veins, as if even the cells were jittery with nerves. "What did he say? What did *you* say?"

"For the first hour, it was mostly me doing the talking. I told him everything. All of it. About Lindsay and you and the work you're doing. And I told him how I felt."

Tiff pulled the blanket off the back of the chair and wrapped it around herself, hoping to ward off some of the chill that seemed to rush over her. This was unheard of. She and Bruce hadn't talked for an hour straight their entire marriage. And talking about how he felt—that just was not one of his things.

"It really helped me to get some stuff straight in my head, but I realized tonight that I'm still angry. I feel left out of your life. I told him that it seems like you left with Lindsay." The muscle in his jaw pulsed as though the effort to keep his own anger at bay was nearly overtaking him.

Tiff's gaze dropped from her husband to the arm of his chair. He was right. She'd done this to them, to him. "I'm so sorry. I never meant to put a wall between us." In her effort to love others, was she pushing her family away?

His hand touched her shoulder. "I know that now. Pastor Jim helped me to understand where you were coming from. He's a big fan, by the way."

"A fan of what?"

"You and your ministry. I've made light of what you're doing. It's important, but at the same time, it's hurting me. I need a balance. And I can't lose someone else." There was a catch in his voice. "Can you understand that?"

Unsure what this would mean, she nodded and finally saw what she'd been running from. It was easier to put distance between herself and the people she loved than take the risk of losing them. "I do. And I am really sorry." She covered his hand with hers. "I'm going to work on this."

"I appreciate it. And I'd like us to talk to Pastor Jim together. He says there's a grief class he and a counselor have been working on. They're hoping to get it started in August. Maybe we could go."

All their hurts out there for the world to see. Tiff would be lying if she said she really wanted to do that, but her husband was right in front of her. He'd been brave and he was fighting for their marriage alone. She'd join in the battle. "Okay. I can do that."

His mouth curved into a slight smile. "I saved you some cake."

Tiff's heart hammered. "Words that speak to my soul."

Over cups of decaf coffee and slices of German chocolate cake, they talked about Lindsay openly for the first time since losing her. They remembered all the silly things she'd done as a child, all the talents and intelligence, even the horrible moments after she'd begun to twist away from them. They laughed and cried and connected for the first time in ages. And Tiff wondered what this marriage and her love for her husband would end up costing her.

FRIDAY MORNING, ZARA WAS READY to collapse, and no amount of coffee could cure her mind-melting tiredness. She'd had two hours of sleep the night before, finally falling over on the sofa after installing the pointless carbon monoxide detector.

At midnight, she'd insisted Chad go to bed because he had work the next day. His boss had been as understanding as they could expect with the honeymoon so quickly followed by random days off to work on the house and prepare for the kids. Chad going into the office half asleep seemed like taking advantage of the boss's patience. Another company—and there weren't many around there—might not be as generous.

When Abby came by, they would get the okay. Every cupboard in the house had a childproof latch. Zara just had to remember not to wait to use the bathroom. Those potty locks were no joke. The stove—which would arrive soon—was being delivered by a man from church. And if those goats were able to get out of their pen, well, they might as well move into the house, because they were smarter than any human she knew.

The place might not be pretty yet, but it was safe. The only thing Zara could do now would be to line the entire house with bubble wrap, but of course that was a choking hazard.

As a last-minute thought, Zara had added a hook high on the door that led to the room where she stored her supplies and assembled products. Zara flipped open the latch and stared at the accumulation of projects, all untouched since this major life change. The first thing she needed to do after Abby left was get a large batch of soap brewing. She'd received a new order from a specialty shop in Sisters. It was an opportunity to get her natural products into a new market—and she didn't want to miss it.

Zara was determined that she'd figure out how to manage the business and children—other women did it. It would require scheduling and dedication, but one of those was a strength of hers. The other, well, she was working on it.

In the kitchen, Zara poured her second extra-large cup of coffee and opened her laptop. There was an email from the company she'd bought five hundred lavender starts from. The delivery that was supposed to happen that morning was delayed and wouldn't arrive until the following Thursday, nearly a week off schedule. They offered a discount on her next order, assuming she used their company again.

Tapping her fingers on the counter, Zara reassessed her timeline. If she got them in the ground right away, hopefully the plants would take off and she'd still have a good harvest. Those flowers were one of the most popular additives to her soaps. And she'd been toying with the idea of distilling some oils from the lavender to mix in bath bombs, hand soaps, and her organic laundry detergent.

Also, the goat and puppy incident had torn out a number of sage and thyme plants. She needed to check on those again, make sure they were surviving.

Her eyes were heavy, and the cup of coffee seemed too weighty to lift to her mouth. Maybe if she took one of those five-minute power naps she'd be able to be more productive. The couch was calling her, and she answered by going to it and lying down again.

Someone was hammering. Zara sat up and wiped drool from the side of her face. Something felt different, like the lighting had changed. It was warm, and . . . there was the pounding, except she realized now it wasn't a hammer. It was someone at the door.

Lifting the puppy from where he'd been cuddled up on the sofa, she ran her fingers under both eyes and headed to the front door. In one of the nine little windows at the top, she saw Abby looking back at her car, then checking her watch.

Zara glanced at the clock in the kitchen and found a stove there where the hole had been. This was a weird dream. She bit her bottom lip to snap herself out of the trance but got only a sharp pain in return.

All the little parts of this mystery started to find their places. She hadn't dozed off for five minutes. It had been hours. Before thinking any further, Zara swung open the door and forced her voice up an octave in hopes of disguising the sleepiness. "Hello, Abby. I hope I didn't keep you waiting."

"I was getting worried. I didn't wake you up, did I?"

Her instinct was to deny it, but the way Abby stared at Zara's cheek made her hand rise, and she felt the dent left by the edge of the sofa pillow. Heat pulsed up her neck. "I'm sorry. I thought I'd close my eyes for a minute, but I guess I really went deep. Please come in."

Abby's expression didn't change. She still seemed as if she were judging Zara's actions and having a hard time reaching a conclusion. Maybe Zara should be sure to breathe in Abby's direction to at least prove she hadn't been drinking, but of course there was the issue of morning breath. Why, oh why had she lain down?

"I see you've had the stove installed."

Zara patted her hand on the range. "Just today." She would

really be embarrassed next time she saw the guy at church. Knowing he was on his way, she'd left the front door unlocked. He must have let himself in—and seen her drooling all over herself. Should people capable of sleeping that soundly even be allowed to be in charge of the lives and safety of children? She made a point to keep that question to herself.

This time, the inspection took only a fraction of the effort and length. "Everything looks good. I've been in touch with Cheri, the kids' caseworker. She and Rita feel it's best to move the kids in this weekend. That will probably mean moving in on Saturday and a visit from Cheri on Sunday. Does that work for you?"

Alarms echoed through Zara's head. Maybe she still wasn't awake. Saturday was tomorrow. The children would be there, living in this home, in one day. "Yes." She nodded. "That seems fine."

"Your certification is temporary for now. You and Chad still need to take the Foundations Training course. That will be over an entire weekend. There's a woman in the office who takes care of the registrations. She'll be in contact with you soon."

"Is there childcare for the classes?"

"No. You'll need to get that worked out. Sorry. We just can't manage that on a weekend." She brushed her hand along one arm. "I have a couple homes I need to check in on this afternoon, so I need to be going. Please feel free to send me an email if you have any questions or concerns. Cheri will be in contact with you too."

If she had any questions? Zara was so far past that. She was a mountain of unformed and unanswered questions. "Thanks." There was a catch in her voice, but Abby didn't seem to notice and kept walking down the path to her car.

ZARA GOT THE CALL the next morning that Charlotte had been vomiting throughout the night before. The plan they'd devised with Rita was a long visit on Saturday, with her returning to leave the children on Sunday morning. Instead, they'd now arrive Sunday afternoon with all of their things. The kids' permanency caseworker would come Monday morning. If nothing else, this was teaching Zara to be flexible.

The missing step slowing the transition had Zara distracted during the sermon and unable to make coherent conversation after church. Time ticked loudly toward their change in reality.

Chad took her to a nice lunch—a kind of tribute to their time as just the two of them, the shortest newlywed period imaginable. But the meal was wasted on Zara. Her mind wouldn't calm, couldn't focus on her husband when two children would soon be buckled up and heading toward them.

Excitement and fear mixed like dueling sword masters, one taking the advantage only to be bested by the other.

When they got home, Chad took Zara into the living room and pulled her onto his lap and the sofa. "Let's just lie here for a few minutes and enjoy each other."

She sat up. "Last time I lay down on this couch for a minute, I almost missed Abby, and I did miss the new stove installation."

He chuckled. "I can't believe you slept through that. I told Ben at work. He thought that was awesome."

"Thanks a lot. I love being your workplace amusement."

Chad wrapped her up tight in his arms. "You were tired. You have the right to be sleepy after all we've been through this week."

"I have a feeling this is only a small sampling of what's to come."

He kissed her temple. "I'm sure you're right. But how hard could it really be? They're so small, I can carry both of them at the same time."

Zara shrugged. "I have no idea. I keep wondering what they'll go over in that weekend class, and if it's really a good idea to give us two young children without that information first."

The puppy bounded into the room, somehow having escaped his crate, and peed on the rug.

Slapping her forehead with the palm of her hand, Zara let out a stress whine. "We can't even housebreak a puppy."

Chad was up. He took the dog to the door and deposited him outside, then went to the kitchen and returned with carpet cleaner and a rag. "We'll figure it out. People have children all the time. They can't all be experts before they start."

"But newborns can't move, and they can't use words to tell you how bad you are at parenting. I doubt Charlotte is going to hold back on her criticism."

He looked over at Zara from where he knelt on the carpet. "She likes me." The way his eyes twinkled made her want to launch herself off the couch and tackle him, but . . . dog pee.

Chad and Zara managed to waste away the remaining time doing nothing more than watching television and eating chips. She was sure there were many things they should have been doing, areas that could have used further childproofing, repairs they could have made, but they didn't do any of those things.

When they heard the sound of a vehicle pulling up to the house, Chad and Zara stared at each other for a few too many counts before easing off the sofa and plunging into their new lives.

Rita drove a van—not a minivan, but one of those passenger ones. When she pulled open the side door, seven sets of eyes stared at them. "Sorry. I had to bring the crew with me. My husband got called in to work on an emergency."

A line of guilt coursed through Zara. Rita took on this whole crew with a husband who traveled for work and got called in for emergencies. She made the choice to be there for all of them, and it wasn't like she had a wayward sister who'd put her in that position.

If Zara would have kept up with Eve, she could have stopped this before the state became involved. And if not, at least they would have known the children. Charlotte and Sammy wouldn't be coming to live with strangers, one of whom happened to look like their mother.

"Do you mind if they get out and stretch their legs? It's only an hour's drive, but that's a serious road trip for children."

Chad held Zara's hand. "Of course. The more the merrier."

Don't get too comfortable with that many, buddy. She squeezed her fingers around his. As the children came out one by one, she thought again about the fact that, before last week, she wouldn't have recognized her niece and nephew if they'd walked right past her.

"Here you go." Rita handed Samuel into Zara's arms. "He's been squirming since we started the drive. I bet he'd love to run around the yard."

She took him to the flattest patch of grass and set him down on his feet, her arms outstretched to catch him if he were to stumble. With the speed of an Olympic figure skater, Sammy twisted and took off, weaving this way and that through the yard. In her imagination, he did a face-plant, with blood and dirt and all the horrible things she'd never want to happen, especially in front of a superhero mom like Rita.

But somehow his legs stayed beneath him until he found a patch of weeds to explore. Before she could reach out, he had a seeded dandelion in his mouth, fluffy tufts of white clinging to his lips. "Oh no. Sammy, those aren't for eating." She scooped him up and ran her thumb over his mouth, then attempted to extract the remaining pieces with her finger.

"See, you're a natural." Rita patted the head of a little boy with chocolate-brown eyes, then came closer. "You cleaned him up like you've been doing it his whole life."

A bit of the tension held in her shoulders loosened. "What if I do this wrong?"

"You will."

Her heart hesitated in its beats. Hadn't Rita just given her a compliment?

"We all do. The main thing is to love them no matter what the situation. And of course, to keep them alive." She grinned, her eyes sparkling. "With little boys, that can be a challenge."

A tear welled up in Zara's eye. "I want to give them everything they've been missing. I want to make up for the time I should have been there."

"You can't. Your job isn't to wash away the hurt. You can only heal the wounds, and you do that with consistency, safety, and love. Scars will remain, but a scar is proof we've come through something. In a perfect world, Samuel and Charlotte will someday be adults who wear their scars with pride because they've overcome."

Fullness spread through Zara's chest, a feeling that God had honored her by making her a part of this story. She needed to write it all down, remember that this wasn't a punishment or a trial, but a chance to serve in a real and beautiful way.

"You can always call me. I don't guarantee I'll have the answers, but I can listen." Rita kissed Sammy on the top of his head. "I've really enjoyed these two. There's a special spark in Charlotte. She's going to give you a run for your money, but believe me, she's worth it."

Time slipped away, and before Zara was ready, Rita and the other kids were packed into the behemoth of a van. Zara and Chad stood side by side, a child in each of their arms as they waved good-bye and watched them all the way around the corner.

And then there were four.

Eve

June 2, 2019

I know she saw me. I couldn't avoid her forever. But Bonnie ignores me like we've never met. I hope it's because she forgives me and we're both trying to get our lives together, but I'm guessing, especially after what I heard her say the other day, that she's just waiting for her chance.

The rules are posted all over the place. Any violence and you're no longer welcome here. That may be the only thing standing between me and another pounding. It seems like everyone in here should be working together to get their lives back on track, but there's an undercurrent of jealousy and judgment.

I miss my kids. I don't even have a picture of them to look at. The caseworker took one at the meeting and told me she'd get me a copy. I think about that picture all the time. I was holding my babies tight. I'm sure my face was a mess, but I can cut myself out of the shot.

I can't remember ever being as lonely as I am now. There's one thing that would take away the pain, but I keep reminding myself that using will only make the time until I get my babies back take longer. I've given up everything for that stupid drug. One moment at a time. I have to make it.

The caseworker told me the length of time is really up to me. It could be a couple months or forever. If they want, they can terminate my parental rights and give my children to another woman. Maybe Zara, maybe someone else. These are the things I need to remember.

I'm going to keep writing that down. They can terminate my rights and give my children away. The law says this can happen if I don't do what I need to do to provide a minimum standard of living for my kids.

I don't want to lose them. Charlotte and Sammy are the only people in the world who love me.

THAT NIGHT THEY ATE THE DINNER Rita had suggested— pasta, peas, and chicken drumsticks. After three attempts at Googling the safe size for a one-year-old's pasta, Zara finally smashed it all with her fork until Sammy had a pile of goo on his plate. As for the chicken, she wondered if he'd eat it if she ran it through the blender first.

Zara set the plate on the tray of his high chair, handed him a small child's fork, and stepped back to watch what came next.

"Sammy doesn't use a plate." Charlotte tasted the chicken with a tiny, hesitant bite.

"What do you mean?" But as she asked the question, Zara felt something hit her in the back of the arm. Something plastic. Something covered in goo.

Charlotte's mouth cocked into a familiar smile—just like Eve's—just like her own.

Zara picked up the plate on the floor at her feet and set it on the table. As she rose, she caught a glimpse of her husband, her ally, sharing an amused look with the five-year-old.

Sammy started to grunt. Smashed pasta covered his chin, but that was about all that had survived his plate launch.

"He wants more." Charlotte shoved the drumstick into her mouth with gusto now.

Zara looked at Chad with her *duh* look.

"I think she's right." Chad put a bite of pasta in his mouth, his face showing disappointment at the bland food. "Hmm. I think this needs something."

"Rita puts butter and salt on it. It's so much better when she makes it." Charlotte cocked one eyebrow.

"I don't remember her saying that part." Maybe Zara was stretching to find a flaw in Rita.

Chad left the kitchen table and brought back the butter, salt, and pepper.

Charlotte's hand shot into the air. "None of that. I don't eat foods with pepper on them." She planted her fists on her sides.

"Easy now. The salt and pepper are buddies." Chad set them down well out of Charlotte's reach. "My mom always said they shouldn't be separated, even if you're only going to use one."

"Your mom is kind of weird, huh?" Charlotte's mouth twisted.

"She can be."

"Where is she?" Charlotte looked around.

"She lives at her house. It's a few miles away. Not too far." He sliced a slab of butter and put it on her pasta while Zara inserted tiny slivers of chicken into Sammy's mouth. "She wants to come meet you soon. Would that be okay?"

Charlotte shrugged as though it didn't matter to her what happened next. And Zara wondered what kind of loss left a child so uninvested, yet at the same time, defensive.

CHAPTER TWENTY-ONE

ZARA AND CHAD GAVE EACH OTHER a round of kudos for getting the kids in bed, stories read, and prayers said. Both Sammy and Charlotte had actually fallen asleep, and it was only eight o'clock. They had a few hours to watch a television show and relax together.

Settled onto the couch, a gray knit blanket over them, Zara rested her head on Chad's chest, the remote in her hand. Almost as if their celebrations had caused it, a thump came from upstairs at the same time that she pressed the power button. "What was that?"

"No idea." Chad leaned her up and got to his feet.

Zara clicked the TV off again and followed him. Tiny voices carried into the hall, then hushed. They listened at the door before Chad finally peeked his head around the corner. He motioned for Zara to look too.

Charlotte had climbed into the crib and lay next to her brother, a light blanket covering both of them. Sammy slurped on his Binky while Charlotte ran her little fingers over his fuzzy hair.

Zara and Chad eased away, sneaking down the stairs as if attempting a perfect getaway.

Chad headed back to the couch, but Zara tugged on his arm. "Shouldn't we put her back in her own bed?"

"I don't know. They look content. And it's their very first night here. Maybe we should just let them be. It might be what they're used to."

"But what if she rolls over on him? He could suffocate."

Chad pulled her into a hug. "I don't think that little sprig up there could manage it. Don't worry so much. Kids are tougher than you think."

Maybe that was true physically, but Zara had seen the invisible damage that broke her sister, convicted her mother, and still plagued her to this day.

She checked on the kids at least five times in the night, unable to sleep through visions of Sammy smothering. Each time, they were snuggled up together, Charlotte's arm lying like a shield over her brother.

Before the sun had vaulted the mountain range to the east, Zara was fully awake. Not knowing what to expect with the kids, her brain wouldn't allow her to sleep. She eased her feet to the floor, careful not to rouse Chad or the dog, but as soon as she took her robe from the chair beside the bed, Pickles pounced, grabbing hold of the hem.

"What are you doing?" Chad's voice was heavy with sleep. "Are the kids up?"

"No." She spoke in a hushed tone as she unwound the puppy's teeth from the fabric. "I just woke up early. Go back to sleep."

"You're going to be exhausted today. You were up half the night too."

"How would you know that if you weren't also awake?" She smiled in the dim light.

Chad started to get up, but she put her hand on his bare chest. "Lie back down. I'll take Pickles outside and start the coffee."

"No way. Your coffee is weak. We're going to need my recipe today."

She poked her head into the room next door to theirs, assuming she'd find the kids in the same position they'd held through the night, but this time Charlotte was on her bed. Zara hadn't heard her move. What if she'd taken a wrong turn and fallen down the stairs, or managed to get outside and lost? How did mothers cope with all the things that could go wrong?

The puppy started to wiggle in her arms, his gaze set on Charlotte.

Zara hustled downstairs and put him in the yard before he could wake up his new playmates.

Dishes from last night's dinner still sat alongside the sink. She wasn't a great housekeeper in the best of circumstances, but with all this sudden parenting, she'd fallen completely off her game. Before Zara could fill the sink with warm, soapy water, Chad was behind her, wrapping his arms around her waist. She leaned her head back, letting his warmth comfort her. Living in the same house, being husband and wife, was still so new and fresh. Her heart was fully his, yet it needed to stretch and make room for Charlotte and Sammy too.

Chad started the coffee, its rich scent filling the air as Zara dropped dishes into sudsy water to soak. He brought two mugs down from the cupboard and retrieved the creamer from the fridge. "We did it. The first night."

"It might be a bit premature to celebrate. At least wait until we've completed twenty-four hours. Plus, Kelly, the kids' new caseworker, is coming today to check in on us. I can imagine a hundred ways that could go terribly wrong."

He shrugged. "Or it could go great."

"Easy for you to say. You'll be at work." She gathered her hair over her right shoulder.

Chad poured creamer into her mug, then coffee. "I'm really sorry about that. If there was a choice, I'd be home today and for at least a week or two, but I've used the majority of my vacation time, and I've only been at this job a few months."

She took the warm cup from his hands. "I know. It's not your fault. Actually, none of this is your fault. They're my sister's kids."

A flash of sadness or maybe disappointment ran across his face. "I wish you wouldn't do that."

"What?"

"Make this a problem you're responsible for and . . . leave me out."

She put down the coffee and took his hand. "I'm sorry. I just don't want you to feel burdened. We're supposed to be newlyweds."

"We're also supposed to be a family. Your people are my people and all that. I want to be as much a part of their lives as you are."

"How did I get so lucky? You are a precious man."

He nodded, an impish smile on his face. "I like you too." He kissed the top of her head.

The sun flooded the field out the window with vivid light, and Zara was reminded of the beauty of God's amazing creation. A girl like her didn't end up in a place like this. But here she was. And though she and Chad had been given a hard blow when they found out she carried the Hunter gene, they still had children to love, even if only for a short time. By next summer, they'd be back to just two again. There'd still be questions about how they would eventually grow their family, but at least they'd know how much or how little they wanted to pursue children.

Zara thanked God for Sammy's obvious health and the doctors who would have checked him thoroughly at birth. What a blessing that he'd beat the odds—Eve had to be a carrier if she was. Fury burned as Zara thought of how irresponsible her sister had been to get pregnant when she could have passed on the gene. But like Zara only a short time ago, Eve probably had no idea this danger lurked in their DNA.

Chad headed upstairs with his coffee.

Zara followed to check on the kids once more. As she hit the top step, she heard Charlotte reassuring Sammy that everything was okay. How sweet. She was so caring when it came to her brother. But as Zara turned the corner, her mouth fell open. Charlotte was back in the crib, trying to secure the tab on a dry diaper she'd put onto Sammy in a crooked way that was still impressive for a five-year-old.

"Hey there. You don't have to change Sammy. That's my job."

Charlotte started, her hand reaching across the toddler as if she could protect him from some unknown danger.

"I'm sorry." Zara moved slowly forward. "I didn't mean to scare you."

"You didn't." Her eyes were rounded and intense. "I'm sorry, Zara."

"You can call me Auntie or Aunt Zara if you want."

She shook her head but didn't say anything.

"Can I help you out of the crib?"

"I can do it myself."

"I know you can, but I'm still learning how to take care of a five-year-old. I need all the practice you can give me."

Her forehead creased, but she stood and let Zara lift her out.

She was thin but strong, and Zara ached to hold her for a minute, but Charlotte tugged her body away. Someday, maybe that grit and determination would serve her in a healthy way. As for now, it felt like a wall Charlotte kept to guard herself from others.

CHAPTER TWENTY-TWO

KELLY ARRIVED RIGHT ON TIME. It wasn't possible to be that punctual without parking alongside the road and waiting for the exact right moment to drive the remaining bit.

She was a middle-aged woman, slightly thin for her frame, with gray streaks coming in around her face and oddly smooth skin.

Zara had put the puppy in his crate to keep the distractions to a minimum, but the way Charlotte had looked at her since then was hot enough to shrivel the hardiest plant. She knelt down in front of the little girl. "Listen, I promise I'll let Pickles back out as soon as our visit with Ms. Kelly is over. Okay?"

"I wouldn't want to be locked in a box."

Kelly knocked on the door about three feet from where they stood.

"Of course you wouldn't. And that will not happen to you."

"But you did it to the puppy." Charlotte fisted her hand on her hips, her mouth a straight line.

This was not how Zara wanted to welcome yet another case-worker. She stood and answered the door. "Come on in."

Sammy leaned from her arm, trying to reach the edge of a picture frame, and toppled it before she could move.

"Oops." The blush that must have covered Zara's face in scarlet heated her as it rose. "I'm sorry." She moved to the side so Kelly could come in, then replaced the photo on the shelf.

"Hi. I'm Kelly Pratt, the permanency worker. You must be Zara."

She held her free hand out to shake Kelly's. "And this is Charlotte and Sammy." Zara turned to find Charlotte missing. Internally, she slapped her hand against her forehead about ten thousand times. "Charlotte?"

"Let me take this little guy while you get her." Kelly took Sammy, and Zara's arms sang at the relief.

Turning around the corner, she found Charlotte sitting on the floor, her arms crossed against her chest. "Hey, what's going on?"

"I want you to let Pickles out. It's making me sad."

Zara sat down beside her and took a deep breath. "How about you come in and meet Ms. Kelly, and when she leaves, I'll give you a special treat to give to the puppy?"

Charlotte cocked her head. "How about two special treats?"

"Deal." Zara stood and reached down to pick Charlotte up, but the look the little girl shot her way was a strong warning to keep her hands to herself.

They reentered the living room and found Kelly and Sammy sitting on the floor with a ball. She must have brought it in her oversized woven bag. They pushed it back and forth, Sammy's face lighting up each time she returned it to him.

"Kelly, this is Charlotte."

The little girl went right over to the caseworker and hugged her around the neck.

Zara could have choked on the shock. She'd been trying to get the tiniest bit of affection from Charlotte since she'd arrived, and nothing. But the moment Kelly came in the door, she was treated like an angel.

"I've met the kids once before." Kelly returned the hug, then got up and sat on the sofa. "Kids, do you remember meeting me at Rita's house?"

Charlotte nodded, but Sammy threw himself on the ball and laughed.

"Charlotte, do you remember what my job is?" Kelly bent forward, putting her at eye level with the little girl.

"You help keep kids safe." She bit at her lip. "Do you help moms too?"

"I try to. I want to help your mom get healthy so she can take good care of you and your brother."

Charlotte threw Zara a scowl, then sat down to play with Sammy.

The rest of the conversation went by in a blur, with mentions of upcoming visits and the plan for reunification. The only true detail that shot out at Zara was the timing. According to Kelly, if Eve did all she needed to do, it was possible—but highly unlikely—for the kids to go home in the early fall. All the same, Zara found herself wondering how she could make an impact on Charlotte before she was gone. And once Eve took them back, would Zara and Chad ever see the kids again? Would Eve allow it? For the first time in forever, Zara would be at Eve's mercy.

"Could you give me a quick tour of the house? It's beautiful. I understand you and your husband have plans to restore it."

"We did . . . we do." Zara stood, getting Sammy as she walked toward the hall. "Come on, Charlotte, let's show our visitor around." She couldn't help the way she wanted Charlotte to be hers, not Kelly's. The tug was irrational, but it was strong. She led them into the hall with a bedroom and a bathroom they hadn't yet made usable.

The closer they got to the spare room, the stronger an unpleasant scent grew. Zara pulled Sammy's diaper out the way she'd seen mothers do, checking for contents, but there was nothing.

"It smells gross." Charlotte reached one hand into Kelly's and used the other to plug her nose.

One glance at the ceiling confirmed Zara's suspicions and drew everyone's attention to the darkening spot on the drywall. Something, maybe a squirrel, had died in there, and the situation was bleeding into their home. Tears tickled Zara's nose, but she would not let them win. "I'm sorry. It looks like we have an issue." She swung around to look Kelly in the eye. "I'll get this taken care of as soon as possible."

"Zara, please don't worry. I've seen so much worse than this." She motioned for them to keep moving. "I trust that you'll handle it in a timely manner. After all, you have to live here too." She grinned. "Life happens. I'm not here to worry you. Please. I want to be an advocate for your family."

"Thank you." It was the first time someone aside from Chad had called them a family. The words warmed her, giving Zara a dose of hope that she needed, because the fatigue of a night with little sleep and the frustration of one more house problem were about to push her under.

They finished the tour without any more unfortunate encounters; then Kelly left to see another family. Zara didn't envy her the job. Yet somehow, Kelly managed to keep a positive attitude. Zara would remember that.

"Oh no!" Charlotte ran in from the kitchen and huddled behind the couch, her body shaking.

Kneeling, Zara reached to touch her. The contact between her hand and Charlotte's shoulder seemed to cause her screaming to start. "What is it? Do you miss Kelly?"

"There's a thing outside. Something wild." She buried her head in her hands.

Zara stood, Sammy still clinging to her side, and went to investigate. All they needed was a cougar or coyote. That would be more than even Kelly's graceful nature could tolerate.

Clicking sounded from the back deck. With deeper exploration, Zara found a small, fluffy goat staring through the back door.

Sammy burst into giggles and squirmed to be let down. He pounded his palms on the glass, and the goat responded by jumping and twisting as if he were performing some kind of dance. Sammy's face colored as his laughter increased.

Around the corner, Zara found Charlotte still pressed against the side of the sofa. "Come with me. I have something to show you, and I promise I will keep you safe."

She seemed to calm enough to hear her brother's giggles and agreed to take Zara's hand.

In the kitchen, Zara knelt and pointed toward the paned-glass door. "It's a goat. See? He must have found a hole in the fence. That one still needs a name. Would you like to help with that?"

She crawled up beside her brother and placed a hand on the door. "We could call it Jane."

"I'm pretty sure he's a boy."

A sharp glare snapped Zara's way. "There was a lady in our last building who had a beard just like that goat. She was called Jane."

"I think that's a perfect name." Zara looked away. Any expression could send Charlotte into a meltdown. The learning curve was steep. How had she ever dared to think college was tough?

By the time Chad returned home, the house was barely inhabitable. How the rodent bomb went from *What's that smell?* to *I can't breathe!* in the course of eight hours was a mystery.

The first thing he did when he walked in was turn and walk back out. "Wow. What died in there?"

"That's what I'm afraid we're going to have to find out."

"Should I ask how the caseworker's visit went?"

Zara peeked around the corner. Charlotte was still playing with Play-Doh at the counter. Sammy had fallen asleep after crying in her arms for forty-five minutes. "It went surprisingly well; however, that's when the smell started. And Charlotte likes her,

176

so apparently she just can't stand me." Zara shrugged, trying to look like this was no big deal, but it was. She was Charlotte's aunt, after all. Wasn't there supposed to be some kind of biological connection? But then she remembered her mother. Zara had loved her growing up, but her mom had always seemed disconnected, as though there was something better out there for her and kids were the anchor holding her back.

"I'm sure she likes you." Chad winked.

"Daddy!"

Zara turned away from her husband in time to see Charlotte launch herself into his arms. *Daddy?!*

"Well, hello there, sweet girl. How was your day?" He scrunched up his nose and kissed her forehead.

"It was okay. Zara doesn't know how to play many kids' games like Rita." She sighed as if she'd put up with about all she could for the day.

"Charlotte?" Zara put a hand on her back. "Why did you call Chad 'Daddy' a minute ago?"

Charlotte's eyes looked as if Zara was hopeless. "Rita told me that I could call foster parents whatever I want. I want Chad to be my daddy, so that's what I'm going to call him."

Zara started to explain that Chad was her uncle, but she'd been on the accelerated path to learning there was no arguing a point with this five-year-old. Instead, she sent a text to Rita.

> Newbie foster-parent question: Is it okay if Charlotte wants to call Chad *Daddy* even though he's her uncle?

> That's really up to you, but I'd let her. She's trying to make a connection, and that's very important for children who've been removed from a parent. She's never had anyone she could call Daddy before. I think she's just trying to say she likes him.

There was one more question Zara wanted to ask but couldn't. Why didn't Charlotte like *her*? It was too embarrassing to put her insecurities out there for anyone else to see, especially with the way a child was playing them like a fiddle.

Before she could even text back a thank-you, Sammy howled from the place she'd left him on the carpet with a blanket and pillows forming a makeshift crib. She'd been too paranoid after all that screaming to even try an advanced move like slipping a sleeping toddler into his own bed.

Chad held up his hand. "Let me get him. Oh, and Mom is coming over."

Zara looked around at the chaos that their house had already become. "When?"

He gave her a bashful smile. "In about twenty minutes."

This time, she slapped herself on the forehead.

"Why are you doing that?" Charlotte asked.

"No reason. Grandma Mahoney is coming over soon. Should we change you out of that dirty shirt?"

"Is she your mom?"

"No. She's Chad's. My mom is the same as your mom's mom." Zara cringed at the twists and turns of that sentence.

"What?"

"Grandma Mahoney is Chad's mom."

Charlotte rolled her eyes around in circles, then went off toward the chosen members of the family.

Eve

June 3, 2019

Reasons to stay clean and sober:
1. My kids
2. Having my children back

3. *Teaching my kids not to live like this*
4. *I have no idea, but there must be other reasons. I miss my kids so much.*

CHAPTER TWENTY-THREE

ZARA MANAGED TO GET A BASIC MEAL of hot dogs and store-bought applesauce together while Chad changed the kids into clean clothes. She'd found a box of macaroni and cheese in the back of the cupboard and decided it would make a decent companion to this kid dinner.

In her imagination, she'd always fed her kids fresh, organic home-cooked meals. Yet here she was, one day in and already resorting to the processed chemical wasteland of Chad's bachelor days.

A little pitter-pat came up behind her on the linoleum. She turned to see Sammy, drool covering his chin with a shine, a wet spot already spreading on his clean T-shirt, and a perfect four-tooth smile on his face. Zara would never be able to explain the feeling in her chest when she looked down at this little boy. He melted her. Took her words, her thoughts, and mushed them all up in a happy mess.

She picked up her nephew, held him tight against her chest, and inhaled the sweetness of his skin. Before she could even think, Zara was blowing raspberries into the crease of his neck, and Sammy let out the perfect roll of giggles.

That's how her mother-in-law found them. Zara didn't know

how long she'd been standing there, but the look on Sharon's face told Zara she'd already been touched by this child.

Sharon covered her mouth, tears in her eyes. "Isn't he the most precious thing you've ever seen?"

Zara held her hand on the back of his head in a proprietary way. "He really is."

She lifted both arms, slung with gift bags. "I've got grandma goodies!"

Sammy twisted in his aunt's embrace. Apparently, he had a solid understanding of the word *goodies*. When he saw the brightly colored bags, his little hands started opening and closing like he was squeezing the air in his excitement.

"Mom." Chad, with Charlotte slung over his shoulder, kissed Sharon on the cheek. "You didn't need to bring presents."

"It's a grandmother's privilege, and I plan to take it as long as I can." She set the gifts on the floor, and in a second Sammy was out of Zara's arms and tipping over a pink-and-purple sack. "Hold on, little one. That's for your sister." Sharon scooped him up and moved him near the green bag.

Sammy leaned over the edge and let out a long, excited squeal. "Twuck." It was the first word he'd said in their presence. When Zara had spoken with Rita at the park, she'd said there were concerns about his delayed speech but she hoped it would come as he became comfortable.

Chad helped him extricate a ridable Tonka dump truck from the packaging.

Within a minute, Sammy was climbing into the back, making wet engine noises.

But Charlotte stayed back, watching the excitement with a straight face.

"Charlotte, do you want me to bring the gift to you?" Zara asked.

Her chin quivered, and she buried her face in Chad's pant leg.

Zara knelt down at her eye level and rubbed her hand on Charlotte's back. "What's wrong?"

She pulled away and went to the present, taking out a baby doll that smelled of powder. Charlotte held it close. "How long can I have this?"

"Forever." Sharon's eyes washed with tears that she worked hard to blink away. "This dolly is for you because you're special, and we all love you."

"My mommy loves me." Tears streamed down Charlotte's face as she stared into the eyes of the baby. "I miss my mommy."

Though Zara had been sure her heart couldn't break any further, right then, it split apart.

Eve

June 4, 2019

I've found a place where I can be alone, away from the stares and danger of Bonnie, but still in the safety of the house. I'm not strong enough yet to make it to anywhere in town, and I'm so scared that being out there, where I know what's available and where I can get it, I wouldn't make it an hour. So I hunker down in a little nook that leads to the supply closet, just me and my journal.

The days are so long. Minute after minute of longing, of needing a hit. Honestly, I want to die and be done with all of this. I can't be a mom. I can't even be a decent girlfriend. My life has brought horrible pain to everyone who's ever been close to me.

My brother died after I told him I was embarrassed of him. He choked and died only an hour later. My mother couldn't handle anything after that—not that she'd ever been happy. Now she sits in jail and probably blames me for everything, especially losing Tyson. And Zara. We were supposed to be a team, but I bailed. I thought sinking into a fog to forget it all was more important than caring about my sister. If anyone is an embarrassment, it's me.

It wasn't long after Tyson's death that I crashed while running cross-country. I was good—the school record was within my reach—but the injury that I got from the fall landed me in surgery. During the recovery, I learned what it was like to float away from all the hurt. The medications I was prescribed fogged my brain. I didn't think of my shame. I didn't think of anything. And I loved it.

Now I've given my children a horrible label: foster kids.

I just want one chance to see them again, tell them I love them, and say good-bye.

Someone just called my name. I have a phone call. I can't imagine who would want to talk to me.

ZARA BRAVED HER NEW WORLD, imagining herself as Wonder Woman as she took the kids on their first outing together. Did anyone say *outing* anymore? When she'd used the word on the kids, they'd both looked at her like she'd stepped out of a black-and-white movie. But they were going to have a visit the next day with Eve. A practice run seemed like a good plan.

She had three things on her list. None of them was grocery shopping. That she was not ready to tackle, but having married the best man in the entire world had its perks. Chad had volunteered to pick up the things they needed on his way home from work.

Today's first objective was to join the library's preschool story time. Zara had stared at the schedule for a while, trying to figure out if they were supposed to attend toddler time or preschool time. Obviously, most families must have more than one kid.

She finally chose the older. Scoring points with Charlotte had become somewhat of an obsession.

Unfortunately, that had to be followed by their first trip to the pediatrician—a state requirement. They'd be okay, though, since she planned to tell them about the stop at the park while they were at the doctor's. It was a reward kind of thing. That was supposed to work with kids.

At the library, they parked as close to the building as possible, though still a distance. Judging from the packed parking lot, story time was a hit in this community.

After turning off the engine, Zara looked in the rearview mirror from one face to the other. They were snuggly secured in their car seats, the safest place for them . . . ever. It took actual minutes for her to come to a decision on the order for car evacuation. First, she unbuckled Sammy and slung him onto her hip, her purse hanging on the other. Then she went for Charlotte.

"Listen, before I let you out, you need to understand a couple of rules. They're very important."

Charlotte nodded but started trying to manage the buckle on her own.

"You must be beside me at all times. Do you understand?"

"I want to get out. Sammy's out."

"Charlotte." Zara lifted her chin with one finger. "Listen. Stay right beside me. Do you understand?"

Her face tipped to the side, and she gave a *duh* look that made Zara's seem pathetic. Patience wasn't on Charlotte's list of talents. She squirmed back and forth as though she'd been chained for a week.

"I don't think you're listening."

"I did. Let me out." Her voice rose to a level that would draw attention. There was no need to provoke the judgment of strangers.

"Fine." Zara's teenage-level response slipped out. "Do not let go of my hand."

They made it into the library without Charlotte even attempting to tug away. This was serious progress in an area that had felt hopeless. Inside, the quiet Zara had expected was consumed by the sounds of little kids. They followed the voices and easily found the hallway leading to the room for story time.

Zara was ready. Ready for Charlotte to pull away. Ready for Sammy to squirm from her arms. Ready even for a tantrum for no apparent reason. But she wasn't prepared for what actually happened. As they got close to the room, both children grew quiet. Sammy nuzzled into her neck as Charlotte held tighter to her hand, her body pressed along Zara's leg.

Taking them back a few paces, Zara bent down, looking Charlotte in the eye like Kelly had. "Are you feeling unsure about this?"

Charlotte kept her gaze on the others and nodded.

"I'm going to be with you the entire time. I promise. And we'll sit near the back in case you feel like you need to leave." In one way, everything Zara said seemed ridiculous. How would Charlotte ever be okay if she didn't just move forward? That's how Zara had survived, right? But on the other hand, this was a chance to give Charlotte what Zara now knew she'd really needed as a child: compassion, care, and acceptance. But the worry remained. How was she to love Charlotte through her fears and still keep her from seeing herself as a helpless victim? There were no perfect answers, only the best in the moment.

She wrapped her arm around Charlotte, bringing her close, then forced herself to stand up while bearing the weight of two children, her bag, and those few extra pounds she carried around just for fun.

A few steps closer to the room, and Charlotte started to kick, her hands fisting the fabric of Zara's shirt, nearly leaving her exposed and with no hands to recover. "No. No. No. I'm not going in there. You can't make me." The tone grew high and deafening.

Everyone turned to look, their stares shooting judgment that penetrated Zara's weakened armor. "Okay. Calm down."

Charlotte's response was a scream that left Zara with a ringing ear and a permanent case of mortification. With the muscles in her arms burning, she turned and headed for the nearest exit. They had no business anywhere close to a quiet zone.

The warm summer air rushed over Zara. Exhausted, she set the kids down on a bench and shook out her arms.

Charlotte's face was scarlet, with white blotches along her eyebrows. She held her jaw tight, the vessels in the sides of her neck protruding.

"That's not the way we express ourselves."

Fire lit the little girl's eyes.

Sammy took the opportunity to scramble off the bench. When Zara took hold of his hand, he went limp, dangling from one arm like a yo-yo.

"I don't like you." Charlotte's words rang out, calling new people's attention their way. Then she was up and running.

Zara flung down the bag, scooped Sammy under her arm, and took off after Charlotte. The little girl moved as if she'd trained for this moment, but the street was only twenty feet ahead. Zara screamed for her to stop, but she didn't even look back.

Charlotte's right foot came off the sidewalk and into the street.

As Zara yelled again, her body moving at top speed, a stranger reached out her arm and snagged Charlotte around the middle.

Zara watched the rescue with a mixture of horror and relief, her heart hammering, her face and chest wet with perspiration. Even on the worst days, she'd never known fear like she'd just experienced. Zara's body sagged onto the curb in front of Charlotte and the woman. She pulled the child into her arms and held her tight. "Charlotte, don't ever do that again. I was so scared. You could have been hit by a car."

Charlotte's lip quivered; then she burst into tears and body-wracking sobs.

With her hand on Charlotte's soft curls, Zara snuggled her tight.

Even Sammy was stunned into squirmless silence. He reached out his hand and covered Zara's.

"Thank you so much." Zara looked up, but the woman was gone, hopefully not to report them to Protective Services. So much for story time. Her stomach clenched as she thought about their next stop, the doctor's office. Exactly how was she supposed to manage that with only two arms?

CHAPTER TWENTY-FOUR

ZARA'S DAY LASTED THREE HUNDRED FIFTEEN HOURS before Chad pulled up to the house with take-and-bake pizza. Even though it was only six, she had the oven preheated and the kids in their pajamas. There'd been no warm-up period to parenting, no chance to read all the books, no newborn who couldn't move of their own free will. She'd known it would be difficult. But tonight, Zara was beaten.

Sometimes the hours flew by, and she ran around trying to get things done before the day ended. But at other times, it was like the seconds took an eternity to click around the clock. Her brain was either on fire with the rapid pulse of keeping up, or teetering on the edge of a coma due to boredom. And when was it that she felt grateful? Thinking about that just added to the guilt.

Chad entered the house and was swarmed by two little munchkins. His face lit up, and he engulfed them in his long arms, giving the kids everything they needed with just his safe and steady affection.

He came close and kissed Zara's cheek, but she felt herself pull away, forcing some distance she didn't really desire. "I'll take the kids for a quick walk down the field and give you a breather."

His sweet smile and offer that felt more luxurious than a two-hour massage brought tears to her eyes. "Thank you."

The dog trailed after them. She watched her husband, Sammy on his shoulders, Charlotte holding his hand, walking toward the sun. It was beautiful. The way the light silhouetted them was an image more glorious than any piece of art, but it was a picture Zara didn't seem to fit in.

She peeled the plastic wrap from the pizza and slid it into the oven, half of it only cheese, the other half everything.

A family had always been in her dreams for the future. Yet she'd never imagined feeling so lonely and incompetent.

The doctor's appointment had made the disaster at the library feel like a vacation. Both kids were terribly behind on vaccinations, so Dr. Kiddle thought this would be a great time to stick needles into them—many times. There were warnings posted in workplaces with loud noises, but no one warned about the risk of hearing loss faced in the first weeks of foster parenting.

To top it off, while the doctor was able to get access to their immunizations through the online database, he didn't have their other medical records. A caseworker would have to find out who'd seen them and make a request. With Sammy so undersized for his age, Dr. Kiddle wanted to know if this had been true since his birth, or if he'd been losing weight recently.

They would have to come back in a month for a weight check. Getting them into the office again would be a challenge even for Supernanny.

Zara rubbed her hand over an ear. If only it were just the hearing she could lose. In the four days since the children's arrival, she'd fallen two months behind schedule. The math didn't work out, but this was where she landed. Zara's Garden, the business she'd been babying for three years, was finally taking its own steps. And Zara wasn't able to keep up.

The tension started to ease as the tears found a way to escape. She was so overwhelmed, so tired her bones ached, so beaten and heartsick and also so totally in love with her niece and nephew. Eve might be the other half of her, but how would Zara ever gain the strength to hand the children back and trust that her twin would be able to protect them?

Eve
June 6, 2019

She came at me. Not like a physical attack, but I wish it had been. Bonnie walked right into my personal space and whispered in my ear, "He knows you're here, and you better know he's mad you sicced the cops on him." Then she walked away as if she hadn't just thrown a threat at me.

I don't know how to get to Joey and tell him I don't have anything to do with the police wanting to arrest him. It's not like I called Tiff to come get me. I didn't even press charges or give the cops his name. They can't make me, and I'll never testify.

The caseworkers said I won't get the kids back if I'm living with Joey. It's part of the requirements. I don't know what to do. I still love him.

I love Charlotte and Sammy too, and they're my kids. I'm supposed to be the one who cares for them and keeps them safe. But I'm not even doing as well as my mother did. I can't be with Joey anymore. And I'm afraid he'll kill me if I don't come back.

At least today I'm still clean, and I get to visit my kids. That's what I'm thankful for.

TIFF AND BRUCE SAT WITH PASTOR JIM in a cool gray room with the scent of lemon hanging in the air, and all Tiff could think about was how she'd failed so many people in her life. They were two questions into the appointment when the tears took over, leaving her as surprised as her husband.

"What's wrong?" There was an edge of defensiveness in his tone.

Pastor Jim leaned forward. "Bruce, do you think her tears are about you?"

He shrugged. "I guess."

Tiff wiped her face with the tissues the pastor handed to her.

"Tiff, are you upset by something Bruce has done or said?"

She shook her head, unable to put her feelings into words.

"Most of the time I meet with couples, we run into the same problem from different angles. Communication. We get into the habit of deciding what our spouse is thinking without asking them or listening to them."

They spent the entire hour with Pastor Jim coaching them through a conversation. At first, it seemed ridiculous. Why would they need someone to teach them how to speak to each other after nearly thirty years of marriage?

It didn't take long to see they'd let the skill diminish.

Why had they waited so long?

By the time Tiff left counseling to pick up Eve, she was already an emotional time bomb herself. Not the image she wanted to portray.

Tiff adjusted her rearview mirror.

The same conversation between Tiff and Bruce had been on repeat in her mind for days. She owed him her best, but he'd have to love her for who she was now. Compromise was the only way toward reconnection. If pressed, Tiff could at least say she was conservatively hopeful they could find the right path again.

As Tiff neared the women's shelter, a part of her shrank, as if she were cheating on her marriage. She wasn't the woman who'd walked down the aisle to marry Bruce. And he wasn't the same man. Life and loss had changed them, in some ways for the better, but more often, she wasn't sure.

Eve was already sitting out front on the bench. She clutched her bag in both hands, as though she feared someone would steal it out here in the open. It was time to start moving forward. The next steps were helping her obtain a job, stay clean and sober, and learn how to be a parent.

Society possessed a shortsighted nature. In general, it meted out punishment for broken laws, then expected people to move forward changed and never to repeat the problem behavior. If only it were that easy. Eve didn't seem to have any skills. She'd told Tiff that she did graduate high school, which was a great start, but there wasn't exactly a résumé of work experience to draw from.

Today, Tiff had driven the nice car. It made her feel uncomfortable, but the clunker refused to start, and Tiff didn't have time to get someone to look at it. She unrolled the window and waved to get Eve's attention.

Her eyes rounded when she realized who was behind the wheel, but a second later, she came around to the passenger side.

"Thank you for taking me again."

The confidence Tiff had hoped would blossom in the absence of the drug's haze had not appeared. If anything, Eve's words had grown softer, her demeanor smaller.

"We have some extra time. How about a quick lunch?"

Eve's gaze remained trained out the window, as if she'd been released after a long prison sentence. "Sure. That would be nice."

Getting Eve to suggest where and what to eat was a wash, so Tiff chose a place near the DHS offices known for serving amazing hamburgers.

The restaurant had a fifties theme, with a checkered floor and Formica tabletops, but the girl who led them to their booth had a tattoo on her neck and a piercing in her lip that really broke up the atmospheric illusion.

Once they were seated, Tiff was able to look Eve in the face. The bruising had subsided significantly, but she still had a sallow appearance. "How have you been? Is the shelter working out okay?"

She nodded.

"Do you have any plans as to what you'll do next?"

Eve picked at her fingernail. "I don't know."

A server in a red-and-white dress covered with a frilled white apron approached. "What can I get you ladies today?"

Tiff ordered, then Eve repeated it word for word.

The woman nodded, scribbled something on her order pad, and left.

"I really want to help. How about we make a list?" Tiff took a notebook out of her purse. "What are the things you need to do for DHS to return the kids?"

She seemed to sink farther into the seat.

"I know it seems impossible, but I can help you. Eve, you're stronger than you think." A familiar quote about strength and bravery ran through Tiff's memory. They were words she'd repeated to her children so many times. Now she hoped Lindsay had remembered those words and known how special she was.

"I'm not strong at all. I'm not sure I can do this." There was a catch in Eve's voice, as if her throat didn't want to let the words out into the open air.

"How are you doing with your sobriety? Have you been to the class at the shelter?"

She nodded. "I sat in. I'm doing okay."

"That's great. See, you're already making progress." What if Eve didn't pass the drug test before the visit? What would happen then? "When you get further along in your healing, we can help you find a job. The new caseworker, Kelly, said she has a list of employers willing to give women a chance."

"I don't know how to do anything . . . legal."

"And that must be scary, but if you take this one day at a time, soon you'll be able to get additional training and move into a job you love."

They fell silent, Eve staring at her hands. Tiff was a fraud. While her desire to help was genuine, her empathy had been stunted by good fortune. It was ungrateful to even think like that, but how was she supposed to connect with Eve when she couldn't imagine how she felt?

ZARA'S NERVES WERE ALL BOUND UP in knots she couldn't untangle. She gripped the steering wheel, thankful Chad had taken a long lunch and would meet them at the DHS office. In a few minutes, Zara would be in the same building as her sister for the very first time in ten years. Her body raged when she thought of all Eve had put Charlotte and Sammy through. How was she supposed to forgive her twin or even look at her face—a mirror image of her own?

In the back seat, Charlotte sang a song inappropriate for a five-year-old while Sammy thunked the back of Zara's seat with his new cowboy boots.

She made the last turn into the parking lot.

Chad was leaning up against the pickup, waiting.

She opened her door, and Charlotte's lyrics spilled out.

"We really need to get some kids' music playing around the house." Chad gave her a worried look.

"I'm doing the best I can."

His hand settled on her arm. "That's not what I meant. You didn't teach her that song. I meant *we* need to teach her some new ones. Are you doing okay?"

She took in a breath; it sounded like her lungs were having a seizure as she tried to blow out the growing tension. "I'll be okay. I promise."

"No worries. I'm here to help."

She touched his cheek, stubble already growing out from this morning's shave. "Thank you."

"Oh gross," Charlotte hollered, breaking the moment. "Are you going to kiss?"

Chad laughed and kissed her forehead.

Both of Charlotte's chubby hands covered her eyes, and Sammy laughed, though Zara doubted he understood what was funny. To him, this was all a game designed for his personal amusement.

Before she was ready, Chad unbuckled Charlotte while she got Sammy and the diaper bag. They'd learned a lesson or two already. One of those was never leave the house without diapers and wipes. For some reason, that mistake was as good as giving a month's worth of fiber to a little boy.

They walked to the entrance, a child in each of their arms and Chad's free hand around her waist. To anyone who didn't know them, they would look like a normal family, but this building was their truth. These were not their children. The facts followed Zara like a black cloud, pelting her with condemnation. *You're a fraud. You could never be a decent mother. And you'll never get the chance to try.*

The stream of nagging words told her she was not enough with such power, they might as well have been real. When Zara first became a believer, thoughts like those were pushed to the background, replaced by the understanding that God did not see her that way. To Him, she was a precious daughter. Yet thoughts of Eve and the current situation were shoving her back to old ways. In Zara's mind, her sister was stealing from her, taking her peace and letting her hold these children for a short time, only to rip out her heart and destroy it.

Cold air—too cold—met them as they opened the door. The waiting area was a near-empty void. She stepped up to the counter and waited for the woman sitting there to acknowledge her, but she kept typing away at her ergonomic keyboard.

"Excuse me."

The woman held up a hand, palm out in a stop motion.

Zara gave Chad an eye roll the receptionist couldn't see as he shuffled the kids to the corner where a few toys were set up.

Her inner germaphobe wailed at the thought of the bacteria and viruses that must have plagued that play cube.

"Okay. Now, how can I help you?"

Zara shifted her attention back to the woman. "We're here for the kids to have a visit."

"You're the foster parents?"

That label irritated Zara. It separated the children from them, as if they didn't belong at their home. It meant substitute, not as good, a last-ditch alternative. It was a divide that she couldn't stomach. Zara might not have known Charlotte and Sammy until recently, but she loved them. "Yes. For Charlotte and Samuel."

The woman stood. "We don't usually have the foster families up here. Didn't anyone tell you about the other entrance?"

Zara shook her head. Now they weren't good enough to enter through the front door?

"Let me get someone to take you back to the foster parent waiting area."

As the receptionist disappeared, Charlotte's voice rose above the layer of tension. "Mom!"

Zara spun. And there she was. Her twin. The image that stared back at her was one she'd longed for and one that broke her. Behind her, a woman stood off to the side.

Charlotte launched into Eve's thin, scarred arms.

Something held Zara's feet still while her heart begged to go forward. Her brain was scrambled between loyalty and love for her sister and fury as she watched Eve hug the child she'd chosen drugs over. Her jaw tightened until it ached. There was a real longing to hate Eve for what she'd done and who she'd become. But hating Eve meant hating a part of herself. They were not just sisters but identical twins.

Eve's eyes rose, and her gaze found Zara's, a connection binding them together across the room.

Through the filter of tears, Zara saw her sister, thin and weakened. Yellowed bruises marred her face and neck, accentuating the brown circles under her eyes. She didn't wear makeup, and her clothes fit like they belonged to a larger woman.

Eve had been a partier, and Zara had known she was abusing the medications from her knee surgery, but she honestly hadn't thought it would come to this. Zara had left a bit of herself behind to die.

Chad's eyes begged Zara to join the group, so she forced one foot, then the other to make the journey from where she stood to her sister. "Eve."

Charlotte remained twisted around her leg.

But Sammy was lost in the similarity. He stood between them, his focus bouncing back and forth like a game of Pong. Then his eyes filled with tears, and he started to wail.

Eve and Zara bent at the same time, their shoulders colliding as they reached for Sammy. In unison, both stood. Zara gasped. It was like watching a reflection of herself after a battle with the flu, their movements matching.

"I'm sorry." Zara backed away, but so did Eve.

"No." She curled her lips over her teeth. "I'm sorry. I put you in this position. I'm sorry you had to take the kids." She lifted Sammy, her movements stilted, as if it were a struggle.

Placing her palm across her collarbone, Zara bit her tongue to hold back a wave of emotion.

Kelly appeared from out of nowhere. "Okay. Eve, I'm going to need to take you with me for a minute. One of my coworkers will take the kids and foster parents to the other waiting area while we visit." She placed her hand on Eve's back, urging her to return Sammy to Zara, then led her toward a door.

Charlotte climbed into Chad's arms.

"Eve?" Zara's voice was as weak as her heart.

She turned, her mouth forming a sad smile, then left with Kelly.

Before Zara could crumble, Chad had her. Sammy and Charlotte clung to their hips. Where was the happy ending going to come from?

"Chad and Zara, will you please follow me?" A man with spiked dark hair and a DHS badge pointed to the door at the back of the room.

But before they could get far, the woman who'd brought Eve in slipped her hand into hers. "I just want you to know, I'm praying, and I'll help however I can." She stepped back, leaving something pressed into Zara's palm.

CHAPTER TWENTY-FIVE

"I DON'T GET IT." Zara paced back and forth in the tiny room. "Why are they keeping us separated? Is it something I've done? Did Eve ask for it to be that way?"

Chad sat in the corner of a worn beige couch and glanced at his watch.

"Seriously?"

"What?"

"I'm in the middle of a crisis here, and you're checking the time?"

"It's not because I want to leave. It's because I don't. But you know we need my income to pay the mortgage. You're not working anymore."

She froze, her fists burrowing into her sides. "No. I might not be making a regular paycheck, but we agreed to give this business a go. You and me."

He wiped his hand across his forehead. "That's not what I meant, either. I mean, we need the money. And let's be honest, you can't handle any more orders and the kids. No one could."

That might be entirely true—for her. But Rita would be able to do it. Zara hadn't even opened her business email account in four days. If something didn't change soon, she wouldn't be able to fill the orders she already had.

Taking a seat next to him, she tugged at her tight ponytail, letting the pain give her focus. "I don't know what's happening here. Sometimes I want the kids to stay forever, but a minute later, I can't wait for them to go home to Eve."

He rubbed his hand up and down her thigh but didn't say anything. Really, what could he say? Her nerves were frazzled, leaving her ready to use whoever she could to relieve her personal stress. She needed a minute off, a break and time with her husband. But even if she had that precious time, she'd be unable to appreciate it. Her heart and soul were with her sister and her children. She just wanted them back and safe. *What kind of person considers her sister to be unsafe for her own children?* Evidently, the one who had suddenly become a foster parent rather than getting the time to mourn her own loss of future children. That couldn't be healthy.

Standing again, Zara reached into her pockets. A finger grazed the edge of the paper the woman with Eve had placed in her hand. Zara pulled it out and read the name and phone number. Even if DHS didn't want them connecting here before visits, she had a way to contact Eve. But should she?

Chad was still there when the door swished open and the kids returned. The man who'd led them to this room was with them. So many caseworkers and other staff—how were they supposed to keep everyone straight? He explained his role as a supervisor for visits. It was his job to sit in the room with the biological parent and the children, observing how they interacted, watching for any red flags.

Zara wanted to remind him that they'd learned her sister was in this position because of addiction and her violent boyfriend. There'd been no report as far as she knew that Eve had ever actually hurt the children, at least not physically. Yet she remembered their mother's depression. It made their home a silent battlefield and left scars on Zara, and surely on Eve too.

Eve
June 15, 2019

Reasons to stay clean and sober:
  1. The smell of Sammy's head
  2. To earn Charlotte's trust
  3. To make my sister proud of me, if that's even possible
My time with the children this week hurt even more than last time. Charlotte went on and on about Zara's husband. She kept referring to him as "Daddy." I looked at the guy who was watching us, but all he had was a sympathetic smile.

Charlotte has never met her father. I'd like to keep it that way. He owned me, leasing me out to anyone willing to pay him for the time. Even though he said I was free to go whenever I wanted, I knew there'd be a beating if I tried. He would have killed me before letting me go.

I wasn't sure that Chaz was her father at first, and I hoped he wasn't, but a couple weeks after I found out I was carrying my girl, there was a bust. Chaz went to jail on a five-year sentence, and I was given my freedom.

It was my chance. I did my best to stay clean. I moved to a different town, closer to Zara, and found housing with the help of government assistance. I pushed all thoughts of Chaz and what had happened to me into the back of my mind, until the day I gave birth and the child they placed on my chest had the same eyes as the man who'd used me in ways that wouldn't be allowed for an animal.

I brought her back to the studio apartment and sank into a blackness I'd never gone to before. Every heartbreaking moment of my life pressed me further down. Out of desperation, I contacted my mother for help. I thought maybe she could stay with me for a bit, watching the baby while I tried to get myself up again.

Instead of congratulations, she tore into me about the stupidity of having children when I wasn't even able to care for myself. Her words destroyed the fraction of hope I had left. That was the day I wrapped my baby up and took her with me to find a hit. I needed it to make the agony fade enough to care for her. That's what I told myself; it's what I believed.

I learned in my addicts' meeting that it can be helpful to get my story out and onto paper. I want to heal, to give my children a future, to have them back, but reliving these moments of shame has my sobriety hanging by a thread.

I want to move forward, but I can't erase the distance I saw in my sister's eyes. It tugs me back. There's no one more like me in this world, yet we're so far apart. I guess seeing her made that clear.

Tiff has invited me to go to church with her family tomorrow, but it's Father's Day. I don't want to intrude. I've done enough of that already.

Instead, I'll stay here, avoiding Bonnie the best I can.

ZARA BRACED HERSELF. They were going to do it—take the kids to church, face the wondering eyes, answer the questions in vague ways that made them look like they were covering up a juicy truth. Last week, they'd stayed home, watching the sermon online, but it was time to take the next step. Sharon had bought a frilly dress for Charlotte, who had oohed and aahed about it for an hour, petting the lace as if it were a kitten. Sharon had even gotten Sammy a bow tie that buttoned underneath the collar of his shirt.

Zara checked out the clock and realized they needed to be in the car within fifteen minutes if they wanted to make it to the nine-thirty service on time.

Charlotte was still sitting at the table, sliding pieces of French toast around her plate, only eating the bites that were cut into squares.

Syrup ran in rivers down Sammy's chin.

Chad looked up from the griddle. "That's his third piece. Should I cut him off?"

As if he understood, which maybe he did, Sammy looked up and stuffed three more bites into his mouth.

"Slow down. You're going to choke." Zara wet a washcloth and cleaned his face. "We may need to call this one. We can go to the eleven o'clock service."

Chad nodded. "Next week, we'll have this mastered."

She smiled, letting him live in his made-up world where people became parenting superheroes in the span of two weeks.

"Mom wants us to have lunch out with her after church. I told her that would be fun."

Zara's mind was blown. How could that be fun? She could barely get them through a meal within the protection of their own home.

"The look on your face says I made a mistake." He handed her a plate of breakfast.

"I'm not sure we're ready to try a meal at a restaurant."

"We can make it a family-friendly one. How about the pizza place with the ball pit?"

Charlotte dropped her fork, which clattered to the floor. "Ball pit?"

"Maybe." Zara gave Chad a look.

He shrugged. "Wherever we go, it will be fun, and there will be yummy food and Grandma."

"I like Grandma. I've never had one of those. I hope I can keep her forever. Do you think I can? And Jane too. I really like Jane the goat."

"Unfortunately, that's not a question we can answer right now." Zara sat down beside her. "We'll just have to be patient and see what happens." Charlotte loved Chad, Sharon, and a goat, but Zara was still on her to-be-determined list.

"My mom says we're going to be back with her in a little while." Charlotte looked down at her plate. "I don't want to live with Joey."

"You don't have to. Your mom will find a place that's safe, without Joey." Zara should have controlled her tongue, but how could she let Charlotte sit there in her worry without trying to ease her fears? Eve was supposed to stay away from him. It was part of the reunification plan. But would she really? How much control would DHS have after the kids were back in her care? And what was stopping her from packing them up and leaving, never to be seen by Chad and Zara again?

Investing in the children's lives was like sacrificing a part of her heart. With each day and each struggle, their lives merged. When Zara had left her family behind so she would have a chance at a life of her own, she hadn't taken time to think about what and who else would be missed.

ZARA WOULD CALL THIS SUCCESS. They had arrived at church—never mind that Jane was wandering around the farm, out of the fence again somehow, and never mind being fifteen minutes late for the eleven o'clock service. Never mind, too, that Sammy freaked out when they put his little tie on. And definitely never mind the mismatched shoes that Charlotte insisted were too pretty to pick between.

As it turned out, it was Father's Day. Having grown up without one, and with Chad's father deceased, it wasn't a day Zara had ever paid much attention to. But here they were, and she hoped it wouldn't send Charlotte into some kind of spin.

Debra Jasmine met them at the door. "I heard the whole lot of you would be joining us this week."

Zara's face warmed. How many of these people were talking about them? If it were someone else, she'd have so many questions. There was nothing that made a finer lesson against gossip than being at the wrong end of it. "We're here." She lifted an arm as if she'd performed a magic trick.

"You'll need to fill out a tiny bit of paper work when you get them to their classes. Just about allergies and stuff like that." Debra started walking, and Zara got the feeling they were supposed to follow.

She looked to Chad as they hustled after her. "I wasn't positive we'd be leaving them in class. It's their first week here."

"I understand, but it will get harder if you don't do it now." Debra spoke with such confidence; she must have understood this far better than Zara.

They arrived outside a classroom filled with kids who looked about Charlotte's age. Debra put both hands on the door frame and leaned in.

"Well, who do we have here?" Their pastor's wife, Fern, greeted Charlotte first.

"I'm Charlotte. This is my dad." She pointed up to Chad.

Every time she called him Dad, Zara sunk further into the wasteland of worry. Charlotte was getting attached. So were they. Zara had called him Uncle Chad a hundred times in front of Charlotte, but they were always Zara and Daddy when she referred to them.

Fern smiled but remained on her knees. "That's wonderful. My name is Mrs. Fern. I help out here in the pre-K room. Would you like to join us? We're just about to do a craft."

Charlotte looked back at Chad, her eyes filled with excitement. He nodded.

As if she'd known Fern and the others all her life, Charlotte dove into the classroom and started talking with a blond girl in ribboned pigtails.

Zara held Sammy closer.

After giving all the information needed, they moved on to the nursery, assuming Sammy would have a similar reaction. But no. He screamed as soon as the teen helper reached for him. They tried a second time, and Sammy's tiny fingernail cut a line across the back of Zara's neck. No way. A few minutes alone was not worth traumatizing Sammy further.

Zara reassured him the entire walk to the sanctuary that he'd stay with them. By the time they walked in, the sermon had already begun. Sammy was quiet, but his fist was wound into Zara's hair. They couldn't separate if they wanted to.

For the first time, she and Chad sat on the right side of the sanctuary, where all the real parents sat, ready to make a quick escape if their babies acted up. There wasn't a single toddler in the mix.

For five minutes, they listened to the pastor preach about Jacob's attitude of superiority and his inclination toward deception. At that point, Sammy finally felt secure enough to release her hair and start giving raspberries on her cheeks. Very loud raspberries. It sounded like an airplane was taking off from their row.

"Shhh." She pulled him back and looked him in the eyes. Sammy had beautiful eyes, the kind women ooh and aah over, wishing they had just a bit of those long lashes. He'd been growing; she could already tell. A tiny bit of skin now folded along his neck. When he grinned, the nubs of his new top teeth were visible.

Shushing a one-and-a-half-year-old little boy was apparently equal to tickling the same child. Sammy placed both hands on his tummy and let out a resounding laugh.

Just like that, every eye was on them.

Chad leaned in. "Do you want me to take him out?"

Zara probably should have taken him up on the offer—after all, she was with the kids all week—but even though Sammy had no regard for proper church etiquette, his giggles brought her to life. He made her feel totally in love.

Standing, she held the bundle close and edged past Chad.

"Bu bu." Sammy waved his hand in the air as they passed by people. "Bu bu."

While she probably should have felt embarrassed, all Zara could think was that Sammy was speaking. She wanted to stop and holler back to Chad, *Did you hear that? Sammy said bye-bye.* Pride swelled in her chest, and as she walked out with her head high, her nephew said yet another word. It was a miracle right there in church, and she was thrilled everyone had the privilege of hearing it.

As late as they'd been, she played with Sammy in the foyer for only a few minutes before the closing music started.

He didn't hesitate but started bobbing up and down in time with the drum beats.

"What a good dancer you are, Sammy."

He grinned back. This little boy was coming alive before her eyes, the image of the carefree child he deserved to be.

When Chad filed out with the rest of the people, they went together to get Charlotte.

She burst out of the classroom, something held behind her back, a purple marker line streaked down the middle of her face. "Daddy, Daddy! I have a surprise for you."

"Well, I can't imagine what it could be. Hmm." Chad looked up, tapping his finger on his chin. "Is it another goat?"

"No."

"Is it a tractor?"

"No. A tractor wouldn't fit in my hands." Her mouth went slack, as if she was exasperated with having to take care of them. "Look." She pushed her hands forward, exposing a colored rock with the words *My Dad Rocks!* written in the middle. Charlotte had drawn wavy hearts all around the words. She placed it on Chad's outreached hand and waited.

Kids and parents filtered around them, but they were in their own bubble.

Chad stared at the artwork, his lips tight.

"Oh, Charlotte." Zara put her hand on the little girl's shoulder. "That is beautiful."

Her husband, all strong and tough, nodded but couldn't speak. He leaned down and hugged her.

CHAPTER TWENTY-SIX

Eve

June 16, 2019

No one in the shelter mentions that today is Father's Day. I guess most of us don't know our dads, wish we hadn't, or feel too much shame to acknowledge they exist.

I wish I'd given my children fathers they could look up to. As far as I'm concerned, Charlotte never needs to know who hers is. I didn't know mine, and not knowing didn't seem to leave Zara any worse in the end. Charlotte can be like her aunt, safe and happy.

If he knows it's Father's Day, Joey will be wondering where Sammy is today. He'll want to see his son. The way he talked about Samuel sounded like he's his possession . . . much like I am. Maybe that's better than nothing. I know Joey loves us. He's told me. But I really messed things up this time. If I can fix things with him . . .

The phone is so public. If I could, I'd call his cousin, get a feel for how Joey is feeling toward me right now. I'm not sure how to survive without him. Joey picked me up when I was a mess and *gave me and Charlotte a place to stay. He was right when he said I wasn't very grateful. I just want to tell him I'm sorry.*

TIFF AND BRUCE CELEBRATED Father's Day alone. Tiff had invited Eve to join them before thinking it through. Fortunately, she'd declined. Bruce would have been rightly offended if Tiff took his special day away like that.

They did something new this year, something they hadn't done together since the day they'd placed the memorial plaque. They sat together at the edge of the neighborhood playground on the bench that held their daughter's name. From there, they watched children play in the same place they'd once taken their own little ones.

Lindsay had leapt from the swing here and cut open her chin, requiring stitches, but she'd wanted to come right back the next day. She loved to fly as high as she could go, scramble along the monkey bars, and whip down the slide. Lindsay had been fearless. She'd been strong and brave and, Tiff thought, impenetrable. But everyone has vulnerable places. Her daughter had been pierced in hers.

Tiff wove her hand into Bruce's. "I miss her."

"So do I." His voice was heavy.

"Are we going to make it through this?"

"I hope so."

If only he'd make a declaration, say he'd fight to assure their victory over the grief, but his hope was all he had to offer. Tiff had little more. Her heart was a bundle of ragged and torn pieces. All she could do each day was follow the course God was giving her. If she stopped working with the women, if she walked away from Eve, she wouldn't make it. How would that make things better with Bruce?

"Are you going to be free for the day?"

"I told you; this is all about you." There was a bitterness in her voice that made her cringe. "I'm sorry. That came out wrong."

His head bobbed. "Do you see that little girl? The one on the play structure that looks so much like Lindsay did?"

"I do."

The child bounced up and down on the bridge connecting two sections.

"Those were good days." Bruce ran a hand through his hair.

"They were."

"I often wonder what I did wrong. I wish I had the chance to do it over."

"Don't do that to yourself." It was easy for Tiff to say that to him, but she'd had the very same thoughts every single day since realizing Lindsay was using. "We did the best we could."

He looked away. "Maybe. I'm not sure I did. I worked too much."

This honesty was good and important, but when had talking about the naked truth become so painful? "There are a lot of things I'd do differently too."

"I've been thinking about your work on the streets. I don't want you to stop. I'm glad you found something that makes you feel like you're making a difference. I think I'm jealous. Not just of the time you spend out there, but also that you're able to do something that honors Lindsay in a special way. I just keep doing what got us into this in the first place."

The little girl flung herself down the slide, landing hard on the ground at the bottom.

Bruce jerked as she hit the bark mulch, his fatherly impulses still very much intact. "Sometimes I wish we would have had more children, not because that would make up for losing Lindsay. I think they would have made our family . . . fuller." He put his arm around her for the first time in what seemed like a long and arduous journey. "And less of a business venture."

For them, there'd been a turning point. She'd have to say it was somewhere near the beginning of the middle school years. They'd started taking the activities and the successes and failures more seriously, prioritizing awards over character, wins over compassion. "I'm not sure more children would have changed us, but maybe. We could have been too busy keeping up to push them like we did. Why did I become that mother?"

"It was both of us. It's a shame we don't get to try again now that we have more perspective, but that's the thing about parenting: You can only do the best you can with what you know at the time."

Tiff squeezed his hand in hers. "So, I've been thinking a lot about what you said. I want you to know I love you, and our marriage is worth fighting for." She wiped a stray tear from below her eye. "But I need you to experience what I see so you'll really understand how important the work I'm doing is. I'd like it if you'd come with me. See the women and get a glimpse of what I'm seeing."

"You told me once that I shouldn't go. They wouldn't trust you if you had a big man along with you. What's changed?"

What had changed was her perspective. She'd been holding on to her time alone with a double helping of pride. The ministry was her thing—her penance, even. And she didn't want to share it with anyone, especially not with the man she'd shared a daughter with. "I was selfish. Your coming along might push some people away, but we're a team."

He pulled her near, and she laid her head on his broad shoulder. "We'll see. I'm not really sure I'm up for that, not when I think about Lindsay and what happened to her. I'm not the strong one. I can't look at what she went through. I can't face it."

Tiff's phone buzzed, and she pulled it out. The number on the display was unfamiliar.

"Go ahead and answer it. You'll be distracted if you don't."

She leaned up and kissed his cheek. Something she hadn't done for a long time. "Hello?"

212

"I'm sorry. I didn't know who else to call."

"Eve?"

"Yes. It's me. I didn't do this. I promise I'm clean."

"Slow down." Tiff stood and paced back and forth in front of the bench. "What happened?"

"Someone put a balloon of heroin and a stolen ring under my pillow. When I came into my room, Lyla was standing there, holding them. She called the police and told me I couldn't come back to the shelter. I promise you, it's not mine. I want my kids back."

"Okay." Tiff tried to think while her heart thundered and Bruce stared on. "Are you under arrest?"

"I was, but then they let me go. I have to come back for court. How am I supposed to prove I didn't do it?" The panic in her voice made Tiff believe her even though she knew better than most people that taking the word of an addict was a mistake ninety-nine percent of the time. Somehow, even after being fooled by Lindsay and so many others, Tiff knew Eve was telling the truth. And even if she wasn't, she needed someone to believe in her. Tiff could be that one person.

Her gaze caught on her husband's questioning stare. She'd just promised to put him first, and yet Eve needed her. What was she supposed to do?

Bruce stood and fished his keys from the pocket of his khakis.

"Eve, where are you right now?"

"At the courthouse. They let me use the phone."

"I'll be there as soon as I can."

The line clicked off. Tiff licked her lips and felt a wave of heat rush over her.

"That's the woman you've been working with?"

She nodded and waited for Bruce to take the next step.

He twirled his keys around his index finger. "Sounds like she's in trouble."

"She is."

Time edged by them in slow motion. The sounds of the

children playing, the creak of the swing sets seemed distant and hollow.

"Well, we'd better go get her." His face was as unreadable as at any time in their relationship, but he'd offered, and she wasn't about to refuse.

She reached her hand toward him.

Bruce stared down at her fingers long enough that she almost pulled them back, but she waited, and he took her hand.

Eve
June 16, 2019

This journal with the picture of my kids taped on the inside cover is the only thing I was able to grab before being taken away from the shelter. They gave it back to me after I finished all the intake stuff and was released. I thought I'd lost the pen, but the officer, a man with oddly kind eyes, found me and returned it. This is my lifeline. It might be thin, but my words on the pages are the only strength I have right now.

I'm tucked into myself at the bottom of a small tree. The courthouse casts a shadow over me, keeping me almost too cool. I didn't take anyone's ring, and I didn't buy those drugs. This time, I really am innocent. What if I get away with my many screw-ups just to go to jail on someone else's lift? What will happen to my kids then? Will I see them if I'm in prison? Do I even want my kids to see me there?

The thing I'm afraid of much more than doing time is someone finding out that Chaz is Charlotte's father. If I was put away, they might give my daughter to him, or someone in his family. They could separate my babies from each other.

I haven't done a great job as a mother, but I'm seeing more clearly now. I want to give them a chance to not end up like me. With Joey or Chaz in the picture, that's gone.

Joey never loved me. If he had, he would have gotten word to me at the shelter. He must know that's where I was. If Bonnie knew, everyone did.

I bet she planted the stuff under my pillow.

Tiff is a lifesaver. She talks about God like my grandmother did. I want to believe what she says. I want to have the kind of life and hope that allows a person to believe there could be something or someone out there who holds all the power but doesn't want to crush me. If that were true, maybe I could change. Maybe my kids and I could be all right.

So, God, if you're out there, show me a miracle. Let me see that you really do have love for losers like me. I just need some kind of sign.

CHAPTER TWENTY-SEVEN

CHARLOTTE MUST HAVE ASKED CHAD a hundred times if he loved his Father's Day gift.

Zara remembered what it was like growing up thinking about her dad and fantasizing about who he might be. She wondered if any of a dozen movie stars could be the one man who'd been looking for her all her life. Had he known she existed? Did her mother steal Zara and Eve away from him? Her imagination ran wild with scenarios in which she was a hidden princess and the king would someday come to her rescue.

Of course, as she got older her mind became more jaded, and she began to assume her mother was being honest: Their dad was nothing more than a responsibility-shirking narcissist. Even now, she sometimes thought about what it would be like to have a dad, so she couldn't blame Charlotte for latching on to Chad. If someone like him would have walked into her life, Zara would have grabbed him too. Actually, she did, knowing he would make a perfect father for her future children. Charlotte had a good eye for value.

By the time they drove up to the house, it was well past Sammy's nap time. Noodles clung to his shirt and hair. They got him out of the restaurant by letting him take a few more on a napkin with him to the car. Zara couldn't comprehend how a child who ate as much as Sammy could be underweight. He ate all day long, but Zara had the fortune of available food. They weren't rich, but they always had enough. She wasn't too old to remember going to bed hungry because there wasn't anything in the house to eat.

Zara's stomach soured. Eve had been living in much of the same way they'd grown up. She'd never had the opportunity to see there were other options. Zara should have been the one to show her. What kind of sister finds a treasure and keeps it all for herself while her twin suffers and starves? She'd never thought seeing Eve again would give her such a strong dose of guilt, but it had been her constant stalker since seeing Eve face-to-face at the DHS office.

Zara switched sides with Chad as they got out of the car. They didn't even need to say a word. She went for Sammy, and he got Charlotte. When the kids' emotions were high, it was easier to give them the parent they desired.

Sammy clung to Zara's blouse with his filthy, food-crusted hands. He pressed his face into her neck the way he did when he couldn't seem to get close enough, or feel safe enough. She patted his back as they went into the house, careful to keep the dog from jumping up and licking a meal off the sleepy boy. By the time she'd gotten to the top of the stairs, she could feel his hot breaths growing longer and deeper. Sammy was about out, and she'd have to lay him down with the thin layer of food still on his skin or risk waking up a tired toddler. Zara went for the crib.

In a move she felt a great deal of pride in, Zara leaned over the crib railing and deposited the sweet boy onto the sheets in one smooth motion. He shuffled in his sleep, finding the right position and curling an arm around the soft blanket Sharon had brought over. She'd said it was a little something she'd been knitting for someday, though Zara was sure it had been made especially for this little guy. Sharon wasn't one to admit to late nights creating a gift Zara hoped he would treasure forever.

Outside the window, Charlotte screamed.

Zara lurched for the fan switch, turning on the hum in hopes the noise outside wouldn't wake Sammy. After one last look at his sleeping form, she headed down to see what tragedy had befallen their young princess now.

She found a trail of Charlotte's shoes and clothes heading away from the house. Her gaze followed the screaming and found Charlotte halfway to the barn in a full run, not much left on. Chad was about twenty paces behind, his hands held out at his sides.

She ran after them, catching up to Chad first. "What is going on?"

He looked like a man who had been stunned beyond repair. "A spider."

"She got bit by a spider?" They both jogged to keep up with the panicked and barefoot child.

"Nope. She *saw* a spider." Chad sprinted ahead, turning in Charlotte's path and catching her in his arms.

She flailed, her face bright red and her animal-like screams shocking the beautiful summer day.

"It's okay. Charlotte? Please calm down." Chad sat on the ground, trying to hold her.

Zara couldn't go to them. The scene was every nightmare she had about taking the children. What if they didn't know what to do? And they didn't. Charlotte was so far past being in control, her eyes didn't seem to recognize Chad right in front of her.

He just kept talking to her, his tone even, but Zara could see in his eyes that his own panic rested right below the surface.

Finally, after a long enough while that she thought someone even miles down the road must have heard and called the authorities, Charlotte's body started to relax. Her chest shuddered with emotion, and sweat dripped down her hairline and across her temple.

"You're safe. You're okay." Chad kept repeating the words, and Zara took them in as if they were meant for her too.

How did a child with such a tiny body carry around so much painful baggage? What had happened to her to cause this kind of wild overreaction? The kids had lived in a world where balance was an unknown, and she and Chad were trying to make it hour by hour on the instincts they had, which were entirely based on nothing.

Zara found herself looking forward to the DHS training they had scheduled for the next weekend. Maybe they'd find answers and explanations as to why these kinds of things happened and how they should handle them. She just hoped Sharon could really handle the kids while they attended the training.

No childcare at foster parent trainings.

As BRUCE PULLED UP to the courthouse, Tiff spotted her. Even from a distance, Tiff could see Eve was more broken than she had been the day Tiff had found her in a drug-induced haze. Her hand moved across the page of her journal. She'd been attached to it since the moment she'd been able to hold a pencil again after the beating. Judging by the stack of similar books Tiff was storing for her at home, writing in it was medicine to Eve. Putting her pains and sorrows into words seemed to help her to survive.

"What's she doing?" Bruce's voice was soft, almost as though he knew her and cared.

"She writes everything in her journal."

"Is that what you have stored in the garage?"

"Yes. It's the only thing she's held on to."

He cleared his throat. "That's kind of sad. You know what I mean. Like it's how she makes a mark. I wonder if she feels invisible."

Tiff reached and found his hand, then squeezed it for all she was worth. He was right. In a moment of observing Eve, he saw her better than Tiff had. What that young mom needed was to be seen, known, loved. Didn't everyone need that?

"Do you want to come with me?"

He pulled his hand away from hers. "No. This is your thing. I don't want you to get me wrong here. I think you're in over your head, and I want our focus to be on salvaging what we have left."

"Bruce, what do you think that young woman is trying to do?" She hadn't yet left the protection of the air conditioner, but the heat was steadily rising. "Our lives can't be only about us. We can't isolate ourselves from the rest of the world because that's easier, not when we know what's out there. It would amount to turning our backs on Jesus. Is that really what you want to do?" She heard the edge in her voice, but Bruce needed to get this through his overindulged skull. This, right here, wasn't about them. They had everything they needed. *To whom much has been given, much will be required.*

Tiff swung the door open and, for the first time, wished she was doing this as a member of a team. Now that her eyes were opened to some of her own hidden motivations, she needed to be more fully on an altruistic path, if possible.

Eve must have sensed her presence. She looked up when Tiff was about twenty feet away. The skin around her eyes was ringed in red, and her hair lay all to one side, as if she'd been twisting it around the way Tiff had noticed her doing when she was particularly anxious. She jumped to her feet, holding her journal close to her chest.

"I got here as quickly as I could. What made Lyla even look through your room?" Approaching Eve was sometimes like moving close to a scared animal. Tiff had to take it one slow step at a time to avoid Eve's look of panic and her own fears that the young woman would flee.

"I think the person who put the stuff there told her to look."

"Do you know who did this?"

She looked away.

"Eve, this is important. If you know someone put that stuff under your pillow, you need to say." The heat from the sun directly above them, combined with Tiff's uncertainty as to the next step, made sweat dampen her back and stick the shirt to her skin.

Eve's mouth was a strong line indicating her commitment to silence.

"How about we go by the shelter? We'll talk to Lyla and see what we can do. At the very least, you'll need to pick up your things."

"Thank you." She pulled her zippered sweatshirt around her slender frame.

"Aren't you hot?"

"I'm fine. Thank you."

Maybe Eve was hiding something. Tiff had learned to be careful over the last couple years, but she'd let down her defenses with Eve. If Eve was using her, it would be the perfect evidence for Bruce to throw in Tiff's face.

They walked toward the car, but Tiff stopped and put her hand out when they were halfway there. "Eve, I should tell you that my husband is with me. We were celebrating Father's Day."

The color washed from Eve's face.

"Will you be okay if he goes with us?" Tiff didn't know what Eve's experiences with men had been. Even mentioning Father's Day to Eve made Tiff feel spoiled. Tiff had a wonderful father, a true hero. If only every daughter were that lucky.

"I'm sorry. I shouldn't have called. I messed up your day." She started to turn.

"No." Tiff reached for her. "We can celebrate any time. Let's get you through this right now."

"I can't."

"What about Charlotte and Sammy?" This was playing dirty, throwing out her best card. "There are steps you need to move through if you want to get your children back. Housing is a big one."

"Okay." She scratched at the back of her neck. "I'll go. But Lyla said I wouldn't be able to stay there anymore."

"One thing at a time." Tiff opened the rear passenger door. "Bruce, this is my friend Eve. Eve, this is my husband."

"Nice to meet you," Bruce said. The timbre of his voice had reverted to professional.

Eve nodded but didn't make eye contact.

Few words were exchanged on the drive, but luckily it was only a mile or so from the courthouse to the shelter.

Bruce pulled into a parking space at the front of the building. Since it was a Sunday, Tiff wasn't sure Lyla would be in, but there was always a paid employee in her place who could at least enlighten Tiff on the situation.

"I'll stay out here. I get the feeling not many men go inside." Bruce pointed to the sign that read *Shelter for Women and Children*.

"Thank you, honey. This shouldn't take long."

Inside, the building seemed to have grown colder since Tiff's last visit. She pressed the buzzer at the front desk, and Lyla ambled out of her office.

"I hung around. Kind of thought I'd be seeing the two of you before long." She motioned for them to join her.

In the office, pictures of children, many taken right there in the shelter, lined the walls. Every flat surface held stacks of mismatched papers. For a woman who ran a remarkably tight shelter, Lyla kept a mess of an office.

"Before we all get too comfortable, I want to remind you both that this place has a policy. If we bend the rules for one woman, a hundred will come behind her, asking for the same luxury." Lyla sat behind her desk, her hands clasped together in a teepee on the surface.

"I understand, but what about innocent till proven guilty? What makes you think someone else didn't put those things under Eve's pillow?"

"Number one, Eve needs to speak for herself. She'll have to

learn that if she's going to make a new life. And number two—"
Lyla blew out a breath that lifted her dense bangs—"I can't tolerate any drugs in this house. It's too dangerous to the women trying to get clean, and we have children here. If DHS thinks we're being lenient, what's to stop them from removing those kids from their moms?"

"I understand." Eve rose from the metal chair, filling the room with squeaks.

"Your belongings have been packed. Misty has a key and can get your box from the storage closet." Lyla nodded for Eve to go on, but she didn't rise herself. "Tiff, can you hang on for a minute?"

Tiff leaned back. "Bruce is waiting, but I have a little time." At the core of this situation, they had a young woman who was trying to do what was right, trying to stay clean and sober and get her children back. If a women's shelter couldn't be counted on to help, where was Eve supposed to go?

"I feel horrible, and if Eve isn't guilty, well, it won't be the first time I had to kick out an innocent woman. What you don't know is that I'm in a tough position here. We get most of our funding from a private source, and we've been told more than once that if drugs are tolerated, the money stops. She just can't stay here."

"What is Eve supposed to do now? Should I just throw her out on the street?"

"I'm going to talk to the drug court attorney. There's a good chance Eve can get into their program. Often, they won't go forward on charges as long as progress is being made. It has one of the best outcomes I've seen."

Tiff looked up at the tiled ceiling. "Lyla, how is anything going to help her stay clean and sober if she doesn't have a place to live?"

"That's what I was going to say. The people going through the program have access to Oxford Houses. They offer clean and sober living. It may take some time to get a slot, but it's the best answer."

Tiff brushed off her pants as she stood. "I hope you're right." She walked out the door. Eve needed a place now, and all Tiff could offer was perhaps a couple of nights in a hotel.

Eve wasn't in the open area near the desk.

Tiff wandered outside, hopeful she hadn't taken off. Eve stood near the back of Bruce's car, the two of them looking at the box he'd just slid into the trunk. Bruce saw her but instead of waving, he went to the front of the car and started the engine. Coming back around to the back, he said something to Eve and she got in.

Nerves twisted inside Tiff. Bruce was waiting and would want an answer as to where they were taking Eve, but Tiff didn't have any ideas. For the first time, her husband was out on the battlefield with her, and he'd see what a complete failure she really was.

Tiff shook her head as she neared him. "No luck."

"I have a proposition for you." His eyes were stern enough to make her want to refuse to listen, but that wasn't really the way to mend a marriage. "I think Eve should come home with us. She can stay in Brandt's old room, not Lindsay's."

A burst of adrenaline hit Tiff's bloodstream like a flash of lightning. "You're serious?"

He held up a hand. "This is absolutely not without conditions."

"Of course."

"Here's the deal. Eve can stay with us as long as she stays away from drugs, alcohol, and any illegal activity. She has to do what she needs to do to get herself a job and her own place."

"Yes. That's totally reasonable."

"That's not all."

She bit her bottom lip, anticipating the real reason behind Bruce's kind offer. There was a catch.

"If she fails, you're done. You give up the ministry, and we go back to our lives. Listen, I know this was part of your grief process, but I need you now."

Tiff took a step back. His words felt like an attack.

"Is that something you can agree to?" His jaw tightened, and despite thirty years of marriage, she was left with little room for negotiation.

"It's a deal. As long as Eve is okay with it."

"I already asked her to stay." Bruce turned away from her and got into the car.

Tiff stared at the place where he'd just stood. How did he know she would agree?

CHAPTER TWENTY-EIGHT

Eve

June 17, 2019

I'm staying with Tiff and her husband. I didn't want to, but I couldn't think of another place I could go, at least not one that wouldn't make me go back on my promise to my kids. I have to stay clean.

When Bruce drove up the driveway, I found out real quick that people who say Tiff is rich are right. The road up the hill was worth more money than I'd seen in my whole life. Bruce is some kind of lawyer. I guess it really does pay to stay in school.

Tiff has told me a little about her daughter, but not much. It's part of why I was scared to come here. Why would a girl who had so much throw it all away? It doesn't make any sense to me. I had nothing when I took my first dose, but it made me feel like I had everything. It's never been as good as that first time, though. I've been chasing the freedom it gave me, but it's like a dream I can't get back into.

Flipping back to the beginning of this journal and staring at the faces of my babies is the only thing that gives me hope. I need to show them another life before it's too late for them.

I've spent most of my time here camped out in this bedroom that's nicer than my old apartment. There's a small dresser and a lamp by the bed. The comforter seems like something too nice to sleep under, and the mirror over the desk does an amazing job of showing me how out of place I am.

Bruce doesn't talk much to me. I'm glad he's gone most of the day, but I'm not sure what to say to Tiff, either. I owe them so much, but how do they expect me to pay them back?

———

WOMEN HAVE WORKED IN THE FIELDS *while minding their children since the beginning of history. Isn't that what we're told?* If that was really the case, Zara should be able to get the lavender plants into the ground with Charlotte and Sammy in tow.

There was nothing like the feel of grass for Sammy. He loved to run in it, pick it, and try to eat it. He was a lot like the goats in that way—though Zara would be sure to keep that observation to herself. A caseworker might not get her humor.

She set Sammy with a bowl full of plastic cups in the shade of a maple tree, then started bringing plants around the house as fast as she could make a trip. Each time she came around the corner, Zara checked to be sure he was still there and not choking on something.

Charlotte pushed her baby doll in the swing Chad had hoisted into the tree. Zara could have asked her to keep an eye on her brother. That was probably what those ancient superwomen did, but Zara had been doing all she could to get Charlotte to be a five-year-old, not a little mother to her baby brother.

By the third trip around, her arms ached and the rows of plants near their final growing spot were still small in comparison to the mob of seedlings still waiting to be moved.

Sammy had turned the bowl over and was smacking the cups against it with vigor.

"Can I carry some?" Charlotte took her baby out of the swing and laid her on the steps to the back door.

"Sure." This wasn't going to make the job any easier.

Zara hefted Sammy onto her hip. In response, he howled until she realized he wanted one of his plastic cups. The three of them went to pile number one. "Charlotte, just take one at a time. It's very important that the plants don't tip over." Zara put one container in her hands, and Charlotte actually smiled back at her. With one in her own left hand, Zara used that arm to hold Sammy and took four more in the right by pressing a finger into each one's dirt and squeezing tight, like a waitress with a bunch of dirty water glasses. Halfway around, Sammy started using Zara's head as his personal drum, pounding the cup on the back of her skull and singing a tune with unrecognizable words. "Stop hitting, please." Her words fell on ears attuned only to his music.

By the time they got to the garden, Zara was sweating, Sammy had drifted halfway down her side, and she had aches in her head and fingers. She set down the toddler and collapsed onto the cool grass next to the edge of plowed earth.

"Nap." Sammy thunked her on the head again.

He was coming up with new words every day, like a pin had been pulled out, activating his vocabulary. "No. I'm not taking a nap. I'm just resting for a minute."

Charlotte set her container down alongside Zara's head. "This is easy."

Ha.

Sammy toddled over to a young fruit tree. He looped his arm around the trunk and ran around it in circles.

"Charlotte, would you like to help me plant these?"

"Yes." She jumped up and down. "Can I?"

"Of course." Zara's imagination went wild with ideas to get Charlotte her own tiny gardening gloves and miniature tools, but this was the same kid who nearly lost herself at the sight of a spider. Better to keep expectations to a minimum.

She took her trowel out of the bucket, leaving her own gloves in there. If Charlotte was going to do this bare-handed, Zara had better work that way too. "This is what we need to do." She showed Charlotte the lines she'd already marked with the use of string tied to wooden stakes at the ends. "If we dig our holes under this twine, it will keep our rows nice and straight." As she dug the first hole, Charlotte wriggled next to her.

"My turn." She took the little shovel and started digging. Dirt flew every which way, but there was a smile on her face that lit up the entire farm.

By the time Chad returned home from work, Charlotte and Zara had planted twenty lavender plants in a zigzag line. Zara had fished at least twelve assorted things from bugs to flowers out of Sammy's mouth. She looked at the kids. They were filthy, and she wasn't much better.

"Daddy!" Charlotte flung herself into his arms. "We had the best day ever. I planted the garden. Do you want to see?"

"Of course." He put Charlotte down and let her lead him by the hand to show off her big accomplishment. As they passed, Zara couldn't help smiling at the two brown handprints on the back of Chad's best button-down shirt.

After baths, dinner, and stories, Chad put the kids to bed and came downstairs, where Zara was getting caught up on orders. She'd have to make soap tomorrow, even if it was in the middle of the night while the rest of the house slept. They'd be gone all weekend for the training.

"That was one happy little girl." Chad bent over and kissed her neck. "I don't think I've ever heard her talk so fast and excited."

"I know." Zara swiveled around in the desk chair. "I think I really got somewhere with her today. And we accomplished something. It felt really good." She leaned back, basking in the glory of her first somewhat successful day since the children had arrived.

"That's great. It kind of opens the door for something I was wanting to talk with you about." He took her hand, and they went into the kitchen. He pulled a gallon of mint chocolate chip ice cream from the freezer, a sure sign that something big was coming. Chad knew her weaknesses. "What if Eve isn't able to get her life on track?"

"What do you mean?" It's not like it was that complicated. All she had to do was what most of the population did every day: stay off drugs and get a job and home. Zara shook her head. Her brain knew this was not at all simple, but her heart took another path.

"I'm just wondering, would you want to keep the kids?"

"Like foster them forever?"

"Or adopt them."

Zara's heart felt so tugged in two it would surely tear. Adopting meant losing her sister—and not like she'd already experienced. There had always been hope that Eve would come around, that they would restore their relationship. But Eve's recovery would mean losing Sammy and Charlotte, and that was going to kill a piece of Zara too. There was no way for this situation to conclude without a devastating heartache.

"I don't know." That was the truth. She could never choose between Eve and her children. There had to be a way to keep both.

Eve

June 19, 2019

Tiff and Bruce hardly speak to each other. I don't know if it's because I'm here or if they're always this way. I thought people with money didn't have problems like this, but he doesn't ever touch her. At least she's safe from him, but he doesn't touch her in nice ways, either.

CHAPTER TWENTY-NINE

Eve
June 20, 2019

> *It's a Thursday, and I'm seeing my babies today. I hope I get a chance to talk with Zara this time. I blew it big-time the one time I saw her. I want to tell her that I'm sorry and I appreciate all she's doing for me and my kids. I know I don't deserve it.*

IT TOOK TOO LONG, but Tiff finally got Bruce to tell her what happened at the shelter. He'd overheard a couple women talking about how Eve got what she deserved and Joey could finish her off, for all they cared. They didn't come right out and admit to planting the ring and the drugs, but he felt sure they had. It's not like her husband was overly sympathetic to addicts, but his sense of fairness was fully intact. He couldn't and wouldn't walk away from something he felt lacked justice. In his world, there were no versions of gray—only black and white.

That was one of the first things she'd loved about Bruce. He'd fight for the underdog if it was getting kicked without cause. At the time, she hadn't anticipated the many rules that went along with these traits. She did now.

"I'm ready." Eve came out of the spare room freshly showered, her hair pulled back into a ponytail. Tiff itched to get her a little makeup, something to make her feel pretty and help her see how beautiful she was, but fear that the gift would been seen as an insult stopped her.

"Eve, you're looking healthier by the day. I'm so proud of you." She looked away like she always did when Tiff complimented her.

"Why do you do that?"

"What?"

"You stop looking at me when I say something nice to you. Do you think I'm lying?" Tiff stepped closer.

A flush colored her fair face. "I don't know."

"What did you see when you saw Zara?"

Tears filled Eve's eyes. "I saw what I should have been if I were stronger. What my kids deserve to have."

"Do you know what I saw?"

She shook her head.

"I saw you in a few months."

Her chin came up.

"You're just as beautiful and capable as Zara. You came from the same place, and even though you've had a hard detour, there's no reason you can't have a perfectly gorgeous life."

"I'd be happy just to give my kids a shot at a future, you know?"

"I do." That's what Tiff had wanted for her children too. All the pushing was to give them every opportunity possible. "What your kids need most is your love. I learned that the hard way. If I could go back, I'd stop the lessons and extra tutoring and just spend time loving my kids. You can do that."

Before she turned away, Tiff thought she saw the beginnings of a smile. Her heart expanded as it brought Eve into it. Eve was not

Lindsay, but she was special to Tiff in a way that only a daughter could be.

ZARA HAD JUST GOTTEN THE CHILDREN BUCKLED into the car when she got the call. Sharon was being rushed to the emergency room after falling off a ladder. Her heart hammered, and she cringed as the realization hit her that her first thoughts were of her own needs. How could she make it through the coming months and the loss of the children without Sharon by her side? She closed the door and pressed her hands to the glass, then prayed God would make her a better person and Sharon would be okay.

Zara couldn't be two places at once, but right then she needed to be at the hospital and at the DHS office.

That's when she heard the click.

Her spine went straight, and she searched her pockets, not finding the keys. Zara yanked at the driver's door—locked—then all the others with no success. She peered into the back seat. Sammy was gumming the keyless remote. "Hey, Sammy. Can you push the buttons?" She did a little happy mime for an example. "Push the button, Sammy."

Apparently her routine was pleasing, because he grinned, losing interest in the keys and dropping them to the floor.

Both kids stared at her from buckled car seats that she'd worked hard to ensure they couldn't escape from. Was there a bigger fail than this one? Chad was on the way to the hospital to be with his mother. Eve and all of DHS were at the office, waiting for the kids to show up for their visit. And the sun was beating down on her. Zara was literally cooking her niece and nephew in a mobile oven.

Sweat dripped down her neck. "Charlotte, can you unbuckle like a big girl?"

She shook her head. "I'm not allowed to do that."

Perfect time for her to choose obedience. "Just this once, it's okay. Please."

Her forehead wrinkled, and she looked at Zara as if this were a trick.

"The doors are locked, honey. I need to get in."

Charlotte's eyes went round, and Zara immediately regretted her words. Behind her, a loud bleating began, over and over—a goat with a hero complex. That's all she needed right now.

"It's okay. This is no big deal. I can fix this." She looked around as if another key would magically be lying there. It was not. "Can you reach the button on the door?" With her index finger, Zara pointed toward where Charlotte's lock would be, then remembered her other move she'd been so proud of—engaging the child safety locks.

Charlotte's chest rose and fell faster, like the ticking of a time bomb. She was getting close to an explosion.

"Honey, this isn't a big deal. Just let me think for a minute." She turned so Charlotte wouldn't see her Googling what to do when you lock your child in a car on a hot summer day. The number of results temporarily boosted her ego until she saw how many times dying children were mentioned. That was it. No child died on her watch. Zara picked up a large rock from the edge of the driveway, walked to the back of the car, and slammed it against the window. It cracked, a tiny circle marking the point of impact. She slammed it again, aiming for the same spot. This time, she pinched the flesh on the side of her pinky. Within seconds, a blood blister had formed.

Charlotte and Sammy were both crying.

Zara went to the side of the car again and assured them that everything was okay, while inside she was farther down the path of panic than they were.

Pulling out her phone again, she Googled how to break a window. It turned out a rock was not the best answer. She ran into the garage and found a hammer, then, using the claw end, she punched away at the edge of the back window like the instructions directed. A few minutes later, the window caved, and she was able to push the majority of the glass into the back of the SUV.

Zara climbed through the hole and pulled herself over the seat, then unbuckled both children and held them in her arms. "See. We're okay. It only took a minute to get the car open again."

Sammy was quickly soothed, but Charlotte kept asking what she was going to do about the window. Zara had no idea.

Eve
June 20, 2019

I passed the drug test. I don't know why that always surprises me. It's like I'm so sure I'm not going to. I think I've used and forgotten, or that maybe I did it in my sleep.

We're sitting in the waiting room, and I'm glad I brought this journal along in my bag. Zara is late. She's never been late to anything. She was even born first. Writing helps me with my nerves, but I'm still scared she won't show. What if she took the kids and left town? Who would even take up my case and look for them? They'd be better off with my sister.

This is such a scary place. The people here hold my future in their hands. Tiff says it's up to me, but it's not. They can take my kids forever, them and the judge.

When I went back for my previsit appointment, Kelly already knew about my arrest. She said I was lucky to have a friend like Tiff, but I needed to be proactive and look for a job and a place to live. It wasn't going to work if I left everything up to Tiff.

I'm not. I try to help out. There's not much I can do, but I offer every chance I get. I don't know how to get a job when I have visits and stuff. Who would hire me? And how would I get there? I've never even had a driver's license.

Where are my kids? It's twenty minutes later than the meeting was supposed to start. What has Zara done? Even though she's only eleven minutes older than I am, she's always thought she was better than me. But it's me who's gone out of my way to prove her right.

CHAPTER THIRTY

ZARA TOOK THE PARKING SPACE farthest away from the back entrance of DHS and backed in. With the shrubs tight against the rear of the car, maybe no one would notice the gaping hole. Foliage actually reached into the vehicle. She covered the front window with the screen even though the sun shone from the other direction.

Trying to keep the kids from thinking about the events of the morning, Zara kept up a steady stream of conversation, unbuckling them and keeping their progress facing away from the broken glass.

"Charlotte, what do you want to do with your mom today?" Zara helped the little girl out of the car, Sammy already on her hip.

Charlotte shrugged.

"Are there any special games in there you two like to play?"

"No. There's just boring stuff. I want to go home and plant the gardens." Charlotte leaned her head onto their joined hands.

"Maybe we'll have some time this afternoon." She really should take the car in for the window repair before too many people saw her driving around with extra ventilation. "Is that your favorite thing from this week?"

Charlotte looked up to her left, as if trying to find the right memory. "No. I think that was when you crashed the window to save us."

Regret snaked all the way to her core. Zara pressed the button by the back door and waited for someone to buzz them in. After a couple of questions through the intercom, the door clicked open.

Kelly met them in the hall, a smile so fake it could have been plastic stapled to her face. "I'm glad you made it."

Zara forced a smile back. "So am I." There was no way she would elaborate on the situation that caused their tardiness. This wasn't middle school, and Zara was doing her best even if it was nearly fatal.

She took Charlotte's free hand and reached for Sammy. "I'll get these two into their meeting. Maybe we'll have a chance to talk later."

Oh. Did they really have to talk? Based on the vast array of answers Google supplied to her question about locking children in cars, Zara was far from the first person to make this mistake. Maybe Charlotte wouldn't mention it.

While the kids were in the visit, Zara spent some time looking up places that would repair car windows. It appeared to be a costly act of heroism on her part. With the slowdown in her product creation and all the time Chad had taken off work, they weren't exactly making great strides in house repairs and student loan repayment. Though DHS offered some compensation for child-care, that was only for foster parents who worked outside of their homes. With Zara's business being home based, they expected her to manage the workload and the children at the same time.

She couldn't afford to hire help with the children or with the business. She'd just have to manage later hours, but that also meant forfeiting sleep and some of her precious time with Chad.

Leaning her head back on the couch, Zara tried to brainstorm solutions, but her mind wouldn't let her forget that somewhere in this building, her twin sister was with Charlotte and Sammy. They were kept away as if there'd been some kind of violent outburst between them. This back room was a kind of prison.

How was Zara supposed to reestablish a relationship with Eve when they couldn't even be in the same room? She paused. The piece of paper the woman with Eve had slipped her . . . what had she done with that? To think a perfect stranger was a connection to her sister. Honestly, though, Eve wasn't much different to her. If they hadn't shared the same features, they'd know nothing about each other except for the times they'd shared as children. And what were those, really? It was a lifetime ago, the hurts and sorrows. Zara wasn't the same child who grew up in a home of uncertainty and tragic loss. She'd become strong, grown wings.

What had happened to Eve since then? Had she experienced moments of joy and excitement? Had she accomplished things she never thought possible? Did she know what it was like to be truly loved by a man?

Zara doubted any of those things had happened for her sister.

They were two people created out of one, and Zara had taken all the fortune, while Eve struggled through what remained.

TIFF PACED BACK AND FORTH by the window facing out of the DHS waiting room. If only she could just have a few minutes to talk with Zara. When she asked the receptionist where Zara was, she informed Tiff that there were confidentiality issues, and Tiff did not have the right to that information. She struggled not to stomp her feet as she made her way back and forth.

Reunification was the key word around there, but how could reunification take place when nothing was being done to mend the relationship between sisters? Charlotte and Sammy would be best served by having both Zara and Eve in their lives.

The kids must be bonding with Zara and her husband. How could tearing them away to be returned to Eve be a benefit? Wasn't it possible for Sammy and Charlotte to have their mom *and* their aunt and uncle?

Her phone buzzed, and she took it out of her pocket. A text from Bruce. *Call me when you can.* There'd been an odd feeling between them since Eve moved in. It wasn't like he was angry— this was his idea after all. It was more like they didn't know how to find their new roles. Eve wasn't Lindsay. That was a mantra that played over and over in Tiff's head, and she wondered if it did for Bruce too. Why couldn't she just ask him?

She swiped at her phone until it was ready for her to hit the call button, but she hesitated. Maybe he'd had enough and wanted Eve out. She couldn't go back on their promise to let her stay. She'd done nothing wrong.

Tiff made the call and lifted the phone to her ear as she exited the building. The receptionist didn't need to hear her personal business. Confidentiality pertained to Tiff too.

He answered on the first ring, which startled her. "Hello."

"Hi. What's up?"

"Well . . ." She could picture him sitting back in his desk chair. "I might have a job opportunity for Eve."

Tiff's mouth fell open. "Seriously?"

"It's not much, but it's a start. One of the custodians in the office quit suddenly. She had to go out of state to take care of a relative or something. I've already spoken to the lead. He says he'll give her a try. It's part-time right now, but there's a real likelihood it will become full-time in the next couple of months."

Tiff's throat tightened. Her husband wasn't a bad man. Not at all. He'd gone far out of his way for Eve. She'd even be working in his building, which in Bruce's mind, would make her a reflection of him.

"What's wrong? Did I do something wrong?"

"No. The opposite."

"So, you think she might be interested?"

"She's in her visit right now, but yes, I'm sure she will be. I'll talk to her on the way home."

"All right, then. See you tonight."

"Wait." Tiff struggled with the words. There seemed to be more emotion than could fit into any combinations of letters. "Thank you. You didn't have to do this."

"I'll see you tonight." He disconnected.

Bruce was a man with a big heart. She'd nearly forgotten. When things had started to get rough with Lindsay, there had been so much tension—blame, even. They'd thrown it at each other without uttering a word when, really, it was pain that plagued them. They were broken by what they saw happening to their daughter and powerless to fix what they couldn't understand.

Through the window, Tiff saw Eve enter the waiting room. Tears streamed down her face, and she looked around like a child who'd lost her mother in a crowded store.

She shoved the phone back into her purse and went to Eve. "Are you okay?"

Eve sniffled and nodded.

If Tiff had the chance to do things over again, she would pry into Lindsay's life more, ask the questions, insist on communication. But Eve wasn't her daughter. She couldn't force her to tell what was going on inside her mind. Instead, Tiff tried to make the moment lighter. She looped her arm through Eve's. "How about some ice cream? I have some great news for you."

CHAPTER THIRTY-ONE

ZARA LAY IN BED AT FIVE A.M., watching the sky change from black to deep blue. So many thoughts swirled in her head, too many to be contained by dreams.

She and Chad couldn't show up to the DHS training in a car with a missing back window, and they couldn't go in her old pickup. Chad had been very patient in driving the beast to work since the kids came home. She sighed. She really needed to be careful about thinking of their house as *home* for the children.

Scrolling through her phone, Zara finally found a place with online reservations that could take care of the window that morning. Chad could drop it off and pick it up on the way home, but they still needed to locate a babysitter. From what she'd Googled, the going rate even for teens was more than they could afford. When life fell neatly into place, Zara automatically braced for something terrible to happen. Yet, when her life was in chaos, she showed up, better equipped to face a challenge than not.

Pickles jumped on the bed and started licking her face.

"Not yet," Chad grumbled, then rolled over.

"I've got him." Zara slipped out of bed and pulled her socks back onto her feet. Scooping the dog into her arms, she avoided the mess he'd make on the bare wood stairs.

In the kitchen, Pickles agreed to go outside but immediately wanted back in for breakfast. This wasn't a good habit to start, but neither was waking the kids before dawn with the whines of a hungry puppy.

Chad's phone buzzed from where it sat on the counter. She looked at the screen. It was a text from Sharon.

What was her mother-in-law doing up so early? The doctors had confirmed a break in her ankle, but she was fortunate that was the only fracture. Even so, they'd kept her overnight for observation and to monitor her blood pressure, which had risen to concerning levels since being there. Zara swiped the screen and read her message. *I'm so sorry I can't watch the kids this weekend.*

Zara's heart sank. Even confined to a hospital bed, Sharon was worried about them. Since first meeting her, Zara had wondered how her life and Eve's would have been different with a mother like Sharon.

A noise caught her off guard, and Zara's toe caught the lift of the floor going into the dining room. She stumbled and hit her right knee hard, sending a jolt of pain up her leg that left her queasy for a minute. She steadied herself and made her way to the bottom of the stairs, straining to hear it again.

Nothing. She'd banged up her knee out of sheer paranoia.

Then it came again—Charlotte crying out, "No. No. No."

Zara took off, motivated by the fear of Sammy waking up and also by her need to help Charlotte. When she got to their room, Chad was one step ahead of her. He knelt by the top of Charlotte's bed, and Zara took a seat by her feet.

"Hey, sweetie, wake up." Chad brushed the hair from her face.

Her eyes opened slowly; then she sprang fully awake, looking back and forth between the two of them as if they were strangers and she'd been abducted.

Zara fumbled with the right words to say, not wanting to scare her any further. "You're safe. You're at the farm, remember?" She longed to hug Charlotte, but that seemed to hold its own dangers.

Anger flamed in the little girl's face. "Get out of my room! I don't want you in here."

"Okay." Zara stepped back a couple of paces. "We wanted to help. You seemed like you were having a bad dream."

Sammy began to wail, and Zara turned to pick him up, leaving Chad to figure out how to deal with the irrational five-year-old. They'd seen this kind of thing before with Charlotte. Any time she got hurt or felt like they were laughing at her, she'd slip into a rage. It seemed to be a defense against embarrassment.

Sammy was the opposite. He reached for Zara when anything distressing happened. She took him in her arms and walked into the master bedroom.

Their kids—these kids—were vulnerable. They needed such patience and love. Where was she going to find someone who could take care of them while she and Chad were at a mandatory training? It couldn't be just anyone. Zara needed to trust that person.

That's when her phone buzzed. She reached for it and read the text, Sammy slumped over her shoulder while slurping on something, probably the neck of her pajama shirt. Trinity had heard about Sharon being in the hospital and wanted to know if there was anything they needed.

Could she really ask? Trinity had said before that she wanted to support them in fostering the kids. She said she'd do whatever it took to make this easier for all four of them. And she'd done such an amazing job with getting them through the home study process. They couldn't have done it without Trinity and the rest of the crew from church. Maybe Zara *could* ask.

But this wasn't the kind of thing you sent in a text. Charlotte's screams had quieted, so she made the call.

"Hello?" Somehow, this woman sounded cheerful all the time. As if every single conversation was a privilege for her to partake in.

"Hi, Trinity. This is Zara Mahoney."

"I know. Your name popped onto my screen. I'm so sorry Sharon is struggling. Is there something I can help with?"

"Well, maybe. Chad and I are supposed to be at a mandatory foster parent training this weekend. Sharon was going to keep the kids."

"Foundations Training. Yes. I've actually gone through the process. My husband and I do shelter care from time to time."

That sounded like something to do with the Humane Society instead of kids. "What's that?"

"Temporary emergency foster care. Do you need me to help with childcare this weekend?"

It was kind of like she made the offer without Zara's even having to ask. Could she really be that lucky? "Well, yes. Could you?"

"I'll have to move a few things around. Can I get back to you in the next hour?"

"Of course. You'd be doing us a huge favor."

"And I'd love it. Thanks. Talk soon." She hung up.

That was too easy.

Charlotte and Chad walked into the room. Her eyes were still red, but she was now up in his arms and seemed to have settled. "Who was that on the phone?" Chad asked.

"Trinity. She offered to watch the kids this weekend if she can adjust her schedule."

"That's great news!" He looked at Charlotte. "Did you hear that? You and Sammy get to spend some time with Miss Trinity." His tone was so light and cheery, Zara almost gave in to the enthusiasm. But what did they even know about this woman?

Eve

June 21, 2019

Yesterday was hard. The kids didn't seem to want to be with me. Charlotte asked three times if she could go now. Apparently, she and Zara had plants to put in the garden. My daughter never had the opportunity to dig in the dirt or play on a farm until I messed up and my sister was able to give her every child's dream. And here I am, doing my very best to get her back and take her away from all that. I know in my heart that what I'm doing is right, but my brain keeps reminding me I'm the worst person I know.

Bruce got me a real chance at a job. I meet with the boss tomorrow. It's cleaning, but it's during the day, which makes it easier to get childcare when the kids are back with me. I'll also have random drug tests. I like that. The pressure of having to stay clean—I need it.

Tiff took me to a meeting for addicts after the visit today. She waited in the car the whole time. That's the kind of mother I want to be.

ZARA WAS MORE THAN A LITTLE JEALOUS that Chad had visited his mother during his lunch hour. But taking the kids to the hospital seemed like a bad idea for everyone in the building. By five that night, she was full of jitters about their childcare arrangement. Both Trinity and Chad should be there any moment; then Chad and Zara would be off to their first night of training. They'd never left the kids with anyone. The panic and fear caught her by surprise. She'd counted on at least the first time being with Sharon. What if something happened? What if Sammy and Charlotte needed them?

Her husband was the first to arrive. He walked in smelling of coffee and hand sanitizer. Zara crinkled her nose.

"I know. I stink like the stuff from the front desk. There's a nasty stomach bug going through the office." He kissed her. "I thought you'd rather I stink than give you that yuck."

"Smart man."

Sammy pounded on the tray of his high chair. Mealtime for

this boy had become an event. He tried to convince Zara at least ten times a day that they should eat. She had a strong feeling his underweight days were coming to a quick end. Monday they would see the doctor again. Excitement bubbled in her belly when she thought of that appointment, as if she'd accomplished something heroic by putting some fat on a toddler.

"Is Trinity here yet?" He looked around.

"No. I let Charlotte watch a program while I made dinner."

"Aw. That explains the relative quiet." He took a sliced carrot from the cutting board and popped it in his mouth, then gave a couple slices of apple to Sammy. "You are growing up into a very big boy."

Sammy responded with a smile that shone with the sliver of a new tooth that had finally popped through his swollen gums that morning.

"I was wondering about that." She stared at the rounding face with chunks of apple clinging to his chin. "I gathered from bits and pieces of information that the man who beat Eve was his biological father. Do you ever wonder what he looks like?"

Chad shrugged. "I'd be very happy if I never have to know. The kind of man who would do that to a woman—and the kids were in the house. It's sick."

She was about to respond in agreement when Trinity's cheery voice sang through the open door. "Hey there." She went right to Sammy. "How are you doing, little man?"

Zara's first instinct, one she'd learned to mostly stuff, was ready to answer for Sammy with a snide retort. *Bite that tongue.* Instead, she went with what she'd rehearsed for their first babysitter. "Thank you for getting here early. I've made out a list of how the nighttime routine goes. The kids can be tough." Zara went on to explain Charlotte's overreactions and Sammy's need to be within sight of her at all times.

"No problem. It can be rough with kiddos who've been through traumatic experiences. Last year I was certified to teach TBRI classes."

Zara looked to Chad, who shrugged. "What's TBRI?"

"Trauma-Based Relational Intervention. They may bring it up at your training. I'll make sure you're on the email list if you're interested. We always have childcare on site, and the classes count toward your learning hours for DHS."

Trinity had just spewed out more information than Zara's exhausted brain could take in. The class tonight could be an all-out waste of time for her. She did all the nodding and thanking she knew she should, then said good-bye to the kids. Chad and Zara were finally off together, alone.

How was it possible that, after only a few weeks, she felt a rise of panic at leaving them behind? And how must the extended time of separation feel for her sister?

CHAPTER THIRTY-TWO

By Sunday afternoon, Zara couldn't listen to another word from another person. They'd gone through a training manual the size of a compact car, and yet she didn't feel any more prepared to care for Charlotte's and Sammy's needs than she had before the weekend of endless lectures.

The most helpful source of education came from the foster parent panel on Saturday morning. After that, Zara was both scared and encouraged. Seasoned foster moms spoke about the devastation and grief, as well as the joy they'd experienced when children were reunified with their parents. They talked about the incredible changes they saw in children living in their homes, and they told about the trials of getting everything done. These were her people, the ones who had no issue admitting they were barely keeping their noses above the surface of the to-do list.

To top off her exhaustion, each night they'd come home to glowing reports about perfect childhood days. Then Trinity would leave and the chaos would resume. Bath time. Pajamas. Just one more story. And another drink of water. Prayers while hoping everyone was still there when they opened their eyes.

All the craziness just served to remind Zara that their home could be very empty in a few months. She'd seen the caseworker on Saturday. Kelly wouldn't give details, but she said Eve was promising to be one of her greatest success stories.

Chad and Zara drove home in near silence, each mulling over what they'd learned during the training. Zara reached her hand into her purse and found the folded-up paper from Tiff, its edges softened. What was stopping her from making a connection that could be a step toward her sister and seeing these kids grow up?

When they got to the house, even the dog barked at them, a bad start. Apparently, they'd been gone so long they were being replaced by Miss Perfection.

Inside, all Zara's horrible, rotten, never-let-them-out-of-her-head dreams came true. Sammy was crying, his only consolation being in her arms. Charlotte lunged into Chad's embrace, and Trinity—Zara felt bad for even thinking this—looked like the kids had run her over repeatedly with a Tonka truck.

What did it say about Zara that she could take joy in the pain of others? She didn't know. But she fully intended to blame it on pure exhaustion.

"How did it go today?" Her guts tightened with a tiny dose of shame at asking the question when she could see the answer written on Trinity's face.

"Well, we didn't make it to church. I don't know how you do it. We usually only have one at a time. I think I've had my workouts for the week. But, Zara, please don't hesitate to call me if you need any more childcare. It's hard, but you're a hero, doing it every day. I really want to be there for you."

All of Zara's superiority faded away, leaving her a touch scuffed up by her own self-centered nature. "We couldn't do it without you." No truer words, as they say. She and Chad wouldn't have passed even the first steps to bring the children home if it wasn't for Trinity. So what had made Zara so snarky when it came to her?

Eve immediately popped to mind. She'd always told Zara she had to be the best, and there was no room for anyone else. Oh, Zara wished she hadn't remembered that right then.

She'd do it tomorrow. She'd call Tiff Bradley and see what she could do to help her sister get Charlotte and Sammy back—even if it meant ripping them from her heart.

Eve
June 24, 2019

My first day on the job was amazing. The building where Bruce works has real security. I was safe and felt like I belonged. Even the people in the offices treated me kindly.

For now, I work alongside the boss. He's respectful, and I really like him. He told me that once, about ten years ago, he was living on the streets, using a bunch of meth. It's hard to believe he isn't lying to me. This guy is the boss of a whole crew of janitors. He makes the schedule, does the hiring, and orders the supplies. It's obvious people here trust him. I wonder if I'll ever be trusted like that.

I work only part-time, which allows me to make my court date today and have visits with the kids. Even though I'm innocent of the charges I'm facing, it's not like I haven't committed the same crimes in the past and not gotten caught.

Bruce drove me back to the house after my shift. He's a nice man, but he's all bottled up, like someone who might have a deadly heart attack. I was glad to hear him say that he doesn't think I'll be facing any jail time. I sure hope he's right.

IN THE TIME TIFF HAD BEEN WORKING with women on the streets, she'd never gone into a courtroom. There was a line drawn there, a mark she didn't cross over. Tiff saw her role as someone who offered a few needed things, let them know she cared, and provided information about the resources available to change the patterns of their lives. In a way she hadn't considered before, she had been keeping herself protected, not getting too close.

Bruce had pulled her aside when he came home for lunch. Eve had gone in to take a quick shower after work and before they were to head out and appear before the judge. In the few minutes they had, her husband gave her a rundown of all he'd learned from a friend of his who was a criminal attorney. This could go one way or another. If Eve didn't get the offer to participate in drug treatment court, she was looking at possible jail time.

It was naïve, but Tiff was certain Eve did not steal that ring or buy the drugs.

Eve was quiet during the drive to the county courthouse, but she sat straighter than any time before. Bruce was right—getting a job was good for her.

They found a place to park a block away. Tiff paid the meter, and together they walked under the maple trees that lined the path to the front steps. "Are you nervous about today?"

Eve shook her head. "There's nothing I can do about what happens in here." On the top step, she turned toward Tiff. "Do you think I'm doing the right thing—with the kids, I mean?"

"I don't understand. From all I've seen, you're working very hard to get your children back. You're staying clean and passing your weekly drug tests. You have a job. Soon, you'll be able to get your own place. You're going in the right direction, Eve."

"I know. And I'm proud of what I'm doing. But I just wonder if I'm being selfish . . . if the kids would be better off with Zara." She stepped through the giant door and up to the security officer.

Tiff put her cell phone, keys, and purse in a tray and set them on the belt to the scanner. "Do you even know if Zara would be willing to keep the kids forever?"

Eve's mouth opened, but she couldn't seem to find the words she wanted to say.

"Ms. Brookes, Mrs. Bradley." The attorney that had been assigned to Eve walked toward them.

Tiff picked up her belongings at the end of the row.

"You're right on time." The lawyer wasn't a tall man. He topped out at about Tiff's chin level, giving her an unfortunate view of his thinning hair. "Judge Carmen is a fair man. I think you'll like him."

He led them down the hall and turned into courtroom two.

This building was historic, one of the oldest still in use in the state of Oregon. The woodwork spoke to the age and the commitment once held to promoting law and order. If the people who planned this fine courthouse had known what the future of their beloved community would be, they might not have bothered with the hand-carved detail work that surrounded them.

They took their seats on the first row of benches.

Eve fingered her journal, which poked out of the top of her bag. She didn't go anywhere without it.

When the judge entered, they all rose, no doubt looking like a scene from a television drama.

At the call of her name, Eve went forward.

"Ms. Brookes, I see here you're charged with possession of stolen property and possession of a controlled substance." He laced his fingers and leaned his chin on his knuckles. "Do you have children?"

Eve nodded.

"And I assume you want to stay out of prison and away from drugs for the sake of those children?"

"Yes, your honor."

"I've spoken with the assistant DA as well as your attorney.

We'd like to give you an opportunity, but it will involve hard work on your part. Do you understand?"

"Yes . . . Your Honor."

"I'm agreeing to give you drug treatment court in lieu of going forward with these charges. If you fail at any time, the drug court judge, who just happens to be me, has the right to go forward with prosecution. Is this something you'd like to agree to?"

Eve looked back at Tiff, a slight smile bringing life to her features.

Tiff nodded, hoping that was enough to convey her approval and confidence in the future Eve was claiming.

Looking back toward the judge, she cleared her throat. "I would like that. Yes."

"Great." He didn't smile, but his deep eyes gave away his pleasure. "Your attorney will inform you of the requirements. We meet in this courtroom every Wednesday at one o'clock. Do not be late. Do not be absent."

Tiff wished Zara were there to see this new beginning. If she would call, Tiff was sure she'd be able to help her see what Eve had been through. Reconciliation could be the answer to happiness for both them and the kids. There'd been times when Tiff felt so much anger toward Lindsay for her addiction. She hadn't been able to understand then why her daughter didn't stop using and become the girl she'd been before. The expectations and reality were so out of line with each other. Maybe that was what kept Zara and Eve apart.

Eve

June 24, 2019

Tiff's enthusiasm was contagious. I left the courtroom today feeling like I was at the beginning of a new life, one that would be healthy and happy. It was going to be a life I could give my children and that would leave them with good memories of growing up loved.

If only I hadn't needed to use the restroom. If only Tiff had gone along with me instead of having a conversation with a police officer she knew. If I could turn back time, I'd go back and hold it until we got home.

But I didn't.

The bathroom is in the bottom of the old building. It feels like walking into a dungeon down there, so I was already on edge. When I came out of the stall, a woman I know who worked for Joey's cousin stood by the sink, blocking the door. My first reaction was to look for cameras, any kind of security, but even in a courthouse, the bathroom is considered too private for that kind of access.

I started washing my hands as if nothing was out of the norm.

"Do you know who I am?" She turned on the water in her sink, then leaned forward, one hand on each side of the porcelain.

I told her I did as I finished up, trying my very hardest to seem calm as I rinsed and dried.

"Joey says you've got the police after him. He says if they arrest him, you'll pay the price."

My heart thundered. I was so scared. At first, I thought she meant that he was going to kill me, but then she got specific. I would be going to prison for a whole lineup of crimes he'd conveniently tied to me. And he had people willing to say they saw me selling drugs to minors and stealing from a neighborhood near our old place. Apparently, there was also a storage locker somewhere rented under my name filled with some of my things and boxes of stolen merchandise. Even the owner there was willing to testify against me.

When I didn't say anything, she leaned close. "He's the father of your boy. If you go off to prison, what's to stop him from taking the kid?"

Those are the words that have been screaming through my head since I left that cell of a bathroom. Even if I do every single thing to get clean and sober. Even if I do great at my job, get an education, and bring my kids back home, I'll always be under someone's thumb.

Yet Joey told me he loved me—once upon a time.

CHAPTER THIRTY-THREE

EVE WENT TO BED RIGHT AFTER helping Tiff clean up the dinner dishes. Tiff asked if she was feeling okay, but she insisted she was only tired. There'd been a lot of changes for Eve, and so she figured that could be true. On top of the new job and court, leaving heroin behind seemed to make her very prone to periods of sadness. Having the children out of her care probably didn't help either, but Tiff planned to ask her in the morning about getting a doctor's appointment.

Bruce entered the kitchen with his empty milk glass and set it in the clean sink. "Patrick went on and on today about Eve. He says she works twice as hard as any of his other employees."

"That's great." Tiff gave him a look, but he didn't seem to understand her meaning, so she sidestepped an argument and put the cup into the dishwasher herself.

"What happened at drug court is really good news." He leaned up against the counter. "Do you think she'll make it through?"

Tiff shrugged. "I think so. There's a lot on the line."

His head bobbed up and down like a bobblehead. "I suppose that's true, but she can't do this to get the kids back. Remember how we tried to push Lindsay to get her act together? We even offered her trips, a car, anything."

"A new car is hardly the same thing as a woman's children."

"True enough, but I still believe, if she's to be successful, she needs to do this because she wants it. You and I both know that things happen. Kids grow up."

"And she'll be alone."

"Maybe. Maybe not. We're not alone." He took her hand and kissed it gently, like he had when they were dating. "I'm praying that somewhere down the line, she finds a wonderful man to share her life with, like you did." His face brightened with a teasing smile.

Tiff walked into his embrace. "We've made it through some tough stuff."

"That we have, sugar." He kissed the top of her head, and she relaxed into the echo of that term of endearment she hadn't heard since before Lindsay started slipping away.

Eve
June 30, 2019

I'm scared every minute of every day. If I didn't feel like my taking a hit of heroin would be a huge kick to the Bradleys and my children, I would. But I can't take any risk of Sammy ending up in Joey's care, or Charlotte in Chaz's. What was I thinking? Two children by two different men, and both are at best, dangerous.

I told that woman when she approached me in the bathroom to let Joey know I had his back. I wouldn't testify against him or help the police locate him. It's not like I was ever able to find him when I needed to anyway. I pose no threat to him.

Joey has already spent time inside. He's actually done a

couple of stints. I guess he's worried about how long they'll give him if they get hold of him. Maybe he should just disappear. That would be best for all of us.

Or maybe I should.

The longer I stay clean, the more things I remember, the more I want to use so I can forget. Tiff is all faith and forgiveness. I pretended I was too tired this morning to go with them to church. The lie left a bad taste in my mouth all morning. I should have gone. Being alone brings temptations I would never admit to anyone else. This place is full of pricey stuff that would get me back in good with Joey and get me so high I wouldn't have the capacity to feel bad about what I'd done. All it would take was a phone call, and I could have the place emptied.

But I didn't do it. Not this time.

Reasons to stay clean:

1. To protect Charlotte from Chaz

2. To protect Sammy from a life like Joey's

3. To thank Tiff and Bruce

4. To show Zara

5. Because I'll lose my job if I use

SHARON HAD BEEN STAYING AT HOME with the help of one of her other daughters-in-law and Walter, but the doctor said she was in great shape. The break was clean, and the recovery should be fairly straightforward.

While Zara took Sammy in for his follow-up doctor's appointment, Chad took his lunch hour with Charlotte at Sharon's house, which meant less trauma for their girl and for Zara. She couldn't handle another pediatric meltdown for a while.

Zara checked in with the front desk, being sure they'd received

Sammy's records from the last doctor he saw. The woman at reception nodded but didn't seem very friendly today.

From the weight pulling on her left shoulder, Zara could already guarantee that Sammy had gained significant weight. She set him down, and he ran to the fish tank in the corner of the room. At some point, he'd lost that adorable toddle, replacing it with speed and balance.

"Fissy." He pointed to the glass.

"That's right. You're saying so many words now." She wondered if he was showing off his new skill to Eve at their visits. "Look, there's a blue fishy."

"Boo fissy." Sammy jumped up and down like a lottery winner.

"Samuel. We're all ready for you." A nurse in pink scrubs held the door open.

She ushered them into the same examination room they'd had before.

Zara's first thought on entering was the memory of Charlotte's panicked screams, her red and sweaty face. She didn't know how, but she'd do anything she could to keep the little girl healthy to avoid extra visits.

"Let's get a weight, then Dr. Kiddle will be in to talk with you."

Zara knew the routine now, which made her feel like a real mother. She stripped off Sammy's clothes.

He giggled as she tugged on each sock.

When he was bare naked, Zara set him on the scale, making funny faces to keep him from climbing off.

"Look at that." The nurse nodded toward the digital readout. "He's gained a couple more pounds. You must be feeding him bricks."

She picked him up and got the diaper on before they had an unfortunate shower. "I think bricks are about the only thing he isn't eating. I'm afraid of what he'll put away as a teenager." Even as the last words were working their way out of her mouth, she felt the sting of loss. Zara wouldn't be there when Sammy was a teen, when he went from sweet little Sammy to tall and broad Sam. She had to find a way back into Eve's life if only so she didn't miss watching the kids grow up.

"Dr. Kiddle will be in here very soon. He had to calm down a new dad after first shots. You know how that can be."

Zara didn't know. She hadn't even known Sammy or Charlotte when they were that tiny. She'd missed too much, and all because she'd thought Eve would get her life together and search her out. Her sister was right. She was a self-centered jerk.

When the doctor came into the room, she could see concern in his eyes. Was she feeding Sammy too much? Could he gain too quickly? Zara would have thunked herself in the forehead if she were alone. Of course he could. Obesity had to be worse than being underweight, or at least as bad.

"We received Samuel's medical records." Dr. Kiddle sat on the short stool and pressed his palms together. "There wasn't much there. Unfortunately, he's had little in the way of medical care since birth."

The air in the room grew thin, and she gasped for oxygen. "What about the test for Hunter syndrome? He had that, right?"

The time between her question and his answer stretched out across the room, taking out all the hope and joy and replacing it with fear.

"But he's healthy, right? You'd know if there was a problem, if he had Hunter?"

"I know you were hoping for more. As we talked about before, having a negative test on file would be the perfect answer. But that's not what we have. We're left with an unknown for the time being. But you're right that Samuel is healthy—now. I've done a little research into the syndrome, and it appears that there are no visual ways to tell if he will get the disease at this age. We can do a urine test. It won't be definitive, but it will give us a clue. If there are signs in the urine, we'll move on to the more complicated test."

"Okay. Let's do that." She held Sammy tight until he started to squirm and whine. "Is there anything we can do . . . if it's positive?" Embarrassing tears blurred her vision. She couldn't stop them from streaming down her face. Zara wasn't an emotional person. She was controlled. In charge. And now, a complete wreck.

"I'm not sure how this works with a child in foster care. We're going to have to check on the insurance coverage, and honestly, there's a lot of strange thinking when it comes to kids and genetic testing."

"But we need the information. I have to know if he's . . ." She couldn't hold back anymore. "I need to get home. I have to get Charlotte from Chad. His mom has a broken ankle." Why was she saying all of this? The need to get away from Dr. Kiddle was like the need to breathe. It consumed her and forced her to comply.

Losing her son—her nephew—wasn't an option.

She grabbed her bag, keeping Sammy held to her chest, and bumbled from the exam room, through the hall and waiting room, then into the fresh air.

He had to be wrong. Dr. Kiddle was just a smallish-town doctor. Maybe he'd made a mistake, or they didn't get all the records. Eve was a mess, but she wasn't an idiot. She'd have had Sammy tested. Even the hospital would have thought of that when he was born. It had to have happened. Yet Zara hadn't considered what caused Tyson's death until she was about to be married. Why would Eve, with all of her other problems, suddenly be so responsible?

The receptionist watched her through the large window.

Zara opened the car and buckled Sammy into his seat, taking an extra minute to examine his facial features. There was a slight broadening along the bridge of his nose, and he looked remarkably like Tyson. Why hadn't she seen that before?

Leaning down, Zara kissed his forehead. Safety had evaporated. She'd assumed Sammy was secured by medical testing, but there was little in life that came without risk.

As Zara climbed behind the steering wheel and drove out of the parking lot, her thoughts drew back to the moment she found out she was a carrier, how her fear of watching another child die was so encompassing that she would have left home and lived as a recluse in the mountains to keep her genetic flaws from leading to another round of grief.

Yet here she was, her heart attached to the little boy behind her. In any circumstance, she couldn't walk away from him of her own will. He had become part of her, not because they shared DNA, but because she'd held him, cared for him, and given him the part of herself that Zara had kept guarded.

If it meant watching Sammy live and seeing him die, she would do that. This must be what motherhood really came down to.

Eventually, somewhere down the line, when Chad and Zara were ready to build their family, Zara would have no doubts about adoption. Charlotte and Sammy had taught her that love was not biological. She'd seen it with her husband. His love for these two was nothing smaller or less than hers. And the fact that she didn't give birth to them didn't diminish the depth of her love, either.

When they arrived at Sharon's, Sammy was sound asleep in his car seat. Zara texted Chad that they were there, but she couldn't leave the car. A few minutes later, he and Charlotte popped out of the front door.

Chad buckled Charlotte in, then looked Zara over carefully. "What's going on? Did something happen?"

She bit her bottom lip until her emotions were forced back

down. "Sammy didn't have the testing. We don't know if he'll get Hunter."

Chad's mouth fell open, and tears flushed his eyes. He pulled Zara into his warm embrace. "We're going to be okay. So is Sammy."

"Your faith is mighty big."

"As big as a mustard seed."

She smiled a little at the reference to something the pastor had said at their wedding. He'd read the Scripture about the mustard seed, then reminded them that faith in both God and in each other would help them to live their best lives together. Zara sure hadn't thought they'd be tested on that so soon.

When they finally pulled back, she and Chad shared knowing smiles. They were a team, and together they'd fight whatever came their way.

"Do you have a minute to sit with the kids?" She ran her fingers through the side of his hair. "I'd like to see your mom."

"Of course." He glanced at his watch.

"I'll make it fast."

Inside, the house was immaculate, like always. A tiny bit of her might have been hoping to find at least a couple things out of place, maybe just a spoon in the sink. She found Sharon in the living room, leaning back in her recliner. Though the chair had been in this place near the picture window since the first time she'd come to Chad's childhood home, Zara had never seen her mother-in-law sitting there. "Hey, Sharon. I wanted to see how you're doing."

"Oh." She started to get up, but Zara motioned for her to stay seated, and to her shock, Sharon complied. "I didn't hear you come in. I'm doing much better." There was a frailty in her voice that Zara had never heard before. "The doctor says I'll be back to my old self in a few weeks."

"That's so great to hear. I hope Charlotte wasn't too much to have around today."

A precious smile glowed on her face. "No way. She was the

highlight. Exactly what I needed. If I wasn't so tired and sore, I'd be begging you for some time with Sammy too."

"I know you would." Zara swept her gaze around the living room. Sharon had been married to Chad's father for nearly forty years, until he had a massive heart attack and died in front of her. They'd had all sorts of plans for retirement, travel, and grand-children. Sharon hadn't planned her life like this—living alone, none of her four kids having kids of their own yet.

His death had happened the year before Zara arrived on the scene. She'd never known the man who everyone said was a mountain of fluff and love, but she saw him in his son. Sharon had always been so strong, yet Zara wondered what it had been like during those first weeks of widowhood. Had she wept? Did she manage to keep the house perfect when her body felt crushed under the weight of loss? She wondered about those things be-cause she'd been running from any chance of grief since the day of her brother's death. She'd even run away from Eve because, in her heart, she'd known how far her sister had strayed. She couldn't stand to be there when Eve finally went too far and they couldn't bring her back.

"Can I come back and talk with you sometime soon? I need your help understanding a few things."

Sharon reached out her hand, still bruised from the IV, a re-minder that she'd only just been released from the hospital.

Zara covered it with her own.

"You are welcome here any time, Zara. You're one of my kids. I hope you really understand that."

Zara's nose tickled as emotion tried to work its way out of the depths. "Thank you. I'd better get out there so Chad can get to work."

She nodded, a smile in place as it always was. "Take care of yourself. I'm praying for the four of you."

Outside, Zara found Chad leaning in at Sammy's window, his forefinger stroking the skin of the sleeping boy's arm. Next to him, Charlotte pretended to change the diaper of her baby doll. Not much time had passed since the children had come to live with them, but they'd all changed. Zara's heart was open for the first time in years, and it would almost certainly lead her to grief, but when she let herself take in the beauty of these children, there was no doubt they were worth it.

A therapist might have said Zara was finally healing. Truthfully, she thought she'd only just begun to grow up.

CHAPTER THIRTY-FOUR

TIFF'S HOUSE FELT VACANT AGAIN, empty without Eve. She'd gone to work that morning along with Bruce, the two of them deep in conversation as they left, each with a take-along coffee mug. Tiff's heart was warmed by the way they'd developed a kind of friendship. It had been great for Eve, showing her what a man could be like, but it was even better for Bruce. He was healing . . . finally. When she looked at him, Tiff saw the open wounds of Lindsay's death slowly turning into scars.

While Eve was doing better than she ever could have imagined, Tiff found herself lonely when she was gone, as if her presence had become something Tiff had become a little dependent on. It wouldn't be long before Eve moved into her own place. She'd gotten more hours already, and her boss was eager to move her to full-time. When she wasn't working, Eve was at Narcotics Anonymous meetings. She called them NA, and they seemed to be giving her a new measure of hope.

Tiff set her own coffee cup in the sink, not bothering to rinse it, and walked to the wall of windows, where she stared out at the valley below their home. Comparisons were being made in her heart, though she knew she shouldn't allow them. Tiff wondered what was different between Eve and Lindsay. Why couldn't her daughter have made the strides she'd seen in Eve?

Most of the time, Tiff ended up with the same conclusions. She was the difference. She hadn't known how to help her own daughter. Tiff was selfish, so worried about how the world would see her if her child was known as an addict. She should have cut through all that static and solely been Lindsay's mom, her advocate.

Tiff's phone chirped with the new ringtone Eve had helped her install.

When she checked, the number wasn't familiar, but she answered anyway.

The voice that came through the cell sounded so much like Eve, but without the hesitations she'd grown used to. "Hi. This is Zara, Eve's sister."

"Zara. Yes . . . I know who you are." Tiff thought back to the slip of paper she'd given her with this number. After all this time, she'd figured Zara didn't want any contact. "How can I help you?"

"Is Eve with you?"

"No. She's at work right now. Do you want me to have her call you back?"

"I don't know. There are things I need to tell her, but I . . ." Tiff waited so long, she wondered if Zara was even still there. "I'm not sure how. It's been too long."

"It's never too late, as long as you're both still breathing."

"Do you really think that's true?"

Tiff wandered through her own memories, looking for a map that would lead Zara and Eve together. Addiction didn't come with an easy path. But hope still existed. How could she make Zara understand this when she hadn't been able to herself when it mattered most? "Would you be willing to meet me for coffee?" As soon as she offered, she wanted to pull the question back. Why would she? Tiff was a stranger.

"Yes, I'd like that. A friend is coming over to watch the kids this afternoon so I can get groceries. Could you meet in an hour?"

"Absolutely. Do you know that artsy shop on Buchanan?"

"Coffee Dreams?"

"That's the one. How about there?"

"I'll see you in an hour." She hung up.

Eve wasn't there to ask, and Tiff wasn't sure she'd be okay with her talking to Zara, but there were so many pieces to this. She needed to share her experience, because it spoke more to what Zara was going through than to Eve's situation.

Tiff arrived early, ordered a latte, and sat toward the back of the coffee shop. It was a trendy place, designed more like a rustic art gallery with tables, stools, and couches. Most of the people here seemed to be hard at work, tapping away on laptops and tablets. A few chatted with friends. Near her was a table of four older men, each taking turns ranting about how he could fix all the problems of the world. She couldn't help but wonder why all their issues still existed if these guys had the answers.

It wasn't hard to spot Zara. As Eve grew healthier, the resemblance expanded. There was something so sad about identical twins who no longer had identical faces. Eve looked like the older sister, with scars and lines etched by hard times and poor choices. When Tiff had first met her, she was gaunt, her hair thin and damaged, her features hidden behind a mask of makeup.

Zara seemed to prefer a natural look, and it suited her. The brilliant blue of her eyes sparkled against her summer-tanned complexion. Her hair, soft and smooth, was pulled into a ponytail like it had been the last time Tiff had seen her. It wasn't hard to envision Zara with a baseball cap on, working in the garden. Tiff had looked over her website. She'd done well for herself.

"Tiff?" The smile on her face seemed more than a little

forced, but who wouldn't have reservations with all she'd been through?

Tiff stood, felt awkward, and sat back down. "Do you want something to drink?" Cupping her hand around her mug, Tiff let the warmth calm her. She should have waited and bought Zara's coffee. Her ability to act civilized was slipping.

"No. At least not yet. I'm feeling pretty jumpy already, without caffeine." She pulled out a chair, scraping it along the floor, and sat. "How's Eve really doing? Kelly says she's making progress, but that's not much of an answer."

"Eve's done better than I ever could have hoped for. She's strong, and she loves the kids so much."

Zara looked away, casting her gaze at a painting of two men and a cow.

"I'm sure losing her the way you did had to be hard."

She nodded.

"I understand."

Zara turned her face back to Tiff, her eyebrows furrowed. "I don't think so. No one really understands where I'm coming from. There's a team for Eve, and I'm so glad you're there for her. Everyone at DHS understands what it's like for women who lose custody of their children. They seem to know all the steps and have the whole process of reunification down to a science. But who gets what it's like to meet two little people you didn't know existed, to see your own eyes looking back at you, and know they could be ripped away at any moment, never to be seen by you again?"

"You're right." Tiff clasped her hands in her lap, trying to hold them back from touching Zara's arm the way she would with Eve. "I don't understand all you're going through. I never should have said that. What I understand is what it's like to lose someone very close to you to addiction."

Her head tipped to the side, but Zara had no response.

"My daughter, Lindsay, started using heroin and meth during

her junior year of high school. We knew she was hanging out with a guy we weren't fond of, but we thought we'd raised her to make good decisions. We thought this could never happen to us." Feeling the waves of grief riding up her body once again, Tiff took a deep breath. "It wasn't a matter of making good or bad decisions after that one time. That's all it took. She tried heroin while she was supposed to be at a sleepover with her best friend. It wasn't just her—a few of the other girls tried it too—but for my Lindsay, it stuck. For some reason, she got a bad roll of the dice. Lindsay spent the rest of her life searching for the high she got that night."

Zara rubbed her finger back and forth across her right eyebrow, much like Eve did when she was processing. "How did your daughter die? Did she overdose?"

"I guess I was prepared to have the police come and tell me she'd died that way, but it didn't happen as I expected. Lindsay had been out of the house for less than a year when we received the news. We had tried to keep in touch with her the best we could, but she stopped returning our calls and texts. A year later, a guy in jail confessed to seeing her killed. Now we just wait for her remains to be found, so we have something to bury."

"I'm sorry." A pink flush colored her cheeks. "I've been waiting for the call that Eve has overdosed since I left for college. I always wondered how the police would find me, but I knew they would. And I knew she'd die, but I didn't do anything to try and stop it." She leaned forward, holding her forehead in the palm of her hand.

At least a minute ticked by without another word, but grief, even unwarranted grief, needed time to settle.

When Zara looked up again, there was a shimmer in her eyes. "I can't step out of the guilt. I feel like I failed my sister, and it destroyed her. I left her with our mother and went on with my life, starting over while she crumbled."

Tiff did it then; she reached across the table and put her hand on Zara's arm. "That's the thing about loving an addict. It comes with overwhelming guilt." Tiff waited until she looked her in the eye. "This isn't your fault. There was nothing you could have said that would have made Eve stop using before she was ready."

"But there's something I might have to say that could cause her to go back."

Tiff felt the blood drain from her face as she stared into Zara's eyes. There was a blow coming, and it was going to be huge.

"Has Eve told you about our brother?"

"She mentioned he died young."

A sad smile stretched across Zara's face. "He had a disease called Hunter syndrome. It affects only boys. I was tested a few months ago and found out I'm also a carrier."

"And since you and Eve are twins, that means she's a carrier too?"

"Yes."

"I don't understand. Sammy seemed perfectly healthy to me."

"Symptoms don't appear until the child is between two and four."

The pounding of Tiff's heart had reached from her chest to her ears. "And it's fatal?"

"Life expectancy is short. At the very best, if Sammy tests positive, he could live to twenty, with cognitive and physical decline. More likely, he would die younger." A tear slid down her cheek, and she brushed it away with a slap of her hand.

"Oh, Lord, please no." Tiff's body had grown heavier as Zara relayed the news. She explained there's a procedure to test for some kind of enzyme in the urine, then bloodwork or skin biopsies. Everything she said swirled around like the tornado that took Dorothy to Oz. "When will you know?"

"There are some complications because he's in foster care. The doctor needs approval. But here's the thing: The caseworker has to tell Eve what's going on with the kids' medical care. I haven't talked to Kelly yet because I don't want this to come from her. Right now, you know my sister better than anyone else in the world. Do you think she can handle this?"

Tiff reached into her purse and drew out a couple of tissues, one for herself and one for Zara. "I don't know."

CHAPTER THIRTY-FIVE

Eve
July 8, 2019

Patrick moved me to full-time much earlier than expected. He says I'm doing a great job, and he couldn't ask for a better employee. I can't help but feel a little proud of myself. I know it's no more than what most of the rest of the world does every day, but it's new for me. I have a job, a support system, and a plan.

When I meet with the kids this week, I'm going to tell them all about what I do. I want them to know I'm trying. I want them to see me as hardworking and committed.

I've decided to stay quiet about Joey. No matter what the police say, I won't tell anyone what he's done or where to find him. If I keep my head down and my nose clean, maybe over time he'll just forget about us and move on. It's not like he doesn't have other women. He always did. I was good at looking the other way.

Bruce suggested a few programs at the community college. He said he'd help me get funding so I could take classes and have the kids in a good childcare. I'd really like to be a vet technician. Can you even imagine me with a job like that? I won't share

*those ideas with my kids yet, in case I can't do it, but maybe
someday.*

*Tonight I'm making dinner. It will be simple spaghetti,
but it seems like Tiff could use a break. She's not as perky as
usual, and I wonder if it's something about losing her daughter.
I know that, for years, the grief of losing Tyson came back
whenever I didn't expect it. It still shows up every now and
then.*

LOOFAH PODS WERE LENGTHENING along the hog panels that
Zara had bent over into upside-down U-shapes. Some of the flowers had fallen, but most still hung on. She couldn't help but run
her fingers along the plants, imagining the harvest of actual loofahs. Charlotte would love the process of cleaning out the seeds.

Her heart stilled. Charlotte might not be there when fall arrived. She could be back with Eve and moved on to who knows
where. The fact that her sister had been this close for the last few
years and Zara hadn't even felt her presence remained a shock.
If she wasn't able to sense her that close, how would she know
when Eve was gone again?

Suddenly, the loofahs lost her attention. She watched the kids
play in the sandbox Chad had installed over the weekend with
the help of Trinity's husband, welcome new friends. Charlotte
and Sammy couldn't get enough of the sand and had dragged
out half the kitchen implements to use as toys.

Charlotte still fell apart at least once a day, but they were able
to manage her emotions and help her to calm the storm earlier than before. She was starting to really trust them—not just
Chad, but both of them. Would she feel that way after she left?
If by some miracle they were able to stay in contact, if Eve would
forgive Zara for not loving her the way she should have, would

Charlotte want them around? Or would it feel like Zara and Chad were getting rid of her?

The thought of that little girl hurting gave Zara a physical pain in her chest. She'd thought she'd had all the grief she could bear for a lifetime. She'd lost her brother, her sister, and the hope of having children. None of that seemed worthy of her tears now as she faced the truth that she was soon going to lose her niece and nephew. They had become walking little pieces of her heart.

Charlotte waved, a measuring cup in her hand. "Mama Zara, come see our restaurant."

Mama Zara. She clutched her chest. Zara should correct her. She had no right to take Eve's place in that way, but the words filled her up with so much love, she thought it would kill her. She blinked away the emotion as she neared those two sweethearts, Sammy with his increasing vocabulary and Charlotte with her growing optimism.

"Would you like a piece of pie or some cake?" Charlotte passed her hand over the creations like a tiny salesgirl.

"Cake. Cake." Sammy rubbed his rounding tummy with both hands.

Charlotte tipped her head down, giving him a serious look. "Sammy, this is for pretends. You don't really eat the cake, okay?"

"Okay. Cake."

She looked at Zara and rolled her eyes, as if Sammy was such a child and she, Miss Charlotte, was a grown woman.

"I would love to have a slice of pie. What kinds do you have?"

She tapped her index finger on the tip of her chin. "We have apple, grape, and peanut butter."

"Grape pie? That's a new one for me. I think I'd like to try it, please." Zara sat down on the grass just outside the sandbox.

"Here you go, ma'am." Charlotte used one of the plastic plates they'd acquired right after the kids moved in to serve up a pile of sand with a few blades of grass poking out the top. "I hope you like it."

"Oh. This looks delicious." Zara pretended to take a bite with a fork she found beside Sammy's leg. She should probably do another check on all the items Charlotte had brought out here. "Mmm. This is the very best grape pie I've ever had."

"You're silly. You've never had grape pie."

"Maybe so, but I think you're the very best sand cook in the whole world." Zara held out her hands.

"That's because you love me so much."

She wasn't sure why, but Charlotte's words right then nearly undid her. "You're right, sweetie. I love you a ton."

"Can you adopt us, then?"

Zara's heart turned over and headed out on a race. "Adopt you? Where did you hear about adoption?"

"Miss Candy, at Sunday school. She adopted a baby boy because his mama couldn't take care of him. So she is his mama now."

Zara remembered Candy having the baby with her when she taught last week. Surely some of the more observant children, Charlotte for one, had noticed she hadn't been pregnant. "It's not that simple, Charlotte."

"But my mama can't take care of me. Don't you want to be my mom?" Round eyes blinked up at her, the enormity of the entire future there in the image of Charlotte's hopeful nature.

Zara did want to have that role, more than she should. She wanted to take Charlotte and Sammy, with all their issues and potential medical problems, and make a permanent home for them here. She wanted to protect them from the world and never let another person hurt them in any way. How could she explain to this five-year-old that what happened to her was not up to Zara? That her mother had a right to her because she'd given her life?

Yet, given a standard DNA test, Zara would have shown up as her mother too.

"Charlotte, there's nothing I would like more. You are such a special and wonderful little girl. It's not up to me—your mom is doing such a good job of trying to make a safe home for you."

"I have to go potty." She jumped up and ran toward the house, a trail of sand following her.

Eve
July 11, 2019

I don't want to keep doing this. Every day is so hard. I need a break. I need to leave this reality and sleep for a day or two.

Tiff got me a cell phone so that I can stay in touch with work and stuff, but the numbers on the screen make me think of how I can punch in a combination and get a fix. I have the money.

Sometimes it actually hurts to be clean. I feel like my body is aching for heroin, crying for it.

How am I supposed to do this for the rest of my life? When will it get easier? Will it?

A guy in my meeting got his thirty days yesterday. He'd been clean for five years before that and fell. Five years! I don't know how I can possibly be encouraged by his story. This is hopeless. Addiction is forever. I might as well be in prison. I'll never have freedom.

CHAPTER THIRTY-SIX

WHEN THE POLICE KNOCKED on the Bradleys' front door, Tiff was initially shocked. She'd forgotten to close the gate. It was so rare to hear someone at the door when she didn't already know who was on the way. The image of them waiting under the security camera, all business, sent her thoughts wandering to places she tried to avoid.

Her second instinct was fear.

She'd known her daughter was forever gone for years now, but there was this tiny string of hope that remained as long as Lindsay's body—whatever was left of it—still hadn't been discovered. There were nights when she'd woken in a sweat from nightmares that started like that moment had, with the knock at the door.

The knob was cold against her palm. Tiff twisted and it opened easily, revealing the uniforms she'd seen on the camera. This wasn't a dream. "Yes." She tried to force a smile, but all she could manage was holding back a mother's agonized sobs.

"Mrs. Bradley, we're here to see Eve Brookes. Is she available?"

Tiff's heart started to beat again, pounding in her chest with absolute relief. "Sure. Come on in." But what did they need with Eve?

There were two of them, a man and a woman, both wearing the same serious composure that gave police added authority. They walked through the door and stopped in the entrance.

The woman reached into one of her many shirt pockets and pulled out a card, then tapped it on the side of her opposite wrist.

"I'll be right back."

In the hall, Tiff knocked on Eve's door. She'd been home from work for only twenty minutes.

Eve opened the door and stood there in jeans and a T-shirt, a towel wrapped around her hair. She'd gained a bit of weight, which gave her a healthy glow, but a darkness still circled her eyes.

"A couple of police officers are here to speak with you."

Eve took a step back. "Why?"

"They didn't say. I'm sure it's nothing serious." But Tiff really wasn't. In her experience, police only came to the door when it *was* serious. "I'll let them know you're coming."

Nodding, Eve shut the door between them.

Eve must have felt the same way Tiff did about surprise visits from authority figures. Between the two of them, they were likely to look as if they had something to hide.

"She'll be right out," Tiff told the officers. "Can I get you something to drink—water, soda?"

"No, thank you." The female officer responded for both of them.

"Please come sit down."

The woman nodded her agreement.

Tiff led them into the living room, where they both took chairs, and Tiff sat on the couch. Her brain was unable to conjure up a topic of conversation, so they sat in awkward silence until Eve joined them.

She'd towel-dried her hair and combed it into a ponytail, making her look more like Zara than ever before. Tiff had planned to talk with her about Sammy's condition this afternoon, but she'd wait on committing to that until she found out what was happening here.

"What's going on?" Eve edged closer to Tiff and sat near the middle of the sofa. "I haven't done anything."

"Ma'am." The female officer, Officer Talbot, took the lead, and Tiff wondered if that was a purposeful tactic to gain Eve's trust. "We'd like to talk with you about Joseph Crawford. We understand you and Joseph were involved in a relationship for at least a couple of years."

Eve nodded. "Joey and I were together for almost three years, but I don't know where he is now."

Talbot tapped a pen on her notebook. "Listen, I understand you're refusing to press charges against Mr. Crawford for domestic violence. We know he was the one to send you to the hospital, but without you, we have no proof aside from talking to your daughter. But we're not here about that. This man—and I know you know what I'm talking about—is seriously bad news. We need him off the streets, and you have the chance to make that happen."

"What about my kids?"

The male officer, Pittman, shrugged. "What about them?"

"How are you going to be sure Charlotte and Sammy are safe?"

He crossed his arms. "Seems to me the safest they can be is if he's in prison."

The color in Eve's face washed out, as if all her energy had gone down the drain in her shower. "I don't know anything." She stood. "I'm sorry, but I can't help you."

The officers took her lead and rose too.

"Listen, you can play it this way, but there will be trouble to come for you and the kids. It's a guarantee." Pittman proceeded to the door, his boots loud against the hardwood floor.

Taking the card she still held between her first two fingers, Officer Talbot held it out to Eve. "You can call any time if you change your mind. We can help."

Eve held her gaze on the card, her mouth silent.

———

Eve
July 12, 2019

I almost did it. I almost told the cops everything I know about Joey and his network, about the women, the drugs, the violence . . . but I couldn't. He's been able to get to me so easily. What if they didn't have time to reach the kids before he did? He can find them anywhere. No one around here says no to Joey.

I can't believe I thought he was my savior. Sure, he was better than Chaz. Chaz is very willing to look the other way when a girl is clearly a child, selling her to whoever will give him a buck. I took Joey's line in the sand as goodness. But there's no goodness in either one of them. Only danger.

When I get my kids back, we'll get out of here. Not to another supposedly safe little town, but to a city where we can disappear. No one is going to know who we are or where we came from, and they won't care, either. We'll just be another family, nothing to sound the alarm over.

It means leaving Bruce and Tiff. That's the worst part. Bruce treats me as if I have something important to say, and not because he's trying to get something from me. He's careful not to be alone with me except when we drive back and forth from work. He's the first man I feel like I can trust, and he'll be the last.

This starting over means no more men in my life, ever. I can't be trusted to choose wisely, and I can't risk my kids or my sobriety on some guy who'll never save me.

Tiff says the only man who has that kind of power is Jesus.

CHAPTER THIRTY-SEVEN

TIFF RECEIVED A TEXT FROM ZARA. The caseworker was coming over for the monthly check-in on Monday, and Zara would have to tell her what the doctor said. Tiff and Zara were on the same page about wanting Eve to know first. This left Tiff with no choice but to bring up the subject now, only thirty minutes after the visit with the police.

"Eve, could you come out here?" She didn't usually holler down the hall, but she wasn't ready to look Eve in the eye.

A minute later, she sensed a presence behind her. "Is there something I can help with?"

Tiff took a deep breath as she finished wiping the counters clean. "There's something I want to talk with you about."

"I'm so sorry about the police coming here. I hope none of your neighbors saw."

Tiff turned. "It's not that. And I really couldn't care less what the neighbors think. Let's have a cup of tea and some cookies." This was something her grandmother would have done when getting ready to tackle a tough subject. Tea and cookies had a way of smoothing the harsh edges of life.

Without waiting for a response, Tiff retrieved her nice teapot from the display and began adding tea leaves. Using the instant hot water tap, she filled the container and set it on a trivet in the middle of her small kitchen table.

The sun shone into the room, drawing bright brushstrokes of light across the tangerine-colored tablecloth.

"What should I do?" Eve's voice held an edge of fear, and knowing her as Tiff now did, she imagined Eve was probably wondering if she and Bruce would kick her out of their home. What at one moment was devastating could become trivial in the next. That was one of the lessons Tiff had learned along the way—one she wished she would have understood earlier.

"Can you get the nice teacups from the china cupboard? We'll make this special."

"I've never had real tea before." Eve pulled open the cabinet door and took one cup gently into her hands. "Did you do this with Lindsay?" Her eyes shot up as though she'd let something slip out that should have remained buried.

"No. I wish I had, but back when we still had Lindsay, I didn't realize that you have to make moments special, even hard ones." The words were out of her mouth before she could swallow them.

The stillness that followed brought the heavy weight of loss into the room.

"What's going on?" Eve set the cups down and stared, unblinking, into Tiff's eyes.

There wasn't much to do now but lay it all out. "Sit down." Tiff poured tea into her cup even though she doubted there'd been enough time for it to fully steep. "Everything is okay."

Still standing, Eve gripped the back of the chair. "That's not true."

The Lamaze breathing Tiff had used so long ago to work through the birth of her children came back on instinct. "I'm not saying this isn't going to be a rough conversation. Please . . . sit down."

Like the child she was in so many ways, Eve did as she'd been told. Her hands wrapped around the delicate china cup as if the warmth could save her.

"I met up with your sister earlier this week."

Shock colored Eve's face red.

"I'm sorry. There was no intention to go behind your back." Tiff sipped from her delicate cup, waiting for the right words to find her. "Zara loves you. She wanted this to come from me, because she wants to do everything she can to help you remain healthy."

"You mean she thinks I can't handle whatever it is because I'm a no-good addict who will turn to drugs when she gets the hiccups?"

"No. It's not that." Though Tiff had to question herself. In a way, wasn't that how she and Zara were both treating Eve? "I'm going to be straight with you. Zara had some testing done this spring. She discovered she's a carrier for Hunter syndrome." Tiff waited for the news to find its way into Eve's understanding.

A flush ran up Eve's neck and into her face.

"Your brother had Hunter."

"I remember hearing that. But he died because he choked to death."

"Apparently, that's a common concern with kids who have this syndrome. His life expectancy wasn't long, even if he hadn't choked that day." Perspiration dampened the back of Tiff's neck. She thought about Brandt. How had they supported him through Lindsay's struggles and her death? What had she and Bruce missed in their own grief?

"Is Zara sick? Is she dying?"

"No. Being a carrier doesn't mean you have the disease; it just means you can pass it down. In her case, it means that any child she has—any boy—has a fifty-percent chance of having the disease. There's still no cure."

Tiff saw the moment when it all came crashing down on Eve. The moment when she realized how this was personal. Her mouth fell open, and tears rushed her eyes. "Sammy."

All she could do was nod.

"I didn't know. I thought Tyson was just different because of something my mom did, or something his dad did. He was so great. I miss him." Tears fell down her cheeks, landing on her crossed arms. "What have I done to my son?"

"Sammy will need to have tests done to determine if he has Hunter. There's a chance he won't, but the doctor is concerned. Zara and I felt it would be better for you to hear this from me than from the caseworker. She's held off notifying Kelly so we could talk first."

Eve's head shook with tiny bobs. "Is there anything we can do if he has this?"

"The doctors will do everything they can to give him the best life possible, but the realities are tough. I don't think we should go there until we have a definitive answer."

Her head tipped to the side. "I don't need to. I already know what will happen to my son if he has this. And I know how it will affect my daughter. Don't forget: I've lived this."

Tiff reached across the table, past her untouched tea and the plate of cookies, and took Eve's hand. "No matter what, it will be different for your kids. You're making a safe and happy life for them. They have a future because of the hard work you're doing." She gave Eve's hand a squeeze. "I'm so proud of you."

A sad smile graced the beautiful young woman's lips. "No one has ever said that to me."

Eve

July 14, 2019

Tiff and Bruce are so good to me. Tiff took me out to see a matinee at the community theater. I told her once how, before

I started using, I used to love acting in high school, and she remembered. She makes me feel important.

Bruce met us for dinner at a restaurant I could never go to without their special treatment. I know they're trying to make me feel better, and I love them for the effort.

The speaker in my NA meeting yesterday talked on and on about how important it is to not compare ourselves with anyone else. At the time, I hadn't thought the message applied to me. But it does. I've been comparing myself to Zara my entire life, not just when we were growing up. I've found myself doing it a lot since Tiff and I talked about Tyson.

Zara knew why our brother died. She was responsible and had the test done before having children. She did everything right.

Then there's me.

I had children because I got pregnant. There was no more thought to the action than that. I didn't think about what they would need, how I could give them a decent future, or what my actions meant to them. I was selfish.

Not much has changed. I want to free myself of this place and get as far away from Joey as possible. But my kids, they've formed a bond with Zara and her husband—I hear it in all the things Charlotte says during our visits. If I'm really thinking of them first, how can I move away with them?

And if Sammy is sick . . . what am I going to do? He'll need so much that I don't know how to provide. I need Tiff and Bruce in my life if I'm going to take care of my son the way he deserves. And my kids need Zara . . . just like I always have.

CHAPTER THIRTY-EIGHT

ZARA'S HOUSE WAS A MESS of toys, Charlotte's half-made recycling box crafts, and the packing material that had just arrived and needed to be filled with products to ship. None of this bothered her today as she awaited the arrival of the caseworker. Today Zara's mind was stuck on a repeating loop. *Sammy may have Hunter. Sammy may have Hunter.* She'd thought losing a sibling was the worst kind of agony until she was faced with losing a child she loved as her very own.

"Sammy is poopy . . . again." Charlotte rolled her eyes. It had only been a few weeks since she was the one who wanted to provide all her brother's care. Now she trusted Zara to make sure his needs were met. It was a victory. "Mama Z, did you hear me?"

Zara cringed at that awful nickname, a suggestion from her husband, who thought Mama Zara was a mouthful. She'd gone from maternal figure to hometown rapper in record time. "I heard you, Chuck." She winked as she used the nickname she'd given Charlotte in response.

Zara slid her hand under the couch and grabbed a diaper and the box of wipes. To a seasoned mother, this move might have seemed amateur, but she was pretty proud of it.

Sammy, however, had caught on to her little trick. He grabbed two of his trucks and ran at a speed that indicated a future track star in the making. If there was going to be a change in his body, it hadn't slowed him yet. What Zara could give him now was the opportunity to experience all the joy in life, even if he wouldn't remember it.

She jumped up and went after him, delighting in his squeals and giggles. When she caught him, she turned his body and held him to her chest. "Got you!"

He threw his arms around her neck and kissed her jaw.

Could there be a greater gift in the world than the sweet kiss of a child? In giving joy to him and to Charlotte, Zara was gaining far more.

Only seconds after the diaper change was finished, there was a knock at the door. Zara let Kelly in and welcomed her to the chaotic, messy, love-filled home.

Eve still hadn't chosen to contact Zara, but she had gotten word from Tiff that she'd shared the news. Zara dreaded having to tell the caseworker. It was another step toward a possibility that was so much better ignored. But to have the testing begin, she needed approval from DHS.

"I know you're busy," Kelly said as she held the plastic teacup and saucer Charlotte had served her with. "Let me run through my questions, and I'll get out of your hair. I can see the kids are well cared for and loved."

Zara took Sammy onto her lap, holding one of his trucks in her hand while he explored the wheels and the fire ladder. "We went to the doctor again with Sammy."

"Oh yes, you had an additional weight check. How was that?"

"He's gained and is now nearly where he should be for his height and age. The thing is . . ." She hesitated. Should she say anything in front of Charlotte? But if Eve and Zara had known all that was really going on with their brother, wouldn't they have been more prepared for his death and their own futures? "Sammy didn't have a test I'd assumed he would have early on." Hindsight being as crystal clear as it was, she realized it was unrealistic for her to assume that Eve, with all she'd had to contend with, would be more on top of understanding the hidden dangers in their genetic blueprint.

"What test is that?" Kelly started flipping through her notebook for information she wouldn't find.

"Hunter syndrome. Eve and I had a brother with it. We're carriers."

"Your brother." She looked at Charlotte. "He passed, correct?"

Children had bat ears when it came to information that wasn't meant for them. "He passed what?" Charlotte looked up with bright eyes.

Zara ran a hand over her hair. It had grown at least two inches this summer and lightened in the sun. "Passed means that he died. He's in heaven."

"So is Mirna's cat." Charlotte started to dig in the box of blocks given to them by a woodworker in the church. "Mirna was very sad, but now she has a puppy. I think puppies are better, except when they chew on your toys."

"That's for sure." Charlotte had no idea how many of her toys had been replaced during post-bedtime runs to the store so she wouldn't have to know that Pickles had done it again. Zara stood and retrieved the paper work from the mantel above their still-to-be fixed fireplace. "The doctor needs these papers signed before we move forward with testing."

She examined the forms Zara handed her. "I'll have to check with my supervisor on this. I'm not sure how we handle testing, or how we make sure Oregon Health Plan will pay the bill."

"I understand. There's something else. Eve has been told already. I know you don't want us having any contact, but I asked her friend Tiff to give her the news. I felt it was important she was supported."

Kelly's lips cocked to the side. "Why would you think I don't want you to have contact with Eve? That's not a problem as long as the kids aren't involved."

"I just assumed that, because we aren't allowed to see each other at visits, it was some kind of policy."

"No." She rolled her eyes. "I'm sorry. Sometimes information gets confused in the process of conveying instructions to the visit supervisors. The only reason we keep people separated is when there's interaction that's unhealthy for the children. I can't see that being the case here."

"I don't understand." The rage Zara had felt every day she'd spent in the back room grew and ignited. "She's my sister. If she's supposed to get better, wouldn't it be helpful to have us in her life? I've heard over and over again that the goal here is reunification. How can it be reunifying when they're about to get ripped away from another family?"

Kelly looked from Zara to the kids, her eyes wide.

"I'm sorry. I don't know what I was thinking. Please excuse that outburst." The last thing she needed to do was look like a crazy woman and have Kelly wonder if she was really the best person to be caring for Charlotte and Sammy.

"I understand. Trust me. This process is frustrating for those of us who work in it too." She shifted the stack on her lap. "I'll do what I can to help you and Eve reconcile. I fully believe that's the best thing for all of you."

"Do you want to see my ballet moves?" Charlotte started twirling before the caseworker could answer.

"That's very good." She looked back at Zara. "When was the last time you and Eve had a good relationship?"

She wanted to say they were close when she'd left for college, but that would have been a lie. They'd started to drift apart their freshman year of high school, when Tyson died. Grief had a life all its own, and with that life came the ability to drive in hard wedges between relationships. "It's been a very long time."

"But you miss her?"

"I do." At least Zara missed the part of Eve she wasn't sure still existed. She missed the sister who had played horses with her for hours, who weathered the storms and chased the rainbows at her side, the mirror image of herself.

"In some counties, they have mediated family decision meetings. If you're interested, I'd like to see if we can arrange for something like that. It's a chance for all parties to sit down and talk about how the children will be best served."

Zara nodded but couldn't seem to get her mouth to work.

"It's looking like reunification will take place at the end of the summer." A sympathetic look crossed her face.

The news hit Zara with a force, making her turn her gaze back to the toddler on her lap. "If they could have both of you in their lives, imagine how great that would be for them."

"I'll do whatever I can. These two mean the world to me." Zara's voice cracked, and she held her fist to her mouth until the emotion passed. Everything in her life had spun out of control from the moment she'd gotten the letter from DHS. And still, someone else would be making the decision about where the kids went, who would raise and love and care for them every day. Her heart would break in half when she handed them back to her sister.

How could she trust Eve to keep them safe?

Eve

July 22, 2019

Court went well. The judge is pleased with my progress. If I do what I need to do, they'll be giving my kids back to me soon. I just need a place to live. Bruce and Tiff said they'd help me with that, but I don't want to leave here. For the first time in my life, I know what it feels like to be cared for. I wonder if I would have made the same mistakes if I'd had a dad like Bruce. But Lindsay still fell, didn't she?

If Tiff and Bruce couldn't protect their daughter from the temptations of drugs, how am I supposed to do that for my kids? And what will happen if it turns out that Sammy has Hunter? How will I care for Sammy and make sure Charlotte doesn't get lost along the way?

I don't know how to take care of my kids, take care of myself, and give us all a future.

Maybe I could learn. Maybe.

But there isn't enough time. All the responsibility and pressure are coming down on me at once. I love my kids so much, but I don't know how to do this.

CHAPTER THIRTY-NINE

Eve

July 29, 2019

I think we found the place today. I can't believe it. I'm about to have a legitimate I'm-paying-the-bill apartment. It's in a secure neighborhood with homes that aren't new but aren't dilapidated, either. The landlord lives in the connected house. It's just an over-the-garage situation, but there are two bedrooms, one for the kids and one for me. As Sammy gets older, I'll figure out something. Maybe I'll share Charlotte's room or sleep on the fold-out couch in the living area.

And it's furnished! Like, there are beds and that pull-out couch, and even a table and chairs for meals.

The older couple who own the place go to Tiff's church. They said they'd drop the rent even further if I would take over mowing their lawn. Of course! It's all too good to be true.

The only thing that matters is that it will be a perfect home for my children. It's safe. And Joey won't know where we are, but Zara and Tiff will.

I've decided I can't do this on my own. I need to humble

myself and ask my sister to forgive me. I hope she'll be willing to help out with the kids until I can get reliable childcare.

I'll know soon. Zara and I are having lunch together on Thursday.

BY THE TIME ZARA RECEIVED THE CALL that Sammy could have the testing, she'd about given up. Nothing moved quickly in the foster care system, except expectations on her time. Those came up frequently and with a pressure that could have burst a Goodyear blimp.

There were a couple of options for the urine sample, as there was no way Sammy was going to tinkle on command. The doctor had recommended a kind of sack with sticky edges. For a woman who was just getting the hang of diapering, this seemed like a stretch, but it was better than more invasive procedures.

Zara clicked on the television and started an episode of *Doc McStuffins*. Charlotte would stare at the screen with a look of awe until the program ended. At first, Zara had felt a twinge of guilt at using TV to entertain her, but it was a lifesaver, and she'd take the help. She slung Sammy onto her hip and went to get the lunch items out of the refrigerator.

All she had to do now was wait for Chad to get home, and together, they'd head to the doctor's office. No problem. It was just a urine sample—not a test that would tell them if Sammy had a future. *One step at a time, right?*

Chad came into the kitchen to Pickles barking like the house was being invaded by an army of cats. He set a white bag on the back of the counter and picked up the dog. "Hey, buddy. Chill out."

Pickles changed his tune and started licking, his tongue moving at mesmerizing speeds.

"You're going to hate me." Chad's face cocked into a lopsided smile.

"What?" That pressure was mounting again, like her chest was ready to blow, but Sammy patted her cheek and kissed her chin. Within a second, he'd changed his focus to the counter, where the string cheese waited for his lunch to be served.

"I can't go with you. One of the clients I took over is in some serious trouble with the IRS." Chad pulled the tray from Sammy's high chair while she put him in and fastened the buckles.

"But." Zara's mouth went dry. "But that's not your fault. You just started. And what about the little bag thing? And how will I get Sammy to sit still while we do this?"

Chad slid the tray back into place and handed Sammy a cheese stick. "The guy before me was fired. It's my job to clean up his mess." He shook his head. "Didn't they say this would be easy? They just clean the area, take the strips off the sticky tape, and stick it on." He shrugged. "Once he goes, that's it."

"Oh yes. Simple"—Zara rolled her eyes—"if you're doing this on a baby doll. Sammy is a very mobile toddler who can't even stay still for a simple diaper change. I can't imagine what will happen when they trade his diaper for a stick-on bag."

"I think the diaper goes back on. Or maybe not. I don't know." He kissed her cheek. "I'm really sorry."

She deflated with a long exhale. "I know. Good luck with your client."

"You're the best." Chad ducked back out the door, and she was all alone with the kids again. Guilt ate at her when she wanted her freedom, yet fear had its way when she let herself love the moments with the kids. There was no way that all would be perfect in the world ever again. Zara was on a raft heading for a waterfall, with no oars or even a life jacket.

"Mama Z, it's over!" Charlotte's voice bellowed from the other room. "Quick—another one is starting. I'll have to watch it."

Zara couldn't help but chuckle. Charlotte was making a lot of headway in the honesty department. And she clearly understood her weakness for *Doc McStuffins*. She walked into the living room and clicked the television off. "Let's have some lunch, then. We need to go to the doctor."

Charlotte's eyes went wide, but she didn't run. Another improvement.

"No worries, kiddo. This is an appointment for Sammy only. I may need you to be my helper."

"What are they going to do to my brother?"

"They need a urine sample."

Her mouth twisted, asking the question without having to utter a word.

"Pee. They need some of Sammy's pee."

"That's disgusting. Why do they want that?"

She had that right. "It's not such a big thing. They test it to be sure he's healthy."

"I don't want anyone testing my pee."

Zara turned around before Charlotte saw her grin. "Let's get some lunch."

They arrived at the office twelve minutes past their appointment time, but by the looks of the waiting room, it wouldn't make much difference. A kid was slumped over a phone, continually wiping his nose with the side of his arm. Near the fish tank, another child stared at the water, tear tracks streaked down his dirty face, a large bandage affixed to his forehead. A little girl sobbed uncontrollably in her mother's arms. And a lady held her newborn tight in the corner of the room, looking like she would fight back an army to keep her child safe.

Charlotte started jumping from state to state on a rug designed as a map of the United States. A boy joined her, and they seemed to be getting along well, until his face turned a greenish hue and his mother lunged forward with a garbage can.

Zara took Sammy and Charlotte toward the entrance and

doused them both with an ample amount of hand sanitizer. How could there be so many germs during the summer?

The nurse finally called them back. The exam room, though small, seemed sterile. There was a safety in the confines of these walls that kept vomiting children at a distance. Zara had never been good with sickness, and since joining the mothering team, she'd only gotten more paranoid.

"So, if you could get him undressed, this shouldn't be too bad." The nurse prepared the bag while Zara got Sammy ready for this odd process.

Once his skin was cleaned, the nurse removed strips from the outside of the bag and attached it. "Okay. It's all up to you now, Samuel."

And they waited. What seemed like a constant any other day was now turning into a dry spell. Charlotte peppered Zara with questions about the bag, the urine, the testing. None of which Zara was able to answer in a way the five-year-old found acceptable.

Forty minutes later, at about the same moment that both children began sobbing from the exhaustion of being stuck in a room the size of a closet, Sammy gave up and produced a sample.

Zara hadn't cheered so much since watching Chad run through the finish line of his half marathon last year.

It took the doctor only a few minutes to come in with the news: Sammy's urine showed elevated levels of sugar molecules. Dr. Kiddle scrubbed his hands through his thick graying hair. "I think we should go ahead with a blood draw for the next level of testing."

Zara looked from the doctor to Charlotte and back again. Her mouth fell open. This couldn't be happening.

"I've asked a pediatric phlebotomist to come in. It shouldn't be more than a few minutes. I was thinking Miss Charlotte might want to watch a video with one of my nurses. Would that be okay?"

Zara nodded. At least they could get through this by only traumatizing Sammy—and Zara.

Eve
July 31, 2019

Soon, I'll be independent. I'll have my own apartment, paid for by the proceeds of my own job. I have a feeling that my rent is not what it should be, that Bruce and Tiff have done something to help, but I'm still proud. And I know they're proud of me. That's one of the things that has made the difference. I know Bruce and Tiff are excited for me, and they really believe I can do this.

Today, I bought a frame and put the picture of me and the kids in it. I already look so different from that day, but it's a reminder, and I want it to hang in a place where I'll see it and remember where we've been.

TIFF FELT LIKE A CAT BURGLAR as she and Bruce entered the above-garage apartment. With the windows having remained shut for who knows how long, it was warm, nearly hot. She pushed one open and felt the soft breeze float in, bringing with it the sweet scents of the jasmine plant that grew underneath.

Bruce dropped the first box on the counter and turned to head back out for another. There was a lightness in him that had been absent so long, she'd forgotten to even miss it.

"And here's another." He dropped it in the middle of the living room floor. "We'd better get this stuff unpacked just in case Eve happens by." His cheeks crinkled with his smile.

"It's a little like the night before Christmas." She remembered the late nights she and Bruce had spent putting together gifts and a stocking for Lindsay and Brandt. It was always a special time with her husband, a time where they shared secrets and surprises, relishing the excitement of the season.

Bruce set his mind to the art of toy assembly, while Tiff removed tags from clothing and placed them in the dresser that came with the apartment. She made the beds with freshly laundered sheets and blankets. The crib would be delivered the day before they moved Eve into the apartment.

When they were done, Tiff looked around. It was a home waiting for a family.

She'd gotten involved. Too involved. And she wouldn't change a thing.

CHAPTER FORTY

Eve

August 1, 2019

There's so much on the line. I'm having lunch with Zara today. Tiff asked if I wanted her to come along. I do, but I think this is something I need to do on my own. If I can't face my sister, it's like not being willing to face my mistakes and the people I've hurt. My counselor, the one they assigned me at drug court, says I have to tell the truth even when it hurts. The truth is, I made the choices that got me here, but it's also me making the choice each day to keep getting healthy.

That last word stops me in my thoughts every time. I wish it weren't such a common word in recovery. Healthy. I have the chance to get healthy, mentally and physically, but Sammy might not. He has whatever genes I forced on him.

For days after Tiff told me that my son could be sick, I struggled to keep moving forward. It felt like God was punishing me, like even if I did everything right from here on out, He was reminding me of His ability to crush my soul any

302

*time He wished. Tiff says that isn't how God works, but from
where I sit, it feels like I'm in constant danger.*

ZARA STOOD JUST INSIDE THE CAFÉ when Eve pulled up to
the curb in a battered Toyota. They'd seen each other at the visits
off and on for weeks now, but the passing of information about
the kids and the small talk that environment allowed didn't leave
room for any depth and real reconciliation.

Looking around at the simple establishment, chickens painted
on the walls, people eating breakfast at an hour past lunchtime,
she wondered, would this setting be any better?

The bell jingled as Eve came through the door.

They looked at each other, staring into eyes they should know
as well as their own, but neither spoke.

"I have your table ready." A young man with a Disney tattoo
peeking out from his right sleeve collected two menus and led
them to the back of the restaurant. "You two must be sisters."

Zara nodded. What had happened to the days when people
had automatically recognized they were twins? Any time they
went out, people would stop them, tossing question after question their way. Did they like to do the same things? Why weren't
they dressed alike? Could they tell what the other was thinking?
Zara had felt like a freak show.

They sat and took the offered menus; then he was gone to get
water.

"Thanks for coming." Zara peeked over at her sister.

Eve nodded. She'd always been the quieter of the two. Always
the one to wear darker colors, less likely to introduce herself. She'd
been Zara's shadow more than her equal, and Zara had liked it,
so she'd encouraged those roles.

When the man returned, Zara ordered a coffee and the

vegetarian omelet even though she was a serious meat lover. Eve ordered a Danish and plain black coffee.

Eve fiddled with the cuff of her long-sleeved T-shirt. "I hope you know that I'm very grateful for you and Chad taking the kids like this. And I'm so sorry you were put in this position."

"I'm not." Zara steepled her fingers, then laced them together. "Not that I wanted you and the kids to go through the things you've been through." Every word that came out of her mouth had the potential to ignite the tender string of hope between them. "I'm just glad that I got to meet them, that you're getting better, that . . ."

Time spread out before them. Zara wanted to say what came next, but she didn't have a firm grasp on the idea or the words.

"I love my kids."

"I know. I love them too."

That brought tears to Eve's eyes. "I don't want to take them away from you, but I can't live without them, either. Do you understand?"

Zara's chin moved. She did understand, because, for the first time in years, she and Eve were exactly the same. They both loved Sammy and Charlotte. Neither could imagine a life without them.

"Is it possible for Chad and me to stay connected to them . . . and to you?"

"I want to say yes. I really do."

Zara's heart thundered. "What's stopping you?"

Eve looked away.

The man returned with their food.

Warm scents of breakfast formed a new wall between them, and it turned Zara's stomach. "I know I made bad choices, and I'm sure you feel like I abandoned you, but I thought I was doing the right thing."

Fire flamed in Eve's eyes. "There you go, telling me what I feel. You always did that."

"What are you talking about?"

"I spent most of my life having you tell me what I wanted to do, wear, and feel. Didn't you ever wonder why I chose the opposite every time? I wanted to be me, not a version of you."

Zara ripped the top off two packets of raw sugar and dumped them into her coffee, then poured in cream. "You could have said something." She stirred, then lifted the mug to her lips.

"Really? And what do you think you would have said?"

"I don't know, because I'm not the same person anymore." Her words grew softer. "I've changed. I want us to get to know each other for who we are now."

Eve cut into her Danish. "When will the results be back from Sammy's test?"

"The doctor said there was a good chance we wouldn't get an answer from the urine test, and that turned out to be true. There was sugar in the urine, but not an amount that would make him think we're definitely looking at Hunter. They went ahead and took a blood draw. Now we just have to wait."

"And if he has it?"

"There are some treatments available. They aren't cures." Zara stuffed a bite into her mouth to help swallow down her fears and grief. "Eve, I know we have a lot of hurts between us, but Sammy and Charlotte need both of us."

"I know. I just don't know how to be healthy and move forward with such a big piece of my past."

"I'm your sister. Not your dirty laundry."

A small smile lifted the corners of Eve's mouth. "That's funny. It sounds like something I would say."

THE NEXT WEEK BROUGHT NEW CHALLENGES, almost sequestering Zara's old fears to the corner.

Court was no place for children. They might as well have asked

Zara to take the kids for a visit to the state prison. Yet she had no real authority, and when the state made a request, she and Chad were bound to follow.

They stepped out to the car, and Zara tied the ribbon in the back of Charlotte's dress. It was too much for this event, but Charlotte wanted to look pretty for the judge. Seriously, what was going to be gained by frills and lace? It was the law that mattered inside the courthouse.

This courthouse wasn't plain or simple. It was the kind of place one remembered visiting. It towered above all else in the downtown area, surrounded by a lush lawn, as if the building were more of a monument than a place to put away criminals.

Zara knelt on the sidewalk and reached out her hands, waiting for Charlotte to place her own little hands into hers. When she did, Zara knew she had her attention. "Do you have any questions about what is going to happen today?"

"The judge just wants to see us, and she'll say what happens next." Charlotte leaned forward and hugged Zara. "Don't worry, Mama Z. I'll be there with you."

Zara's throat tightened. She felt Chad's hand on her shoulder, and Charlotte's fingers brushing along her back. What right did she have to be sad or worried? Zara was the adult here. She was a grown-up.

"Will we have to leave today?" Charlotte's words were muffled in Zara's neck.

She held the little girl out. "No, sweetheart. When the time comes, Chad and I will help you get settled in your new apartment with your mom. But that's not today."

"Does the judge know I don't want to see Joey ever again?" A tear rose in her eye.

"She does." No matter how many times she and Chad reassured Charlotte, the same worry continued cropping up. If Zara ever saw Joey face-to-face, she'd likely end up in the courthouse on her own charges.

TIFF AND BRUCE WALKED ON EITHER SIDE of Eve, up the courthouse steps and into the building. There was a quiet hopefulness that clung to them as they made their way to courtroom number two.

Eve's attorney, a middle-aged man with thinning salt-and-pepper hair and a tie the color of pumpkins, met them in the hall. "Thank you for being early. It means a lot to the judge when you show that you respect her time." He held his hand out in greeting to Bruce. "Thomas Darling."

"Yes, Mr. Darling. I recognize you from the bar association dinner. Good to see you again."

"Likewise. Your wife has been a great deal of help. Her support and presence here give Eve a great deal of respect in the eyes of the court."

"Well, my wife is amazing, but Ms. Brookes should receive the lion's share of the credit. She's abided by the orders of the court and the plan set out by DHS. I'm sure you will see to it that she's given more frequent and less supervised access to her children."

"My thoughts exactly."

Kelly came down the hall, along with another man in a suit and tie. Mr. Darling ushered Eve to the other side. "Is there anything you need to share with me before we go inside?"

"No, sir. I've passed all my drug tests, gotten a great job, and I'm moving into my apartment soon. I'd like for the kids to see it."

Tiff placed her hand on Bruce's back. In turn, he slung his arm over her shoulder. She guessed they looked like two proud parents ready for their daughter's graduation.

ZARA SAT FORWARD ON THE BENCH. She hadn't known to prepare the kids to sit with their attorney rather than her and Chad.

By the look on Sammy's face, there were only a few more seconds that he was going to allow what he surely saw as an injustice.

The attorney, a woman who'd had only one contact with the children before today, had taken Sammy out of Chad's arms and Charlotte by the hand, leading them away as if they were mindless puppets.

Charlotte looked so tiny up there, and so far away.

The judge introduced herself to the children and made sure they each received a teddy bear. She spoke directly to Charlotte, asking her questions about how she spent her time and what she liked to eat.

By the time the state's attorney had the chance to speak, Sammy's bottom lip was quivering. One tear trickled down his face as he reached for Zara.

She couldn't hold herself back another second. Zara rose and walked to the railing separating the spectators from the court participants. She reached for Sammy and got a solid glare from the kids' attorney. So much for having their best interests in mind. Charlotte jumped up from where she sat and joined Zara too.

"That's fine," the judge said. "If the children are more comfortable with the foster parents, there's no reason they need to be up here."

Zara smiled, hoping she was transmitting her thankfulness adequately without making it look like she was a child snatcher, as she'd heard people in the DHS waiting room say about foster parents.

When she returned to Chad, pride shone in his eyes. Who cared what everyone else thought? Charlotte climbed into Chad's lap and laid her head on his chest. To Zara, all was right with the world—until she looked up and saw the pain in Eve's eyes.

Eve

August 5, 2019

I'm finally able to sit down and explore my feelings about today. After court, there was a lunch with Bruce and Tiff, an NA meeting, and I had a physical. My attorney thought a clean bill of health from a doctor would show I was serious about my new life.

The judge said I was doing very well and that it was time to start reunification. The kids will start having "community" visits with me. We can meet in a park or somewhere like that, without the guy who sits in the corner of the DHS visitation room scribbling notes about our every interaction.

Community visits mean leaning on my sister or Tiff to be a kind of supervisor. I feel like I've already taken so much from both of them. But I can't wait to see my kids without all the restrictions.

On the other hand, I'm nervous. Charlotte and Sammy have completely bonded with Zara and Chad. They look like the perfect family.

I did some research on Hunter syndrome and twins who are carriers. From what I understand, Zara shares nearly as much DNA with my kids as I do. She's like another mother, except I'm the one who had them grow inside of me and who brought them into the world. It would be easy to say that's why they love her so much—it's simply science. But how does that explain the way Charlotte takes comfort in Chad's arms? I've never seen her like that with a man. She trusts him. She trusts him more than she trusts me.

CHAPTER FORTY-ONE

SATURDAY MORNING, THE SUN SHONE on the wide expanse of lawn, still glistening from the moisture from the underground sprinkler system at Bunyon Park. Zara was the first to get out of the car, leaving Chad with the kids so she could approach Eve on her own.

Eve sat on a bench, her gaze on the playground, where Charlotte would soon be an explosion of excitement. She was alone, no Tiff today, and Zara wished for the extra buffer the older woman granted with her kind demeanor.

"Hey there." Zara slid onto the seat next to her sister.

Eve looked around. "Where are the kids?"

Time and distance hadn't evaporated the connection between them. Zara felt Eve's anxiety, her fear that she was being tricked or laughed at. "They're in the car. Chad will bring them over in a minute. They both took their shoes off on the drive over." She rubbed her hands up and down the denim covering her thighs. "I need something from you."

"What?" The sprinkle of alarm was still present in Eve's voice.

"I need you to promise me, if it gets too hard, if you start to struggle or make choices that could hurt the kids, that you'll let me know."

"I've never hurt them. I wouldn't."

"You know what I mean."

Eve tugged on the end of her ponytail.

"I don't want to find out they're in trouble through a state agency again. Just let me know, and I'll be there to get them. No questions asked."

"They're my kids." Her voice didn't carry the conviction needed for her words. Then she added, "I will."

"I feel like I let you down. I didn't protect you the way I should have."

"It's not your fault."

"Maybe, maybe not. It doesn't change how I feel. I want to do better, especially for Sammy and Charlotte. And . . . I love you, Eve."

Eve leaned forward and crossed her arms against her lap. "I'm part of you. And you're part of me. I'm not sure how to be separate and connected."

Chad and the kids walked toward the playground, hand in hand.

Zara looked up at the cloudless blue sky. "I remember thinking that exact thing when we were about thirteen. I had a major crush on Brian Weber. Do you remember him?"

Eve nodded. "His hair . . . how could I forget?"

"I was so afraid he'd like you more than me."

"We were thirteen. All he cared about was our looks, and we looked the same."

They both turned at Charlotte's squeal. She didn't give Zara or Eve a glance but bounded through the grass until she reached the slide.

Chad jogged along behind her, Sammy bouncing and giggling in his arms.

"You're lucky," Eve said. "Chad isn't like most men."

"I used to think that too, but my experience was limited. Chad is very special, but he's not the only good man out there." Sharon had found not just one, but two men who loved her and treated her as if she were royalty. And there were the men from church who brought in her new oven while she snored away in the next room. And the men who volunteered their time to get the house ready for inspection. "Our mom only exposed us to the kinds of men who hurt others. We missed out on knowing what was really out there."

"I did the same thing. Joey could have killed me right there in front of the kids. I don't know how I can ever forgive myself for that."

Zara grabbed her sister's hand. "Eve, I don't know how I would have forgiven myself if I'd lost you. I'm sorry."

Eve leaned into Zara's side, just like they had as little girls, before they'd gotten lost looking for their own ways.

Charlotte's scream broke the moment to pieces. Both women jumped from the bench and lunged forward, their shoulders crashing into each other as they moved to get to her, a cut on her arm bleeding through the edge of her sleeve.

Chad was there first, Sammy clinging to his side.

By the time Zara and Eve reached Charlotte, Sammy was sobbing as if he were the one injured.

"Charlie, honey, what happened?" Eve scooped her up.

She stiffened and pointed to a stick at the end of the slide. "Who did that? Who would put a stick where a little girl could get hurt?" Tears formed rivers down her cheeks. "I don't like this park. I want to go home. I want Pickles." She pushed away from her mother until Eve relented and set her on the ground. Charlotte grabbed Zara's hand and pulled toward the car.

Eve's mouth was wide open. She seemed so much smaller than Zara at that moment. "Okay. I think you should go ahead, then." She took Sammy in her arms and gave him a quick hug, then passed him back to Chad. "Thank you for meeting me here. Charlotte, I'm so sorry you got hurt. I'll see you soon, okay?"

Charlotte's body leaned at a right angle away from Zara, their hands still firmly attached, but she didn't acknowledge Eve's words.

Zara knelt. "Charlotte, you need to say good-bye to your mother. I realize you're upset, but she came out here to see you."

The little girl let go of Zara and wrapped her arms around Chad's leg. "Daddy, can we go now?"

"Go ahead," Eve said. "We'll have another opportunity soon. I love you, Charlotte."

"Bye." Charlotte didn't make eye contact.

Zara turned to Eve. "I'm so sorry. She doesn't mean anything." She remembered the deep hurt she'd felt when Charlotte first moved in and gave Zara less than a stranger's worth of attention. How horrible that would feel from your own child.

"No worries. You need to get that cut cleaned up, anyway." Eve's smile was sad, but she made a true effort to let the situation just happen, not try and change the unchangeable feelings of a five-year-old. Zara respected that more than she knew how to express.

Eve
August 10, 2019

Our first community visit was a total disaster. I really believed that seeing the kids in a neutral area like the park would give us back our relationship. I thought they'd run to me, hug me, maybe even want to come home with me.

I was living in a dream.

After Zara left with my kids and Chad, I walked around the edge of the park, taking three or four laps. I watched families enjoy picnics, a T-ball game starting up, and a few teenagers sunbathing in the late-summer heat. I looked at the world

*around me from the outside, and it was so big and open, so
many possible paths and life choices.*

*My life has been stunted up until now. While I was using
and being used, all I saw was the moment in front of me—
survival. I don't think that's what life is supposed to be.*

THE LANDLINE RANG, STARTLING TIFF out of deep thought.
They'd kept the phone all these years just in case Lindsay were
to call. But that wasn't going to happen. She'd never call home
again, yet neither Tiff nor Bruce had the heart to disconnect the
line. "Hello?"

Silence.

"Hello?"

Just as every time before, a telemarketer took over after a pause.
She slammed the phone down.

Bruce came and laid his hand on the table beside hers. His eyes
said what she was thinking.

"It's time to get rid of this."

He nodded. "We've had cells for years. Lindsay is gone, and
I'm just about sick of listening to that old answering machine
play back calls from every Tom, Dick, and Harry who wants to
sell us something."

"I'll do it this month."

"I can, if you'd rather. I know it's more than a phone." He
brushed his fingers through her hair.

"No. I want to do it. I think we should start going through her
room soon too. We've been keeping it like a shrine, and instead
of reminding me of good times with our daughter, it's giving
breath to my grief."

They walked into each other's arms, the scent of his soap mixing with her hand lotion, the warmth of his breath on her neck
melting her into his embrace.

Their meetings with Pastor Jim had started off painful, but each time, a little more of the loss was released from her heart, making space for their marriage. It wasn't going to be easy, charting a new course together, but they were committed. Life was meant to be lived to the full.

CHAPTER FORTY-TWO

WHEN THE NEWS ABOUT CONWAY'S DEATH reached Tiff's ears, it was not without a large dose of regret. She'd slowed her work on the street, putting her concentration on Eve alone. But what about the people who counted on her? Conway had gotten better as the summer nights warmed and dried the air, but it hadn't lasted. What would happen to Esther now? Where would she go?

Tiff scanned the block where Esther and Conway could usually be found. There on the edge of their sidewalk, a makeshift memorial had grown up from the gray concrete—notes, flowers likely picked from a nearby park, and even one picture of Conway and the dog, a clipping from the newspaper. But no Esther.

There was an informal memorial to be held around noon. It was the way these things were done. No fees to funeral homes, no catered meal, just friends and allies leaning on one another as they acknowledged the loss of one of their own.

Tiff pulled up to the location and retrieved a box holding fifty bagged lunches. As she was wondering how to carry those and the crate of water bottles, Bruce pulled in beside her.

He rolled down his window. "Hey there."

"What are you doing here?" Her stomach buzzed like it used to each time he'd come to pick her up for a date.

"I heard what you were saying last night about Conway and his wife. I wanted to pay my respects. It sounded like he was a special person." Bruce popped his door open and stood, towering over her.

She tapped her index finger on her upper lip, hoping to disguise the feelings that wove through her—feelings of love, of thankfulness, and of being heard. "You're just in time. Can you help me with this stuff?"

He pointed to his cheek, a grin on his face.

Playing along, she stretched to his height and planted a kiss where he'd indicated. "Thank you for being here," she whispered.

His boyish smile was enough to feed her heart for months.

Bruce loosened his tie and pulled it off, dropping it onto the seat of his car, then hefted the water bottles out of her trunk.

They walked together to a bench, where they placed the items and stepped away. Soon people started to congregate, helping themselves to a lunch and water. When Esther arrived, Tiff wanted to go to her, envelop her in a hug, and share her sympathies. Even though she'd built relationships out here, she still wasn't one of them, so she hung back, waiting for the crowd to thin, for her chance to see her friend.

It was while Tiff helped Bruce collect a few stray water bottles that Esther came to her.

"Dear friend, it's so good to see you here. Conway would have appreciated your thoughtfulness." Esther's clothes had been laundered, and she smelled as if she'd had a recent shower.

"I'm so sorry for your loss. He was a good man."

Esther nodded, tears in her eyes.

"Where have you been staying?"

"I took a bed in the shelter, but I'll be heading out tomorrow morning. My daughter lives in Colorado. She wants me to join her there. It's about time I give up my wandering ways to concentrate on my grandkids."

"You have a daughter? I didn't know." Tiff placed a hand on her heart. "I'm so glad you won't be alone."

She put two fingers in her mouth and managed a perfect toothless whistle. The dog came running. "Never alone. I've got my dog, my God, and my family. It won't be the same without the old man, but we'll meet again."

Tiff mulled over those last moments with Esther long into the night. She had a lot to learn from the people she worked with. Esther, Theresa, Eve—these women knew desperation and contentment. They knew what it was like to suffer, and they knew what it meant to surrender. Tiff was only just getting a glimpse.

Eve

August 15, 2019

The caseworker was here. She approved my place. I can't believe it. I didn't feel this good when I graduated. Honestly, I didn't feel this good when I had my babies. There was more fear then, when there should have been celebration.

I can't help remembering the day Sammy came into the world. I'd tried to stay clean, and I'd done fairly well, but a week before, I'd slipped and used. When I went into labor, I'd actually considered not going to the hospital. I had nowhere to take Charlotte, and I was so afraid that if we went in, they'd know what I'd done and take my babies away from me. Even now, I can't believe they didn't. I left there as soon as they'd release me with a toddler, a newborn, and an addiction that had come back to live with our little family.

318

Tiff says I need to forgive myself so I can move forward. How can I do that? Is there a step-by-step way? Because each time I think I've come into my new life, the guilt covers me, and I'm pushed back under its current.

"THIS ISN'T RIGHT." Zara slammed the metal bowl down on the counter, filling the air with the metallic ring. "Kelly wasn't there at the park. She didn't see how not ready they are to return home."

Chad leaned back on the cupboards, nodding.

"This isn't about the children at all. It's all about Eve and her rights. When do Sammy and Charlotte get rights? We've done so much work this summer. Charlotte isn't running off nearly as often. And Sammy's test results haven't come back. Are we supposed to hand them back to Eve when he could have major medical needs coming? She isn't prepared for that. Seriously, I'm not even prepared for that."

Silence.

"What?" Zara tossed the bowl onto the top drawer of the dishwasher.

"I said nothing." Chad held out his hand.

She slammed the machine shut. "That's my point. I'm telling you all this, and you're over there, quiet, like none of this even matters to you."

"Whoa. That's not fair." He hopped onto the counter. "I figured this was one of those times you just need for me to listen while you verbally process your feelings." A direct quote from premarital counseling.

"No. This time, I actually want you to fix it."

He clasped his hands in his lap, a sad expression dimming his features. "I can't."

Eve
August 16, 2019

It's lonely here, on my own. The kitchen still smells of the gourmet pizza Tiff, Bruce, and I shared after moving in the last of my belongings. They've helped in so many ways, and from the looks of it, I'm ready to have my children again. But caseworkers don't see the fears that rage under the surface. They don't know the doubts that befriend my every waking moment. And they don't realize I don't even know who I am as a clean and sober mother of two.

In a way, Charlotte and Sammy are strangers to me, much like I must be to them. Though my heart knows them, the me that's here in my kitchen, writing in my journal—the me who will line up this bound copy of my thoughts with the twenty-seven others I wrote as an active addict—she is new to this world. She's never lived and loved and existed before. How can I trust her?

CHAPTER FORTY-THREE

ZARA PLACED CHARLOTTE'S FAVORITE DOLL in her new suit-case, keeping her gaze on her tasks and away from the questioning eyes of the owner.

"Can't you stay with us too? Mom is your sister. I know she is. So you should live in the same house. Come with us, please, Mama Z."

Zara looked at Chad.

He shook his head.

"I'm sorry, sweetheart. This is a special time for you, Sammy, and your mom. She's very excited to have you spend the night at the new place. In fact, she told me she was going to have cheese pizza for dinner. Doesn't that sound great?"

"I don't eat cheese pizza." Charlotte crossed her arms, her face flaming red.

Before she could bolt, Chad picked her up. Her body was vis-ibly tense, but he cut off her spiral before it could spin out of control. "Since when? Last week, cheese pizza was your favorite." He tickled her until she gave in and giggled.

Zara zipped the suitcase and turned to look out the window. Just a few months earlier, when she hadn't known what she wanted, this was the window that had fallen open and shattered.

Now she felt like she was the one who was shattering. Reunification was the goal of foster care. It was supposed to be the second chance that parents needed, and the hope that children required. So why, when it was working out like the picture-perfect model of care, did Zara have a giant hole growing in her heart?

She turned in time to see Chad walking down the hall, Sammy holding one hand and Charlotte the other. He was an amazing father, just like she knew he would be. How did someone stop being a parent? How would they go from Mom and Dad to a couple again?

She'd have to ask Sharon. Somehow, she'd survived the death of her soulmate, then in Walter, found another man to share her later years. Through all those times, she'd been the picture of contentment and peace.

How was it possible to want something so completely for her sister, yet want it just as much for herself?

Zara sat on Charlotte's bed, pulling the pillow close to her chest. She inhaled the scent of strawberry children's shampoo. Would Eve use the same brand, the one Charlotte loved because of the happy-faced berry on the bottle? Would she know that a warm bath in the evening calmed Charlotte before bed and reduced her nightmares?

Zara felt the answer.

Eve would know, because Zara would tell her all the things she'd learned. And maybe, Eve would tell her some of the things she'd missed in Charlotte's first five years. Maybe Eve could let her see baby pictures or tell her what the kids were like then.

Squeezing the soft purple pillow, Zara did what she was learning to do since the moment she'd learned about the children. She gave it up. She handed her worries to God and let Him shoulder the burden she and Chad could not. Charlotte and Sammy were in His hands, even while Zara had attempted to hold them, keeping them for herself. Even disguised as the children's best interests, underneath, her desires were pure selfishness. She wanted to keep

Charlotte and Sammy and watch them grow up on the farm. But she wanted her sister too.

Eve

August 17, 2019

When Zara and I were young children, we lived in a small house beside our grandparents' larger one. We ate home-cooked treats from our grandmother's kitchen, and we listened to her read to us, sometimes from our little book of Bible stories, sometimes fairy tales.

As the haze thins, I'm able to remember back to those days without the deep sadness of their deaths, but with the memories of the life they gave us, even if it was far too short. It's like I've been fixed on the losses, not taking in the blessings, and there have been many along the way.

Tonight, Sammy and Charlotte will stay here with me. It's not permanent, but it's one giant step closer. We're still waiting to find out about Sammy from the doctor. If I'm going to be able to handle a situation that took my mother down, I'll need to remember to keep my focus on the blessings.

My blessings:
Charlotte
Sammy
My job
Our new home
Health (even if my Samuel has Hunter, he's healthy now)
Tiff and Bruce
The car that Tiff is letting me use
The framed picture of me with my kids that's in the living room

*Chad, who's shown my children what a man's supposed to be
like*

My sister

———————————

ZARA KEPT LOOKING BACK at the kids, securely buckled into
their car seats. Yes, she and Chad could give them a safer car. They
could provide for some extracurricular activities. They might
be able to afford camps and sports. But Eve was their mother.
They'd been with her from their birth until a few months ago.
They needed to all be together. Zara just wanted to be included
in the family. The five of them.

Chad parked along the curb.

Eve's neighborhood was nice. Her garage apartment was surrounded by single-family homes with basketball hoops in the
driveways and people walking dogs and pushing strollers. They'd
passed a park only three blocks before arriving. It was more than
Zara had ever imagined at the beginning of the summer. For the
first time, she really saw what Kelly and Tiff had been seeing. Eve
had done the work. She was ready to be the mom again.

Zara's heart would break. So would Chad's. But this wasn't
about them. It wasn't even about Eve. This was the best they could
all do for Charlotte and Sammy. And the best was living with Eve
and having Tiff, Zara, and Chad in their lives. This must be what
it takes a village meant.

Eve approached the car, and Zara took in a deep breath, letting
a smile come with the exhale. She opened the door and hugged
her sister. Eve didn't respond at first, but when Zara didn't release
her embrace, Eve returned the squeeze. "I'm proud of you," Zara
whispered in her ear.

She stepped back. "That means more than you could ever
know." Eve tucked a loose strand of hair behind her ear.

"This is where we live?" Charlotte's excited tone broke through the moment. The little girl was looking all around, her eyes lit with amazement. "I love this place."

Eve picked her up and hugged her tight. "I'm so glad. This is the beginning of our new lives." She set her daughter down. "You're getting so big and strong. Aunt Zara has been feeding you good food, hasn't she?"

"Yep. And Sammy too. He has some roly-polys."

"I'm going to do my best to make sure we have good food here too. But I might need your help learning some of Aunt Zara's tricks."

Charlotte took her hand. "I'm sure Mama . . . Aunt Zara and Uncle Chad will teach you everything about taking care of us. They're really good at it."

Zara's heart broke and healed at the new titles. She'd been talking with Charlotte about the role she and Chad would now take in her and Sammy's lives. They were aunt and uncle, just like they'd been designed to be, but the summer had changed her. She'd never be able to look at Charlotte and Sammy as just a niece and nephew. She'd never hear the call for foster parents the same, either. Children were just that—children. Precious children, despite their situations. Not one deserved any less than the next. Maybe her heart would expand to fit more little souls. She believed it would.

TIFF COLLAPSED ONTO HER LOUNGE CHAIR and scanned through the channels on the television. Maybe a movie would be nice. The alarm chimed, letting her know that Bruce was on his way up the driveway. He'd picked up takeout on the way home, to a house with only Tiff there.

Eve's absence had left a hole Tiff wasn't prepared for. The house seemed bigger than it had before her arrival, as though it actually echoed her footsteps in the hollow rooms.

The garage door hummed open, then closed.

She kicked her legs over the arm of her chair so that she could see him as he came in through the garage access door.

"Well," he said. "You look relaxed."

"I don't know about relaxed. Maybe bored would better describe it."

He held up two white paper bags. "I have an answer for that. Come take a sniff of this."

She pushed herself up and took one of the bags from him, the scent of tandoori reaching her nose before she even unfolded the top. Her favorite. "But you can't stand Indian food."

He pointed at the other bag. "But I love a good bacon cheeseburger."

Tiff reached into the cabinet and pulled out two of her grandmother's china plates. Opening the bags, she set his burger on one and scooped her food onto the other.

"This is mighty fancy."

"What's the point of having nice things if we don't use them?" He took down two crystal goblets and filled them with ice water.

They ate in peaceful silence. The phone rang, but neither of them jumped to answer it, and it disconnected without a message.

"I have a surprise for you." His eyes twinkled.

Dread expanded her stomach. Bruce had a talent for gifting her with things she didn't need and really didn't want. "What is it?"

He angled in his chair, fishing something from his back pocket. Finally, he held out a key, the metal ring encircling his pinky.

Tiff forced a smile. Didn't he ever truly hear her? She didn't want a new car. In fact, driving the one she had made her feel wasteful and spoiled. "Thank you. But, Bruce . . ."

"Come on." He stood, holding his hand out to her. "Take a look before you shoot it down. This car has some features you're going to love."

She joined him, the tandoori chicken sitting hard and heavy

in her stomach. A fight was coming. The only way to avoid it was to pretend she loved his gift, and that wasn't honest.

"Close your eyes." He sounded like a child on Christmas.

The light switch snapped, but Tiff couldn't see a thing.

He guided her steps, then stopped her and turned her body. "Okay. Take a look."

With a breath of surrender, she opened her eyes. Almost immediately, tears blurred her vision. A silver Honda was parked where her old Toyota usually sat. It had a couple of dings and must have been at least twenty years old. "What's this?"

"I thought it was time for a new car. Eve can keep the Toyota." He tapped the hood. "I had them put in a brand-new motor. This old girl runs better than her first day on the road."

"Oh, Bruce."

The width of his smile was greater than she'd seen in years. "You know me."

Could there be any deeper connection than to be known?

CHAPTER FORTY-FOUR

Eve

August 18, 2019

Zara and Chad picked the kids up this morning from their first "sleepover" here. I was so tired, but I couldn't tell my sister. I didn't want her to know that the kids cried at bedtime, and Charlotte had nightmares all night. Once, she was screaming about Joey, and the fears it awoke in me sent me running to the bathroom, where I was sick. Sometimes recovery looks so pretty, so peaceful and hopeful. But underneath, there are scars on all of us, deep ones that reach to our cores.

The other thing I didn't want to tell my sister was how much I wanted to use last night. It felt like I needed the hit just to keep breathing. I called my sponsor around the time the sun was coming up. Five minutes into our talk, Sammy woke up.

I'll be at the eleven o'clock NA meeting. I may need to stay for the one o'clock too. How am I going to do this and care for my children? How do I ask for help without being needy?

"Hello, Zara. This is Kelly. I wanted to check in with you about the kids' overnight stay with Eve."

Zara shifted the phone to her other ear and turned on the hose for the loofah plants. Across the yard, Charlotte pushed Sammy gently in the safety swing. "I think it went well. The kids regressed a bit when they came home, but I imagine that's normal. Eve seemed exhausted."

"But nothing that would cause you to have concerns about the children's safety." The sound of papers shuffling was loud enough to hear through the line.

"No. Everything looked safe." Zara let her fingers stroke the length of a loofah pod. They grew down from the hog panel, forming a dome. Soon, it would be time to harvest. She'd need to see if she could have a day with Charlotte then. They could pick the plants together and clean out the seeds.

"Well, then. I'm setting the reunification date for August 25. How does that sound?"

Zara's face tingled. She sat down on the grass, water seeping into the side of her jeans. "It sounds soon." She mentally counted out the six days until Charlotte and Sammy would be moving. "We don't have the test results yet."

"That's okay. I'll let the doctor know next week that the children have been reunified and that they should send all information directly to Eve."

The way Kelly spoke, it was like this came down to logistics rather than real people and real feelings. "Okay. Well, thanks."

"And, Zara, you've done a great job. Thank you."

The words that she'd once sought seemed empty now. "Thank you."

"Please touch base with me after the drop-off. I'll be over to Eve's within twenty-four hours to do my first evaluation."

That was it. They exchanged good-byes, but nothing really mattered except Charlotte and Sammy.

Eve

August 22, 2019

My kids will be back in three days. This time, they're staying. I've arranged to take three days off work. That should help them get settled. Maybe I should have taken a week, but I need the money, and my job gives me stability. I'm not sure I could do this if I didn't have my shifts to keep me focused.

The state is helping me pay for their day care. I'm hoping, eventually, once the kids and I have settled in, that Zara might be willing to keep the kids one day a week. It's better for them to be with family.

When I think about what's in my kids' best interests, I'm overwhelmed with guilt for letting so many things slip by before. My little girl has fears and worries no child should even understand. And Sammy, who knows what his future holds?

My sponsor says I need to be honest in my journal. The words are here to help me heal.

This is the truth:

I'm scared.

I feel the need to have an escape plan, just in case I can't handle all of this.

Heroin is still screaming at me—not all the time anymore, but it cries out when I'm not on guard.

Each day, I've made the choice to stay clean and sober.

Today, I'm still choosing sobriety.

I have people who want to help me.

Joey is still out there.

ZARA STOOD IN THE BEDROOM DOORWAY, watching Charlotte and Sammy sleep in the dim light from the west window. She closed her eyes and let the sounds of their breathing enter her heart. She wanted to remember this, every little thing, because tonight was the last night they'd live here, under her roof, but they would forever be her first children. No matter what came, that wouldn't change.

Her cell phone buzzed. "Hello."

"This is Dr. Kiddle. I've been catching up on some paper work this weekend and discovered the test results for Samuel haven't been given to you. I sent a copy to the caseworker. Did she speak with you?"

"No." Zara walked into her room and sank onto the bed. "Not about that."

"I really am sorry. This was my responsibility."

Blood pounded to the point of minimizing her hearing. She weighed out what to say next but stuck with nothing.

"Samuel's urine test was positive for sugar, so we went ahead with the blood test."

Zara clenched her free hand into a fist. He was taking forever to say the words she knew were coming.

"What we didn't see in the blood was an absence of or even a lower level of the enzyme we would expect in a child with Hunter. I'm a bit concerned about his kidneys, but I think another urine test in a few months will be sufficient. It's not uncommon to have a kidney that spills sugars. But as far as Hunter syndrome is concerned, I think he's cleared."

Her body shot up so fast, she nearly dropped the phone. "No Hunter?"

"Correct." He cleared his throat. "I'm glad we got some good news here."

"Thank you for calling. This is wonderful!"

When she'd finished the call, Zara jogged down the stairs and threw herself into Chad's arms. "No Hunter."

"What? How do you know?"

"The doctor just called."

His grin said more than words could. "Should you call Eve and let her know?"

"Let's surprise her tomorrow. I want to see her face when I tell her Sammy is going to live a long and healthy life."

EVE TOSSED THE THIN BLANKET to the floor. The clock read one o'clock, and up to this point, she'd probably managed twenty minutes of sleep. The only drawback to her little apartment was the heat. The day before had been hotter than any day since she'd moved in, yet Eve kept the windows closed and locked.

She lifted up on one elbow and took a drink from the bottle on the floor near her bed. When she set it back down, her finger grazed over something. She pressed at it.

A shoe. Not hers. Not empty.

CHAPTER FORTY-FIVE

EVE'S HEART THUNDERED in her chest. She pushed away from the edge of the bed, but a hand grabbed her arm, pinching the skin, burning the flesh below. She opened her mouth to scream, but only a whimper made its way out. Tears stung her nose, her eyes.

"Did you really think you were going to get away from me like that? Stupid girl."

"No. I didn't tell them anything."

Joey had her by both arms. He lifted her up, his face close to hers, his breath hot on her cheek. "The best thing for you would be death. Then you wouldn't be a problem for anyone anymore. Trash like you needs to be cleaned up and thrown in the dump."

"No . . . please don't."

He tossed her back, her head slamming against the wall. "I'm not going to need to. I think I'll leave that up to you." He flipped on the bedside lamp, illuminating the sharp features of his face. Joey pulled a syringe from his pocket. He held it up to the light, tapped the side with his finger, and set it down. "I'd suggest you help yourself. You might as well have one last happy moment before the end, 'cause, baby, as soon as I get one tiny whiff of police after me, I'll be sure you're dead, and they'll never find your body.

Hmm. I wonder what that little brat girl of yours would do then? Don't worry. I won't kill her. She'll bring a good price."

Joey reached across the bed and grabbed her by the ankle, dragging her toward himself. He leaned down and kissed her hard. "Consider this a gift. And if you're as smart as you seem to think you are, you'll be out of here and I won't have to hear another word about you. Otherwise, I may come back. And if not me, I have friends who'll be sure you get what's coming to you."

A minute later, Eve heard the door close and his footsteps descending the stairs. She was alone with her old friend.

"I LOVE FRENCH FRIES." Charlotte held one in each hand, comparing the sizes while Sammy stuffed his into his mouth, one followed by another.

Chad winked. "I told you. No point in fixing a fancy see-you-later lunch when there's a perfectly wonderful fast-food restaurant on the way."

Zara could already feel her wedding ring growing tighter as she shoved her own salt-frosted fry into her mouth.

"And they even give you toys here." Charlotte held up a plastic figure, still wrapped in a little bag. "Aunt Zara, did you know about this place before?"

Zara hesitated. Her last moments of being this involved in Charlotte's life shouldn't end with disappointment. "I had a feeling."

Chad tapped the face of his watch. "We'd better get going."

Charlotte's gaze dropped to the toy still in her hand. "What if I don't want to go?"

How was Zara supposed to explain to a five-year-old that what she wanted wasn't part of the criteria that determined her future? "We're only a few miles away. And we'll visit you very soon, okay?"

Her bottom lip quivered, but she didn't argue.

When they arrived at Eve's, Charlotte was still quiet, but Sammy was on a fast-food high, jabbering about everything he saw out the window. About half the time, Zara could even understand him.

Eve didn't greet them in the driveway this time, and Zara was relieved. She needed some time with the kids before entering the apartment, some time to feel okay about leaving and stepping back, taking the role of aunt.

Chad opened the back of the car and took out the kids' new suitcases. "Why don't you head on up? I'll be there in a minute."

With Charlotte in front, just in case she slipped on the steps, Zara climbed the stairs, Sammy a heavy weight on her hip. They made a loud clomping, the three of them, like the billy goats in the story about the troll under the bridge, but Eve must not have heard. When they reached the door, Zara suggested Charlotte knock. She wasn't sure that walking in was appropriate, even if it was Charlotte and Sammy's home now.

When Eve didn't answer, Zara herself gave the door a good pound, but still, there was no sound of movement inside. "That's weird." She smiled at Charlotte, as if this wasn't a completely odd thing for her sister not to be there when her children were moving back in with her. "I'll just give her a call. Maybe she has earbuds in or something like that."

The call went to a voice-mail box that hadn't been set up yet.

Chad hollered up at them. "What's going on?"

"I don't know. She's not answering."

Charlotte stomped back to the top step, sat down, and crossed her arms. "She probably forgot us."

"I'm sure your mother wouldn't forget you. There's an explanation. We just don't know it yet."

"She's forgot me before."

"That was before. This is different." Wasn't it? Zara hammered again, then tried the knob. Locked.

"I'll check with the landlord. Why don't you bring the kids

down?" Chad's concerns were plain in the darkness of his eyes. Could they have come this far, gotten this close to reconciliation, only to lose Eve to an overdose?

Zara hefted Charlotte onto her other hip and descended the stairs sideways as quickly as she could while being safe. The kids wouldn't see their mother if the worst had happened. Zara would protect them from that much. At the car, she buckled them into their seats.

Chad jogged back from the house. "No one's there."

"I'll call Tiff. She has a key." Zara made the call as Chad took the steps two at a time.

Sammy burst into tears.

"It's okay, Sammy."

Tiff picked up. "Hello."

"Tiff, this is Zara. We came to bring the kids to Eve, but she's not answering the door."

"Is the car there? She should have the Toyota." The fear in Tiff's voice sounded like an echo of her own.

"No. I don't see it. Eve said you had a key to her place. Would you mind coming down here?" Perspiration trickled down the back of Zara's T-shirt.

"Of course not. I'll be there as soon as I can."

Charlotte's sobs joined Sammy's.

From the top of the stairs, Chad shook his head. "I saw a ladder around back, but all the windows are closed."

Zara tried Eve's cell again, with the same result, then pulled up an episode of *Doc McStuffins* and handed the device to Charlotte.

Chad met her in the driveway. "I could knock down the door, but what if we're overreacting? Maybe she just went to the store."

"Tiff's on her way. You might be right. The car isn't here." But even with that evidence, something felt terribly wrong. For the first time in years, Zara felt the connection with her twin. It wasn't something magical or mystical; it was understanding. Eve would be here if she thought she could.

TIFF DIALED BRUCE'S NUMBER as she ran for the car. He was on the golf course, but she hoped he'd taken his cell along. No answer. She drove through the gate as it was opening, the keys to Eve's house hanging from one of her fingers. She didn't bother to close the gate again.

The ten minutes it took to drive to Eve's were filled with muttered prayers and pleas to God. She'd come so far. Eve had the chance to be a success story.

Chad and Zara met her at the car, their faces echoing her concerns.

Tiff's hand shook as she handed the key to Chad. "Zara, why don't you stay here with the kids. We'll be right back."

For a moment, it looked as though Zara would argue, but then she turned back to her own car, mother's instinct likely overriding her own fears.

Tiff followed Chad up the stairs. He pounded on the door but got no response, so he inserted the key and opened the door.

There was a stillness in the apartment, a feeling that something not so obvious was missing. Inside, Tiff's heart pounded. If they found Eve, it wouldn't be the first time she'd seen an overdose, but that kind of horror didn't lose its effect.

In the kitchen sink, a syringe lay smashed next to a hammer. Crystalized liquid surrounded it, as though it had been full at the time of impact.

Tiff crossed the small living room and tapped on the bedroom door as she entered. The bed was made, with an envelope lying in the middle, Zara's name written in block lettering on the outside. Tiff picked it up and held it to her chest. Maybe Eve wasn't dead, but sharing the news that she wasn't here, either, was going to break both her heart and Zara's. And then there were the children.

"What did you find?" Chad entered the room.

She held out the letter to him.

"It's thick." He weighed it in the palm of his hand. "Aside from that unused syringe, I didn't see anything of concern."

They walked back out to the living area, where Tiff stopped as a sudden rush of unease hit her. Then she saw it. The photo Bruce had helped Eve hang was gone.

CHAPTER FORTY-SIX

Two weeks had passed without a word from Eve. Zara and Chad had packed up the few things she had in the apartment, most of which had been clothing for the kids. But Eve's journals—she'd given Zara permission to read them in the letter she'd left—were far more valuable than any other token.

Zara set down the last of the twenty-seven volumes. Her heart had been shredded as she waded through the pages of her sister's life. She felt the sorrow, the isolation, and the helplessness as if it were happening to her. But she'd also gotten tiny glimpses of Charlotte and Sammy in the years before she knew them, and she saw Eve's love for her kids.

She set aside the questions that visited every day since finding Eve gone and headed outside to join Chad and the kids. It was time to harvest the loofahs.

Eve

September 17, 2019

I've picked up a new phone and a new journal. They represent my hope for a new life. My first move was to download the NA app. Sometimes I watch the minutes tick by, showing me each one that I've managed to stay clean and sober.

The heroin Joey left was a wake-up call. I held the syringe in my hand for what felt like the whole night while the drug called to me in a soothing whisper. Even as I crushed the plastic, making it impossible for me to use, I became aware of how far I still was from healthy. I need a lot of help, a lot of counseling. Someday, I might be a stronger woman. I might even be able to be a good mom. But it's not fair to make Charlotte and Sammy wait on me. They're children. That time flies by. I won't waste another minute of it on my addictions.

I talked to Patrick this morning. He's become more than my former boss. He's my mentor and my friend. He's set me up with a group near Chicago that will help me get a job, a place to live, and the help I need.

There's no way I can doubt that God is real. Not after all I've been through, and still, I have the chance at a future—and so do my kids. It's my prayer that, someday, I'll be able to give back a little of what I've been given.

LEAVES FELL FROM THE TREES, and the air had turned from warm breezes to a wind laced with an icy chill. Though Zara and Chad had hoped and prayed for something different, they hadn't had a single word from Eve for over two months.

Tiff and Bruce had gotten a call from Eve the week before, though, and they assured Zara and Chad that she was well but wanted them to go forward with the plan she'd set out in the letter. They all had to move forward. It was the best thing they could do for Charlotte and Sammy, who still remained in the legal custody of the state.

Each day, Zara prayed for Eve's return, yet she understood what her sister was doing. She was being a mother to the children in a deeper way than Zara ever could. Eve had sacrificed everything for their protection and future.

Chad and Zara walked into Kelly's office alone. They'd left the kids with Sharon, who was fully recovered. No doubt Walter had a lot to do with it.

"Hey. Thanks for being willing to come to me." She swiveled to the side, away from her computer. "What did you want to talk about?"

Zara held out a thick packet of paper work.

"What's this?" Concern drew lines between her eyebrows.

"Eve did this before she left. We wanted to give her a chance to return before we went forward. She's signed over her parental rights to us."

Kelly leaned back. "I don't believe it. Seriously? And you are willing to adopt the kids?"

Zara's jaw tightened, and she couldn't speak. How could she feel joy when her sister was somewhere out there, living the life of a fugitive because she believed this was the only way to ensure the children were safe?

Chad pulled her to his side. "We are."

"All right. I need to talk with my supervisor, but we'll get this moving to the next step." She stood. "Listen, I know this is tough. But the kids need you, and I want you to know you're doing the right thing for them."

"Thanks." Zara turned away. She didn't want Kelly to see her tears and decide she was unstable.

Besides the initial testimony she'd left in her apartment, Eve had sent in detailed statements, giving the police more than enough evidence to arrest Joey and keep him incarcerated for life. She wouldn't be returning to testify, but she'd been able to provide enough in the way of places, physical evidence, and other witnesses to assure his conviction even without her.

Since Eve hadn't indicated a father on either child's birth certificate and Joey was hiding from the police, the attorney said they should be able to move forward with the adoption. Once it was complete, Joey would have no reason to come after the kids.

Zara and Chad walked out of DHS hand in hand. Sharon had insisted they take a few hours to themselves. The sky had turned a dark purple, and cool air raced over Zara's skin. Hiking was out of the question, but they could enjoy a meal with no ketchup for a change, knowing they'd be a family again when they returned home.

TIFF AND BRUCE CAME IN FROM THE GARAGE, having spent the greater part of the morning organizing the shelves of supplies. Bruce had added a few of his own touches now that he was meeting with a group of young men in the foster care system. His hope was to help them gain the skills to be good husbands and fathers, changing the course of the next generation by becoming the kind of man he would have wanted for his daughter.

"Iced tea?" She held up the pitcher she'd taken from the refrigerator.

Bruce pulled two glasses from the cupboard. "Absolutely."

"It was sure nice to hear from Eve again this morning. I thought we'd lost her." Tiff blinked back tears.

Bruce put his arm around his wife. "You're not the only one. I'll admit it now—Eve's disappearance brought back sour memories for me. I really questioned why God would allow me to let my guard down, just to be hurt again. But it seems the Big Guy knows better than I do. I'm really proud of Eve."

"Me too."

He squeezed Tiff tight. "I think she's going to make it. In a perfect world, that could have happened here, with Zara and the kids, but I believe Eve knows very well what she's able to handle right now, and what's just too much."

The phone rang from the living room. Their eyes met in the

hesitation. Eve had that number, as well as their cell phone numbers. That had been enough to convince them to put up with the solicitors a bit longer.

Tiff left the pitcher on the table, the refrigerator door open, and went to the phone, hope lightening her steps. "Hello?"

Silence.

Tiff's shoulders dropped.

"Mom?"

Tiff's body dropped to the floor, the phone still in her hands, tears washing over her cheeks.

"Is she okay?" Bruce knelt beside her.

"It's . . ." She handed the phone to Bruce.

"Eve, are you okay? Can we come get you?"

"Daddy . . . it's me. It's Lindsay."

Epilogue

Zara

January 19, 2020

I got a card in the mail today from my sister. They come regularly now, always assuring me she's confident in her decision and that she's praying for all of us. I'm amazed at how she knows I need to hear those words. Eve also wrote that she's doing well. She's very happy in her job, and she's going back to school. She still hasn't told me where she is, but the envelopes are postmarked from Chicago. Even when we were children, she'd always wanted to live in the big city. I've always wanted to live on a farm. I guess we both got what we were after.

There was one huge surprise in Eve's letter. She's been writing to our mother. I don't know if I'm ready to believe this, but Eve says she's gotten a lot of help in prison. She's being treated for her mood swings, and she's really involved in prison ministry. Maybe I'll contact her, or at least read the next letter that arrives. We all need another chance.

Charlotte has grown so much. She's halfway through her first year in kindergarten, and I'm proud to say, it's been a success. She had so many questions when Eve disappeared. We continue to talk this through, assuring her that her mom is still part of our family. She also sees a counselor each week, which has helped us all to understand one another and the changes we've been through.

Sammy remains healthy. There haven't been any other indicators of a kidney issue. He talks in full sentences now and is steadily increasing the grocery bill each month. We may have to take out a second mortgage when he's a teen just to feed him!

Tomorrow, we go before the judge. He'll make us Charlotte and Sammy's legal parents. There will never be a moment I'm not grateful for this, yet at the same time, there is loss.

I'm not fully me without Eve. I didn't realize this until I lost her for the second time. Wherever she is, I hope she knows that we love her, we miss her, and there will always be a place here for her.

This isn't the way I dreamed of starting a family, not that I don't love the kids. I couldn't love them any more than I do. My design had only one way I thought could lead to happiness. I know better now. God has a plan that is far outside of my own reach. And no matter what it looks like, I'm learning to see that His way is the way it should be.

Author's Note
and Acknowledgments

ADDICTION IS A TOUGH SUBJECT to tackle in fiction. This one area is tied to so many of the greatest hurts in our country. I would be doing a disservice to those who have suffered in bondage to addiction if I tied this story up in a neat bow.

Maybe you've gotten to the end of Eve, Tiff, and Zara's story and you're wishing that Eve could have stayed, that she and the children could have moved forward into a beautiful future together. While that kind of ending does happen, it's not common within the timeframe of this story. I too wish it could be that simple. But healing takes time, and childhood does not wait.

I hope you walk away from this book with the realization that addiction does not define a person. I hope that when you see someone battling drug dependency, you will stop and pray for healing. There are miraculous stories of men and women who've turned their lives around. I count it as an honor to know a few of those people.

While doing research for this novel, I had the opportunity to sit down with a woman who has lived through many of the things we see Eve face. She told me her story with such clarity and transparency, I will forever be changed. Thank you so much, Kristina. I'm so proud to call you my friend.

We often hear about how broken our foster care system is, and I'm not arguing that, but there are people with genuine hearts who work each day to make the lives of the children in our communities better. I'm so grateful for the caseworkers who put in hours around the clock, and the court-appointed special advocates who volunteer their time to assist kids.

To the parents who do the hard work necessary to reunify their families, you have my respect. And to the foster parents who give their hearts to kids for as long as they are needed, there is no way to adequately say thank you.

I'm honored to be a part of Every Child Oregon, an organization that strives to support children in care, foster parents, and families.

Thank you to Bethany House, Baker Publishing Group, and Raela Schoenherr for allowing me to tell these stories. Rochelle Gloege, you are an amazing editor. I've loved getting to know you better through this process. You teach me so much along the way. Thank you to Amy Lokkesmoe, Noelle Chew, and Brooke Vikla and the rest of the team for their marketing genius. And thank you to the Bethany House design department. I love this cover!

Once again, Jodie Bailey talked me down from the cliff so I could finish this project. Without her, I'd be hanging on the edge, trying to eat an elephant all at once.

Marilyn Rhoads, Karen Barnett, and Heidi Gaul spent many hours helping me to hone my prose into a story. My sister, Kaitlin Boyce, read early drafts and didn't give up on me. Thanks.

Thank you, Cynthia Ruchti, my friend, mentor, and agent. You both inspire me and push me to be better.

Over the course of my writing this novel, my husband has increased the number of dishes he knows how to cook. I don't deserve you, but I'm glad I have you.

Thank you, Lord, for allowing me to spend my days creating stories. It's the perfect job for a girl who could never fully wake from her daydreams.

About the Author

Christina Suzann Nelson is an inspirational speaker and the award-winning author of *If We Make It Home*, *Swimming in the Deep End*, and *More Than We Remember*. She writes and speaks about hope after dysfunction. Christina is over the top about her passions, including the stories created somewhere in the twists and turns of her less-than-focused brain. When she's not writing, she's working with the Every Child Initiative, chasing escaped steers, reading, breathing in the sweet smell of her horse, hiking with her dog, or enjoying her just-as-crazy family. Visit her website at www.christinasuzannnelson.com for more information.

Sign Up for Christina's Newsletter!

Keep up to date with Christina's news on book releases and events by signing up for her email list at christinasuzannnelson.com.

More from Christina Suzann Nelson

After a life-altering car accident, one night changes everything for three women. As their lives intersect, they can no longer dwell in the memory of who they've been. Can they rise from the wreck of the worst moments of their lives to become who they were meant to be?

More Than We Remember

You May Also Like . . .

In this epistolary novel from the WWII home front, Johanna Berglund is forced to return to her small Midwestern town to become a translator at a German prisoner of war camp. There, amid old secrets and prejudice, she finds that the POWs have hidden depths. When the lines between compassion and treason are blurred, she must decide where her heart truly lies.

Things We Didn't Say by Amy Lynn Green
amygreenbooks.com

When deaf teen Loyal Raines stumbles upon a dead body in the nearby river, his absentee father, Creed, is shocked the boy runs to him first. Pulled into the investigation, Creed discovers that it is the boy's courage, not his inability to hear, that sets him apart, and he will have to do more than solve a murder if he wants to win his family's hearts again.

The Right Kind of Fool by Sarah Loudin Thomas
sarahloudinthomas.com

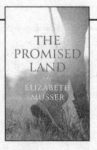

Desperate to mend her marriage and herself, Abbie Jowett joins her son in walking the famed Camino pilgrimage. During their journey, they encounter an Iranian working in secret to help refugees and a journalist searching for answers from her broken past—and everyone is called into a deep soul-searching that threatens all their best laid plans.

The Promised Land by Elizabeth Musser
elizabethmusser.com

⬥ BETHANYHOUSE